APOK

BY MICHAEL WALTON

Chief Editor - Danney Hamilton
Editor - Catherine Walton
Photographer - Carrie Duncan of Four Bees Photography
APOK 'Sniper Font' supplied by Billy Argel

Produced by:

FriesenPress
Suite 300 – 852 Fort Street
Victoria, BC, Canada V8W 1H8

www.friesenpress.com

Distributed to the trade by The Ingram Book Company

CHAPTER ONE

Bang! Bang! Bang!

A wall-mounted mirror shakes, distorting a woman's reflection, as a man's voice cuts through the drywall, "come on Carrie, that was Steve, he's waiting for you on the roof."

Digging carefully with manicured red nails through a little hand bag, she pulls out a lipstick, "yeah, yeah, I'm almost done."

"Did you do your homework on this guy? This isn't going to be a walk in the park."

Glossing over her crimson lips with cherry red, she kisses the air, "Yep."

The baritone voice continues nagging, "I'm serious. The boss is counting on this interview. This is your last shot Warren. You better not screw this up."

Stepping out of the washroom Carrie stands beside a host of desks. Hiking up her mini skirt revealing more of her slender legs, "I told you not to worry, one way or another I'll get him to talk."

Glistening under intense lights is a man's olive complexion, accentuating a film of sweat and grime coating his body. Wearing fluorescent orange coveralls he shuffles his feet, rattling the long chains that bolt his ankle and wrist tethers to the floor. Lowering his head down to his hands, he rubs his unshaven face, and scratches his scalp through short dark hair. The prisoner growls, "I have nothing to say to you."

Sitting on a thick metal chair Carrie readjusts her position, tugging on the bottom of her black mini skirt trying to insulate her thighs from the sting of the cold steel. Crossing her sleek legs, she

1

seductively tosses her wavy dark hair out of her face and over her shoulder. Her lips begin to move as her crystal blue eyes interpret the writing on the notepad held in front of her.

"Mr. Miguel Mejia, you have nothing to say? A vicious trend of police brutality appears to be seeping through the force and many are pointing the finger at you, starting with the murder of that school teacher."

Keeping his head down he snarls, showing his teeth, "Perhaps you didn't hear me the first time, I said I have nothing to say."

Glancing at the chains holding Miguel at bay Carrie continues, "Mr. Mejia after two years in prison, you have completely exhausted your appeal process. Facing the remainder of your life in prison, you finally have the opportunity to tell your side of the story. Why don't you want to talk?"

Waiting for a response she loses her patience and looks up from her notepad. Speaking with red lips growing a little tighter and speech a little harsher, "Miguel! Sorry, I mean, Mr. Mejia. With nothing to lose, why don't you want to talk?"

Rubbing his chin against his chest, he whispers, "I have nothing to say."

"Mr. Mejia, I was assured by the warden that you were going to cooperate with this interview." Pressing her hands together she feels the sweat building up. Looking for some assistance, her eyes scan the wall-sized mirror.

Tilting his head up, Miguel's cold dark stare pierces Carrie's soul to the core, "Assured?"

A sudden unconscious body jolt followed by skin tingling fear, shot through Carrie. Strengthened by the added security measures, Carrie's widened eyes and enlarged pupils slowly resume their natural size. Pressing the point, "Mr. Mejia, I need you to answer these questions."

Extending his arms and legs, he finds resistance from the chains as the slack disappears; he frowns as he glares at her. A labyrinth of spiteful emotions washes over him. "Listen to me. You and your friends have done more than enough damage. I'm not playing these games anymore."

A heavy iron door creaks open, interrupting the conversation. A straight-faced jail guard enters and confidently saunters over to Mr. Mejia. Putting his hands on the back of the prisoner's shoulders he whispers in Miguel's ear. The Spaniard nods, his body slumps and the guard retreats from the room, closing the door.

"This is such bullshit!" Yanking the chains, his biceps bulge through neon orange sleeves. Glaring over at the mirror, knowing his every move is being monitored, Miguel relaxes his muscles and lowers his head, speaking very sharply through clenched teeth, "Okay Ms. Carrie Warren, *apparently*, I will answer your questions now."

Jolted awake, sitting bolt upright, Carrie's heart races as the strands of the nightmare wear off. Trying to understand the noise and re-orient herself, her eyes scan her familiar miniature bachelor apartment. The siren sound in the room is not a prison escape lock-down alarm from yesterday's jail interview; it's her morning enemy, the alarm clock. Slapping the snooze button drains the rush of energy that lifted her out of her sleep. Carrie falls back into the warm seas of her duvet. Feeling a little uneasy as her head sinks into her pillow, she negotiates with herself to find the will to get up. "Ahhhhh," she whines, "that was too short."

Turning the radio on, she waits to hear updates of the current weather situation. "It is brutal out there. I don't know where this cold front came from but be prepared to receive the shock of your life. Jack Frost is back early and with a vengeance...now more of your top six at six."

Carrie shuts it off, "Okay, maybe just ten more minutes."

The morning sun had yet to rise to wipe Jack's ice-covered smile off windows. Cars travelling into the city still appear to be frozen over. Drivers hunch over steering wheels, straining their early morning eyes through frost cleared hand-wiped streaks.

The road and sidewalk congestion signals the start of the hustle and bustle of another workday in the city. Early morning heads still suffering from sleep lag, make their way to work, similar to a computer start-up program; on, but not completely ready for use.

Among the pedestrians getting off the subway is Carrie, dressed for the elements. Wearing fashionable black knee high leather boots with a practical heel, she prepares for her trek to the office. Walking out through the turn-style she places her gloved hands into the pockets of her black wool double-breasted jacket. She tucks her face down into a tan Persian scarf loosely thrown around her neck. The scarf softly rubs against her skin reminding her of the warm duvet she left only an hour ago. Her dark damp hair hangs down, framing her face.

Climbing the stairs leading to the city streets above, the air hangs thick with every breath she expels. Bothered by her decision to spend a little more cozy time in bed, she feels her damp hair begin to freeze as she adjusts the sliding backpack on her shoulder. This morning she doesn't try to give herself the get up early pep talk, 'early to bed early to rise.' Nope, truth be told, she will probably steal ten minutes tomorrow as well. Carrie's mouth forms a guiltless smile, "it's only frozen hair."

Weaving through the familiar streets, Carrie makes her way towards the upper floor office. Bopping in her own world to newly released music on her cell phone, she ignores the occasional text beep news reports, summoning her back to reality. In the 'information age' and in particular in a city so large, she, along with everyone else, is subject to information overload. Ironically, the more the news feeds people intravenously, the more it is blocked out like white noise. She watches as a van stops and the driver drops off a stack of news papers on the curb in front of a corner store.

Glancing down at the tightly bound news paper, Carrie studies the head-line, 'The Birth of Killer Cops!' In bold colour photos, two Metropolitan police officers are handcuffed on public display, found guilty of murder. The recent conviction of these officers, the second in just over two years, has the force bracing itself under heavy scrutiny. Commentaries from social justice advocates and police critics heat up in public debates addressing the increase in vigilante justice. The political pundits argue that there is a dangerous and lethal trend finding its way into modern day policing. Should the public be concerned? The Police Chief, under public and media pressure, read from a prepared speech, 'these isolated incidents are not consistent with the philosophy of the police department and our legal system. These men acted of their own free will, outside the law. Justice has been served in both cases. It's time we advance from here as a city.'

Energized after skimming the cover story, Carrie moves along, seeing pedestrians buying up copies of the newspaper and thinking, *my story is going to blow that one out of the water.*

A rough looking seasoned police officer drives by Carrie. She studies his profile, getting a quick mental shot and shivers, reading the words written on the side of the squad car, 'To Serve and Protect', *protecting our city huh? Who's protecting us from you?*

The senior patrolman's dark baggy eyes, fatigued from a long career and the night shift's demands, widen as he listens to a popular talk radio show.

"Vigilante police officers, should they be electronically monitored? After all, these are public servants being paid by my tax dollars and yours! Callers, tell me what you think about the way this government is using our money to defend these so-called police officers."

The officer now fully awake, starts yelling at his radio, spittle spraying the dash, "You sons of bitches! Why label us all with that bullshit? Who do you think arrested the first one? None other than yours truly, Saduj Toiracsi! I am a hero, the last thing I need is your ass monitoring me all the time."

In full rant, he accelerates, rounding a corner as wide eyes suddenly capture his environment. Reflexes slam on the brakes as the cruiser lunges forward, skidding across the pavement. His vehicle comes to a violent stop, smoking tires rest across two lanes. Saduj releases the carbon dioxide from his lungs taking another breath yelling, "What the hell is going on here? For fuck's sake I just want to finish my shift. I don't have time for this shit."

Re-positioning his cruiser squarely behind the tanker clearly displaying a trade mark emblem on the back, Saduj ignites his emergency lights, remembering his latest lecture from his supervisor, and anticipating a new one. Rocking his head back and forth he mimics his superior, "Saduj get into my office I'm sick of you sleeping all the time..."

This time he wants to make it abundantly clear he is not behind some factory sleeping again. Using weight and momentum, Toiracsi shifts his bulk out of the car as gracefully as a wild hippo. Fully annoyed, he notices the tractor trailer partially blocking two lanes without any flashing hazard lights. *What an asshole. Who does he think he is?*

Distastefully obscuring the early morning sky is the concrete highway overpass. The stainless steel tank flashes intermittent reflections of the red and blue light emitted from the police vehicle. Now standing behind his open car door Toiracsi reaches in, grabbing the radio mic and calling in to dispatch, "301 out with a vehicle".

The dispatcher responds, "go ahead 12-301."

"301, corner of Lakeshore and Yonge, Alpha Bravo X-ray Echo 405." Reluctantly, he slowly bends down, checking the information streaming across the onboard computer in his car.

'Special Interest Police' boldly flashes. 'Vehicle reported stolen during a gun point robbery.' The fact that it happened three days ago catches his attention.

Toiracsi hears the dispatcher requesting a second unit to assist. He pulls his pants up, readjusting his gun belt around his large belly, and waits for back-up. Closing the car door the senior patrolman approaches the arriving squad car. His back-up is an eager young fresh face straight out of the academy.

Putting on street-wise veteran bravado, Saduj lowers his vocal tone a notch, "Don't worry. The Mafioso crony who stole this rig is long gone. As soon as it broke down he would have left it. We don't need anyone else to assist. Come on we'll save everyone time if we just do it ourselves."

The young officer looks around, stalling. "This is by the book, sir?"

Saduj slams on the hood of the rookie's squad car. "What's a matter with you rook? Get your ass out here!"

Jittery, the young officer gets out of the car. "Sorry, I just thought we were supposed to..."

"Man, you're stupid, I just told you we're not waiting, now let's go."

Following the veteran officer's lead the rookie shadows Toiracsi's approach. Guns drawn, sirens coming from a distance, the two officers start advancing slowly toward the driver's side door. Using the vehicle's side mirrors to peer inside the cab of the truck the veteran officer scans for hostile occupants.

With eyes searching the area in textbook fashion, the young officer's feet move closer together, heel to toe crunching frozen sand under boot treads. His heart beats a little faster, veins pulse a little harder, he feels like a rookie. Ears strain to hear familiar and uncommon sounds. Squeezing his gun handle, his hands start to sweat...

Carrie reaches the news building glancing at the 'WBC Network' sign wondering, *when are they going to update that logo?* Breathing easier now, she looks over her shoulder, timing her entrance through the spinning glass doors. Entering the front reception area she pulls out her WBC identification card. She wishes she could re-take her picture. It was a very bad hair day. Nevertheless, showing her card with her name in bold print, CARRIE WARREN, was a badge of honour, small town girl making her way in the big city.

Approaching the security desk in the grand lobby of one of the largest buildings in the heart of the city, an aging security guard greets her as she shakes off the cold. "Good morning Miss Warren. You're in rather early on a cold day like today."

Carrie smiles and the elderly man's face nervously flushes in her presence, much like a school boy.

Oblivious to the security guard's embarrassment, she swipes her card. "Hi Ted. I was having one of those nights."

Fumbling for something to say the security guard asks, "Did you watch the news last night? That rich guy, what's his name again, oh yeah Mr. Nomed, went to Egypt negotiating with the rebel leaders again, he's been busy."

"No sorry, I've been busy too working on my own story."

"He's really making headlines but I'm sure your story will be fantastic too, Miss Warren."

Carrie rolls her eyes and starts to walk away, "Thanks Ted."

"Oh, Miss Warren, your part of the building is still pretty quiet. You shouldn't have too many distractions for a couple of hours especially with people travelling in this weather."

"Perfect. I think that will give me enough time to polish up my facts. I'll talk to you later Ted, have a nice day." Carrie steps into an elevator.

Commuter traffic on the highway overpass listening to the latest Top 40 and hot topic talk radio stations is completely oblivious to the police officers approaching the stolen tanker below. A radio host drones on, "... more arrests have been made in the use and construction of magnetic generators..."

Radio news-casters banter about the validity of these arrests and suddenly become quiet as the radio reception ends abruptly. The shiny tanker truck below transforms into a huge mushroom cloud of fire, creating a massive shock wave felt for miles. Flying heated sheets of metal slice through the traffic above. Cars burst into flames, and fly through the air. Broken bodies and vehicles crash into the crater's abyss where a senior officer and rookie once stood.

From a distance, more mushroom clouds take shape, rising from ground level, dwarfing the buildings below. The magnitude of the fires from each chain reaction explosion creates a vacuum of oxygen in the areas around them, fuelling their growth. The initial shock that shattered windows and blew people and objects away, reverses its energy. Anything remaining nearby is sucked toward the brilliant hot light growing in intensity.

Working inside one of WBC's editing booths, Carrie feels the floor sway, and the rumble as the walls shake. Her insides churn wondering in a panic, *is this an earthquake?* Quickly exiting the room, she finds the answers the hard way. Unexpectedly, fighting for air, her skin temperature rapidly rises as the supreme radiance forces her to fall to her knees. Carrie realizes that this is something far worse than a simple earthquake.

Gasping for life, Carrie's lungs fill with forced air as it returns to the room. Her strength swiftly follows. In a series of fluid movements, the reporter grabs a television camera and sprints to the nearest window. Instinctively setting up the device she captures the most terrifying events as they unfold. Mesmerized, she keeps shooting as the heat from the explosions ignite nearby businesses and residences, turning them into bright orange and black walls of fire. The shock wave caused nearby structures to crumble under the stress. A chain reaction of motor vehicle collisions gridlock the streets. Car alarms compete with the mayhem of sound attempting to summon help that won't arrive any time soon. Making a disastrous situation worse, are the suffocating dust clouds filling the air, bringing visibility to near zero.

Carrie frantically pans from side to side trying to capture as much as possible. As the dust and debris settles she continues to document the aftermath. The devastating collapse of nearby buildings and gaping smouldering holes expose compromised natural gas lines beneath the streets. Swarms of frantic people run cluelessly through clouds of the rotten egg smelling gas.

The earth violently erupts again as broken natural gas lines feed deadly fuel to hungry flames liquefying asphalt, blackening earth and sky, while annihilating nearby survivors. The lights in the WBC building flicker again. Through eye-stinging tears and ringing ears Carrie watches the city burn itself into darkness. Clumsy fingers search her purse for her cell phone as her camera captures the flaming Armageddon. The dead space on the other end of her cell phone punctuates the seriousness of the situation. Fighting a natural urge to panic, she takes three breaths. *Come on. I can do this. Just relax.*

Wondering when the city will be in total electrical and communications blackout, she tries in vain to find a new signal. The reality of her world was falling fast. Should she be leaving town like any rational thinking person would? Could she make it out of this horror? How could she survive? She didn't want to think about how the uncontrolled sewage spilling out from destroyed pipes will affect clean drinking water.

The reporter struggles to recall the combination to unlock the camera's ability to transmit images directly to the WBC satellite. *Come on Carrie, this is nothing, you've done this before. What's that stupid code?*

Punching in a series of numbers, a sudden whir brings the camera system to life. The words 'live feed active' appears on the camera view screen, causing the reporter to exhale for the first time in a long while. Suddenly Carrie sees the camera screen blacken and the green light fade away. She slaps the side of the camera, and nothing changes. *Don't panic. I probably just need a fresh battery.*

Rushing to the tech closet, Carrie grabs two spare batteries, shoving one into her backpack and replaces the one on the camera. Lugging the video equipment down the stairwell to the street below, she's happy her muscles didn't give out from the additional weight. It's horrible to think about it but she knew broadcasting from ground zero could provide vital information to the panicking public and put her faltering news station on the world stage. It wouldn't hurt if she emerged as the face bringing the news to the globe. With a few more frustrating tweaks and a lot of begging to the tech gods, the green light comes back to life and Carrie is live.

Walking quickly, reporting the events as they happen, the reporter manages to eke out short phrases as her lungs fill with soot, "...as we approach one of the explosion sites... I will try to keep up and describe what is going on..."

Rounding the corner of a building, the camera's eye stops moving, "Oh my God! There is someone trapped inside this car!"

Clicking is heard and the camera focus adjusts for a moment before it captures a clear image. Running out from behind the camera Carrie tries to open one of the car doors. Inside the car is an unconscious person and a crying toddler strapped in his car seat. Carrie starts screaming but her voice drowns in the cacophony of chaos. "Someone, help me! Please someone help me!"

Her muscles and tendons strain as she pulls and pulls to no avail. She starts scanning the ground for something to assist. Glass shattering nearby and metal on metal crumpling causes her to worry that she may have put herself in danger. Scanning her surroundings for help, Carrie spots a team of firefighters. Out of breath, she runs stumbling through rubble waving her hands in the air grabbing their attention. Pointing to the victims in the car, the firefighters quickly assess the safety of the area and follow her into uncharted territories of carnage. Not missing a beat, Carrie captures their heroic efforts live on camera.

It took the firefighters a split second to realize that the mangled body in the driver's seat was a young woman who didn't believe in seatbelts. Extracting the woman and child from the twisted steel frame, the firefighters begin trying to revive her as the child screams while watching the barbarous pounding on his mother's chest. Beads of sweat form under the helmet of the young fireman physically giving everything he's got. Determined to resuscitate the crying boy's mother he pushes on, as his female colleague repeats, "Otis call it. She's gone. Otis!"

Jolting the woman's chest with intertwined hands under his body weight, the young fireman continues. Otis' partner grabs his arm, raising her voice even louder, "Otis come on, you have to call it. There are others who need us."

Drenched in sweat and blood, the young man looks up at his partner's face fighting back tears. He sits back on his heels as she comforts him. "You did your best but there was nothing you can do. We have to keep moving."

The fireman reaches over to the crying child and wipes tears away from his little face. Gently picking up the boy, the toddler kicks and wails as he carries him away, leaving the mother on the cold pavement. Carrie's throat tightens, witnessing the little boy's outstretched arms, desperately trying to reach out to his mother who isn't responding, "Mommy, wake up! Mommy, wake up!"

Carrie braces herself against a wall to maintain her poise, thinking to herself, *how many others are in that same situation? How many people right now are without any help?* The weight of her reality seems to sit squarely on her chest. Battling for emotional control, she makes a feeble attempt at a motivational speech. *Be strong, you're a professional, Get it together girl.*

Slowly picking up the microphone and walking in front of the camera, she begins to tell the story to the WBC web audience. Sniffling and coughing between words, "Burdened with the care of a motherless child... they continue their heroics, as they make their way to different fire locations.. The search for survivors continues." Slowing her speech, "I don't envy what they will find today."

A man dressed in a dark suit, clutching a cellular phone in full stride hurtles himself around the corner of a dimly lit hallway. Two large men with earpieces curled up behind their ears hold up their hands yelling, "Whoa, whoa, whoa!"

The running man screeches to a halt exclaiming, "You have to wake him right now! We're under attack!"

Awoken by thrashing at his door, the Prime Minister glances with heavy eyes at the red digital glowing numbers slowly coming into focus. "It's 6:35 a.m."

"Mr. Prime Minister, we're under attack! Toronto has been hit, Toronto has been hit!"

Adrenaline rushes into the Prime Minister's veins. He jumps out of his bed as though someone had just electrocuted his warm Egyptian cotton sheets. Trying to calm his racing heart and make sense out of the morning's abrupt wake-up call, he hastily attends the door and tries to appear dignified, wrapping his housecoat around himself. Gathering himself calmly he addresses the excited man before him, "Clint, what are you talking about? What's under attack?"

Catching his breath Clint sputters out, "The entire city of Toronto, sir."

Standing there devoid of emotion the Prime Minister digests the information.

Clint points down the hall and starts sidestepping away from the Prime Minister's bedroom doorway, "Sir, we must act quickly."

Without a word spoken the Prime Minister accompanies Clint down the hall into a chamber. Grabbing a remote, Clint depresses a button lowering a large screen from the ceiling. A crackly older voice describes the scene. "In all of my years reporting the news, the atrocities and mass destruction seen here can only be compared to that of war. My heart and prayers go out to the families suffering in Toronto this fateful morning."

Continuous news footage displays videos of the fires engulfing Toronto. The Prime Minister's eyes close as he turns away from the screen's images. Absorbing the flood of emotions overwhelming his body the Prime Minister rubs his eyelids and wipes his hands across his housecoat. His glassy eyes open, scrutinizing the room, he locks onto Clint's pupils, "What's our status?"

"I've attempted to contact the mayor, and the premier, but telecommunications has been interrupted. I haven't been able to reach either of them. Sir, we cannot wait any longer. We need a response."

Looking up at the television screen watching the mayhem, the Prime Minister mutters, "Blackstar?"

"What's that sir?"

"Clint, you have to go wake everybody. I want them here immediately."

"Right away, sir."

As Clint dashes out of the room, another government aide enters before the door fastens shut. Ignoring the aide, the Prime Minister coaxes his eyes back to the screen.

"Mr. Prime Minister, is there anything I can do for you?"

"Mark." Pausing for a moment, the Prime Minister turns to face his aide.

"Yes." The aide responds, waiting for instruction.

"Get General Hamilton on the phone right away."

Mark's perplexed face now in full scowl reflects the confusion and disbelief ripping at his boss, "Sir?"

The Prime Minister, lacking patience given the situation shouts out, "Mark, did you hear me? I said get General Hamilton on the phone right away!"

Alienating Mark with the severity of the order, the aide nods and quickly leaves the room. The Prime Minister slouches forward, elbows on his knees, running his fingers through his uncombed salt and pepper hair. Mentally wrestling with the natural human response, fight or flight, he struggles to speak. "We need...We need...We need..." Grabbing a piece of stationary off his desk, the leader of the country scribbles out a note. The silence is only interrupted by the scratching of the pen.

The crash from a slamming door makes the Prime Minister jump, as the aide fights to speak, panting, "Mr. Prime Minister.. General Hamilton is on line one."

The Prime Ministers deliberately rises slowly, handing Mark the letter. Holding it up Mark reads it over quickly. His eyebrows rise as the Prime Minister speaks in a softer tone, "prepare that letter for dissemination. We need to act quickly."

"Yes, sir." Mark leaves the room making sure not to question any more decisions.

The Prime Minister calmly sits down at his desk, hesitates, than picks up the phone, "General, I apologize for the early hour. Have you been watching the news?"

"Mr. Prime Minister, turning it on now, sir."

"General, let me speak frankly with you. I am aware that it was my predecessor who terminated your employment here, and for that I must apologize. Your reputation is above reproach and we need your expertise now like never before. I would like to reinstate you immediately. You know I wouldn't ask if I..."

Interrupting the leader of the country, General Hamilton speaks, "Mr. Prime Minister I would be honoured to serve my country once again."

"Thank you, General. I will have you reinstated immediately. You are hereby authorized to provide direction and support in whatever capacity to the City and its officials. The paper work is being sent to you right now!"

General Hamilton wastes no time. Dialling in his new security clearance code, he sends his first order to the Centralized Military Department. A very formal female voice verifies the authenticity of the call, "How may I be of assistance General Hamilton?"

"Nancy, I need you to deploy the army to the city where they will await further instructions. Authorization code Blackstar. Have all reservists summoned to their nearest military base and prepared for deployment."

Knocking out communications will disrupt infrastructure causing public panic and chaos in the first twelve hours. Public utilities are next. This smells and looks a lot like a war. "We've got to be ready. Get some birds in the sky and contact the British and American Ministries of Defense. We need to see what's coming!"

Her formal voice responds on cue. "Yes sir, right away. I'll contact them immediately. Sir, it's good to have you back on board!"

Thinking about the strategic importance of the next few hours, General Hamilton walks to his closet to dust off his old uniform. Catching a glimpse of himself in the mirrored door he stops, momentarily examining his tall thin frame. The last time he wore his country's military gear, his hair was light brown. With his hand he brushes his hair off to one side. The grey strands seem to be winning the battle of time. Rubbing the sharp lines of his square jaw he inspects his aging face. His cold calculating eyes are a little dimmer than they used to be as they unite with their reflection. *There's still lots of fight left in this old body.*

Pictures hanging on the wall beside his closet distract his thoughts. Faces from platoons over his tenured career stare at him standing there. Young vibrant faces once proud to defend their country served as a cold reminder of what followed. Every soldier that died under his command left an emotional scar. Over time, the pain of that memory became tolerable. Political attacks by people supposedly on the same team cut deep and seldom ever healed.

Not so long ago, Hamilton lost his ability to stomach the political stage. Many good men and women lost their jobs at the hands of elected officials, under pressure from civilians. These people have little to no understanding of the job, let alone understand some of the decisions made in the line of duty, yet they sit as judge, jury and executioner when a lobbyist group threatens their office. Now was not the time to think about that. Hamilton reluctantly reaches for the closet door to put the past behind him. The door swings open covering up the pictures on the wall, shielding him from the eyes of those he let down.

The General reaches in, pulling out a black suit and not taking any further time to locate his uniform that he packed away long ago. White gloves fall to the floor as he frees the hanger off the rack. Bending down, his back cracks as he scoops up the gloves. He takes a couple steps back, sitting on his bed straightening out his torso. Staring at the gloves in his hand he places them next to a wedding picture of his youthful self standing with a beautiful young woman. The photo sits alone on his nightstand.

Getting dressed, Hamilton knows in a few moments he will be forced to answer the world's questions with few answers.

Standing in front of her camera, a visibly weary Carrie is draped in the coat of a fireman. Shades of ash speckled gray sit atop her dishevelled dark brown hair.

"For years we have known that Canada has been a potential target of terrorist attacks. Nothing brought this to light more than the arrests made of the now infamous 'Toronto 18.' They were a group that plotted to bomb downtown Toronto and storm Parliament Hill to assassinate the Prime Minister. The idea of this occurring was at best a vague concept to many who have never experienced such horror. Now without electricity, water, sewer, and problems with the phone systems, the citizens of this once majestic city are panicking. EMS flood to the affected areas and attempt to maintain order and provide some direction for those running through the streets..."

Carrie's cell phone rings. Surprised, she answers the phone and a voice speaks through patchy reception, "Carrie...great job...keep up the good work...we are sending up a chopper but I want you to keep rolling on the ground...there is a lot to be seen and heard at your level."

Despite the poor reception, Carrie is able to decipher the voice as the CEO of her news corporation, Mister Clifford Bernard Wilson.

An awkward moment of pride almost makes her feel guilty. She had briefly questioned how much trouble she was going to be in, not having authorization to do what she was doing. Her off-the-cuff running commentary on the events gripping the city appeared to be exactly what he wanted. Pleased, she responds, "Thank you, sir. Of course."

Looking to the sky the reporter sees domestic helicopters battling for position. Every news agency with local resources is attempting to expose the horrors to the world.

Feeling safe for the moment, Carrie allows herself to relax briefly. She is given permission to stay with a new group of firefighters as they drive around the wreckage. Closing her eyes, Carrie wishes she had help carting her tripod and camera around. Carrying it from her work van to an event scene never proved to be a problem but lugging it around for blocks on end, tends to make soft muscles scream. She reaches back, rubbing aching shoulders and wishing she never cancelled that gym membership. The fire truck rolls to a stop.

With unexpected assistance from one of the firefighters she manages to set up her camera in time to get a statement from a winded fireman covered in the familiar gray flakes.

"...without any water through the system... we have done all that we can possibly do firefighting...... we are now trying to pick up the slack assisting... other Emergency Services in caring for the injured and evacuating people..."

Carrie's camera continues rolling, capturing images and sound bites of pain, anguish and triumph. The next location is a grim site of horror and suffering. Close to what seems like ground zero of another explosion, the truck rolls to a stop. Putting the camera down again her eye picks up hundreds of people along this street, injured, dying and dead. The sickly smell of burnt hair and flesh permeates the air. Taking in the devastation she begins walking ahead of her camera as if in a trance. A cry for help snaps Carrie out of it. Approaching a downed light standard, she notices a teenage boy speared to the pavement by the metal construction. The large glass bulb had shattered when it hit the ground, which shot spikes through the boy's body. He is alive, but just barely.

The boy looks directly into Carrie's eyes, "Miss, can you please help me, I don't want to die."

Needing to scream at the situation and herself for getting emotionally involved, Carrie shouts for any firefighter within earshot.

One fireman from her truck runs to her aid. Panicking, she grabs onto him, "Please can you help him? Please!"

The fireman looks and candidly responds, "Carrie, he's not going to make it. Look around here. We need to focus on the people who have a chance. Once that is done, we will do everything we can to help whoever is still alive. I am sorry, but, I have to go."

The reporter knows the boy heard every word, and returns to the boy trying to think of what she can say to comfort him. Like the glass and metal through the boy's spine, the fireman's candid truth was a crushing blow. How could she just leave him? Carrie flips from pity to rage thinking, *who gave these emergency workers the power of life or death? Who?*

Watching from a distance as the other firefighters go from body to body Carrie realizes, like it or not, these situations force us to play God.

The boy watches out of the corner of his eyes, as the fireman walks away. Tears start flowing down his cheeks, "Miss, please don't leave me. I'm so scared."

"Don't worry, I won't leave you." Is the only response she can muster. She is speechless as she looks down at the puddle she is standing in. It's the pooling of the boy's blood that's spilling out across the ground. Her heart wrenches as she runs her gloved fingers through his hair while holding the boy's hand.

"What's your name?" Carrie asks trembling. The young man's face rolls towards the reporter, as the life disappears from his eyes.

Carrie holds on to the cold lump of flesh that used to be the young man's hand. Reluctantly she lets go and slowly walks back to her camera, finding an odd comfort in its familiarity. Her camera's microphone captures a kaleidoscope of noise coming from every angle including that of her vomiting.

Hunched over, spit hanging out of her mouth Carrie enjoys a brief moment of solitude from her stomach's heaving convulsions. Using her jacket sleeve she wipes away any stray chunks and fluids clinging to her face. Looking back at the boy she sees his dead eyes staring at her, *he had a name. He had a name!* She repeats, as if pleading in anger to a greater force that has suddenly gone mute in the universe. *That was somebody's child! How dare you!*

Knees too weak to hold her aching body, the reporter falls on them, crying for the young man, crying for herself. Suddenly, things don't make sense anymore. Getting the courage to stand up and face her camera she begins to speak. Carrie hears herself reporting the events as if she is looking at herself from outside of her body. The words come out without thinking, narrating events that could only come from a horrible fairy tale,

"...the injured in the streets, are confused and lost... Firefighters, paramedics and police have too many people to attend to and their ability to transport is nonexistent...Focusing their time and attention on those without life-threatening injuries, they are able to care for more people and those people receiving assistance are now empowered to care for others as well. We are truly grateful out here for any miracle, great or small."

From a window seat overlooking the devastation, the General surveys the city. The images are as familiar as home, in a brutal war sense. He assesses and decides where he will set up his Central Command Center. Choosing a nearby military base just outside of Toronto, he places a call to make it happen. Hamilton speaks loudly to overcome the noise of the military helicopter, "Colonel Renniks, this is General Hamilton. Listen carefully, my authorization has been sent to you personally. As such, I have identified your base as the Central Command Center. From this point forward your base will be completely shut down. Absolutely no outside persons will be permitted to reside on the base, and anyone staying will be subjected to further screening and must submit to fingerprints, DNA and new photo passes. I've already contacted Captain Nolin to produce a new security pass. They will be issued to required personnel only. Those failing the background check, refusing to submit to the new security measures, as well as anyone not required must vacate the property until further notice. I should be landing there within the next couple of hours. Make it happen. The authorization falls under the jurisdiction, code Blackstar."

"Yes, sir. Thank you, sir. It is a privilege to have the opportunity to work under your guidance."

Dust and debris smother the air as the General lands at the Central Command Center. Armed guards escort the General to the tactical room as he makes a careful note of his surroundings. Entering the boardroom, Hamilton begins scanning and studying the faces of military personnel, the city's top officials, including the Mayor, the Police Chiefs, Fire Chiefs, paramedics, engineers, and planners.

Approaching the General is a man standing at approximately five foot nine inches in height, with an erect stature and well-built physique. His shaved head conceals the fact that his dark hair had begun to recede along the top exposing the majority of his scalp. His muscular physical attributes are complemented by the manner in which he maintains his uniform. From top to bottom it is absolutely pristine, including his name tag shiny and polished establishing him by both name and rank as Colonel E. RENNIKS.

"General Hamilton. I hope your flight wasn't too terrible. If you ever need an excellent pilot I would be happy to do the job myself." Gesturing to the others in the room, "everyone here has passed an emergency security clearance prior to your arrival. As you can see I've obtained the security passes that Captain Nolin created at your command and handed them out accordingly."

Without delay Hamilton starts going to work, "Thank you, Colonel."

Turning to everyone in the room, "Unfortunately, this is why the people of this country pay for us to be around, to care and protect them when times are at their worst. Due to the damage sustained we must also consider an evacuation of certain city sectors and possibly the entire city. I have already taken the liberty of summoning a great portion of the military and equipment to protect the city. They should be arriving and setting up as we speak. We will show the public what we get paid to do."

Everyone stood staring at the General. He grabbed a chair and sat down addressing the room as they began to follow his lead, "Ladies and Gentlemen, it's time to take back Toronto and restore order."

WBC news anchor Shawn Gurl, a plump aging man who had long ago lost his charming appeal, had become comfort food for the country's eyes and ears. Having spent over thirty years in broadcasting, people know who he is and regardless if they initially liked him or not had accepted him as the voice and face of the local and national news. His calm voice and well-spoken words continue to sooth and hypnotise his viewing audience.

"Temporary shelters are emerging along the streets of the city as people long for shelter, warmth and food. Schools, certain government complexes and high-rise corporate buildings running on auxiliary power are being used as temporary shelters. Roaming emergency services and military vehicles continue to announce to those in the vicinity the location of the nearest shelter locations. Air transports flock to the sky carting necessities to these locations."

Radio stations acquiring rights to use Shawn's voice, broadcast his message through their frequencies. Shelters listen to small scratchy boxes belting out updates and useful information. Shawn's message fills the empty silence of people crowding these locations. Still in shock, there was no denying it, nor attempting to lighten the mood, people are demoralized and devastated!

Shawn's broadcast is abruptly interrupted. "My fellow Canadians." The voice of the Prime Minister broke over the airwaves. Everyone within earshot flocked to the nearest radio, stopped and listened to the most anticipated message since the carnage began.

"Words cannot express the profound shock each and every one of us feels this day. To say the least this is a grave day in our history. Our hearts go out to those who have suffered a loss, and to our emergency workers battling through this trying time ensuring what can be done is done. Never before have we experienced such devastation within our borders. The military is currently investigating the events of the last twenty-four hours. Rest assured we will find out who did this to us and bring them to justice. We will bring back our way of life. We will repair the damage. We will survive. Please help one another during this trying time, and may God help us all."

After the Prime Minister's address to the nation the minister of National Defence announces, "a team led by our own national hero General Hamilton is heading the investigation and also the organization of the clean-up and rebuilding efforts in the city. He has been the strength behind our Armed Forces in both action and leadership. In the world community he is a sought after voice of knowledge, and we are fortunate that he has come out of retirement to help resolve the Toronto situation."

Hamilton still wearing his business suit sits at a large desk in a sterilised white office brightly lit by fluorescent bulbs lining the ceiling. Atop his desk is a laptop computer streaming live news reports from the city. Stacks of paper waiting for his review fill the table's surface. Pouring through these documents, highlighting the problems plaguing the city, he is unable to keep at bay the flood of memories.

Thirty years of havoc rip through General Hamilton's mind. While stuck in a daze, his muscles twitch reliving each sound, image and sense as a lifetime's encounters fast forward through his memory. Jumping from planes, explosive entries, returning gunfire, women screaming, children crying, and men dying are worlds he grew accustomed to. This Toronto situation is looking too familiar.

Shawn Gurl's image hits the screen. "Before we connect to a panel of experts out of the United States who assisted in the investigation of the September 11th, 2001 terrorist attacks, I'm being told that we have breaking news from our reporter at ground zero."

The graphic banner across the bottom of the screen reads, 'Toronto in Turmoil.'

"Now over to Carrie Warren."

"Thanks Shawn, we have just received unconfirmed reports that nearly one hundred gas stations, three major landmarks and four major routes were destroyed by explosions while the number of hurt, injured or killed continues to rise. As you can see here, the collapse of the CN tower has forever changed the Toronto skyline, which stood as its iconic image since the 1970s."

Carrie disappears behind her camera scanning the scene showing the demolition of the CN tower. The camera pans out and focuses down a street, as she comes back into sight, "Shawn, I'm being told that there have been numerous clashes between groups of citizens. They are fighting for basic needs, food, water and shelter. Without police intervention these clashes will add to the overwhelming casualties."

"Watch out!" A voice yelled in the background. Carrie's camera is knocked over feeding a stream of information to the viewers from its side.

A speeding truck slams through a store front. A group of bandits wearing masks jump from the truck through the gaping hole in the shattered glass. Within seconds they emerge with arms full of merchandise as the getaway driver speeds off with the loot.

Carrie's voice comes back near the camera standing it up, "Shawn, my tripod is broken, they ran right at me, I just barely got out of the way..."

The General watching these events is interrupted by Colonel Renniks. "Sir, I apologize for disturbing you but we are receiving information about more hostile civilian activity occurring in the city. Police and our forces are trying to deal with the situation but there are too many occurring."

Pointing at his computer streaming the news, "Colonel, I see that. Do what you can but do not spread our people out thin. We will not sacrifice our people's safety sending them into such volatile situations without enough back-up."

"Yes, sir." Renniks departs, leaving Hamilton in his room alone once again.

Turning to the news, Hamilton shakes his head as new images appear on the screen. A banner forms at the bottom of the screen identifying the speaker, this time it is a Doctor of Psychology from Harvard,

"War-like catastrophes have two significant affects on the average untrained person. Like magnetic poles, people are drawn to one side or the other. In this case, the one side is compassion, love, and understanding. The other is full of fear, hate, and selfishness. When such a disaster occurs, there are those who prey on the weak."

From multiple conversations, inquests and investigations, General Hamilton knows the western world could not fathom an attack like this ever taking place in their back yard. No one was prepared mentally or emotionally for the ripple effect these horrific acts produce. Instead of watching these events on the nightly news safely disconnected from the tragedy of some poor war-torn county; modern society is now witnessing Darwinian Theory up close and personal: 'survival of the fittest.'

CHAPTER TWO

The smoke from burnt flesh, torched buildings, and water evaporation, mingle above the streets as clouds into the sky, suffocating the moon's glow. Using mechanical illumination military troops march through the streets showing the scars on the face of the city the world once called pretty. There was no avoiding the raw sewage smeared across the streets, and the stench lingering thick in the air forcing stomach acid into the back of mouths.

What was once a main street is now a picture of a grotesque lunar landing. Under large spotlights, emergency services in homogenous white bio-suits, wade through broken concrete, and twisted metal. Ironically, the disease-ridden sewage water and sludge, cools down iron beams still glowing molten red. It's impossible to tell the difference between military, scientist, police and fire personnel. Just as well, because under the heavy bio-material covered helmets, soft tears fall from even the most hardened veterans. It is here under the sweat stained domes, they mourn in anonymity and ask for forgiveness.

The voices of the trapped and dying have subsided. Tough decisions were made today. The drone of the diesel generators used to power up the lights mercifully fills the air with a tone of emphatic and monotonous absolution.

Each arm of the emergency response units sift through broken teeth, body parts, photographing undistinguishable remains. The sum of human lives scooped up, catalogued and dumped in non-descript plastic bags. Sophisticated multi-band cameras carefully scan the area to reproduce accurate three dimensional computer images. With any luck, the remains contained in plastic bags may one day find justice.

Reporters and camera crews wait nearby in ghoulish anticipation, broadcast-vultures, ready to devour any morsel of new information. The viewing audience, like newborn birds, wait impatiently to be fed by their parents through regurgitation.

Carrie looks at the candy covered table in her office, realizing she can't eat enough to stay awake. She closes her eyes for a couple of hours on a coffee-stained brown leather sofa when the sound of her cell phone beeping insistently forces her back awake. Her eyes skim over the messages telling her one thing: Mr. Wilson is drunk from the staggering jump in WBC ratings and insists that she, his new star reporter return to the street and continue her coverage.

She reads the most recent message, 'A star needs to shine. Get out there and do your thing. I have my best camera man assigned to you exclusively. Thank me later!'

There was a moment in time when that text would have been framed and hung on her wall. Carrie is grateful for the camera man, rubbing her shoulders that hold the memory and imprints of the weight she carried for hours. Her heart is still gun shy from the pain of human tragedy she has already faced and will face again once she leaves the safety and comfort of the WBC tower.

Come on Carrie you can do this, you've seen worse...okay, no I haven't but when this is over everything will pay off, suck it up girl...you can do this. She finishes her pep talk facing the twisted reflection of herself in the stainless steel elevator doors as she reaches the main floor. Carrie's self pep talks never really worked. She never understood why she bothered. It was moments like this she wished her mother was around doing the talking, but she knew this would never be.

The waking nightmare begins as Carrie's camera man counts her in. "You're on in 5-4-3-2."

On cue, the trained smile shines like the artificial area lights surrounding her. "We are live outside a demolished building that used to be...the Eaton Center." Her words echo and ping from ear to ear as she reports on the team of bio-suit wearing workers carrying a stew type substance in plastic bags.

Getting close to the bomb blasted open crater, Carrie tries to shake the feeling of being the ring master of circus dementia. "There is a hole in the middle of Dundas Square that could easily fit three transport trucks side by side."

Pointing to the hole, she motions to the camera man to get a better shot of the abyss. Following orders he moves in. The pavement gives way under his feet. He falls backwards managing to save himself and the camera. Carrie crouches down and cautiously approaches to assist. The camera man shouts, "just stay there!"

Inching away from the hole he retreats to his former position before he reluctantly stands up. Shaking off the incident he resumes filming and flicks his index finger at Carrie to continue. Standing there, staring at her camera man, she couldn't believe his determination. She snaps out of her awe and dramatically emphasizes the phenomenon, "Ah...ah...the ground is unstable, fires that raged underneath although now extinguished, have weakened the area, particularly around blast sites. These holes are even bigger than they appear!"

The world tunes into the up-to-the-minute news report, 'Toronto in Turmoil.' Television screens bleach insomniacs' faces watching the events unfold. Shocked gazes of horror etch onto the faces and sear into the minds of the curious viewers. Terror is brought home by, an over-the-top music score and ten-second sound bites. Carrie, playing the role of the harbinger of bad news, continues to broadcast, "history is replete with many acts of terrorism, but none can compare to this event in recent memory."

The Prime Minister awakens red-eyed from wrestling with warm pillows and chilling nightmares. The early morning ring of the telephone is a welcome change. Knocking over his reading glasses and a stack of books off his night stand he searches for the phone. Locking onto the plastic receiver he presses a button, stopping the noise from disturbing his wife even further. Feeling her roll over he answers the phone. "Yes" is the only salutation he can squeeze out of a sandpaper grizzled throat from the countless meetings the day before.

"Mr. Prime Minister." General Hamilton begins speaking hands-free nearly drowned out by the sound of his car engine as he drives through the streets nearing the Command Center, "I apologize for the god-forsaken hour of this call, however I have disturbing news. Suburban Montreal has just sustained a similar attack."

Silenced and fighting to stay detached from an emotional scream, he leaves the comfort of his blankets, looks around his dark room and then sees the clock. "It's 4:59 a.m. What's the situation?"

"Sir, there are no reports of any victims caught in the explosion. Considering the time of day and the location of the blast, casualties will be minimal. There appears to be no motive for this location to be attacked, it was, for the most part, a vacant facility. I've already sent a couple of our top military investigators to the site to assist the police."

The Prime Minister finds himself at a loss for words as he leaves the confines of his room wrapped in his house coat once again. He's immediately brought back with crystal clarity to his most memorable experience, the moment he accepted the position as leader of the country. Moments after swearing the oath for the highest office in the land, he met with the minister of defence. As the newly-named Prime Minister he was briefed on the ultimate terrorist scenario, codenamed 'Blackstar.' Until now, he questioned and fought with the idea that billions were secretly reallocated and spent to train specialized teams and personnel for such an event. No one expected this to happen in North America, not again. The so called terrorist scenario, a leader's worst nightmare, was now unfolding in text book fashion.

The adrenaline pumping through the PM's body rapidly dismantles the tempered cool veneer he liked to project publicly. "What? We had no warning of these attacks? How could that be? Toronto alone must have required a lot of planning. What about the intelligence community? What assistance have they provided?"

Slamming on the brakes, Hamilton's jeep screeches to a halt, narrowly avoiding a tank pulling onto the road. Breathing hard, he slowly releases his death grip on the steering wheel and shoots back, "Sir, everyone knows that Canada was on the terrorist hit list! There was no conclusive information to suggest an attack was about to occur!"

The General regains his composure and patiently follows slowly behind the tank. "Whoever planned these attacks has maintained a tight circle. Forensic scientists, bomb experts and military personnel are examining seized materials from each of the major blast sites as we speak."

Taking short quick steps, the PM enters his chambers and sits back into his desk chair that had barely cooled down from hours earlier. He turns on the television, "what about civilian unrest?"

General Hamilton gives a by-the-book response. "Infantry are divided in squads and are patrolling with police trying to suppress the looting and rioting in the streets. We are devoting a large amount of resources to keep damage to a minimum. Shelters have been set up and being manned around the clock. Once the Montreal fires have been contained, forensic scientists and investigators will sift through the wreckage. We are actively searching for evidence that links the attacks."

Watching the flickering images of Montreal on the screen the PM stands up, and lodges his Bluetooth ear piece into his ear. Pacing back and forth, he runs his fingers through his hair. Staring at the ceiling, as if waiting for a solution to fall, "General that's all very good, but listen to me, if they succeed..."

Looking back at the carnage displayed on the screen, he shakes his head, "no, No, NO...YOU'VE TOLD ME NOTHING I CAN'T FIND OUT FROM WATCHING THE NEWS!"

Through clenched white-knuckled fists, the PM grapples against his natural instincts to panic. Folding his arms across his chest he lowers his voice, "I expect, no, I DEMAND, more than textbook responses from you, Hamilton. For someone who has fought sorties throughout third world countries, you know exactly what you have to do to survive and win! You, above all knows what happens if we fail to act. Do you hear me?"

Shutting off the jeep engine, he pulls the key from the ignition. Hamilton grew tired of listening to this amateur talk like he knows war, "Mr. Prime Minister."

"I need to know that we are on the same page General. Losing is not an option. ARE WE ON THE SAME PAGE?"

Who is this man yelling at me like a child? Squeezing the car keys in the palm of his hand Hamilton attempts to swallow a humble pill, desperately fighting the urge to tell this politician to go to hell. Swallowing deeply, the General forces himself to answer in the manner that he knows the PM wants to hear, knowing full well they would never be on the same page, "Sir, yes, sir! I will do whatever it takes. There are some other matters that need your attention."

"General, as long as it is brief." The PM opens the window in his office and listens to the silence of the moment, feeling the fleeting sense of serenity as the cold air enters the office dropping the room temperature.

"Very well, sir. Many of the United Nations countries are willing to support us. However, given the large scale of these assaults, they are devoting a great deal of their resources to their own potential threats. Some countries have begun arresting persons of interest. The fact that our global network failed to see these attacks coming, has every country on high alert. Unfortunately for us, no one is sparing any resources."

"What's the next move, General?"

Hamilton reaches over, grabbing a portfolio off the passenger seat, and tucks it under his arm as he walks to the front of the building.

"Currently, I am compiling a strong investigative team. Every phone in the country is under surveillance. All texts sent electronically are scanned for key words. Our country's prime interests are under 24-hour military watch."

Speaking in a cynical voice the Prime Ministers returns, "You know this will have to be approved in the House of Commons."

Security officers open the front doors as the General approaches in full stride speaking through the mic attached to his earpiece, "Mr. Prime Minister, with all due respect, that's your problem. I've already set in motion what needs to be done. I'm following 'Blackstar' protocol."

Hamilton reaches the Command Center, absorbing the positive energy emanating within the room, and proceeds to his office in the back. Scanning the room he sees fluidity in motion, with his subordinates doing all that can be done. "Mr. Prime Minister, if you're really serious about the nation's security, allow me to implement the 360, the independent system that I developed for..."

"General, you know I can't, not without full parliamentary support."

"Yes sir."

"General, I have provided you with as much authority as I can. I'm not sure what your personal philosophy is, but here is mine. We can always ask forgiveness from a thankful country, but if we lose, no one is going to be looking for an apology."

"Well put, Mr. Prime Minister."

"Pull in whatever resources, people, computer programs, whatever you think will work, whoever you trust to get the job done, just get it done General!"

Pulling the ear piece out. Hamilton locates the document bearing the PM's seal and reads it over one more time. For the first time in his coloured career, the General feels the political might that is required to fight such an enemy. Using this strength he plans to undo a wrong that he never had the power to fix until now.

Stepping out from an elevator's opening Hamilton finds himself in an underground warehouse. Aisles upon aisles of shelves fill his sight. To the side he sees his next appointment standing and saluting him.

Hamilton returns the gesture, "At ease, Officer Khan."

The officer lowers his arm and points with an outstretched hand to an office, "General if you could proceed this way, Captain Nolin provided me with this space for now."

Upon entering the room, Hamilton observes oversized computer screens fixed to all four walls and a single desk with two chairs. Behind the desk stands a stack of banker's boxes in the corner. The General takes a seat on a chair, and swivels around surveying the information displayed. "Captain Nolin tells me good things about you. Apparently if you and your team don't have a confidential human source on the inside of an organization, they basically don't exist."

Khan enters the room, and leans against the desk, "General, I only wish that were true."

Grabbing a report from the desk top, Khan hands it to the General. He walks toward the monitors, pointing at the information displayed, "General, as you're well aware, almost every country has suffered some sort of terrorist attack. Leading up to this event the intelligence community has always been able to hear a rumour, gossip, something. Considering the large scale of this event, we haven't heard a word, absolutely nothing to suggest it was going to occur, nor did any of our counterparts."

Shifting his eyes away from the screens the General leafs through the report in his hands and asks, "Are you saying this is a new group?"

Hanging his head, Khan explains, "I'm sorry sir, I can't say. It could be a new terrorist group or it could be an existing one that has kept a tighter lid on things. I wish I had an answer. It's killing us but we are calling everyone we know and so far nothing."

Sympathy is something Hamilton rarely feels. Seconds seem to stop as he realizes what's causing his chest pain. All too familiar with the pressure placed on each individual under normal circumstances the General knows how tremendous this incident must be for this officer.

'Euphoria' might be too strong a word. However, after the General retired and the weight of the Miguel Mejia political storm was lifted off his shoulders, that is the only word he could think of. Doing the job was never the issue, politics was. Not ready for retirement yet, Hamilton decided to take on the life of a mercenary working for governments on projects that would never be revealed to the public. The job was simple, puppet master a nightmare and stop an uncontrollable one from happening.

Using a remote, Khan skims through numerous pictures. Surveillance photos of known extremist groups take shape on the screen as he continues the briefing, "...most active terrorist groups have gone underground to evade detection from authorities. They have resorted to mouth to mouth communication instead of using any other modes of communication. Circles are tighter and fewer people are in the know. Without this information we are having a hell of a time infiltrating their layers. We have been able to photograph them, but determining their malicious intent is near impossible."

Rising to his feet, Hamilton moves with a slow and deliberate gait across the room. Sluggishly he turns and faces the intelligence analyst, "I know you guys are always coming up with the latest and greatest methods of information gathering and extraction. There will be no criticism here. I need to know what your gut feeling is telling you. How do you propose we begin to protect society from a very real bogey man?"

Recalling the cabinet for an emergency session has political pundits and respectable social media mavens discussing the possibility of the War Measures Act being invoked.

"We haven't heard these words in this arena for a half-century."

"True, spoken by any politician would automatically result in career suicide."

"Certainly this situation justifies its use. This extends well beyond Canadian borders."

"I agree this is much larger than the political terrorist group the FLQ kidnapping politicians and killing one. However, I don't agree that we need to resort to such a level of force."

"Mr. Prime Minister the media is waiting, sir," the Prime Minister's aide Clint announced, before noticing one of the most powerful men in the free world wrestling with his neck tie. "Sir, may I help you with that?"

Walking over to the PM who is standing in front of the mirror, the aide grabs the short end of the neck tie and proceeds with the tie ritual. The PM watches the aide, distracted by his thoughts, "Clint, isn't it funny that a simple piece of cloth can command so much time, attention and respect?"

The aide, thrown off by the comment, fumbles and restarts the process. "Sir?"

"So many intricate and delicate moves to yield the perfect result. The irony is that even after every perfect move is made, the tie could still come up short." The PM gives a pseudo-reassuring smile and places a soft hand on the confused aide's shoulder. "It's time to go."

Behind his reading glasses, the Prime Minister's eyes focus on the papers resting on the lectern in front of him. The solid oak table top easily sustains the weight of the sheets lining its top and that of the PM's upper body. Gripping its sides, the PM steadies his hands from overtly shaking. Although in his element, the leader couldn't be any more distraught wondering, *where are they going to hit next?* as he reads his speech,

"We stand together, Canadians with families and friends spread out over this magnificent country. We have an enemy out there who shows no mercy. Semantics is a luxury we cannot afford. Please, for the sake of every resident within our borders let's work together. Right now each of you is being provided sensitive material; there are questions we need answered."

Standing in the corners of the House of Commons military officers monitor page boys handing out stacks of paper to each Member. Bold red ink coats the cover page classifying the document 'Restricted.'

WBC news anchor Shawn Gurl is interrupted with sounds coming through his ear piece as he scrolls through past and present images of Toronto. Looking down, listening to the voice, he nods and faces the camera, "we turn now to our on scene reporter Carrie Warren live on the streets of Montreal. Carrie, could you please explain what you're seeing right now."

"Yes, thank you Shawn. Authorities aren't saying much about the recent explosion rocking sleepy Montreal suburbia. Fortunately this eruption was isolated to a relatively small area. We still haven't been provided with any reports of any casualties. The massive hole left here displays the magnitude of the blast. Currently, there is no information confirming whether this was carried out by the same group that struck Toronto."

Through the doors of the Command Center enters an officer, who despite all those coming and going, stands out from the rest. Several women have been assigned to the team, yet this soldier commands attention. Although wearing standard military issue clothing designed for a man, she cannot mask her feminine physique. Restrained blonde hair pulled tightly into a bun, make-up by minimalist design, demonstrates a concerted effort meant to deemphasize her striking features. It's clear from her athletic silhouette and powerful stride, her masculine walking gait was no accident. Any hint of physical weakness would not be found in her. However, her strikingly intense hazel eyes betray the carefully cultivated don't screw with me image.

Now standing directly in front of the General's office, the hazel-eyed soldier announces her presence with three short powerful knocks. Looking up from a map-strewn desk, General Hamilton flashes a quick smile.

Proceeding directly into the office, the soldier stands at attention on the opposite side of the desk.

"Lieutenant Paula Connie nothing has changed. You do that every time."

Oblivious to his meaning, she asks, "What is that, Sir?"

"You didn't notice you nearly stopped time when you entered the room."

"Sir?" Naturally turning her head slightly sideways as if to avoid the compliment, Lieutenant Paula Connie catches a few periodic glances from soldiers at their stations.

"General, you can't help yourself can you? Always testing. Can we move along?"

"Lieutenant, knowing someone's mind is a powerful tool. Something that you are quite good at, it's your mouth that keeps you from advancing."

"With all due respect, advancement doesn't interest me if I have to sell out who I am."

"Well said, please take a seat," he said, motioning to the chairs opposite his large desk.

Sitting erect, not resting her body against the back of the chair, Paula displays a modest smile, "it's good to have you back. It's been a long time."

"Hopefully it won't be for too long, we don't have much time. Thank you for coming to see me on such short notice. I apologize for having you reassigned, but your expertise is needed here. You've been briefed on the current situation?"

"Yes sir, on the way down."

"Your new assignment is to closely monitor the progress and restoration development of the Toronto downtown core areas."

"Control the chaos, minimize the fiscal damage, and restore public confidence, got it."

Standing up and leaning on the desk as if to emphasize every word. The General looks directly into the Lieutenant's eyes. "This country cannot afford a financial collapse. Foreign investors need to know we have the ability to protect both our assets and theirs. We have extremely short deadlines with a very impatient audience."

"General, I won't let you down. Can I get the personnel files for my new team?"

Settling back down on his chair, confidently the General explains. "You've been given the best officers we can spare. Their files are being transferred to your device." His stern face shifts and begins to resemble a grin, "Talking about team members, I am about to pick up a game-changer, a star player, if you will, to kick start this assignment into overdrive."

Lieutenant Connie was never one for games. She also knew that the General never played them. "General, I have worked with investigators throughout the world and know all those assigned to your team. Sure they have earned their reputations, but I wouldn't classify anyone as a star. They aren't as capable or creative as you."

A sadistic smile stretches across the General's face, "Well thank you Lieutenant, I'm a little shocked at your comment. I've never known you to be the political kiss ass."

Snapping back at that insinuation, Paula corrects the General, "That was not designed to be a compliment. It was an empirical fact-based assessment. I don't believe this is the situation where you test drive amateurs. I am quite pissed off with the notion that you think someone else can do a better job than you. No one lives for the job like you do. I'm here to win and I'm for damn sure not here to kiss your ass."

Amused at how easily he got under her skin, Hamilton admits, "Lieutenant, I understand your position and respect your thoughts. If you have learned anything from working with me in past it should be this; I refuse to settle for second best. You need to trust me now. This particular person will change the face of the game."

An electronic buzz draws General Hamilton's attention. Metal on metal softly squeals as a thick oversized steel door slowly swings open. Hamilton, seated inside the small plain room, sees Miguel Mejia limping into sight shaking the chains restricting his hands and feet. Dressed in filthy bright orange coveralls with splashes of dried blood over his body, Miguel shuffles his shoes over to the spare chair in the room. A cold dark stare reflects absolutely nothing in the deep colour of Miguel's irises. The shackled man's disposition is eased looking at the concerned face of General Hamilton. Rolling his eyes quickly as if both men share a silent joke, Miguel sits down. The guard that walked him in gets a nod from the General and retreats against the room's wall. Miguel straightens up in the chair breathing out heavily,

"Ooooo. Ouch. It's been a while David... from what I hear you're a busy man working for the government again?"

"Yeah, something like that, and from what I've heard, you introduced a couple of guards to some hospital staff. I was told they had to correct your behaviour."

The General stood up, reached into his shirt pocket and pulled out a folded piece of paper. Bending down he places it into Miguel's hands, "I believe this is yours."

Unfolding the paper Miguel sees the picture of two little boys smiling up at him. Looking over his shoulder, he glares at the guard, "These sons of bitches needed to learn a lesson. Never poke a caged animal."

Hamilton nods his head as he returns to his seat, "What else has been happening?"

"Been tied up lately, you know," holding up the handcuffs. "Hamilton come on, I know you better than that. What's up?"

"Miguel, you were never one for small talk." Rolling his shoulders, Hamilton leans forward, "I need a leader, someone who knows how I think, and one that will do what's right but not necessarily what people assume is right. I told you that I would help you in any way that I can. This is it."

Miguel sits back in his chair stretches and mirrors Hamilton leaning forward. He starts rubbing his temples with his fingertips, shaking the chains, "Boss, I'm flattered.. it's been a long time.. After all that happened who would follow me, or listen to me?"

> Cement barriers and chain linked fencing pollute the downtown streets around a courthouse. Police in black riot gear sweat under the sweltering sun holding a line, keeping angry protesters at bay. Snipers on roof tops survey the crowd.

> The masses chant, "Killer Cop! Killer Cop!" The sound vibrates through the courthouse's stone walls reaching Miguel's ears.

Hamilton whispers, "The country will."

Intrigued, Miguel straightens up at full attention. Cautiously the chained man asks, "What?"

Pausing, glancing over Miguel's shoulder, he looks at the guard standing behind him, he speaks in a hushed tone. "You're it. You'll be my right hand man. Anything that occurs will be a product of our control."

"I don't know, boss. People don't forget, boss, how..."

> News broadcasts featuring Shawn Gurl educated the public on the situation in the heart of the city: "Right wing supporters of the Killer Cop clashed with the left wing peace activists. Several police officers were injured trying to suppress the violence ending in sixty-six people being arrested. The mayor had strong words for Parliament."

> "This is absolutely insane. The security fencing, extra police officers and traffic congestion is costing tax payers millions of dollars for this trial? He was caught on camera, it's pretty cut and dry. Convict him and let's put the money towards the city's children programs."

Hamilton leans in closer to Miguel. "I know you've been through a lot. This can be a new beginning for you."

Looking for and even wishing for truth in Hamilton's face as he continues, "I supported you then, as I do now. I'm offering you the chance at a new start."

Sitting upright, the General feels like a salesman completing his pitch. "Miguel, you know I wouldn't bullshit you. You are exactly what I need to stop these psychopaths from killing thousands of innocent people."

Frustrated, Miguel raises his voice, "after what happened I don't know if I can."

> An explosion and flames occupy the prisoner's mind.

Awkwardly standing up abruptly, Miguel loses his balance and the observation guard quickly approaches. A motion from the General's right hand stops the guard in his tracks.

Shouting Miguel continues. "Why now? Why like this?" Dropping his body, he slumps back onto the cold metal chair in frustration as a tear streams down his face.

"Miguel, look at me. I had your mother... and your, your boys relocated to our base as soon as I resumed command. Lisa stayed with her new husband, you know, fireman Rick? Apparently he didn't want to be around a bunch of your old friends 24/7, can't say that I blame him. They're isolated and should be relatively safe out there on the hobby farm. Do it for your boys at least."

The prisoner's outstretched hands grip his scalp pulling loose skin backwards across his skull. His dark eyes leave traces of tear-stained memories on the grey cement floor. Sniffling, he whispers, "My boys...my boys." Sitting up and keeping his head down Miguel speaks softly, holding back a flood of emotions, "sure...count me in."

Hamilton stands up and with a gesture of his hand the heavy metal door re-opens. He looks down at Miguel, "trust me I have never let you down..."

"Daddy can you help me across the monkey bars?"

"Help me too Daddy, me too!"

Two bright-eyed little boys smile and laugh hanging from the bars. Miguel helps and watches as they gain confidence doing it by themselves. Their tiny heads look back at him beaming with pride at their recent accomplishment.

"General, we're over Toronto now." The pilot announced through the helicopter ear phones, snapping Miguel out of a daydream. Looking down he sees the chains that once restricted his movements have been replaced with a helicopter's seatbelt strap and the fluorescent orange jump suit was exchanged for a uniform he hasn't worn in over a decade.

"It's okay Miguel, take a look," the General coaxes.

Gripping the seatbelt strap, Miguel's veins pop out of his hand as he inches his posterior from the center of the bench seat near the window in the door. With his arm fully extended Miguel stretches his neck, peering out the glass, taking in the defunct metropolis. Bombed out hollow craters interrupt the grid lines spread over the city. The Spaniard breathes heavily as if running a race.

Sarcastically the General pokes, "Miguel relax. This chopper was just maintained. You have nothing to fear."

"Yeah, but what day of the week was it done?"

Laughing the General replies, "just look out the window."

Miguel's eyes survey the rubble. Bombed buildings leave stand-ing sculptures of partial stone walls. A blanket of charcoal gray coats the city. His mind recalls his last free day. It was a beautiful sunny day with the streets congested with protestors yelling at him and his family while surrounded by police officers walking up the stone steps into the courthouse.

Seeing a mangled child's playground littered with crumpled cars and chunks of mortar, the Spaniard mumbles to himself, "sons of bitches."

The General shouts to overcome the noise of the helicopter, "that's why you have to succeed. This is only the beginning. Montreal appears to have escaped a similar fate this morning. A warehouse was levelled and we believe that it was the same group."

Giving a half-nod, Miguel continues to map the destruction while clutching the strap in his hand.

"We are on the brink of financial collapse, another major city going down like this would seal the fate of the country for years to come."

"What am I working with, boss?"

"Whatever resources you need. I will take care of all the political bullshit. Just get to the bottom of this quickly."

Miguel pulls on the strap sliding his body back to the center of the seat, "General, I will give you everything I have."

The General looks out the window at the city, "I know."

Landing at the Command Center, ground crews approach to assist. Normally frenzied in motion, the crews stop and stare at the man accompanying General Hamilton.

Miguel winks as he walks past them and enters the building. He knows their faces. Names often escaped, but a face, he never forgot. They were definitely good guys. The kind of guys he counted on equipping his rigs when he used to run one of his old middle-of-the-night operations.

The sound of military fatigues and heavy boots moving quickly down the hallway made Miguel want to yell 'I'm free!'

Picking up the pace, both men try to reach the board room. General Hamilton was confident that Miguel would choose to take the position and arranged a meeting for this precise time. The tour of Toronto took a little longer than expected but the emotional impact on his recruit was needed to secure Miguel's commitment. Hamilton detested tardiness.

In the absence of the helicopter noise and the constant updates from General David Hamilton, Miguel finds time to think clearly. Reflecting on the past he can't remember a time ever feeling this way. Doing nothing but surviving for two years definitely had its neutralizing effect. Self-consciously walking down the military base hall feels like a dream. Miguel had lost count how many times he had dreamed of busting out of prison one way or another. In the small recesses in his mind he knew he would have figured it out. Accepting the decision he made, and the consequences, wasn't easy but was necessary to remain sane. Now at the age of forty he is back to help save the country that wanted to bury him far out of sight.

The General's stride increases in length and speed seeing two armed guards standing outside auditorium doors. Snapping his hand up, he returns the guards' salute and enters the doors, leaving Miguel outside.

Guards rest their hands on their pistols in holsters seeing the Spaniard trailing behind. Pointing to chairs on the opposite side of the hallway they order, "just sit down over there."

Taunting the nervous base guards, Miguel sluggishly follows their directions. Peering over his shoulders he sees them relax and resume their positions as he descends onto the chair. He shakes his head, *stop it; being an asshole isn't going to help right now.*

Sitting there rubbing his head, Miguel feels a sore lump behind his ear. A gentle reminder where he was only hours ago; and truth to the age old saying that he may win a battle but lose the war. Looking down he sees the scars and fresh scabs across his knuckles.

"Man, that Carrie Warren is one piece of ass. Open up the door," ordered a jail guard escorting Miguel back to his cell after the conclusion of the interview.

Shuffling his chained feet, Miguel follows two escorting jail guards into a secured bricked hallway with standard metal doors blocking each end.

Approaching the other end, one of the jail guards asks, "Have they finished with his cell yet?"

"Yep, Bruno told me to start making our way back. He was just leaving."

Inquisitively Miguel questions, "My cell?"

"You'll find out soon enough. You shouldn't have given that reporter a hard time. You made the Warden look bad."

One guard looks up at the camera and yells, "Open up the next door."

With a buzz the door opens and in through the opening walks another security guard with a name tag sewn on his shirt, 'C. Bruno'. As Bruno recognizes Miguel he smiles at the other guards and taps his pocket. A folded piece of paper extended from the top revealing its brown curled sides. Bruno walks past them and continues to the opposite end.

"You took my picture?" Miguel shouted.

"Just move along Miguel," bossed the guard pushing on Miguel's back leading him towards the open door that was already starting to close.

Miguel steps backwards and pins the guard's foot under his own. In a smooth sweep he spun around and struck the guard in the face with his elbow. With his handcuffed hands he wrapped them around the back of the guard's neck and jumped up with both feet, driving his knees into the guard's face. An explosion of blood sprayed all over and both of them fell to the floor. Lifting his arms he released the unconscious man from his clutches and kicked his limp body towards the other guard charging with his baton extended.

Staggering, trying to avoid stepping on his comrade, the guard loses his balance temporarily as Miguel lies on his back. He curls his legs up towards his head. Just as the guard approached he sprang from the ground kicking his legs up and driving his heels into the guard's chest. With a crack the uniformed officer was thrown back against the wall and crumpled to the floor gasping for air.

Bruno, seeing Miguel standing, began to retreat and was banging on the far door, "Open up! Open up!"

Miguel threw his body backwards and performed two back handsprings closing the distance, reaching Bruno in a split second.

Releasing the door's handle, Bruno whimpers, "Please don't kill me. I have a wife and kids. I was only following ord…"

Double fisting the guard in the stomach ended his verbal pleas. As he slouched to the floor holding his stomach, Miguel reached down and carefully removed the folded piece of paper out of the guard's pocket. Thumping sounds and yelling from a host of voices gathering on the opposite side of the door were only two inches of steel away. Looking up at the camera Miguel puts his piece of paper in his orange coveralls pocket and lowers himself to his knees. Slouching forward he closes his eyes, hearing the buzz of the door opening the lock, "this is going to hurt."

Shaking his head, Miguel looks up at the two base guards standing in front of the large doors that General Hamilton just walked through. *After everything I've done. Everything I've seen. Do I have what it takes to contribute to this team? The only thing that kept my mind active was the computerized chess set that my boys gave me.*

Despite all of his past experiences, Miguel knew this is going to be the largest, most far-reaching operation he has ever been a part of and the biggest question torturing his mind was, *Trust. Who can I trust? Do I even trust myself?*

Inside the boardroom, the General walked in to see all military personnel stand at attention. The civilian members begin to follow suit out of both ignorance and respect. The General advises them all to sit down.

"Amidst all of this devastation, I have secured a strong leader, someone whom I have had the privilege to work alongside. In many situations similar to the one facing us today, he has proven himself honourable and battle tested. He is, in my opinion one of the most gifted natural leaders I know. I trust him absolutely, so much so, that I retired on his behalf and would do it all over again if required."

The General walks away from the podium heading towards the seats in the auditorium saying, "This person only has one interest and that is to see this mission succeed. There's no hidden agenda, nor promotion when complete, the only satisfaction is seeing it through to the end. I am pleased to introduce you to Colonel Miguel Mejia."

The room fell awkwardly silent for the first time. For the majority of the people in the room hearing the General speak Mejia's name seems like an ill-timed joke made in poor taste. Sitting perplexed, trying to determine if it in fact is Hamilton's off colour humour, their eyes pick up Miguel Mejia entering the room. Holding the door open the General hopes this symbolic gesture isn't lost on his audience.

Every face registers the same question and a buzz of activity begins. Questions mumble through the crowd.

"The world is scrutinizing our every move and now we have a convicted murderer going to lead the largest investigation in the country's history?"

"How can we possibly follow someone who escaped prison only because thousands of people died?"

Slowly entering the auditorium, Miguel's eyes sweep the room. Confusion, disgust and complacency paint the picture. Familiar friendly faces are difficult to find among the crowd. Lowering his head down toward the mic, the Spaniard begins to question the General's thought process, *It's a tactical error to stand in front of a hostile crowd. Who here is going to follow me? They'd prefer to watch me hang publically.* A familiar flash and voice in Miguel's head shouts, *Own the battle. It begins here.* He scans the faces again. Young, old, scared, and lost souls make up the array of onlookers as he prepares to speak,

"I know this must come as a shock that I am here to work with you, given my personal circumstances. I cannot take back what I did years ago. That doesn't matter in the here and now!"

Miguel's tone deepens and the look in his eyes becomes more intense as he masters his present situation, "there are certain things that happened to us over the last few hours. Things that someone must answer to. We all have hard choices to make. We are in a battle to regain command of our country. This is what we need to do. That is all we have left in our control."

Stepping away from the podium, he walks towards the crowd. The General gets up and meets Miguel. The Spaniard is met by Hamilton's extended hand. In front of everyone they shake hands and the General leans in, "Good to have you back."

Miguel takes a seat in the general population as Hamilton addresses the crowd once more.

"Colonel Mejia, thank you for accepting this position. I would like to advise everyone that the blast sites have been investigated and the items seized are currently under examination. Montreal is now being inspected by our specialists. There will be an action plan set out for all investigators tomorrow morning at 9h00 by Colonel Mejia."

As the room clears, stragglers approach Miguel welcoming him to the team. Standing up and speaking to them the Spaniard notices others sceptical of his abilities leaving the room, speaking among themselves,

"Taking directions from a convicted criminal?"

"Yeah right, good plan."

Among those walking out Miguel recognizes Colonel Renniks.

Reclined in a chair at his desk in his new office, the former inmate flips through pages contained inside a folder. Stopping and looking around, he takes a deep breath, *I can't believe it.*

On the desk staring at him through the stacks of paper is the picture of his boys now flattened by a pane of glass, and held together by a thin wood frame.

Of the paper making up the landscape on his desk top are three of piles of paper consisting of personnel files of those already assigned to the team, 'Review, Pass and Dismiss.' Grabbing a new file from the 'Review' pile he assesses the potential member by reading their dossier and examining their photo.

Setting the bar at the top of the 'Dismiss' pile is Colonel Edward Renniks. Highlighted in his dossier was an entry when he received a medal of honour. The highlighted text that followed read:

'....while piloting a helicopter extracting an elite team from a hostile environment... took out an enemy's stronghold... began taking on enemy fire... sustained a critical hit... Renniks ejected from the aircraft narrowly escaping with his life...Armed only with an officer's side arm he traversed three days over significant enemy terrain, eventually making it back to the base of operations... Submitted by General Izzov.'

In bold writing across the file is written, 'CORRUPT, COWARD, LIAR'...

CHAPTER THREE

Moving silently towards the front door of a house, faint shadows fight to illuminate Miguel's surroundings. Dilated irises strain to locate objects in the vicinity. Cognizant of the proximity to his intended destination, adrenaline dumps into his system. His beating heart is the only sound breaking the ear piercing silence. Fighting to control his hands from shaking, thoughts begin racing, visualizing the next few steps. Miguel's doubts punctuate the temple throbbing anticipation of his next crucial move. *It's been too long...I'm not ready for this...*

Miguel feels the chambers of his heart open and close with every rush of blood through his veins. *This is it,* he tells himself, *it's now or never.* Entering the door into a darkened hallway, his feet forget their weight, creaking the floor.

Down the darkened hallway, a door opens, and Miguel braces for the confrontation. Slightly disoriented, an older woman follows the sounds and pauses, seeing the silhouette before her.

Weakened by the moment, temporarily unable to move, he watches the woman walking toward him. "Miguel?"

She touches his shoulder before embracing him. "Oh Miguel, it's so good to see you."

Unable to respond, his body shakes uncontrollably as he embraces the most important woman in his life.

"Miguel, it's okay. It's okay. I know."

His hardened body gives in under the weight he's been carrying for the past two years. Inch by inch his body sinks toward the floor as the load increases, unable to fight through this battle, tears flow. Leaning against the wall, the elderly lady holds his hand. Looking up at her, he whimpers out looking down the hall at a closed bedroom door, "Where are they?"

Tears roll down her face, "Miguel, you know they're sleeping. I don't think now is a good time."

"Madre."

"Miguel listen to me. You can't. Not right now. After this is all done you will have all the time in the world to reminisce."

The raw morning sun easily burns through the last vestiges of night. Dust particles accentuated by the new sun float unnoticed through the large gym windows. The gym smells of vinegar soaked cleaning solvent and fresh sweat. Muscles strain against tightened skin as Miguel punishes his body. The intensity increases as fast as last night's memories replay itself over and over again. Miguel grunts lifting the heavy iron, cognizant that eventually, he will have to give in to his burden.

Unbeknownst to Miguel while punishing himself, is a crowd gathered, watching this man, beast, machine, push himself mercilessly, lift after gruelling lift. Thoughts and questions cross their minds but no one dares to break the reverenced silence. Who is this man with the word 'APOK' tattooed across his left bicep? He hadn't been active in years.

How could he be any help? Most disturbing, what kind of power did the General wield? Or better yet, whose nuts did he have squished in a vice allowing him to free a lifer jail bird with zero chance of parole?

This black hooded sleeveless warrior was considered by world leaders to be the top field agent on the planet. Many only knew him by name or reputation and few ever caught a glimpse of his face until he left the military. He wasn't concerned about those that could recognize or harm him. Miguel had no time to worry about the dead.

Driving his intensity were the thoughts, and questions that kept coming at him like a boxer caught off guard dodging punches fired in rapid succession. Fighting to overcome years of inactivity, his mind skims and scans every detail of his mission objectives. Sweat pours down every crease in Miguel's aging face as he lands a crushing blow to the punching bag. Visualizing deadly hand to hand combat scenarios with faceless enemies prevented being intruded by painful memories.

He strikes another blow, this time lifting the one hundred pounds of dead weight off the chain momentarily. The punching bag crashes back into place. Miguel's mind creates another faceless enemy and quickly dispatches him with a deadly blow from a swift round house kick to an imaginary skull.

Never before had Miguel been so conflicted. This country with all its blessings, allowed him to kill in its name. Yet, unrepentantly, turned on him when he acted in the names of those who couldn't protect themselves. Something he knew in his heart of hearts was the right thing to do.

Certain lobbyists with malicious agendas and forked-tongued media pundits convinced the brainwashed public he was a bigot and a cold-blooded murderer. The trial was a mockery. There was no way anyone in the jury could have had a clear and unbiased view of the situation. The trial garnered widespread global media attention. Those in government added fuel to the fire, openly suggesting guilt or allowing media leaked, black-markered documents, to imply sinister intent.

Through those long brutal days and weeks of hearings and public outrage, he repeated to himself. *I'm fighting the right fight, that's why I'm here.* This mantra became the bridge between drowning in madness or floating in the pool of sanity. Fighting the 'right fight' was the only badge of honour the disgraced cop wore now.

Miguel remembers the unbearable days when he sat through the court proceedings being branded as a cold, calculating, brutal murderer. However, the toughest days were sitting through the very bright sunny afternoons, suffocating in that stuffy courtroom filled with people staring at him like a circus freak, knowing he was missing fleeting precious moments with his boys. Waiting for the Judge to call it a day, he would tune out the world, wondering what his munchkins were up to.

Ironically, Miguel never thought he would ever be standing at this vantage point either. *Before me is a country on its knees praying for a saviour that's in short supply.* For the first time he notices the onlookers and shameless gawkers, who quickly look away. A contemptuous grin spreads across his sweat streaked face thinking, *life certainly has a twisted sense of humour.*

The next thought slapped any chance of prolonged humour far away from Miguel's face. *Behind every successful man there is a great and supportive woman, or something like that.* Even now he still hears her voice.

"Look at you. Always the hero. They're gonna lock you away now. I'm sure it was worth it."

For a moment, Miguel looks down in pain, like he did at the time he heard those words.

At a time when the woman he needed to believe in him the most, abandoned him. Knowing his children had snuck out of bed and were hiding around the corner was the only reason the broken warrior never offered verbal resistance. *Just let her get it out of her system,* he thought, knowing she has to blow off some steam.

"You're just gonna stand there and say nothing? You're the biggest joke. You let your family down! The ones that you are suppose to protect, REMEMBER?"

The screaming woman invades Miguel's personal space, lowering her voice, "I can't go to the grocery store without a reporter asking me if I think you're guilty and if I'm going to stand by you?" She laughs. "Stand by you...YOU, MIGUEL?"

Miguel couldn't blame the boys when they came running out from around the corner but he wishes he could have prevented it. Seeing the look of horror on their young faces burst into tears as their mother repeatedly slapped him across the face was more than he could bear.

Grabbing her flailing hands in one smooth motion didn't stop her from spitting in his face. While wiping the dripping mucus from his eye with his free hand, the incensed woman softly asks, "Did you save the world Miguel? Do the people love you for it?"

He released her wrists. She steps back towards her sons. The room is silent except for the sobs of two very scared and confused boys. Instinctively, Miguel begins to move in the direction of his boys.

"Don't you dare take another step towards my children," she said, grabbing them.

Now glaring at the woman blocking him from his sons, he motions to speak, only to be cut off by a verbal wall of anger.

"YOU STUPID IDIOT! You did all of this for some asshole. What are you going to do now? Go around killing everyone who you think is an asshole? If you are..." Switching to a new tone of sarcastic soft, the angry woman politely repeats, "If you are...why don't you start with YOURSELF?"

Watching his wife hug the boys as if protecting them from a monster, Miguel had to wonder, *Is she right?*

In front of Miguel, the heavy punching bag erupts into many faceless enemies. Unleashing a deadly barrage of quick and lethal combinations, the onlookers collectively take a healthy step backward. *APOK* became a blur of raw power and speed unseen by most. The shift from admiration to fear from the onlookers was instantaneous.

Jump killer cop jump. The whistle of the skipping rope warns of a nearly invisible speed cocoon encircling Miguel's chiselled body. Barely breathing hard, Miguel's heart works fine for a man creeping up in age. *Jump killer cop jump.* The phrase repeats like a child skipping and singing playground songs, permeating Miguel's subconscious. Those words, those thoughts, fuelled the cocoon.

The media label Killer Cop stuck. *Every news channel and half-wit reporter sentenced me. I was no better than an animal to them. Why not? It's easier to convict a man if you strip away his humanity.*

With machine precision, the rope strikes the floor creating a tapping sound that could easily be mistaken for a machine, monotonously grinding away on an assembly line.

Times were tough after the gavel fell. The weekly penitentiary visits from his sons became bi-weekly, which quickly became now and again then abruptly no more. The only letter from Miguel's wife was sparse and to the point.

'Miguel, I can't keep doing this. It's killing the boys to see you locked up with those animals. We will keep accepting your calls though. Lisa'

Like water on the rocks on the shore, so too was isolation to Miguel. Breaking him down, slowly, forcing him to question himself time and time again. Toying with his mind doubting the things he once held to be true. *Was it the right decision...well, was it Miguel?*

As mercy would have it, the odd piece of mail occasionally found its way to Miguel. It was through these words etched onto paper that provided Miguel the strength to defend from the power of this question. He strikes the heavy bag again with such force that it flies up in the air, the chains barely sustain the stress. *I made the right decision, those without a voice won...I lost. I lost!*

Like so many through the centuries Miguel knows he was expelled from sight, imprisoned without just cause. Like Galileo, highly respected and educated. However, when he contradicted the society's leaders, he was jailed for life. Only recently has the church gone public to say that Galileo was correct and they were wrong. A lot of good that confession will do him now, having been dead for centuries.

The final warning for the onlooker's self-preservation was punctuated by the wretched sound coming from Miguel, "Ahhhh!" Striking the bag with every ounce of energy, his calloused bare knuckles rip open, smearing blood over the perforated leather. Standing there, his hands hang by his sides and drip blood on the floor. With his head lowered, mandible extended outwards, his heaving chest sucks in air. He glares into the mirror hating his reflection.

Day brings to life the toxic smell of black diesel smoke created by the creaking and rumbling of menacing war machines operating through the streets of the Central Command Center. The cold suspends the dissipation of the poisonous clouds lurking in the air. Troops accustomed to the climate pay no heed to them or the scream of jet exhaust filling their ear canals. Sixty pounds of additional weight slow their movements as they congest the rear of large green canvas covered armoured trucks. Hushed by their current situation they begin their procession to the once majestic city, bringing much needed reinforcements and fresh supplies.

Standing outside a military base home, Miguel tugs on the bottom of his tunic straightening out the folds caused during the drive over. He quickly corrects the fit of his hat before marching over to meet Military Police arriving on scene. As they exit their vehicle they couldn't help but stop and notice the Colonel, now dressed in his full military attire with more medals pinned to his chest than notices on a bulletin board at the local laundromat. As they salute him, their eyes keep shifting from his dark pupils down the left side of his chest examining each award that he wore with distinction.

Miguel hands them a copy of the official order he had rolled up, still in his hand.

"Good morning, gentlemen. As I instructed your supervisor, here is our situation."

Allowing them a moment to digest the information was almost too much for him to handle. Miguel couldn't help but think of all the other items he has to complete and grew annoyed knowing how much time is consumed with each little action, *Would these guys just hurry up?* he thought looking down at his watch, wondering if he could finish everything he set out to do this morning. The waiting was over, Miguel catches their faces shift from the complacent uninterested look to their jaw dropping and eye popping, is this a joke expression.

Without wasting any further time Miguel confirms, "Do we have a problem here officers? Do you understand what our mission is?"

Closing their mouths for a moment, computing what he just said, they answer in tandem, "No sir...Yes sir!" Looking at one another for a second, one turns back replying, "We're good."

With a head nod Miguel confirms that he knows how extreme the information may appear but takes no more time to explain. Pivoting around, he begins the approach to the front door, and they follow loosely behind.

The Spaniard takes in several deep breaths walking up to the door. The frost in the air causes his nostrils to temporarily freeze together before the heat overwhelms and releases its grip. His black military shoes reflect the sun's rays from the pristine polishing the former inmate was able to perfect on their exterior. The collaboration of his steps leading to the front door forms a solid beat, a testament to his hours of marching through the years. Stopping short of the door, he stands at attention. Extending his arm out, he knocks on the wood frame surrounding the entrance.

The door opens, with Colonel Renniks stepping into sight. His face, though normally clean-shaven, had yet to be met with a razor. Countless hours in direct sunlight had wrinkled and weathered his skin. Standing in his door frame added another twelve inches to his medium sized frame. Scanning his surroundings, he spots Miguel and the Military Police under his command standing on the cement walkway leading to his home.

Renniks' eyebrows rise as his eyes widen and his body tenses. His hand on the door knob pulls tight into a fist. Using the additional height and security of his home he attempts to intimidate his guests, looking down his nose at them. Tilting his head from side to side, "recently released Mejia and my Military Police."

The Colonel straightens his posture pulling his shoulders back. Raising his head, he barely makes an effort to speak, grumbling, "I do not recall planning a meeting with any of you at this hour, nor do I agree with you attending my quarters. Whatever it is, I'm sure it can wait till the briefing that you, Miguel, set up for later this morning."

Without waiting for a response Renniks completes his sentence and steps back closing the door. Enraged at his arrogance, Miguel shoots out his foot, stopping the door from closing, scuffing the polished surface of his boot, "Colonel Renniks!"

Throwing open the door he smashes it against the inside wall of his house causing the door knob to penetrate the drywall. Miguel pulls back his leg as Renniks pounces from his stoop. Face flushed, eyes bloodshot he snaps at Miguel's face like an enraged dog. "Listen here you fucking convicted criminal. I don't give a shit who you know that can get you out of prison. You don't dare come to a commanding officer's quarters and disrespect him like that, do I make myself clear?"

Steadfast maintaining eye contact, Miguel forces himself to salute Renniks, "Colonel Renniks with all due respect, I am here with an urgent matter that needs your immediate attention."

Colonel Renniks' head bobs backwards. He looks around trying to pick up something that he missed. He catches a glimpse of the MPs who are now several feet away. Squinting he attempts to analyse the situation. His eyes relax and his face returns to its ruddy complexion, sedated momentarily, having received the respect his rank deserves. Renniks steps away from Miguel's personal space, smiles and returns, "If it requires my immediate attention, then yes Mejia you have my permission to continue with your briefing."

"Thank you Colonel Renniks. This document requires your immediate attention." Miguel lifts the document to Colonel Renniks' chest height.

Renniks snatches the document away, turning his body back toward his house. He stops mid stride. The Colonel's body begins vibrating. He rips the paper apart throwing pieces across his miniature front lawn glaring at Miguel. Venom begins oozing from his mouth, "You fucking little prick! I don't think so! This is my base you can't kick me off my own base. No matter what!"

Relaxing the formality in his stance Miguel raises his hands up. He blades his body and ever so slightly lowers his core, *it's your move Renniks, let's see what you've got.* Milliseconds of inactivity seem like an eternity before the first blow.

Refusing to waste any more time Miguel sets and delivers, "Colonel Renniks, I do believe that the document clearly demonstrated that the General had also signed the order relocating you to another base until this particular investigation is concluded. Failure to abide by this direct order will result in charges for insubordination."

The blood visibly drains from Renniks' face transforming it ghost white. Glancing over at the MPs he sees them awkwardly looking away from their former commander's eyes. The Colonel realizes he is defeated. The frosty truth was, he was just another cog in the wheel. He had no control. Before losing all hope he implements a Hail Mary tactic, his tone changes to a higher pitch, "Colonel Mejia, I apologize. I haven't eaten yet, I'm a little bitchy in the morning. If you take a step back, you will realize that you are weakening the investigative team. With all of my contacts I am an asset."

"Don't beg. It's unbecoming. Enjoy your new role Colonel."

Backing up, wobbling from side to side Renniks meets resistance hitting the outside wall of his home. His eyes circle the area, unable to focus. Lowering his arms to steady his body, he braces himself against the side of his residence.

Watching Renniks in full retreat, Miguel turns to the MPs looking them straight in the eyes, "Make sure he leaves the base."

At a moderate pace the Spaniard marches to his jeep periodically looking over his shoulder to ensure that Renniks hasn't moved. Jumping into the driver's seat, Miguel speeds off to his next meeting.

As the jeep gets further away, Renniks begins rebuilding a backbone snarling, "we'll just see how long the government wants a convicted murderer running the show. Don't get too comfortable in your uniform you little spic, you look better in orange."

Entering the Central Command Center, Miguel is met by an officer. "Colonel, the Police Chiefs have already been spoken to. Jointly they agreed to spare at least thirty officers from every major investigative group: Anti-Terrorism; Organized Crime, Gangs and Guns; and, Intelligence."

"Excellent. Do we know who they are sending?"

"Not yet. They will be submitting their files for your review within the next twenty four hours."

A murmur of baritone voices occupies the space in the Central Command Center auditorium. A military guard enters the room, blending in with the crowd. He stands up straight and hails, "A-TTEN-TION!"

Immediately the voices in the crowd stop, with everyone jumping to their feet. Combat boots of every kind simultaneously slam against the floor resonating in Miguel's ears as he proceeds into the room.

Reaching the podium, the Colonel stands behind it. Motionless, scanning the crowd, his eyes move from side to side. Void of sound and movement, the room is completely still. Miguel feels goose bumps form all over his body, sensing the aura of enthusiasm in the room. *Now this is a group that I can work with.* He licks his lips inches away from the mic and speaks, amplifying his quiet voice, "Thank you. At ease, please sit."

The crest of heads in the crowd, curl and sink to their seats like a wave tumbling back into the ocean.

Clutching a device in his hand, Miguel steps away from the podium and patrols the aisles. With his head up, he looks over his shoulder as he passes by each section of the crowd, shouting. "As most of you have discovered, certain officers are no longer part of the team. There will be rumours flying around about the reasons behind it. All I will say about that is this; forget about spending precious time trying to figure out all that bullshit!"

Using the remote control in his hand Miguel manipulates a projector illuminating the large screen at the front of the room as he continues his pass. Captured on the screen in front of everyone are several pictures of the devastation and victims occupying the streets. "What we NEED to do is remain focused on the task at hand. Know this, I demand one hundred and twenty percent out of myself and will expect no less than one hundred percent from each of you."

The Colonel proceeds back behind the podium. Using the laser pointer Miguel flashes the red dot on the screen explaining the simulations. "Early investigative evidence suggests that the bombs were placed directly into the gas storage tanks of the gas stations. These gas stations are all equipped with surveillance cameras and the recorded video is maintained off site for security reasons. We need to obtain these videos and begin looking for someone who had the opportunity to do such a thing."

The Spaniard shuts off the projector. "Professor Crier will explain some of the findings so far."

A man in a white lab coat leaps unto the stage and slows down as he approaches Miguel at the podium. Pushing his coke bottle glasses back up the bridge of his nose, he lowers his head picking up a test tube with a red label on it. Cradling it in both hands he flashes it in front of a camera displaying it on the large screen behind him. "We believe we have identified the compounds utilized during these events. Certain military groups have been known to use these same explosives, however, because of the internet the range of possibilities are endless."

Slipping the test tube back in his pocket, he lifts up a report, skimming through the pages. "Each of you will be given a list of items to pay attention to. Thefts or large purchases of these elements are key for the development of these bombs. Obtain whatever intelligence you can, police occurrences, sales receipts, anything remotely strange, until we have something to go on. We need to examine and eliminate every possibility."

The professor wanders off the stage as Miguel resumes speaking, "The main reason each of you are here is this." Holding up a miniscule device, he intones, "Each member will be issued micro video and audio equipment. Every action or inaction you make will be recorded to ensure both the safety of the public and the safety and integrity of the team. If you receive an order from me I want you to record it. No one is going to be left to fend for themselves."

Marching underneath a sign hanging from the ceiling, 'Military Intelligence', Miguel uses his custom-made military pass to open the magnetic locked doors. Walking down the hallway he glances from side to side reading the inscriptions on the doors before stopping at his intended destination. He reads the name plate, 'Captain Lorne Nolin – Military Intelligence'.

The glass wall situated beside the door has frosted sections with clear unobstructed portions. The Colonel catches a glimpse of the captain behind his desk. Opening up the door, Miguel steps inside to introduce himself. Spotting the uniform, Nolin stands at attention. At six feet four inches in height and three hundred pounds, Lorne shrinks the decent sized office fitted with an oversized desk and a host of active computer monitors. His once lean muscular build, has obviously gotten soft, apparent from the sight of a belly protruding from the top of his pants. His head of hair cut short shows a solid shade of brown concealing strands of grey, while lines across his face says he's been through a lot.

Pushing up his shirt sleeves Nolin reveals Special Forces emblems tattooed on his forearms. Miguel smiles at the irony of this large, powerful man seated behind a computer all day. "Well, well, well, some things don't change; you're still kicking around, old man."

The captain pleased to see Miguel, steps away from his desk and walks over to shake his hand. "I heard old Hamilton busted you out. Sorry I didn't make it to your introduction or your first team meeting. The General has me busting my ass finishing some things for him."

"You didn't miss much."

"Get over here." Nolin said, pulling on Miguel's arm that he already had in his clutches. His gorilla-sized arms wrap around the Spaniard giving him a bear hug with several loud firm taps on the back. "Never thought I would live long enough to see you without bullet proof plexi-glass between us." Nolin releases the former inmate.

Stepping back a couple of paces, Miguel looks his friend in the eyes without straining his neck too much. "Yeah, strange things happening all over. I was as shocked as you. I need a huge favour old man, think you could help me out?"

"Whatever you need." The captain walks back behind his desk.

"Can you pull together an exhaustive list of all friendly military explosive specialists who have any reason to be disgruntled? I hope I'm wrong but we need to rule out everything."

Sitting down, Lorne moves a couple of things off his desk. The captain starts typing, "Sure thing. Gonna take a little while considering we're dealing with other countries but no problem. Should have most foreign names in the next couple of days but my secretary should have a list of Canadian operatives compiled by the time we're done lunch."

"Perfect! But, you're buying."

Alone in his office, Miguel sits at his war room table leafing through documents separating them into piles across the marble top. Breaking him out of a hypnotic state are the chimes from his desk phone. Repositioning the files with one hand, he hits the speaker phone button with the other while continuing his task. "Colonel Mejia speaking."

"Colonel, it's Sergeant Yalle. I just scanned some documents that you are going to want to read. I'm emailing them to you right now. One of our sites was being investigated just prior to the explosions. More interesting than that, it was a gasoline tanker truck that was reported stolen."

"Get me all the information that you can on the vehicle and incident and come see me at the Command Center."

General Hamilton raps on the Colonel's office door as he disconnects from Sergeant Yalle. Miguel puts down the files on his table nodding, "General."

"Migs. I came by to tell you that Colonel Renniks is leaving the base as we speak. I just finished meeting with him and my head hurts." He laughs as he underhand throws Colonel Renniks' security identification pass to Miguel.

Snatching it out of the air, Miguel looks at the pass for a moment before sitting on his desk top and dropping it beside him. "Good, the sooner the better. I never did trust that guy. That Medal of Honour incident was the icing on the cake for me."

Hamilton sits on a chair at the table, "I know General Izzov, his commanding officer."

Reaching for a bottle of water in the case on the floor beside the table the General continues, "I can assure you he picked up a few tricks from him. He was one of the dirtiest supervisors I know and he has one of the biggest egos. He likes to surround himself with worthless people who idolize him. Obviously Renniks was one of them."

Sliding off his desk top Miguel picks up his laptop, joining his friend at the table. The anger lines dissipate from his face. "David thanks again for supporting me on that. Anyways, like I was saying, the call I was on before you came was with Sergeant Yalle."

Opening up an application on the computer Miguel begins reading, "He was sending me something about the explosions that he believes may be something."

Hamilton moves in closer, trying to see Miguel's computer screen.

With his index finger skimming over the words on the LCD monitor Miguel exclaims,

"You won't believe this. There was a stolen tanker truck being investigated at explosion site forty-four."

"Really?"

"That's not the unbelievable part, the officer investigating it was Saduj Toiracsi."

"What? Your old partner? The guy who arrested you for murder?"

"One and the same."

"I'm surprised he even got out of his car. He was the worst one in the trial."

"Apparently, arresting me and grandstanding about it didn't get him the promotion he was looking for. It's too bad, I always thought so highly of him until that."

"Water under the bridge, Miguel."

Closing the lid on the computer, Miguel lowers his voice. "Captain Nolin is compiling some information for me, all members of the Special Forces teams known to be specific bomb specialists, still active, or retired, and or disgruntled. I have a bad feeling about this one David."

Glancing over his shoulders and around the room Miguel leans in and continues, "This was much more organized than any other attack. These explosions appear to be too perfect for a bunch of terrorists, they all detonated within seconds of one another."

Running his hands through his hair, General Hamilton whispers, "Military precision?"

Rolling away from the table, the Colonel nods.

Hamilton rocks his chair backwards, contemplating the situation. After a moment he stands up straight, "Migs, let me know what you find. I have to go keep some politicians happy."

In coffee shops and restaurants around the globe, the complimentary television screens' illuminated hues are the center of attention. Guests constantly monitor the activity fuelling conversations of what the future holds. Instead of daytime television or night time's reality television, people are turning to the news once again. Realizing this, the WBC network takes full advantage of the situation, cancelling regularly scheduled programming, breaking down their television time slots into edible segments based on previously watched television programming at that time.

The WBC network's email and fax machines were filling up with hundreds of requests to syndicate WBC programming featuring Carrie Warren's image. Without discussion, station managers obeyed

Mr. Wilson's request to have Warren's face as the poster child for those facing the battles in Toronto and using her in every way possible. Analysing ratings, her actions alone during the first twenty-four hours of the incident had drawn in a whole society of viewers tuning in to see her struggles with the disaster. Shop owners quickly follow suit, ensuring their customers were seeing the one person who everyone seems to trust to give them the honest truth.

"Help me Carrie! Help me Carrie! Please don't leave me! I don't want to die." Carrie wakes up drenched in her own sweat, crying.

The voices of the dying continue to haunt her every waking and sleeping moment. She looks around realizing she is locked inside her tiny bachelor apartment. She clutches the duvet, pulling it up to her throat. All she can think about is her mom's lecture,

> "Carrie, I don't know what you're trying to prove. Journalism school? You have it good here. Don't move to the city. Stay here with me. You won't have to pay rent and you have a good job. Do you know how many pretty girls are killed or raped in that city every day?"

Looking at her night table she sees the funeral card with her mother's picture. Tilting her head back her eyes scan the ceiling, "Mom, I know you've been watching over me. I need your help more than ever right now."

The reporter jumps, hearing her phone ring. The glow of the clock's display reminds her of how little time has passed since she left the station seeking some respite. Sleep was a luxury she couldn't afford anymore. If it wasn't her work demands keeping her awake it was the constant nightmares she was now plagued with. Carrie looks at the phone displaying, 'WBC'. She swallows deeply before answering, "Carrie Warren speaking...no I don't mind...of course, whatever Mr. Wilson wants...I'll be waiting outside...thank you."

Hanging up the phone, she pulls her hair back into a pony tail. "Do I have time for a shower? Ahhhh. I wish I could get just three hours of undisturbed sleep." Shaking her head from side to side. *Enough with the pity party. A week ago Mr. Wilson didn't even know I existed.*

Speeding away from her neighbourhood in a taxi paid for by WBC, Carrie gathers her thoughts as she proceeds to her first interview. "Driver could you please stop at the nearest coffee shop, I need something to keep me going."

"No problem."

Removing a package of Tums from her jacket she takes a couple tablets out rubbing her stomach, *This is going to be some concoction.*

Fuelled by caffeine, Carrie moves from one interview to the next knowing Mr. Wilson is following her every move. She performs interviews with various law enforcement and justice professionals and people in the street focusing on the continuing battles being waged between anarchists, police, military and vigilantes.

Standing outside a sanctuary, where a long line of porta-potties fills the background on the street, Carrie reports. "While security at the sanctuaries remains high, the rest of the city is a miniature war zone. Extra patrols by police and military have definitely put a stop to a lot of the property and violent crime, but the battle is not over yet."

The reporter turns to a young mother holding a little girl, "With me today is Tina. Tina is living within one of the many sanctuaries set up, pending the repair or evacuation of the city. Tina, what can you tell me about what has been happening here?" she asked, pointing to the sanctuary behind them.

Trembling, Tina begins speaking, clutching her daughter like a teddy bear, "We are forced to provide a statement to police or military officers stationed here. If we don't they told us that we would be kicked out." Tears stream down her face as she leans against her daughter's head, walking away from the camera.

Carrie attempts to follow but Tina enters the sanctuary and disappears in the crowd. The reporter turns to the camera and continues, "A reliable source inside the government advises that the main reason everyone is being video recorded is to analyse stance, posture and movement in comparison to all of the video surveillance being extracted throughout the city. However, the official statement released from the military's intelligence unit supports the interviewing, stating it is necessary to extract any potential witness information, while identifying numbers to provide adequate lodging, food and services to these locations. There continues to be a battle at the political level over how far is far enough to protect people. Giving up their rights for protection; Is it worth the risk?"

Police and military members are viewed dragging a man from a vehicle in handcuffs, while he screams and yells, being escorted up a set of stairs to a building with armed guards standing every couple feet.

"Shawn, here comes another customer." Carrie announced.

Picking up an item from a table, a woman puts it on Carrie's jacket showing an image on a screen. A man standing beside her starts, "That is pretty much the same device used by police and military right now. Apparently it is mandatory that each member is issued audio and video equipment."

Carrie points to the building behind her, "This place behind us is a special court that has been established to quickly process criminal acts taking place within the city. There is no delay upon arrest, they are taken directly before a judge where the audio video is viewed. The criminal is sentenced immediately."

Images of barriers set up at major highway entry points around the city come to life on screens. City buses filled with people approach Jersey barriers across the roads while military and police personnel are viewed funnelling people through gates as Carrie begins speaking, "Entering the city is a task in itself now. Security check points seen here in the background are at all points of entry. No one is permitted to enter the city without being identified, and searched thoroughly."

Tents set up on the side of the road have a long line of people standing outside of them. Each person is brought in one at a time, before being escorted onto a separate bus on the other side of the barriers. "Public transportation is the only mode of transportation from the check points into the city as there are no personal vehicles allowed to travel beyond these borders. Certain groups are frowning on this stating that it is an invasion of privacy, however the government insists it will save lives."

Working under spotlights that once lit the path for evidence now shines for the reconstruction as utility employees slave on through the night. Military personnel standing with machine guns are met frequently with tanks and other armoured vehicles patrolling the streets. Carrie speaks into her microphone, "Military fatigues, machine guns, and tanks once an ominous sight within any western society city are now welcomed, bringing comfort to those living and working here. I was always told a picture is worth a thousand words. I can't say too much else when I see everyone working in concert trying to bring life back to the city."

A sleek black helicopter soars through the air taking off from the Central Command Center. Before it lifts out of sight the underbelly's red paint forms large font letters 'RENNIKS AIR.' Several years back anonymous, jealous or concerned members reported to authorities that Edward Renniks had a suspiciously large amount of money. After a large scale income tax investigation he was found without fault, having received a large sum of money as an inheritance of some kind.

This inquisition seemed to have solidified Colonel Renniks' keen interest in politics. He spent a great deal of time harnessing this elusive power. Instead of working on his job, he devoted himself to working every angle he could to pull favours, manipulate people, and tap into various resources. One of them involved media and news coverage. Eliminated years earlier from the selection process for the Special Forces, he developed a hatred for those who made it. Once becoming a pilot he began working exclusively with Special Forces teams until he had the ammunition to destroy them.

Using a pseudonym, Renniks leaked information to the media which resulted in the dismantling of one of the most highly respected Special Forces units, the Airborne. Strength and momentum of lobbyist groups hounded politicians to do something about it. In 1995 under Colonel Kenward, Airborne Regiments across the country folded once the media unleashed unfavourable video footage. Afterwards, Renniks fraudulently funnelled money through various sources to secure his very own helicopter.

Snapping and squeezing the controls of his chopper, Renniks redirects it to the roof-top of one of the largest news corporation buildings in the heart of the city. Met by security, he is escorted to a large office. Edward proceeded directly to a wet bar and began pouring himself a drink. Taking his beverage to a large leather chair facing out an open balcony, he sat watching a darkening sky with stars illuminating the Toronto skyline. Bursts of light reflect off glass buildings lining the streets before the sound of each explosion twitch the Colonel's ear.

A middle-aged man wearing a dark blue custom handmade suit struts into the room and smiles, pleased to see Colonel Renniks. His bleached white hair reflects the illumination of the pot lights in the ceiling, giving him the appearance of a figure in a Catholic painting with the circle of divinity around his head. He advances to the same wet bar decanting himself a beverage. While pouring a drink, the glitter from diamond cufflinks shoots rays of light across the room onto the ceiling and walls. He gazes out the open balcony with a sadistic smile across his face, "Magnificent isn't it? Look at that. We are covering it twenty-four hours a day, broadcasting that chaos in almost every country around the world."

Putting the cap back on the bottle of 1926 whisky, he walks over to Renniks, "So, what brings you down here? When I got your text saying you needed to talk I expected a phone call not your helicopter on my roof."

Without facing his host, Renniks stares out over the blackened city replying, "Clifford, we have to be very careful what we say over the phone right now. Everyone and everything is being recorded. I don't know who their main targets are, but they are pulling in more and more people to monitor lines, anyone could be next."

Before sitting down, Clifford samples his drink. He closes his eyes as the fluid runs its course passing over his tongue and warming his throat. Opening his eyes, he slowly takes a deep breath and calmly speaks, relaxing onto a chair. "Don't we have rights anymore? The War Measures Act hasn't been invoked yet?"

Mr. Wilson looks toward the ceiling, "Still, I don't see how we can make this work. No one cares what the government does as long as they think it's in their best interests. So even though that's disturbing, I don't see it helping us out."

Renniks tilts his head back, sucking back his goblet's contents. The ice cubes ricochet off each other clinking against the glass. Emptying every drop into his gaping hole, he answers, "Ahhhhh, how is this for help? Leading the investigation is Miguel Mejia!" He gets up and walks over to the wet bar again.

"The convicted murderer, Mejia?" Wilson's stare fixes on Renniks' who responds by nodding his head in the affirmative. Clifford quivers for a moment, looking around, he focuses on the balcony. He gets up and closes both doors.

"One and the same. General Hamilton got him out yesterday and one of his first actions was to get rid of me." Renniks growled, walking back to his chair with a full glass again.

Wilson sits down on the opposite chair, "Does he know anything?"

"Of course not. He's just an asshole on a power trip."

Wilson repositions his suit, "The military is so tight lipped right now. How am I going to get that kind of information, especially from that base? Everything is locked down."

Edward traces the top of his crystal goblet using his middle finger in a circular fashion causing the chalice to sing. Staring out to the darkness, he stops for a moment. He grabs the goblet with both hands, and leans forward towards Wilson, with a satisfied smile, "The prison isn't."

CHAPTER FOUR

The high-pitched whining chug of the helicopter engine slowing down drowns out the seatbelt's metal clasp striking the window after being tossed over Sergeant Yalle's shoulder. Landing at the Central Command Center, he is eager to get this file out of his hands and into the Colonel's. Yalle steps out hugging his documents against his chest. Crouching forward he lowers his six foot tall frame away from the blades rotating above his head. Blowing snow pelts his freezing skin forcing him to squint. A helipad ground crew member wearing goggles and ear protection escorts Yalle to the doors. Escaping the noise and flying debris he finds himself face to face with Miguel.

"Sergeant Yalle, welcome back."

"Colonel." Yalle salutes and presents a thick manila envelope.

Miguel waves him off, "No you hold onto that, I'm going to introduce you to someone. Follow me."

They proceed directly to the Intelligence wing of the building. Upon crossing the threshold of Captain Nolin's office, their noses are met with the sharp odour of thick black coffee. Their eyes recognize that the room's interior glow is generated by the active computer monitors. The only direct illumination is that of a small desk top lamp revealing a trash can full of empty food wrappers. Miguel reviews the room's contents grinning.

Lorne addresses Miguel without turning around to face him, "Colonel."

Side stepping, opening the floor for Sergeant Yalle, Miguel announces, "Sergeant Yalle this is the illustrious Captain Lorne Nolin."

Nolin stops typing, swivels around and stands. Looming over his desk and everyone in the room, Lorne leans forward, extending his hand. Reciprocating, Sergeant Yalle feels his large hand shrink in size as it fits into the palm of Nolin's massive bear paw.

The Captain begins, "Gentlemen – and I use that term loosely with the Colonel in the room – based on the bits and pieces that you have provided so far, this is what I've been able to put together." He points to the screens. "If you could please provide me with anything else that you might have?"

Yalle hands the envelope over to the Captain who immediately empties the contents into his hand. Dropping his body onto his reclining chair, he leans back and rocks back and forth. He speed reads through the documents, finding one of interest. Grabbing his keyboard, he lays it across his lap and brings to life a large wall mounted computer monitor. Sausage size fingers hover over the keyboard tapping away on the buttons gaining access to a military program showing a bouncing ball on a map inlay. As the ball bounces across the screen, Nolin continues to work while explaining;

"That bouncing ball is a GPS tracker device installed in your truck. Military Intelligence satellites have had technology far superior than internet based earth and street views for years constantly recording information. That said, I should be able to find that vehicle anywhere in the world displaying anything around it."

The screen zooms in displaying the transport truck parked, being refuelled at a depot located outside of Detroit. Nolin speaks freely, "This is the day your truck was stolen, and if we continue watching we'll see where it goes from there."

Grabbing a book from the shelf behind him, he drops three inches of literature onto his desk top. The name on the cover: 'Blackstar.' Pointing at the book Nolin continues,

"After September 11th, western governments formed a covert coalition military group to establish fictitious companies, buying up small parts manufacturers. They were able to fabricate new parts with hidden GPS units inside that were placed into every new vehicle off the line. I don't have to tell you that the intelligence gathering purposes are endless."

Exhaling loudly, he leans back in his chair, "And, in closing, here is your vehicle." As he holds up his hand pointing at the monitor, the screen displays a blue bouncing ball.

"What happened to the real image of the truck? Why are we seeing the blue bouncing ball again?" Miguel looks at the screen puzzled.

Rocking in his chair Nolin replies, "Colonel, the satellites are the ones capturing the images, should the vehicle enter a building, go under a bridge and so on, we lose the visual feed however the device remains operational detecting movement and speed continuing to display its geographical position. In this particular case," he said, squinting at the screen, "Your vehicle is located beneath a highway."

All watch as the overpass disintegrates before them. An error message appears on the screen, 'Connection Terminated.'

Nolin sits up straight, looking at the screen and starts typing rapidly, speaking almost as fast, "Sergeant, good job! I think you found one of the bombs. Okay, so let's look at the last location it stopped for a period of time. Let's say one hour. "

Zooming in, the Captain deciphers the information on the screen as the vehicle stops moving, "A mall parking lot located in Mississauga near Hurontario and Highway 403. Let's examine a broader satellite image from the parking lot in Mississauga to the overpass where it explodes. "

The occupants in the room are on the edge of their seats, eyes glued to the screen. All watch the vehicle move along in fast forward attending ten different gas stations.

Miguel springs from his seat moving toward the large screen. He inspects each location the transport stopped as it proceeds through the motions. "Each of those stops are locations that exploded as well." Simultaneously, the ten gas stations explode along with the transport truck and the overpass.

Pointing at the screen Miguel orders, "Zoom in to that Mississauga area before the transport left. This is a perfect place for them. Transport trucks are in and out of here all the time. Its close enough to Toronto that even though it was reported stolen as long as it was driven properly the likelihood of it being pulled over by police would be next to nothing."

Feeding off Miguel's energy, Nolin continues punching the keyboard, "Miguel, I can't believe I never thought of this. I'm going to cross reference all of the blast locations with vehicle GPS information for common denominators."

Screens in the room start jumping. Before Miguel and Sergeant Yalle are able to focus on the information, it changes to another.

"Voila!" Nolin exclaimed, transmitting a visual image onto the large screen showing a mall parking lot in Mississauga, while on another screen he displays a similar map with multiple vehicles highlighted at the same location. "This was their spot."

Lorne immediately brings up another screen, and turns to Miguel. "Those highlighted transports trucks are your bombs. They are the ones that attended all of your gas stations and exploded at the same time. And here is the kicker, most of the trucks were reported stolen within three days of the incident and they all attended the same location for an hour before leaving to execute their plan."

Thinking out loud, Miguel sits down for a moment. "Can you zoom in and catch which vehicle they came from or better yet would you be able to lock onto a vehicle's GPS unit that comes into view on the screen?"

"Absolutely." As the video feed zooms in, Nolin finds the wrench in the system. "Look, all of the drivers came from underneath that nearby parking garage. It is impossible to track which vehicle they came in, or if they did in fact come in a vehicle. They could have attended on foot from public transportation or live nearby. We need to get all surveillance footage from the area to identify who these people are."

Miguel turns to Sergeant Yalle, "Sergeant, I need you to devote yourself to get that video and have it analysed."

Yalle gets up immediately, "Yes sir."

"Thanks Sergeant." Miguel receives an approving nod from Yalle as he walks out the door. Miguel continues speaking to Nolin, "Lorne, let's zoom in and see what they did at those gas stations. Wait, wait, wait! Before you do that, can you see what vehicles were involved at the Montreal site?"

Sitting beside Captain Nolin in his office Miguel hovers over a speaker phone blaring General Hamilton's voice;

"Great work gentlemen. It appears we have something to go on now."

"Like I said it will take Sergeant Yalle and Captain Nolin some time before they can extract and analyse the surveillance footage. We were extremely lucky that the ten terrorists died in Montreal but we're confident that the truck drivers in Toronto have survived and are out there somewhere."

Becoming curt, Hamilton's voice changes tone, "Captain Nolin."

"Yes sir."

"I want to know where each stolen transport truck is!"

"Yes sir." Immediately the Intelligence officer begins working, expanding his search.

"With the information obtained from the Toronto and Montreal investigation we need to act immediately."

"As we speak, sir." Nolin responded with the sound of tapping of keys in the background.

The General's deep voice continues to vibrate the tiny speaker, "Any stolen transports especially tanker trucks must be investigated by one of our teams, do you hear me Miguel?"

Miguel starts opening up drawers on Nolin's desk, "Perfectly sir."

"If our teams aren't available, have police attend and investigate. I don't have to tell you what will happen if they succeed with another bombing."

Finding paper he slams the drawer closed and starts scribbling out information, "No sir, I fully understand the ramifications."

"Good, but Miguel, we can't go in there just killing these bastards, we need answers. Capture as many as you can."

Nolin reluctantly re-enters the conversation, "General, ah...sir, I just brought up the GPS coordinates of all outstanding stolen transport trucks. There appears to be several individual trucks in various locations across the country, which could be normal criminal activity. I have not found anything with that same type of grouping."

"Miguel until we rule that out, get on it."

Captain Nolin interjects, "ah...Sir...I don't mean to be the bearer of bad news but there are too many stolen trucks for our limited number of teams. How would you like the police notified? This is classified 'Blackstar' information."

"Captain, really! Right now the lives of at least twenty thousand were lost because of our inability to share information. Figure out a way. I do not want anymore innocent people to die because I failed to do my job, do you?"

Looking over at Miguel, Nolin shrugs his shoulders, "No sir, of course not."

"Captain, just find a way. Gentlemen, I have to go, I have another meeting starting right now. Keep me informed."

With the sound of the line disconnecting, Nolin's keyboard came to life once again. His head shifts from one screen to the next, he battles with himself thinking of different angles that seemed to escape him until now. Miguel sat in awe watching the work horse pull the weight of the country on his back looking for that missing key. Not wanting to interrupt his thought process the Spaniard remained mute until the keys stopped snapping. Nolin stands up,

"Oh shit! Miguel look at this."

The Colonel's head turns slowly away from the screen, looking at the Captain, making sure he understands what's on the screens. Getting a nod from Nolin, Miguel points to a large picture hanging on the office wall, "Get him on the line immediately!"

"Homeland Security, Colonel Pegrum speaking."

Colonel Pegrum answered the secure line and came face to face with Colonel Mejia and Captain Nolin. Frowning faces ease for a moment to familiar smiles. The ten by thirteen portrait hanging on Nolin's office wall had a large contingent of the Special Ops family together training at Blackwater several years ago, but that wasn't where they first met.

Accepting a suicide mission to rescue or terminate a few good men caught up in a revolution was their introduction. The mission was straight forward, the captives possessed secrets so sensitive that their mere existence put everyone in danger. This was a cover your ass type assignment, intended to show the necessity to leap to the next level of force, the bombing of an entire city. Although each assignment possessed significant amounts of danger, in this case, no supervisor expected a successful conclusion. After forty-eight hours, seconds before the bombing order was issued, the crackle of the radio broke the silence, establishing their victory. This mission, like so many others they embarked on, had no pompous celebration, or notoriety. The only item they received as a memento of the situation they faced was the blood stained clothing and the scarred memories. It was yet another file that was to be burned, eliminating evidence of the disgusting orders they were given, things the general public would never understand.

Pegrum, although older, maintained his youthful appearance due to his dark skin and a full head of hair. The only evidence of his age could be attributed to his harsh gravelly voice and the odd grey strand hiding in his glistening black crew cut. His thin precision trimmed beard, sharp pressed clothes and the ribbons and medals on his tunic forming perfect symmetrical lines instruct his subordinates that half-assed isn't good enough. Each accolade pinned to his chest he wore with humility as a token to those that lost their lives during each assignment.

The Homeland Security Colonel hadn't seen Miguel and Lorne's faces look so serious since that mission years ago. "Men, I'm placing you on conference call with the entire room now."

"Thank you Colonel Pegrum. Captain Lorne Nolin here from Canadian Military Intelligence, we have located a situation, refer to coordinates..."

As the room comes alive with activity adhering to the information provided by Nolin, Miguel takes the lead, "Colonel, we don't have time to really explain in detail but, we believe that those twelve stolen trucks are being armed as we speak for an attack on your capital city."

Immediately, the screens in the Homeland Security room come to life displaying twelve stolen tanker trucks in a rail yard just outside of Washington D.C. Awaking the US military was an animal not to be trifled with, however behind the eyes of the beast were these people locked in a control room forced to watch as the gruesome events began to unfold. No matter how hard they worked they could not put their waking nightmares at ease alone, they had to rely on the actions of others.

The twelve terrorists in the rail yard stood out from the regular comings and goings. They were strictly focused on removing packages from a white taxi panel van parked within the fenced compound. In the mix, a young child carrying a race car runs away from the vehicle being chased by the taxi driver.

After the last package was removed from the van, one of the terrorists activates a device, placing it into the back of the vehicle and closes the door. The unwitting taxi driver returns to his van carrying his child who flails about. The child remained pinned by one of his arms, while the other carries the child's toy.

The terrorist approaches the passenger side of the van waiting for the taxi driver to secure his child in the car seat. As the child fights with his father, the terrorist begins counting out cash and slaps the stack of money on the dash of the van. After a brief exchange of words the terrorist walks towards his transport truck.

Pointing to one of the monitors in the room, Pegrum orders, "Don't lose that van from your sight."

"Yes sir."

The Homeland Security Colonel takes charge, "People, we don't have time to waste, each of you will lock on to a separate truck. Get a dedicated satellite for each one and monitor their action, nothing is getting past us."

"Sir, we have rail police on line right now, there are no officers in the area."

Staring at the screen, Pegrum watches each terrorist get their truck ready for the final journey. Sitting in the cab of the transports each individual begins activating bombs. Like clockwork the twelve drivers exit their vehicles and climb their attached trailers dropping devices into the fuel tank. Scaling down the side of the truck they return to the driver's seat. With a puff of black smoke from chrome covered exhaust pipes each terrorist sets his vehicle in motion.

"Colonel Pegrum, air force advises they will have their sights on target within ten minutes."

"Ten minutes, they'll be in the middle of traffic in ten minutes. Forget it. I want a cleaned up visual of the device they are using. We need that for the teams."

A separate screen plays back the visual of one of the devices, trying to determine as much about it as possible.

"Keep visual on that van." The white panel van taxi rolls outside of the train station's fenced yard and bursts into flames vaporizing the taxi driver and his child. Time slows after the explosion in the Homeland Security Control room. Eyes fix on the screen watching the devil's grin grow with intensity in the blaze, mocking their existence.

"Colonel, we are monitoring a bunch of calls coming from the rail yard into 911 call centers regarding the van explosion."

With a small nod of his head, Pegrum mutters under his breath, "A smart distraction while eliminating any evidence."

While police, fire and ambulance are dispatched to the area to deal with the small inconsequential explosion, Colonel Pegrum makes a call.

"Brad, I'm sending you video footage of the bomb to you right now... I know you're not equipped for this but if at all possible we need at least some of these guys alive... As a back-up plan I would prefer a sniper set up on a bridge rather than a helicopter, it's way too unstable especially with the severe wind gusts today, any distance shot we can't risk it...just give me a shout when you have your gun trucks rolling."

As an old special ops member, Pegrum knew better than most that the teams working out of the Washington DC area had more training than anyone in the country. When anything happens on their turf it is broadcast on the six o'clock news and around the world.

Gun trucks, consisting of black suburban SUVs armed for battle with ready soldiers, race against time speeding through the streets while each tanker truck begins its collision course with the capital city.

Jittery eyes, clenched jaws, and biting lips form a barrage of different expressions. Pegrum notices them all as he scans over those in the
room under his command. He's aware of what everyone is thinking
and feeling, having been there himself on countless occasions. With
so little to time to react to an enormous threat, people find it difficult
to hide their emotions.

Soldiers don't quit, they tell themselves, holding onto a belief that
they are stronger than the average person. Reaching deep into their
souls, they yank and squeeze on their innards extracting every drop of
courage they have to stay the course.

As a senior supervisor he knows keeping everyone busy dams up
the flow of questions rushing to fill the void in their minds. The most
obvious being, *How are we going to stop the threat without more innocent
people dying?* Rubbing a thick scar across the base of his neck, Pegrum
feels the reminder of the painful truth, *It is inevitable, innocent people
will die, but now we have to try and limit that number.*

A staunch hater of Washington traffic, the Colonel subtly cheers
as the morning congestion keeps the transports' speed to a minimum.
Every little bit helps, he tells himself, desperately wanting the special ops
team to handle the situation before he would be forced to unleash
Hell on thousands of defenseless citizens stuck on the highway. A
decision he'd rather not make, why were these people any less valuable than those in the heart of the city?

Like the dreaded anticipation of a guillotine blade being raised
before dropping, Colonel Pegrum observes helplessly as the trucks
enter traffic surrounded by other vehicles. Born and raised in a large
Virginian family, Ryan has relatives everywhere. Zooming in from
orbit, satellite imagery displays the faces in peril. To everyone else in
the Homeland Security control room they see freshman students, dads
coming home from work, moms with their children heading into the
city, tourists passing through, while to Pegrum he sees cousins, aunts,
uncles, friends and other distant relatives. Just the thought of it makes
his iron stomach rust.

With hundreds of people waiting on pins and needles for his next
command, there is no time to personally find out where all his loved
ones are. He has thousands of others demanding his utmost attention.
A sacrifice the job requires of him.

Hailing the air force, the Colonel sets his table, "I need your birds
to stay out of sight for now... Affirmative, retain visual from a distance and if Sergeant Scanlan and his team aren't successful....that is
correct....Operation Blackstar is now in full effect."

Pegrum has to exhaust every logical option before allowing the birds to fire missiles on American soil. With each action he calls out, he checks his watch, timing the response, much like the chess matches of his past. For the first time in a long time, he feels uneasy. His only ability now is commanding orders and having them executed, requiring him to have faith in someone else.

The black suburban gun trucks filled with modern day black knights weave in and out of traffic at mach speeds leaving the city limits. Squeezing the button of the radio mic, Sergeant Brad Scanlon addresses his entire team, "Men, this is a kick ass and take names assignment. For the record I have to say no dispatching of these suspects unless absolutely necessary. Each of you know exactly what I think about that. If it's between you going home to see your family and these pieces of shit, don't hesitate."

While sitting in the front passenger seat with a car load of members behind him, everyone in the other gun trucks listen attentively to the radio knowing there is no time for the information to be repeated. Scanlon's size fills the large front seat. His broad shoulders extend well past either side making it difficult for him to turn around to face the troops in the seats behind him.

The Sergeant's history is no secret, once a first-round draft pick after a storied high school football career, he had his NFL dreams shattered when an ACL tear took him out of the running. Determination drove him to succeed, making a brief comeback before being forced to retire permanently. After surgery and a knee brace later, he joined the military where he advanced beyond anyone's expectations. His team, handpicked by him, were no different; sharing his passion to be the best. Readjusting his knee brace sitting in the front of the Suburban, Scanlon extends his leg out, and pulls it back in tweaking it one last time.

Pegrum was beginning to move his human chess pieces around trying to give his close friend Scanlon the best opportunity to act. "Get the police to shut down the highways leading to the city immediately."

Before the Colonel's last order materialized, his opponent added a complexity to the game. On monitors, Ryan watched the trucks separate onto two different highways. Pegrum grabs the radio, "Brad you're going to have to divide your team. They're separating and taking two alternative routes. We're sending you and your team their SAT locations now."

Frustrated and angry, Ryan punches the top of his desk.

Subordinates scattered throughout the Homeland Security Command Center take sidelong glances at the Colonel, as he punches it again. Looking at the screens in front of them, there is no mistake, this is ugly and there wasn't anything that could be done to make it go away. As traffic on the arteries comes to a stop, the static images of people parked beside these vehicles of destruction becomes all too clear.

Tapping the top of his desk like a war drum, Pegrum's mind scrolls through the situation. *What are we looking at... two highways, six trucks per road...estimated casualty loss....advantages of this situation...we have twelve separate individuals to question if lucky....maintain city's infrastructure...*

Sergeant Scanlon announces, "Men, you heard the Colonel. Gun trucks one to four stick with me as team Alpha, Gun trucks five to eight will be team Bravo under Young Blood. Alpha team, on my mark switch your radios to the alternative channel. Team Bravo, good luck men. Alpha team out."

Brad and the rest of team Alpha lull to a stop. Positioned in the opposing traffic lanes, they wait huddled around tablets as Scanlon lays out his game plan. One by one metal gun mechanisms slam together sending shockwaves through the cabin of the Suburbans like a tuning fork ringing in ears. As the final preparations take place, it is the calm before the storm. No talking is heard other than the Sergeant's instructions, adrenaline entering their systems is dammed up by inactivity.

With traffic now stopped for a period of time, people begin to exit their vehicles trying to see what's happening. Impregnable bone-chilling winds drive the gawkers back into their cars, keeping the roadway relatively clear. The Suburban gun trucks rock from the impact of the wind gusts.

Enlisting various posts in Homeland Security, the Colonel has them call radio stations under the guise of frustrated civilians complaining about the motor vehicle collision impeding traffic on the interstate. More time is all Pegrum is hoping for, allowing the military officials he sent physically to each radio and television station to halt transmission relating to the traffic situation. Ideally this was to keep the terrorists at a disadvantage not knowing of their imminent capture.

Military helicopters begin engaging civilian helicopters, forcing them to flee the area as they attempt to catch a glimpse of the chaos below. A reporter strains his neck, looking around the obstructions. "What's going on? What is it they are not telling us?"

Colonel Pegrum watches the exchange with the helicopters on a screen, yelling out, "Remind him again not to use a signal jammer. We don't know what frequency those bombs are set on."

One of the helicopter pilots voices his opinion, "Homeland, if this is going to work, action needs to be taken and quickly. I don't know if we can keep these people at bay."

There was no argument, Pegrum instructs Scanlon, "Brad, ready or not, now is your time to move. Beware of civilians trying something stupid. You just never know."

The Sergeant returns, "Will do. Thanks Ryan. Men, you heard the Colonel, game faces on, let's move."

That said, the Suburban doors open and they step onto the field. The chill in the air pierces through their gloved hands and balaclava-ed faces. Gripping their automatic weapons they take their positions and set for a moment. Brad looks over his shoulder making sure everyone is ready and snaps the ball into play.

People in vehicles around them gasp, and stare awestruck. *Who are they? And what are they doing?* Unable to move, civilian anxiety escalates seeing the hardware carried by these men in black.

Covering one another, the Special Ops members make their way as stealthily as possible, trying to remain out of sight of the terrorists. Eyes water as another frigid gust smacks them in the face. Hunkering down behind a pickup truck they pause for a moment. Moving from one vehicle to the next, using them as shields, the team stays out of sight. Calls to 911 pour in. Panic grips faces as the team passes by.

During the approach, one of the newest team members, Corporal Tim Spader catches a doll dropped out of a SUV window. Handing it back to the little girl in the back seat he hears the parents arguing, completely ignorant of their surroundings. The little girl yells out, "Thanks mister." The parents turn to their daughter as she points out the window. Looking quickly, they see nothing and continue their argument.

As Spader continues to cover the team, he spots one person who did not share that same look of fear. The Corporal voices his concern over the radio, "Alpha team, there is a strange guy back here. White male, about thirty years old, blonde hair, light skin, no facial hair, driving an older SUV with a Kentucky licence plate #456 ALT."

Tim watches this man, like so many, pick up his phone making a call, but this guy is different. Sensing there's something out of place, Spader presses on while keeping track of this stranger in the midst of scanning for any other potential threats, *What's your deal guy?*

Speaking aloud Tim reads his lips, "...Get out! Get out now!"

Before Spader can relay the message the tanker truck door flies open. Jumping from his seat to the pavement is one of the twelve terrorists. As soon as his feet hit the ground he starts running.

Watching the suspect dodging in and out of people and cars on the road, Scanlon yells, "Up to number eight stay with me. Everyone else deal with this mess."

Without a moment lost, half the team stays with Scanlon chasing the fleeing terrorist, while Tim Spader and the others storm the truck to find the other explosive device on the seat now counting down, "We have five minutes before detonation!"

Holding the mic phone up to his mouth, one of the terrorists seated in his truck yells into the phone, "What did you say? What's happening?"

The SUV with Kentucky plates is now vacant. Off in the distance, walking away, the driver speaks into his phone, "Everyone resort to the fall back plan, get out."

The terrorist picks up his CB radio, "I don't know about the rest of you but I didn't come this far to quit now. I'm going for it."

Pumping the gas pedal the truck engine roars, exhaling a cloud of toxin into the air. Without a word, the driver starts his truck in motion ploughing through the occupied parked cars. The other terrorists in the area laugh in disbelief watching their associate breaking trail through the traffic jam.

Spouting through their CB radio, another terrorist yells, "Let's do it."

Without remorse, the remaining terrorists follow suit. Regardless of age, sex or occupation the weight and strength in these trucks crumples the metal exoskeletons of vehicles lining their path, killing, or trapping occupants locked inside.

A bead of sweat rolls down the side of the Colonel's head as he watches the events unfold. With everything in his body Pegrum fights the impulse to terminate the terrorists before they break through the barricade.

Homeland Security members wait impatiently. Sideways glances meet with others doing the same. Peering slowly around the room they look for the one brave soul who will challenge the Colonel.

Taking the initiative, one Captain stands up at his station. Taking a deep breath he approaches Pegrum who stares at a large monitor, while more images of people dying fill the screen. The tanker trucks clear the blockade as police officers shoot at the trucks without success. The transports crush the police vehicles, leaving them incapacitated, "Sir, what are you waiting for? Issue the order."

Colonel Pegrum pivots sharply facing his subordinate. His dark skin conceals the rage-induced flush of blood in his face, the veins protruding from his forehead do not. The Captain braces himself as Pegrum shows his teeth. Glaring at the man in front of him, the Colonel turns and monitors the progress and then shouts into the mic, "Engage birds. Fire at will."

Immediately, the lead fighter pilot responds, "Roger that."

Swooping down from above the clouds the flock of fighter planes quickly targets the trucks. The beeping sounds of their instruments confirm the visual lock on to each target. With the depression of a button, missiles launch. G-forces compress each pilot's mind and body as they pull away, desperate to evade the blast wave about to occupy the sky. Projectiles compromise the tankers' metal shells, bursting into flames. The explosions rock the highway as each truck evaporates into fire and smoke.

The Homeland Security control room enjoys a brief sigh of relief. The Captain retreats from Pegrum's sight, returning to his station. Ryan ignores the interruption and focuses on the task at hand. "Split the screen and maintain visual of the ground team pursuing the terrorist."

Those not affected by the terrorist trucks smashing into them, watch paralysed by shock, unable to render assistance of any kind. Now seeing the explosion those who weren't panicking have now exited their cars facing the cold wind, running in every direction.

Consoling himself with the decision he made several moves ago, Pegrum speaks to one of his superiors over the phone, "With one ticking time bomb left on that route, I am not risking any more men to assist with this evacuation, we're going to need everyone we can to deal with this situation.... If they die trying to save these people we are going to be severely understaffed and under-qualified to deal with any further terrorist actions...thank you sir."

Team Alpha's remaining members rush around the area attempting to vacate anyone trapped in cars, or those foolish enough to remain locked in their vehicles parked near the tanker, "Get out of the vehicle… run away."

Corporal Spader locates one car that was hit by a tanker truck. Between wind gusts he hears the screaming of a young mother with two young children unable to escape the interior of their vehicle. With Scanlon occupying the radio waves in pursuit of the fleeing terrorist, Tim jumps up onto a nearby van's roof waving his hands in the air, attracting his fellow team members' attention, "Guys, come over here, help me!"

Approaching the car again Spader hears the hysterical mother continue to scream, "Eeeeeeeee. Oh my God. Eeeeeee. I don't want to die. Eeeeeee."

Yelling through the pane of glass, Spader explains his plan, "Listen to me, lady. I know you're scared. I'm here to help. Jump into the back seat and cover your children's eyes, I'm going to smash the windows."

Frozen with fear the woman's hands slowly open, releasing her grip on the steering wheel. Moving slowly, the lady cries as she climbs over the backs of the seats and covers the children's faces.

Crash. A host of glass cubes spray the inside the car. Spader turns to the other special op members who have arrived on scene, "Guys, carry them." Looking off to the side, Tim orders, "Just get them behind that small berm." He points off to the right side of the highway.

Seeing the mother convulse from the anxiety of the moment, Spader swings his rifle behind his back and leans in. He pulls the toddler out of her booster seat and hands her off to one of his team mates, "Go now we don't have much time left." The teammate takes off running.

Tim grabs hold of the mother's face, forcing her to look at him, "Listen to me. You have to get out of here now."

He guides the mother out through the window, passing her off to the next member standing by. Hysterically flailing about, the woman shrieks, "What about my baby?"

"I'm going to get him. Don't worry, just go now." Spader replied as he starts crawling in through the car window.

Constantly monitoring Tim's progress the mother is swiftly escorted away. The Corporal negotiates with the straps holding the baby down. Removing the child from the seat, Spader cradles the infant in his arms. Quickly he inches out of car. Looking down at his watch, he begins sprinting toward safety. Last in the group cresting the top of the berm he braces as time stands still.

The explosion rips open the tanker, fire rolls across the ground instantly engulfing everything in its path. Ultimate energy radiates through the air, launching cars, pavement and cement all over. Corporal Tim Spader's insignificant body is thrown through the atmosphere. Landing in an unnatural position he releases the child who rolls from his arms.

A broken laugh exits one of the teammate's mouths, "Holy shit that was close." He looks over at his partner who smirks, "Yeah, I'm ready to get off this ride now."

The mother grabs her toddler's hand and starts looking for her baby. Hearing her baby's cries she tracks down her child. The baby is lying on the ground unharmed. The mother bends down, nestling the baby in her arms. With her eyes closed she clutches her infant, rocking back and forth. "Thank you, thank you, thank you."

The team members follow close behind and see Spader lying there, "Good job Tim. That was a little too close."

As they near the hero, they notice the baby's pant leg is dripping with blood. Scanning the ground they see a slow moving crimson stream flowing from under Spader's body down into the ditch. Rolling him onto his side they see a twisted metal shard extending out from Spader's back.

Five kilometres away from Team Alfa, Team Bravo is poised and ready to strike. Tucked behind the transport trailer, Team Bravo waits, when the sky illuminates with fire from mushroom clouds billowing up through the atmosphere. Black smoke quickly replaces the crystal blue firmament turning day into night within seconds. Debris from the explosion begins landing, crushing cars and demolishing the landscape. Frightened civilians began to panic and flee the area. Pegrum monitors the activity, watching each terrorist driver flee his vehicle, running away with the innocent masses.

Seeing the hordes of people running towards them, Team Bravo crouches down. Facing out, shoulder to shoulder, they brace for the impact. Supporting one another they stand strong against the relentless pounding. The team leader, Young Blood, communicates with the Command Center, "Homeland we need an evac now."

"Negative. Too risky. We'll send evac after the last explosion."

The Homeland Security Colonel takes to the radio, "Team Bravo, the drivers fled with the crowd. I saw them set their timers but we don't know how much time is left. Do what you can to clear the area but get out of there immediately."

Chasing the fleeing terrorist, Scanlon is beginning to feel the weight of the equipment compounding the load on his knee. Noticing that the terrorist was slowing down, Brad pushes past the discomfort. There was no end zone here for this pathetic running back to seek shelter, Scanlon was going to chase him to the ends of the earth if need be. The former football star was on a mission to destroy this menace.

Continuing to monitor the foot chase, Ryan recognizes Scanlon's struggle to keep up, "Brad, don't worry, I've got you covered. There isn't anywhere he can go that we won't be able to see him."

The Sergeant squeezes out between breaths, "You should... be more worried what... what I'm going to do to this little prick."

"Brad, we need him alive. We've lost all of our other opportunities. He is our last hope for answers."

"Yes sir," he rasped, panting between his reply and orders. "Men, you heard the Colonel...like I said in the truck...non-lethal take down."

The terrorist takes refuge behind a concrete pillar hearing his pursuers on his heels. The team starts to spread out, hunkering down.

With his arms crossed watching the monitor, Pegrum updates, "Brad, he isn't going anywhere. He's catching his breath behind that pillar."

The terrorist reaches behind his back and pulls out a handgun. Peering around the side, he fires several shots. Flattening out, Scanlon and his team take cover. Not engaging the threat they attempt to follow orders despite the whistle of bullets flying over their heads.

Sergeant Scanlon fumbles with his words, knowing he is no hostage negotiator by any stretch of the imagination, "Listen, it's over. You're all alone. There is no where you can go that we won't see you. Just give up."

Over the radio, Scanlon whispers, "I don't have him, who has him?" Hearing no response, he repeats with a more serious tone. "Who has him?"

The terrorist bends at the waist, his body unwittingly conceals his action from Pegrum's view.

"Number seven here, I will make my way around to see what I can."

Putting the gun in his front waist band, the terrorist takes a pack of cigarettes out of his front pant pocket.

"Number eight, roger that, me too."

Opening up a pack of cigarettes the terrorist takes one out and puts one in his mouth. From the same pack he extracts a lighter.

Scanlon directs his men, "Roger that. The rest of you fan out. I want every angle covered. I don't feel like running after this asshole anymore."

Sparking the flint the terrorist ignites a blue flame that he uses to light his roll of tobacco. Smoke blows through the air.

Brad orders, "Sound off when in position."

The bomber takes a big drag before exhaling.

"Number two ready, south side."

The terrorist starts taking several big deep breaths, the cigarette continues to smoulder hanging from his mouth.

"Number three, ready, south east side."

The terrorist closes his eyes, and strikes the back of his head off the cement pillar. The ashes from his cigarette dirty his shirt.

"Number four ready, south west side."

The bomber moves the lighter's blue flame under his opposite hand.

"Number five ready, west side."

With his hand now positioned with all of his fingertips together, the terrorist's skin begins reacting to the heat of the fire under them.

"Number six ready, east side."

The sound of skin melting crackles as the sickly smell of burning flesh precedes the agonized scream of the terrorist, "AWWWWWWWWW!"

"Command Center, what's going on? I need to know. What's he's screaming about?" Brad radioed.

"Sorry Brad, right now with his current body position and our satellite set up, we can't say what he's up to," the Colonel replied.

Hearing the driver gasping in pain, Scanlon attempts again to make verbal contact. "Come on, you don't want it to end like this. Come out and we won't shoot."

The driver peers around after glancing at his melted finger tips, now white and starting to bubble. He takes the lighter in his opposite hand and tries to spark the flint. His melted skin smears across the metal and plastic as he lets out another cry of agony, "AWWWWW!"

In the silence that follows, the terrorist hears gravel crunching nearby. He takes his gun back out and fires several more shots towards the sound. Smoke from the barrel gives him an idea. The terrorist places his un-melted fingers along the barrel and holds on as long as he possibly can without succumbing to the pain. He screams, dropping the gun on the ground.

Confused as to what the driver is doing, Sergeant Scanlon communicates to his team. "Number seven, number eight where are you? I need your eyes."

"Number seven almost in position now." Slowly crawling through dried up strands of grass, number seven stops, and peers through the blades.

"Number eight roger that. I could use a little help, bad terrain over here, very noisy." He looks down at the gravel opening to his vantage point.

Scanlon engages the driver speaking louder than before, "Listen we want to talk. Please don't make this any worse than it has to be, we are not here to harm you."

The terrorist yells back, "Lies. Lies. It is always lies with you. Surrender, so what, you can torture me and try to make me turn on my people?"

Picking the gun off the ground the terrorist pulls out the magazine and checks to see how many rounds were left.

Scanlon shouts, "No, that's not it. Maybe there is something we have that you want."

Homeland Security screens display the driver completely again

The driver rests the gun against his lips, and mumbles to himself, "what do you have to offer?" He starts yelling back, "You have nothing I want, and soon you will have even less."

Scanlon peers through his scope keeping his other eye open watching the entire area yelling, "Tell me what you want maybe there is something I can do."

"You guys are all dead. You just don't know it yet. This way of life has come to an end, a new dawn is rising." With that the terrorist runs out from behind the pillar.

The quickening of the terrorist's actions instinctively brings Scanlon's gun sights up on the terrorist's head. His index finger contracts for a split second before overcoming the impulse. The remaining team members gain similar sight pictures.

Facing Scanlon the terrorist holds the gun directly under his chin. A tear rolls down the bomber's face, "FUCK YOU!"

The hammer on guns drop simultaneously and the terrorist crumples to the ground. Satellite imagery displays a faceless man lying on the ground as team members approach from behind barriers.

Homeland Security Command Center people watch as the team members surround the body. Scanlon's voice is heard, "Get us an evac now, he might make it!"

A team member bends over administering a morphine needle to the faceless man. Blast after blast rumbles the ground. Scanning the horizon Scanlon bends down and grabs the terrorist by his leg. The Sergeant drags him behind the same pillar that proved to be such a hindrance only moments ago.

Cowering behind this immense slab of concrete these hardened men take refuge, accepting this as their fate. The ground vibrates their insides with each thud, thumping and bashing of debris against their cement bunker. The shadow of the pillar keeps them in the dark while the heavens shine brighter than the sun.

As the noise recedes and wreckage ceases to fall, there is silence again.

Pegrum's gravelly voice interrupts the peace in the moment. "Brad stand by. Evac is coming right now."

Through the computer's eyes, Miguel and Nolin come face to face with Colonel Pegrum explaining the situation, "...his fingerprints have been completely melted off and the self inflicted gunshot, not only did it take out a good portion of his jaw, he fell into a coma. Even if we were going to make him write out all the information we need to know, we can't bring him out of this."

The Spaniard speaks up, "Ryan, whatever you find out please let me know. We're running out of options..."

Media swarms over Washington DC reporting the chaos. Star reporter Carrie Warren is on the first plane out of Toronto heading down the coast to join in. She lies back allowing the cushioned seat to fill every curve in her back. Raising her phone up in front of her face she taps out a text message, 'Sam, on my way to Washington. Can't stop thinking about our talk the other night. Looking forward to seeing you again and catching up.'

Turning down the volume on her device she closes her bloodshot eyes attempting to coax herself to sleep. Unable to stop the thought of the young man's eyes invading her serenity, she tosses and turns. Loads of caffeine filling her body isn't aiding her ability to slow her mind down either. Focusing on some breathing exercises she picked up during her hot yoga classes, Carrie manages to release some built up stress, allowing her a moment of peace.

Landing in the midst of the chaos and media frenzy, Carrie immediately goes to work attending the blast site networking through a
host of individuals before hitting screens everywhere. "We are being
told very little at this time. There have been some loose numbers
released identifying at least two hundred people who were critically
injured or killed as a result of the recent terrorist attack just outside
of Washington's downtown core. We have received extensive amateur
video footage capturing the events that resulted in what you see
behind me."

Interviewing an older couple who are wrapped in silver emergency blankets, the old man points to the destruction in the background, "You tell me Miss Warren, who are the good guys and who
are the terrorists here? What kind of country fires on its own people?
Where were all the resources that our tax dollars pay to evacuate us
from here?"

Taken aback by his comment, Carrie feels her world is crumbling.

The afternoon rays of sunlight are attracted to Carrie's wavy head
of dark hair, warming her scalp. She runs her fingers through her
brown locks, pushing them away from her face. Standing on the
curb of a subsidiary news station she finds herself alone carting her
oversized suitcase with both hands. Hearing the buzz of her phone
she releases the handle, letting the bag hit the ground. She reaches
into her jacket pocket and pulls out her mobile. Looking at the little
screen she puts it to her ear right away, "Carrie Warren speaking...Yes
Mister Wilson, you got it and like it? Perfect. So when are you going
to air it? ...Shawn Gurl is going to air my story, why?...Yes sir I trust
you... I know I have a lot to learn... Sorry about questioning you I
was just under the impression that you... I will... of course timing is
everything...Thank you sir... I'm just finishing here and heading to
the airport right now... See you soon."

Carries hangs up the phone as a cab pulls up directly in front of
her. The cabbie rolls down his window, "You call for a cab?"

"Y-y-y-yeah."

The cabbie exits his yellow car gesturing to her large suitcase, "Is
this your bag?"

Carrie nods slowly.

He picks it up, and shuffles his feet over to back of the cab.
Heaving on the bag, he drops it into the trunk. The cabbie looks
at Carrie continuing to stand there in deep thought. "Is everything
okay, Miss?"

In a daze she opens the door and glides her body down into the seat in one smooth motion. Her hair feathers under its own wind, as she swings her hair from one side to the next. The cabbie captures every eloquent move. Entering the cab, the taxi driver catches himself staring at Carrie as she finally speaks, "Can you bring me to the airport?"

She sits back as the cab driver nods, putting the car into motion. Carrie doesn't even notice him gawking at her through the rearview mirror. She starts reviewing images displayed on her phone sliding her finger across the screen. Slamming her phone on the padded seat, she removes a small mirror from her purse. Briefly checking her appearance she applies lip gloss to her dry red lips. The reporter throws the mirror back into her bag and pulls out a pair of sunglasses. Placing them delicately on her face, she covers her deadliest weapons and looks out the window. Peering down at her phone one more time she presses hard on the screen as though she is butting out a cigarette ending the application. She loses herself in her thoughts as she stares out the window. *Shawn Gurl? Timing? Allowing a convicted murderer to keep running the military. What is he thinking?*

The sudden appearance of the Presidential Seal interrupts regularly scheduled programming on every channel. People changing channels in rapid succession, realize that they are held captive to the message they are about to hear:

"My fellow Americans, I come before you with great sadness, hope and determination. Recent events have concluded that confirm without a doubt that we are in the middle of a war with an enemy who shows no mercy…"

While the President addresses his country and the world, General Hamilton is escorted by armed guards down a grand marble-floored corridor. The sound of footwear striking the stone tiles echoes off the walls.

David can't help but think of the million things on his mind. *Why is the Prime Minister demanding my attendance in person considering what's going on right now?* He spots two more armed guards standing outside another set of doors. Catching one of the men roll his eyes upon his approach, Hamilton ignores the act of disrespect. He has enough things to work on, let alone taking this insignificant security guard to task for rolling his eyes at him.

With the door closing behind him, Hamilton walks in facing a crowd waiting for his arrival. Scattered throughout the large exquisite board room with twenty foot ceilings trimmed from the baseboards to ceiling in solid oak were several members of Parliament. They all stopped speaking amongst themselves and stood staring at the General. Their faces contort into painful looking manners dissatisfied with his presence.

Hamilton whispers to himself, "This looks like fun."

One coward strikes out from the back of the room, "The most televised news-filled times in our lives and you have a murderer on the government payroll. What the hell were you thinking?"

A wave of questions and comments soak Hamilton before he can even respond. Having spent time in trenches fighting for his life, Hamilton feels quite confident that he can handle this arena. Standing at attention, he takes a deep breath preparing for the political onslaught.

Just as General Hamilton opens up his mouth to speak the Prime Minister stands, "General Hamilton, don't respond to any of those questions. Please General, we appreciate all the work you've done so far and the President of the United States wants me to express his gratitude to you and your team for helping them avoid a full-scale catastrophe. You saved thousands of innocent civilians. Unfortunately, we need to address an issue that has been brought to my attention..."

CHAPTER FIVE

Taxidermic glassy eyes loom in the room and reflect the flickering of flames trapped in a stone cavern. The fire roars as it ravages the sacrificed wood logs. A suspended razor-thin screen located on the wall above a mantel illuminates images of Washington's highways with massive craters breaking up the pavement's once flawless tapestry. Carrie Warren's voice is heard as video feeds, "As you can see, although Washington's infrastructure remained intact the mass population is preparing for the worst. In every major city across North America grocery stores have placed restrictions on food purchases, which have caused physical confrontations on every level." The television screen displays the word 'mute'.

A slurred accented hoarse male voice shouts out, "They think they can stop this? They are no more capable of stopping this than the British were at stopping the U S of A from gaining its independence!"

Moving inside the trophy room is the outline of a man seated in a high-backed chair rotating away from the fire. Dropping an envelope onto a small table, he picks up a cellular phone. Pressing a button brings the small screen to life. The light from the key pad illuminates his hand as he activates his Bluetooth lodged in his ear. "Come and see me at once. It starts now."

Carrie's face shows signs of prolonged fatigue. Her skin is pale, and the bags under her eyes that were once thought of as shadows now extend into the tops of her cheeks. Her image, a popular face now in many countries, shares recent events pointing to a decrepit townhouse complex missing the entire front portion of part of the building,

"Behind me is the scene of another explosion ripping through a Halifax neighbourhood. Every day for the past seven days car bombs have erupted across North America and Europe. No neighbourhood is safe, no time is standard, people are living day to day expecting the worst. While each incident's casualties are low, the overall death toll is rising. Fear is spreading like an out of control forest fire. It's anybody's guess if we can recover from this emotionally, let alone economically. Over to you Shawn."

Back in the studio, on a screen behind Shawn Gurl, a video displays police cars racing through streets with lights flashing. The anchor man picks up the narrative, "Sources advise that the government and their agencies are overwhelmed and overrun with incidents and information. The backlog of evidence to be properly examined is stacking up while the investigators continue to press on from one incident to the next. We move now to New York where world leaders have been convening for the past couple of days. Standing by covering these revelations is Andrew Scott, one of our subsidiary reporters."

Located outside the United Nations buildings, with all of the flags hung at half mast, a man comes into view of the camera, "Thank you, Shawn. As you can see behind me every country is honouring its dead. In memory of the fallen, they are already invoking new laws to the recently introduced world-wide War Measures Act, trying to curb the daily explosions killing many innocent civilians. Please allow me to question the implementation of these new restrictions."

Shawn Gurl responds, "Andrew, I can't agree more, this is not 'good news'. It's anything but and personally I would call it a nightmare. I have a guest that I will be speaking to during my editorial tonight who has more information to share regarding this situation."

Treading inside his dressing room with pictures of him posing with dignitaries displayed over the walls, Shawn Gurl's voice cracks as he screams, "What do you mean they haven't signed my contract yet? Wilson has had it on his desk for over a month. It's that stupid bitch Warren. I know he's grooming her to take my spot."

In the room, slouched on the couch with his shoed feet crossed and resting on a coffee table, a slippery figure with a shaved head and a neatly trimmed goatee speaks, "Shawn, as your agent we have to start looking for other possibilities."

"What are you talking about? I need this job. I have two ex-wives who have taken everything from me. Personally, I could've retired long ago."

"Shawn, I have two words, Voice work."

Shawn glares at his agent.

The agent dismisses the look and points at his desk, "Come on Shawn, everyone loves your voice. You can't keep pushing the envelope with these unsubstantiated stories regardless who gives them to you. One of them is going to bite you in the ass and you won't be worth shit."

"Just let me handle doing my job, and you handle selling me."

A knock at Shawn's dressing room door interrupts the conversation. A stage hand wearing a headset pops her head in the room, "Shawn, you have five minutes."

"Thanks." Looking at his agent, "Listen, stay on Wilson's ass, I've got to go." He picks up a folder off his desk and rifles through the pages, reading as he walks out the door.

Stage lights display Shawn sitting at a desk, his hands extend out on either side of him forming a pyramid platform holding up his body as he leans forward. "Evening all... I come to you tonight with a heavy heart. There is no easy way to break this news to you. As if the daily bombings weren't enough, now unfortunately we have uncovered some disturbing truths behind the War Measures Act that are sure to affect us all. Once a society relatively free of fear, we are now subjected to a constant state of distress by terrorists, and governments forcing us to fight them."

Shawn looks down changing his paper as anthem music plays in the background. Raising his head he begins, "The world-wide War Measures Act, intended to expose the terrorists living among us, has now taken effect and it appears that we, as the law abiding public are the ones paying the price. Tonight we are going to expose the current conditions throughout the world. And this is only the beginning."

Pivoting to the left, facing another camera, a screen behind him comes to life showing the exterior of a penitentiary. Shawn clears his throat, "Ahem...new laws, new punishments, creating criminals out of innocent civilians using their God-given right to not fight are now being locked up here."

Facing the screen he points to the images before he rotates back around bracing himself, "From behind these cement walls comes two stories so disturbing that mere words alone cannot describe them. An employee at one of the prisons risked everything to get us what you're about to hear and see tonight."

The video feed behind him changes, displaying someone walking down a prison hallway with barred windows, "Right now, they are drafting government employees. Who is next? You? Me? And if we refuse, it is an automatic jail sentence with no opportunity for parole. Some say I would rather go to jail then to die in war, well they are not the same jails that they used to be. Due to the graphic content of the video I'm about to show, it may not be suitable for all viewers."

The video begins playing in the background showing the inside of a prison facility, Shawn presses on, "While the outside world appears bleak, in the jails, it is a death sentence. The world-wide War Measures Act, with the implementation of the government employee draft, has reduced staffing to below skeleton crew levels. Remaining members are overworked and exhausted while the inmates are stacked on top of one another and going stir crazy. Just look at the condition of that facility and it's been less than a week. How many prisoners are in that one cell alone?"

"It's no wonder that this man has lost his mind," Shawn points to a visual recording.

It displays a man with a blank stare. The prisoner approaches the bars and attempts to shove his head between them. Finding resistance he backs up and rams his face against the bars splitting his face open. "Wow. So this guy could be your next roommate. And don't try to argue or call for help, because no one is listening."

The reporter sits up straight and snarks out, "Not frightened enough? Don't miss the next segment of our show. We will be back with more about the War Measures Act after this short commercial break."

The camera fades to black and a makeup artist runs to Shawn's rescue seeing the sweat beading from his pores. While the artist dabs Shawn's face, the veteran reporter smiles, popping the cap off a stomach acid liquid medicine bottle. The artist tries to alleviate his anxiety, "You're doing great Shawn," finishing up the last-minute details.

Shawn nods, chugging down the thick liquid. A stage hand begins the count down, "We're back in five, four, three, two, one…"

Shawn resumes his position of strength in his pyramid pose, "I hope you don't mind being fondled by strangers and taking the bus everywhere you go, because that car you just bought has to stay parked, thanks to the new restrictions in place."

Rolling across the floor, seated in his chair, Shawn inspects the images taking up the screen, "Set up at entry points to all major cities are these blockades."

Video displays cement Jersey barriers across the highway diverting vehicles to a commuter lot where military and police are stationed. Parking their vehicles, a long line of pedestrian traffic approaches a station set up where each individual is thoroughly searched in front of the crowd waiting behind them. From there, they are escorted onto public transit on the other side of the barrier proceeding into the city. "Currently, only public transit, military, emergency vehicles and pre-authorized vehicles are permitted to navigate the streets."

Turning to the right, he faces another camera, "Joining us today is a government employee involved with the implementation of this system. For their protection their voice has been altered. I will refer to them as 'X'....X are you still with me?"

A gargled electronic voice begins speaking, "Yes Shawn, I'm still here."

"X, would you be so kind to describe the protocols and systems that people are going to be subjected to?"

"Of course. Governments have spared no expense on security measures. Everyone attending the major cities identified on the WBC website must first proceed through an x-ray machine, then an airflow search machine and if security is not satisfied be prepared for a physical body search. This is stage one of a system they are putting into place. I have heard that more systems will be implemented shortly, such as facial recognition."

Shawn clarifies, "X-ray machines, air flow searches, facial recognition all to enter the city? And once in the city there appears to be no easy or quick way to evacuate if need be."

X responds, "That's right Shawn. If there is a terrorist scare and transit shuts down, unless you're prepared to walk to the check point no one will be leaving the city any time soon."

Shawn interjects leaning towards the camera's eye, "Considering we have been experiencing daily bombing, expect significant delays. X what can you tell us about the supply situation?"

"Thank you Shawn. That is a very good question. Transport trucks carrying goods and services are now considered military vehicles. Military personnel are onboard every transport. Despite the food being distributed throughout the city, many of these trucks have been raided or stolen. It is unknown at this time if the terrorists are doing this or if those struggling are resorting to such criminality. The government's solution is to arm these trucks with military personnel to use deadly force if required."

"X, I would like to thank you for your time and information."

The line is heard disconnecting and Shawn again takes his position of strength, his face now wrinkled, his eyelids slightly closed, as he glares at the camera, "Innocent people going to jail. Tax paying citizens held captive and searched at will. What is the next logical step, releasing a cold blooded murderer? As much as I wish that was a bad joke, through our penitentiary piece we have learned of exactly that. Convicted murderer Miguel Mejia has been recently released from prison."

The photo of Miguel appears on the background behind Shawn's desk. "For those who do not recall Mr. Mejia, he was the Metropolitan Police Officer who executed a male teacher begging for mercy while the world watched through the internet. Unknown to Mr. Mejia the entire situation was being filmed from the victim's laptop in the apartment near the downtown core. The teacher who was executed may not have been a saint, but still that didn't authorize Miguel Mejia to elect himself judge, jury and executioner. This murder sparked huge controversy, which in the end convicted him of murder. I will play a portion of this horrific video."

A grainy video fills the screen displaying a man with his shirt off, on his knees, his hands handcuffed behind his back, beside a bed. The male pleads with someone out of the camera's view, "Please sir, please. Sir, don't do this please. Sir please, sir."

The camera was only able to capture the barrel of a handgun raised up at the male's head. The male's cries increase in intensity, so much so, the volume distorts the sound on the microphone, "Please sir, Please, Sir, Don't do this please. Sir. Please sir. Please sir, I beg you…. (crackling is heard)."

The muzzle flash from the handgun overwhelms the screen with light and once the light has gone; smoke is seen floating in the air.

Shaking his head Shawn continues, "Brutal. Absolutely brutal. Killing is nothing for this former Special Operations member having performed missions so sensitive, that the government during his trial refused to release information due to National Security. So how does this new regime repay such a monster convicted of the most serious criminal offence? They release him. Yes, you heard right, he is a free man."

Shawn points back at the screen behind his desk. "Pictured here is the prison log indicating that Miguel's last visitor was General

Hamilton right after the terrorist attack on Toronto. Currently, the Prime Minister and all of his aides are refusing comments, raising speculation. I shudder to think who is actually running the country. The longer this goes on I fear that we may never experience true freedom ever again. That is this reporter's humble submission. Good night all, until next time this has been Shawn Gurl from WBC."

"Help Daddy! Mommy, help Daddy! I want my daddy." Two young voices scream. Miguel catches a glimpse of his sons crying and being carried out of the courthouse in his wife's arms. Lisa turns, facing him, tears run down her face. Surrounded by a swarm of reporters Miguel is escorted by prison guards in handcuffs and shackles.

Sitting inside his office Miguel shuts off his internet browser streaming the WBC news. Shaking his head, he grabs another file reading its contents. Slamming the file back down, he opens up his computer locating a folder named 'Command Center'. Inside he accesses another file 'personnel recorders' and inserts his password to open all the files. Scrolling through all under his command he checks each folder ensuring that their daily audio video downloads are up to date.

The Colonel picks up his phone and presses a button, "Come and see me."

Entering his door is a timid young Asian man wearing metal dental braces. Miguel did a double take, seeing the youth before him barely looking eighteen wearing the standard military garb with the Command Center military pass around his neck. The soldier cringes in Miguel's presence. "Yes sir?"

"Private, I need you to get a hold of these people and make sure that they comply with the daily downloads." Miguel hands him a piece of paper with names scribbled on the surface.

"Yes sir."

Miguel stands up, "If they give you any grief let me know and I will handle it personally."

Playing with his miniature camera, the young man questions, "Yes sir. Could I ask you something Colonel?"

"Go ahead."

"I never leave here so why do I have to wear one?"

"They all cross over private. These audio video devices are going to save everyone. Who can allege abuse at our hands if there was none. Likewise if there was abuse, that person is going to be held fully accountable."

Miguel stares down at his hands, "Too often people take matters into their own hands when they don't need to."

The private stands at attention waiting for the Colonel to say something else. He reluctantly squeezes out, "Sir?"

Miguel snaps out of a daze, "That will be all private."

General Hamilton stands spinning a globe on Miguel's desk, while the Colonel sits leaning to the left pulling a piece of paper off of the printer.

"General, could you sign off on this order?" Miguel hands Hamilton a pre-typed document.

David brings it up to his eyes, reading it over. "So, you want a number of troops to start manning the farms in the outlining areas."

"Exactly, the raids on our supply trucks entering the city tell me that it won't be long before we start seeing old cowboy crimes, cattle theft, garden raids and other bullshit. Should imports cease we need to protect these grounds."

"Interesting." Bending down the General signs the order and passes the paper back to Miguel. Hamilton starts spinning the globe again. "As I was telling you, myself and two others will be leading the coalition team, working with you and every other investigative body. In my absence I have left you in command despite what some political puppets had to say."

Miguel reaches forward, stopping the globe from spinning. Looking Hamilton squarely in the face he gains his undivided attention, "Really? And they agreed to it?"

The General strolls away from the globe towards a wall hosting pictures of potential terrorist targets. Touching each one he says, "Right now these politicians are squirming. There is so much happening and even though they want nothing to do with you, they can't dispute your excellent track record. I assured them it is in their best interests to keep you working. After all, what do they have to lose?"

"I don't know what to say."

"Trust me, this will work out just fine, just keep doing what you're doing." Hamilton looks over at Miguel, seeing the Spaniard lower his head and ever so slightly shake it from side to side smiling.

David smirks and walks back over to the Colonel's desk, "That said, I am leaving for our central hub operating out of…"

Spinning the globe once more, Hamilton stops it with his index finger landing on Greenland. "From here we have the ability to monitor all."

The former inmate's knowledge of current organized crime increased exponentially from reviewing every file that the police officers stacked on his desk. They were truly untouchable until now. Miguel makes a call on his speaker phone while organizing folders on his war room table, "Lorne summon every available special ops team for a briefing tomorrow in the CCC at 08h00. We have twenty-five high risk targets, so at least that many teams. If we're short, supplement them with tactical police officers."

"Migs, I know it's been a long time but this isn't golf, you don't handicap teams like that."

"No, but the positives outweigh the negatives. Just do it please."

"Okay, but it's your funeral. You know they won't like that idea."

Teams comprised of military and police personnel begin their night approach on million dollar estate strongholds throughout the country. Dressed similar to a mercenary team, each member was in black from head to toe with balaclavas disguising their identity. The balaclava was fitting especially tight tonight. Expelled breaths inflate the thin material around their mouths temporarily before the excess air escapes through the fibers. Sweat soaked into the cloth creating an adhesive property sticking the material to their faces.

Waiting in the darkness, portions of Miguel's speech repeat in their minds, "Gentlemen, we have an opportunity to gain valuable information that will likely provide us with a starting point to begin hunting down these pieces of shit."

Patrolling down a path, an armed security guard slows to a stop. An inverted human arachnid descends quietly down a cable. Hovering over the security guard the special op member lowers his hands along either side of the unsuspecting man's head. The security guard snarks through his radio, "SP9 to base…the perimeter is still clear. Nothing to see here."

Abruptly, the special op member clutches the man's head. A violent jerk snaps the neck. Scanning the area, the operative releases the dead body. Hidden in the shadows other members appear, carting the corpse off the path.

Weighing heavily on each member's thoughts was Miguel's idea of a pep talk, "I wouldn't ask you guys to ever do anything that would jeopardise your safety unless the magnitude of what we have to gain is that worthy."

Stepping onto the grounds was the ultimate test. Eyes of all members were wider and more aware than ever. The night vision scope on the silenced sniper rifle dispatched guard dogs before they caught their scent. Sophisticated electronics disabled laser grids, allowing members free range of the yard. Creeping across the lawn, using cutting edge technology they were able to avoid the electronic eye of surveillance cameras sweeping the grounds.

Miguel's voice reassures each member, "Implementing a segment of General Hamilton's pet project, I will be able to guarantee that your target will be at the location you are attending."

Electronic gizmos bypass electronic locked doors. Gracefully entering through the rear entrance members pause, referring to schematics displayed on a tablet.

Miguel's directions were crystal clear, "Alive is the only demand I make. Damaged, broken, I can live with, but they must be alive and able to communicate."

Using mirrors, members peer around corners. A series of hand signals exchange between the team leader and his subordinates. The result, an immediate response relayed in movement. Leap-frogging through the mansion's dimly lit hallways members advance toward their objective.

The team stacks up outside two large wooden doors. One behind the other they form a congo line waiting to enter. A slow deliberate twist of the door handle releases the latch. Gradually swinging open the door they spot their target in bed. Slow methodical footsteps approach the sleeping giant when the opening of a door interrupts their stealthy movements. The ensuite bathroom's light illuminates their darkened bodies as a woman exits shrieking, "Eeeeeeeee."

Without a moment lost, two members divert to subdue the female.

The mob boss' eyes flicker to life. Tossed blankets trip up approaching members as the beast bolts from his bed rushing to his woman's aid. Jumping from his elevated king size bed, his three hundred pounds quakes the floor under his feet. Continuing his forward momentum his speed increases. Locked onto the men dressed in black wrestling with his frantic woman he snorts. Raising his arms, with his talons extended, the beast reaches to dismember the attackers. Blind-sided, smashed to the ground the animal rolls back to his feet scanning the room and prepares to launch a counter assault.

His wife shrieks again, "Nick Help me!" Fighting, trying to prevent her mouth from being covered with a cloth, she bites through the material clamping down on the special op's hand. Seconds slip away before the rag tainted with a noxious substance tranquilizes her body.

Special op members form a semi circle around the giant pointing their guns, "Giabatti get down. Get down. Get down."

Inching in they attempt to trap the beast following Miguel's instructions.

Grunting and snarling the mob boss sizes up his foes. He spots behind this encroaching wall of flesh, a man zip tying his wife's lifeless limbs. He begins to growl. The caged animal's bare feet claw the ground. Wide panic stricken eyes focus, squint and scurry over balaclava-ed faces. His body lowers momentarily before he explodes, launching his full weight at the closest member.

The operative engages and attempts to throw the man but his mass is too much and they crash to the floor. On top of the military member the beast starts dropping a flurry of bone hammers on his head before a body check knocks him off and onto his back. Pouncing on the beast, team members kick and punch him. Without a reaction to the pain, the animal propels his body off the ground lifting three members at once.

The team leader runs over and faces Giabatti. He clasps onto the giant's neck and jumps crushing the giant's face with his knee. The beast drops his upper body and the special ops boss slips an arm around the large man's neck. Wrenching with every muscle strand, the leader cracks the mob boss' thick vertebrae, wrestling his fighting body to the ground.

Out in the hallway thundering feet shake the floor. A host of the hit men are about to emerge. The members covering the rear set with ready firearms. Brandishing automatic weapons, henchmen darting around the corner are met with single round bursts severing their spinal cords.

Clutching the thin wood frame in his hands, Miguel stares at the faded picture captured behind a pane of glass. Despite the fold lines and curled corners it was his prized possession reflecting an awkward happy moment in the not so distant past. The image of him and his boys with a catch of fish on a wood dock barely reflects the moment. This was his last weekend as a free man.

> Turmoil burned through every lobe in his brain, until the boat left the dock at the marina in the middle of nowhere. Trolling through crystal blue waters, under a sunny sky with the two most important people in his life, Miguel couldn't imagine a better moment. The tranquility in watching his boys lose their worries catching big fish kept him holding on during the ordeals that followed.

Sitting here in this office was yet another cage keeping him and his boys separated. The ringing of his office phone brings Miguel back to reality. He puts down the picture.

"Colonel Mejia speaking."

Wiping a tear off his cheek, his ear is met with an excited male voice, "Colonel, this is extremely important. You need to come down here immediately. There is no time to explain just come to the interrogation building now."

Miguel throws the phone down on the receiver and springs to his feet launching the chair backwards hitting the wall. Snatching his jacket off a coat rack, he jogs down the hallway. Pulling the outerwear on, he reaches the outdoors and sees a jeep and driver waiting for his arrival. Navigating through the streets the driver doesn't say a word.

Slowing down in front of their destination, Miguel jumps from the moving vehicle and runs to the front door. Ten feet from pulling on the door handle, the Colonel slows to walk. Perfectly timed, a couple of deep breaths bring his vital signs back to baseline, preparing him for what he is going to hear. Opening the door he spots a police investigator waiting for him.

"Colonel, I know we have just begun and there is a ton of information that has already come out that will assist us, but this looks most promising. I won't waste anymore of your time; you can make that decision yourself."

Escorted into the monitoring room's head office, Miguel scans his surroundings. The room is long and narrow with staggered fixed cubicles every few feet on each side. Walking through the room, his eyes shift from side to side, examining each office space. Inside each cubicle an investigator sits at a small desk wearing headphones listening and watching a LCD screen secured to the wall. On the desk in front of each investigator is a computer recording the entire event while the officer scribbles details on a notepad.

"Colonel, as you can see every Organized Crime member from every culture has been arrested as per your orders."

The officer walks ahead of Miguel towards his destination pointing to each monitor he passes, "Outlaw Motorcycle Gang members, Russian Mafia, Asian Organized Crime, Colombian Cartels, Tamil Tigers, Klu Klux Klan, Street Gangs and more are coming in as we speak."

Images on the LCD screens appear more like hospital waiting rooms than an interrogation room setting. Whimpering men of every race are on display having at least one noticeable injury. Blood soaked gauze bandaged heads, black eyes with ice packs, and slings supporting broken limbs are some of the meagre first aid measures comforting these suspects. Miguel comments, "Looks like everybody has been busy."

"You could say that. Colonel Mejia, I think this is the one that you will want to see."

A gang of officers huddled into one cubicle separates allowing Miguel a clear view of the screen. Inside the room the former inmate sees a television screen displaying a lone large man sitting in the room. A large fair-skinned balding man, the few remaining strands lingering along the top of his scalp are pulled back into a small pony tail. The man wearing a neck brace with obvious bruising to his eyes and a swollen broken nose whispers to himself, "What am I doing?"

One of the officers from the crowd speaks up, "Colonel Mejia this is Mr. Nicholas Giabatti. He is one of the leaders of the Italian mafia families. At forty-three years old he is the youngest to lead this infamous group. His proficiency with the illegal drug trade has made him one of the most powerful men in the world. It took a lot of persuasion."

The officer raises his hand shaking his fist looking at his fellow officers, "But I think he is finally ready to talk now. All he has said this far is that he believes he knows the guys we're looking for."

Interested, Miguel responds, "Sounds like a good start. Let's see where it goes. Please don't let me stop you. Continue."

One police officer replies with a smile on his face, "Yes sir, there is a catch. He said he wants a guarantee if he talks, he walks, on everything."

"Really! Okay, tell him whatever he wants to hear but keep him talking. Let me worry about the details after."

"Yes sir."

Moments later the officer enters the interrogation room while Miguel and the others watch.

"Mr. Giabatti, you had begun to tell us that you believe you know the guys we're looking for."

"We're on video right? Yes?"

The police officer nods, "Yes, Mr. Giabatti we are on video."

"So, do I have your guarantee then? I get to walk on anything I talk about today, no matter what, right?"

"Mr. Giabatti, I just spoke to my boss and he said that he will take care of all the details, you have nothing to worry about."

Composing himself the large man moves his shaking hands off the table and sits on them rocking his body in his chair, "Yeah... yeah... yeah...so... Where I met them? So, I had this club, 'Cougars', it was where I did a lot of business from."

Giabatti's mind raced to cover all the details. He pictured his club in his mind, located on a busy street in the heart of Toronto with a majestic store front. The street level outdoor patio was always packed in the summer time. Neon lights crackled and danced under the moon-light like a beacon to anyone wanting to indulge their vices.

"I controlled everything in it, the girls, the drugs, and anyone else that came into the place until this one guy started coming in .There was something different about him besides his Brazilian identification."

The crime boss remembers sitting in his office monitoring the club through hidden security cameras and paying close attention to this man specifically. Just the thought of him and his dark skin with slick black hair highlighting his white teeth and eyes under black lights gave Giabatti a shiver.

"His first name started with an A. What was it again? Alfonso, yeah that's his first name. He started bringing some boys with him, and together they would shut the place down every night. They were my best customers. They always took care of the doormen and waitresses. I didn't know where they were getting their money from. I even had someone look into their IDs but no such luck. Clean, too clean. My instincts were telling me undercover cops with a big budget until one day."

The large man sits back tilting his head back. Raising both hands up alongside his skull, he strokes hair back into a ponytail. Lowering his hands onto his massive thighs he closes his eyes and then opens them again looking straight at the officer, "I walk right? After this is over, I walk? No nothing. If not, you better get me my lawyer, and the rest I will say after a deal is hammered out on paper. Other than that, do your worst, 'cause your beating will heal, these fuckers will kill me and anyone around me."

"Mr. Giabatti come now. We're on audio video. My word is my bond. Beside I have already cleared this with my boss. You're a free man, just cooperate and you have nothing to worry about."

"Nothing to worry about? Right. You don't even have a clue do you?" Grimacing Giabatti's eyes fill with tears.

"We will take care of you. Please. You wouldn't be here if we didn't know something, we just need a little help, that's all."

Wiping his eyes destroyed any evidence of his weakness, as he sits up straight, "Fair enough. How about this, you tell me what you know and I will fill in the blanks."

The officer looks through some papers on the desk holding up one in particular, scanning the contents, "Come now. You know better than that. With your rap sheet you've been around the block more than a few times, you know that's not how it works."

Giabatti leans forward putting his elbows on the table, "Fongool." Taking a deep breath, he begins, "One of the waitresses told me these guys were looking for an easy score. I wasn't going to go into business with them unless I had something over them, so I told her to tell them to prove themselves, and impress me."

A little more interested the officer leans in, "Yeah."

"Well they fucking proved themselves and then some. I got GPS coordinates texted to me. One of my boys checked it out and gave me a ring saying I better come down. When I got there, sitting in a car pale as ghost staring at me was the mayor of Toronto. If it wasn't for his eyes blinking I would've sworn he was dead. I opened the trunk and saw wrapped in plastic the same girl that told me that they wanted to do a score."

Stopping to take a drink out of the plastic water bottle on the table, Giabatti chokes out the first couple of words, "Let..(cough).. me..(cough).. tell..(cough).. you, I couldn't believe my eyes. Here before me was my top producing girl, dead. I should've been pissed, but he replaced her with the mayor and my mind raced with endless possibilities. Standing there beside her dead body my phone received a text, 'impressed'?"

The officer scooches his butt to the edge of his seat and leans forward, captivated by the series of events. "What happened next?"

"When him and his boys showed up at Cougars on the weekend, I took Alfonso into my office right away. He dropped a stack of still pictures of me standing beside the dead girl on my desk."

Stopping for a moment, Giabatti breathes out hard. Smiling, shaking his head from side to side, "What a set up. No one has ever made me sweat like that. Blackmail wasn't his gig though. It was far too juvenile, he had grander plans on the horizon. With the mayor's help we began laundering money through building contracts, but that was just the beginning."

The crime boss finished his water bottle, crumpled it up and put the cap back on. Placed on the table he starts slapping it back and forth like a hockey puck, "About a year later, Alfonso wanted me to get him some chemists. It took some work but I got him some great kids right out of university with huge student loans. Six months later Alfonso was supplying me a new drug called Planet X. It didn't take long before X took over. Everyone went nuts for it, from adult junkies to honour role teenagers."

> Memories of working the road in uniform brought
> back many conversations Miguel had with 'Xlings'.
> One kid, 'high' at the time, swore by it, "It heightens
> my senses to epic heights. I'm talking like, when I
> see the colour blue I can actually smell it and feel it.
> It's hard to explain man, you just gotta try it man."

The giant Italian continued, "People could do it all day, operate machinery, go to school, day to day stuff without acting impaired. It was truly a miracle drug."

Miguel bites his tongue making a fist under the table, thinking of the countless people he encountered stuck in that vicious drug cycle. It was no miracle drug from his perspective. People stayed on it all the time because after it wore through the system everything was dull and they became suicidal. Hock shops thrived with addicts selling everything under the sun to support their habit. Completely broke they turned to petty crime which escalated to violent crime, all so that they could buy another pill.

Following through with more details Giabatti carried on, "They eventually handed over the entire operation to us and we kept paying them a set amount. There was one more provision though."

"And what was that?"

"That I keep paying the scientists while they work for Alfonso. With all the success we moved our facilities to the Bahamas. We were the only manufacturers in the world exporting tons of it daily, so much that we couldn't even keep up to the demand. Manilla envelopes full of money padded pockets at the highest political levels slowing down the legal process with red tape while we continued to make out huge."

Mental images of safe houses full of money had Giabatti think of himself as a hoarder, except instead of news papers or magazines his was cash of any denomination. A short snicker slipped from his mouth, "Obviously we continued working with them. We were becoming richer than we ever dreamed. We didn't have to import cocaine anymore. We couldn't even sell it. Everyone wanted Planet X."

"Yeah, so how does that relate to who we are looking for?"

Giabatti slows down and swallows a couple more times. "Then recently, Alfonso's right hand man came to me wanting something out of the blue, tanker trucks. Stolen tanker trucks from a list of major cities in North America."

Looking up at the camera the mob boss pauses and tilts his face away, looking at the floor, "My local boys were on the job right away while the guys out of town took a bit more time. The next thing I know Toronto is taken out. I never made the connection until the following day when Montreal was taken out the same way. I had just finished telling him to pick up those trucks in that storage facility."

The investigator blushes and very calmly asks, "Mr. Giabatti is there anything that happened after that?"

Trembling, the large man proceeds, "I got this call from a phone number I didn't recognize. When I answered it I knew it Alfonso's voice right away. I felt weak around this guy, he always seemed to be one step ahead and I never pushed him and never wanted to. I figured he had blown up Toronto and tried to blow up Montreal. I didn't know what to do. When he asked me for more of those things in Washington DC, I didn't want to say yes but didn't want to say no. I made some calls and had them set up for him at a rail yard."

One of the cops in the next room raises his hand to the other cops getting high fives, "Holy shit! No one knows that information, we definitely have our guys."

Back in the interrogation room the mob boss finishes, "So that's that. That was the last time I heard from him. Listen that's enough, I think I told you guys enough, I'm a dead man if they ever find out. What are you going to do for me? I want total immunity."

The investigator tries to keep Giabatti focused on the big picture, "We can talk about that in a bit but we need more details. Mr. Giabatti what about the explosives used. Who are these scientists that you set him up with? Where..."

"Listen. I think you know full well what I'm worth to you. Now go talk to whoever you have to talk to, and get me my lawyer because I'm not saying another word. I think I am worth more to you if we do this the legal way rather than me taking the stand saying I made up the entire thing because I was under duress..."

The cops in the monitoring room look at the Colonel, waiting for a reaction. Without a word he got up and casually walked away leaving them watching the mob boss make demands. All of a sudden there's a knock at the interrogation room door. They lean in, paying close attention to the monitor. The investigator inside the room stood up raising his index finger looking at Giabatti, "Just one minute."

The mob boss sits back resting his head on the wall behind him, and closes his eyes.

Opening the door the investigator comes out spotting Miguel with his head down accompanied by the two Military Police officers, "Yes Colonel."

Miguel raises his head slowly, revealing his blood shot eyes, and speaks, keeping his voice low, "Great job. If you don't mind, I would like to introduce myself."

Stepping aside the investigator bows his head slightly, "By all means, sir."

Mr. Giabatti's eyes open with the door. He leans back in his chair displaying a smug look recognizing the pristine uniform, figuring it's someone with real authority. Peering at Miguel's face, it twigs a larger smile, "Hey man, I know, I know you. Didn't you come into my club? You liked the ladies didn't you? Oh course you did, I had the best ladies anywhere." The large man fails to see the veins in Miguel's neck pulsing, boiling blood throughout his body.

The Spaniard approaches Giabatti with his hand extended. The Italian shows his contempt lethargically reaching out to shake hands when the Colonel fires his fist, smashing the large man's throat through the neck brace.

Jolted back for a moment, the mob boss lunges forward gasping for air. Choking and coughing Giabatti was unable to recognize Miguel's set up. The former special op delivers an upper cut snapping his jaw closed severing a chunk of his tongue off. The giant's head flies backwards and ricochets off the wall before he crumples to the floor. Taking a step back, the Colonel shells out a devastating soccer kick to the fallen man's stomach.

The Italian's body is catapulted back against the wall. His corpse peels off like wallpaper. His hands instinctively touch his stomach trying to relieve the pain. Wheezing, the large man rolls to his back while fresh blood flows down the sides of his face, staining the carpeted floor.

Miguel sits on a chair watching Giabatti roll over to his hands and knees, as his body heaves. Blood mixed with mucus hangs from his face. The Spaniard waits patiently as the giant regains his ability to speak, panting out, "What the fuck?... I've given you so much for free... This is how you repay me for putting my life on the line?"

Perched on the edge of a seat the Colonel explains, "Listen here you piece of shit. Anyone who opposes you or stands up to you has their home, shop, store or car vandalised at the very least or worse. You will stop at nothing until they finally conform to your wishes. You deserve to suffer and die a slow painful death. The amount that you help us will limit the pain you feel but in no way will it eliminate it. I will make sure of that."

Giabatti raises his face, fixed on Miguel. He slides his body to the wall where he leans his back against it, sitting on the floor. With his legs extended out straight the crime boss pulls the bottom of his shirt up to his face, revealing the marks of a lifetime of eating rich foods. Using his shirt as a tissue he blows his nose. Pulling his shirt back down over his stomach, blood coats the entire front of it. With red bodily fluid smeared across his face, the Mafioso member laughs, "I knew I knew you. You stand here lecturing me. Who are you? You are no different than me. How many people have you killed? You hide behind your cozy government position doing exactly what I do. I will see you in hell."

Miguel jumps to his feet and in one motion snatches the chair and swings it at Giabatti like a baseball bat. The Italian barely has time to shield himself with his arms before the metal chair legs strike him. "Ahhhh!"

The enraged Spaniard smashes the big man once more with the chair and tosses it aside. He throws open the interrogation room door and storms out. The door barely closes when Miguel rushes back in holding a gun in hand lighting up Giabatti's chest with the red laser sight. Before the mob boss can yell the gun pops. Monitoring the interview the officers in the next room look at one another speechless. Forced to look back at the screen they search for answers seeing Giabatti's body laying face down on the ground.

Slowly rolling over to his back, the Italian gradually moves his hand toward his chest feeling the two prongs lodged into his rib cage with the wires connecting to the tazer gun held in Miguel's hand.

Breathing heavily, Giabatti whispers, "That hurts."

Grabbing the chair on its side, the Colonel sets it down properly. Clutching the gun in his hand Miguel sits down, "Okay, so let's try that again." The crackle of electricity fills the Spaniard's ear canal once more as Giabatti's body reacts to the searing pain.

In the absence of the electrical current charging Giabatti's body, Miguel looks down as the mob boss resumes control over his bodily functions, "Perhaps I didn't make myself clear the first time. Mr. Giabatti, I want you to tell me everything you know."

CHAPTER SIX

Dark red specks of dried up blood continue flaking off the crime boss as he sits hunched over with his bottom lip quivering. Resting his arms on the table top, the Italian occasionally sweeps the biohazard material into a small pile. Escaping through the pores of the overweight man is the body odour of a garlic rich meal. Giabatti's body was showing obvious signs of stress, with his legs incessantly shaking.

Flipping through Giabatti's file, Miguel's finger slides across a piece of paper, "It says here you never finished Grade 10. Amazing how gutter-trash like you can run the country. I want the names of anyone that had any involvement with you and Alfonso."

The Colonel's stone-faced stare was driving the large man insane. Pushed by his desire to ward off the military officer's anger he continues to ooze out information, "...I kept ledgers of everyone I had dirt on. I didn't have everyone's name. Alfonso had his own contacts long before I met him, some I never knew. Together we had all the bases covered. Dirty cops kept us informed of raids, while prosecutors, judges and anyone else that could affect us were paid off."

"That's not good enough. I want names."

The large man sits up. Staring at the Spaniard, his eyes bulge. Lifting both hands he tries to slow things down, "Names...names... so... honestly, I don't remember names."

Miguel drops his head down shaking it from side to side, "Nicholas... Nicholas... Nicholas. Why do you keep playing these games? You're really starting to piss me off. I'm going to go to the washroom and when I come back you had better start answering my every question."

"A, a, a, a..." the Italian stuttered.

Standing up, the Colonel straightens his jacket, spins and walks out the door.

Giabatti strains his neck, listening to the sound of Miguel's voice outside in the hall,

"Gentlemen, if you could watch the door and make sure no one goes in or out until I get back from the washroom?"

"Yes sir."

Standing at a urinal, Miguel mumbles to himself while the pain of a full bladder leaves him, *The next logical step is to interrogate these crooked politicians and anyone else captured in these ledgers. Interrogating and torturing Giabatti is one thing but politicians?*

Leaning his head against the cold tiled wall, Miguel couldn't help an unconscious grin from forming on his face while visualizing beating the shit out of some pompous fallacious members of Parliament, but at the same time he knew his freedom would be short lived. After all, they controlled everything. With a stroke of their pen they could send in the military to conquer a country, killing hundreds and thousands. Flapping their tongues has the ability to affect millions, making a healthier, cleaner society while simultaneously robbing people of their hard-earned money, at the same time padding their own pockets. And should anyone resist them or the laws they impose, the police are summoned to jail them.

Zipping his fly, Miguel wanders over to the facets. Washing his hands, he stares at himself in the mirror. Splashing cold water on his face, his mind races through the memory of him sitting in a lavish office while his high priced lawyer lectured him, "Miguel, don't talk to anyone. There are more and more cops coming out against you than for you. Don't give them any more ammunition."

The Colonel couldn't help but think of the six cops watching the Giabatti interview. *How far removed are they from the dirty cops under Giabatti or Alfonso's control?* Drying his face with a paper towel, Miguel takes one last look in the mirror. *Only one way to find out.*

Entering the interrogation room with a folded up piece of canvas, Miguel closes the door behind him. Kneeling on the floor, he begins opening up the material while speaking to Giabatti. "So how is your day going so far?"

The mob boss tries to see what the Spaniard is doing, "Ah."

"Was your food satisfactory?"

Moving side to side didn't ease the Italian's curiosity, "Ah."

"I am quite aware how shitty prisoner food can be. Do you want me to look into that for you?"

Flattening out the canvas across the floor, Miguel rocks his body back and stands up momentarily before sitting on his chair.

Giabatti beholds the canvas on the floor recognizing exactly what it is. "What... what's with the body bag?"

"Get in."

"You're joking."

Closing his eyes, pinching the bridge of his nose for a moment, Miguel opens his eyes and stares at the Italian, "I don't know what I've got to do to get through to you. I just finished asking you four questions, and you never answered one of them."

"ahhh...ahhh...You only asked me three questions."

"I'm only going to politely ask you once more. Will you please get in the bag?"

Giabatti bends down, reaching for the bag pulling it closer to his chair. His grey pants blacken as urine soaks his crotch and runs down his legs. "L-l-l-listen please, give me one more chance. Ask me anything."

"Get! In! The! Bag!"

"I beg you please..."

Miguel sprung to his feet delivering a sharp front kick, rocking Giabatti's head backwards. His overweight frame succumbs to unconsciousness, collapsing on the floor.

Waking up in the pitch black Giabatti tries to scream but feels his mouth closed shut. Trying to move his arms he finds them restricted, tied together. He slides his fingers through the darkness sensing the coarse texture of canvas. His breathing picks up but he can't satisfy his body's hunger for oxygen through his nose. Squeezing his arms up towards his mouth he locates the obstruction. Clawing at his mouth he pulls back the adhesive tape opening up his mouth, gasping the limited air. His eyes begin capturing light leaking in through the cracks in the metal zipper. The sound of a door opens up, and he feels himself being lifted off the ground, and dropped on a hard metal platform.

Miguel exhales loudly, "Holy shit this guy is heavy."

"Colonel what are you going to do now?"

"If one of you could please stay with me while I cart him to the incinerator, the rest of you stay here until I get back."

A chorus of male voices announce, "Yes sir."

The others officers begin to walk away as one middle-aged East Indian officer remains steadfast.

Miguel spots his perfect posture dressed up a generic grade suit with loose strings around the pockets and sleeves, "What's your name again?"

"It's Rabbath, sir."

The Colonel starts rolling the cart. The hum of the hard rubber tires roll smoothly across the seamless floor, "Rabbath, correct me if I'm wrong but you came directly from your department's intelligence unit, right?"

"Yes sir, I did."

"I can't imagine that this would ever change but Organized Crime would infiltrate government establishments using women."

"Yes, Colonel, that will never change. Men rarely think with the right head around the wrong ladies."

"So true. Back in the day I had the unfortunate opportunity to investigate fellow cops. Each story was almost the same, alcohol, testosterone and married cops are never a good combination going to a bar. Easy prey for these assholes."

Giabatti listens to every word. Feeling the forward motion stop, the Italian hears elevator doors open. The trolley moves again vibrating slightly going over the opening in the floor. The elevator begins moving slowly downwards.

Rabbath leans against the wall in the elevator, "Colonel, I've read reports and information on that. I've never had to investigate them personally."

"Getting that horny cop back to her place is all too easy. And for the rest of his life, he is now a piece of property owned by the mob. From there it grew beyond control, no different than the possibilities with any other profession, especially politicians."

"Yes Colonel, it is a tangled web."

"Let me ask you something."

"Yes sir."

"Zero times one equals?"

"Zero."

"Zero times one thousand?"

"Zero...?"

"Right now I am sentenced to life in prison, I'm the zero. If I kill this piece of shit how much more of a life sentence can I get?"

"Sir?"

The elevator stops and the doors open. Heat rolls in through the opening.

Miguel starts pushing the trolley again, "Whoa. That's hot."

Stopping abruptly, the heat in the bag elevates, Giabatti can barely breath. Hyper ventilating and screaming he starts kicking and squirming fighting trying to free himself, "Let me out. Let me out. I will talk."

Blinding light burns the criminal's eyes as Miguel rips open the zipper. Froth around Giabatti's mouth starts to choke him.

Squatting down, the Spaniard eyes Giabatti's body, "If I ask a question I expect an answer. Anything less, I will burn a piece of your body. I will keep doing this until I have heard all there is to hear. Do I make myself clear? I promise you one thing, make me work and I will guarantee that this will be the most excruciating time in your life. Don't worry. I won't let you die to ease the pain, at least not right away."

The Colonel shuddered when he saw the look on crime boss' face. It's been a long time since he'd seen an adult with a child's look of terror in their eyes. Absolute fear seems to evoke rare qualities seldom seen in grown-ups. Miguel knew at that moment that his world would never be the same.

Beads of sweat began to dissipate from Miguel's brow, crystallizing on his tanned skin. The minimal breeze created from walking in the cool clean air has him enjoying every breath. Pushing the dolly carting the lifeless Italian back toward the interview room, the Colonel periodically scans the expression on Rabbath's face. He knew they were both overwhelmed soaking up the wave of information the crime boss flooded their minds with.

As the information settled into the Spaniard's grey matter, he began cultivating the raw details, *The endless supply of explosives are actually being made locally within each country. With every city locked down I pray that we don't suffer any more attacks. The public wouldn't be very forgiving. Under all of these new laws they demand success, can't say that I blame them.*

Reaching the military police stationed outside of the interview room, Miguel stops the cart and glances down at the package on the dolly, "Mr. Giabatti, I would like to thank you for your cooperation in this investigation."

The crime boss is still soaking wet. Drenched in sweat, he lies stationary on the cart. With his head exposed out of the zippered opening he closes his eyes and shakes his head ever so slightly.

Military police standing by, stare in awe, curious about what had happened during the hour and a half that they were away.

The Colonel instructs his subordinates, "Gentlemen, he's all yours. I need two more officers to assist me with something else though."

"Yes, sir. Right away, sir."

Snapping his fingers, Miguel gets Rabbath's attention. "We need to talk."

The appearance of guilt coats the officer's face as he stands off to the side with his eyes avoiding all facial contact, "Yes, sir."

Miguel steps aside as the military police attend to the former mob boss. Pulling on his arms they help him sit up. Giabatti's stomach heaves as his head lunges forward spitting up yellow bile that spills onto his extended stomach. His body falls backwards hitting the top of the metal dolly. Rolling his head to the side drool seeps out from his lips. The MPs look at each other. One takes the lead carting the crime boss down the hall on the dolly. As they disappear around the corner two fresh officers march into the building.

Moving towards the monitoring room, Miguel waves the two new officers over, "Please, follow me."

Opening up the door he sees a number of officers sitting around in the hallway talking. At once they spring to their feet standing at attention in his presence, "Gentlemen, I know it's been a long night but unfortunately it is not quite over. Please accompany the MPs back to my office, I will meet you all there shortly."

The officers nod without complaint and exit the room. Miguel heads over to the recording station and saves the interview generating a copy on a SD card. Pulling the electronic memory card out, he slips it into his pocket.

Escorted by Military Police, the Colonel's office fills with officers. Taking to the seats around the table, eyes glance back and forth. An awkward silence fills the room. With security standing guard they feel as though they had done something wrong by witnessing the interrogation.

Miguel walks in recognizing the concerned looks on all of their faces. He turns to the MPs, "Thank you, if you could please wait outside."

He walked over to his fridge and removed seven beers handing them out to each officer personally. Carting his chair away from his desk, he brings it over to the boardroom table. Taking a seat he looks up noticing that no one dared to open their drink. Miguel sat back into his chair, taking a long deep breath. Rocking backwards he removes the cap of his bottle and gulps down a big swig. Springing upright he contemplates his next words, "Congratulations, gentlemen we are finally showing some progress. Please drink up, we deserve this, it's been a long night. I think this will help take the caffeine edge out of our systems, so we can talk for a minute before getting some very much deserved rest."

With the wall clock in his peripheral displaying 5:56 a.m., Miguel continues stoned faced, "Gentlemen, I am not going to lie to you. That was a lot to take in. If you have any questions feel free to ask me."

Sitting back he takes another drink then puts the beer down on the table in front of him. The clear glass beer bottle stands almost empty. Reluctantly, the officers remove their beer bottle caps and take conservative drinks from them.

"I apologize for the delay. What we have just heard is no doubt very disconcerting. This has been an informative night; however, a lot of what you heard remains to be proven."

Pausing he glances around the room, not a one offers to speak, "There are a lot of people who will be interested in what Giabatti had to say, if he said anything at all. That is why we must keep the fact that he is here a complete secret. Are we actually going to bring these people in and interrogate them the same way?"

Standing up, Miguel steps over towards his wall covered with photos of would be suspects, and rips them down, "First, we need to refocus our sights. Get Giabatti's ledgers, videos and other documents linking these politicians to him. Once we have those we will start our attack."

Black and white photos scatter across the boardroom table. Positioning himself at the front of the table Miguel examines the faces in the room, "Until then, do not speak to anyone about what happened tonight."

He reaches back to his desk grabbing a letter size pad of paper. Turning around he removes leaf after leaf walking around the room handing them out. Speaking like his drill Sergeant in boot camp his voice echoes off the walls, "On this piece of paper, I want you to address any concerns. If you know anyone who was identified, please advise any and all details. There is no shame in pulling out of this portion of the investigation. I want to make sure that the following is well understood. From here on in I will demand your best and more than that, loyalty."

Returning to his desk, he throws the pad down, and grabs his beer finishing the last drink. Slamming the empty bottle down, he makes eye contact with each person in the room. Miguel's intense dark stare forces the officers to blink and shy away, "For those who wish to stay or those who leave, the information that you just heard is classified and if anyone finds out you'll have me to deal with. The lives of hundreds of millions depend on us."

Relaxing his stance and glare he sits on the corner of his desk, "Other than that, I need every one of you to use my computer, access your file and download your audio video recorders of the events of today before you go home. Gentlemen it's been a good night; please finish your beer and get some rest. I will catch up with each of you in twenty-four hours. Drop off your paper later this evening in my mail slot, other than that I will see you in a day."

Roaming through the room Miguel puts his hand on Rabbath's shoulder, "Come with me for a moment."

The East Indian officer straightens up. His eyes bulge for a moment, catching the others in the room stopping and staring. Avoiding eye contact, he follows the Colonel out into the hall.

Whispers begin within the office between the police officers…

"I thought he was going to kill Giabatti."

"I know, my ass started to pucker thinking about it. If he died what would we do?"

"Watching him beat the shit out of known criminals is one thing but taking this maggot crime boss' word and torturing fellow cops, politicians and civilians, I am not going to be any part of that."

"Who's controlling our so-called boss? What's stopping him from killing someone else?"

"I don't feel like following this psycho to jail when this is all over, I have a wife and kids that need me more than this."

Sitting behind his desk in his empty office, Miguel sees six empty beer bottles littering his boardroom table. Looking at the clock hanging on the wall displaying 7:00 a.m. he voices his next move, "Okay, just one more call." Dialling the number using the speaker phone, an answering machine picks up, "Captain Lorne Nolin, Military Intelligence. Leave your name and number and I will get back to you as soon as possible."

Grabbing the receiver he starts, "Lorne what banker hours do you work? It's Miguel. I'm emailing you a list of items that I need ASAP. Get the team that retrieved Giabatti to revisit his residence and collect the items contained in this email. Thank you."

Slamming the receiver down, Miguel collects six files in his hand and puts down one at a time until he gets to the last one. Opening up the file, he holds up the accompanying photo displaying a younger version of Rabbath, "Are you going to be loyal or just another big disappointment?"

Positioned outside one of the farm locations witnessing the added military presence is Carrie Warren and her news crew. Fencing and barbed wire cover the landscape stretching for miles on end.

The aroma of manure is in the air from a recent coating the fields had just received. Controlling her gag reflex Carrie cups the scarf over her face preparing to ignore the smell, "I forgot how bad that really is."

"Hey farm girl, if anyone here should be used to this smell it's you."

"Suck it up Carrie we don't have time to waste," getting the hand wave signalling her to start.

Carrie drops her scarf and turns, facing the camera, "Scenes like the one you see in the background haven't been witnessed since World War II. Instead of prisoner of war camps they are now designed to keep people out. The protection of fields and large barns storing food appear to be high priority."

A train entering the facility squeals and rumbles, advancing toward the large grain barns drowning out Carrie's soft spoken voice. Military members continue to examine each train car walking along side of them.

Lowering the mic away from her face, Carrie looks over her shoulder waiting for the train to come to a stop.

Emerging from one of the train cars is a man with a large backpack who jumps to the ground running beside the train.

"Stop!" Military personnel shout.

Shaken by the scene, Carrie yells at her camera man, "Johnny you better be getting all this!"

"Got you covered Carrie."

The running man stops, crawls under the train, rolling to the other side and then sprints towards an empty military jeep parked on the grounds. Opening the door, he sets to jump into the vehicle when shots explode. Collapsing onto the gravel, his backpack rips open and its contents spill out, covering the ground. Captured in High Definition, the camera zooms in displaying the backpack's contents consisting of potatoes and corn on the cob still in its husks. The man's unremarkable face could have easily been anyone.

Gasping at the screen over her camera man's shoulder, Carrie steps back covering her mouth, "Oh.. my.. God... he was shot... because he was hungry?"

Military men advance toward the gunned down body, investigating for signs of life.

Searching the corpse, the camera zooms in, seeing a hearing aid lodged in his ear.

Carrie lost for a moment, sees her camera man waving her on. She blinks a couple times and steps in front of the camera. She starts running along the chain linked fence towards a military officer arriving on scene in a jeep. As he steps from the vehicle Carrie yells out, "Officer, Officer, could you comment on what just took place?"

He looks out of the corner of his eye and signals a private over to his location. Seeing them speak briefly, she watches the private run over to the fence, "Carrie, you have one opportunity to leave before you and your crew are arrested for interfering with an investigation."

"Breaking news, the world watches the shooting death of a man who stole a bag full of vegetables." Shawn Gurl said with a sharp tone. "Some crime, trying not to starve! This poor young man was an out of work simpleton. We move to our on the scene reporter Carrie Warren, Carrie."

"Thanks Shawn, I have with me Captain Milton. Captain, can you explain what transpired and why so much force for such an incident?"

Milton holds up a backpack showing the camera, "Of course, thank you Carrie. If you were watching the events, it was a backpack like this he was carrying. It could have easily been a dirty bomb, which would have contaminated this land."

Carrie accepts the backpack in her hand.

The Captain continues, "To the viewers who witnessed this, like yourselves at home, there is no way we knew what he was carrying. We acted in accordance with the law."

A military jeep arrives at the front fence where Carrie and a number of other of reporters have gathered. Colonel Renniks scans the crowd standing in front of jeep before descending from the passenger side. Squeezing his lips together he conceals his smile.

As part of the media scrum, Carrie shouts out over her colleagues, "Colonel Renniks, Colonel Renniks, as officer in charge of farm security how does this blatant breach reflect on our new security measures ensuring our safety when this man was able to enter a train destined to our food supply?"

Turning his head he dismisses the question. He looks for another face when Carrie yells, "Knowing now, that he was a hearing and learning impaired person would you have still authorized the use of deadly force?"

Renniks' attention was drawn back to her face. Looking at her media pass, he stares into her eyes and responds, "Well Ms. Warren, in this situation we have seconds to respond. Had it been a dirty bomb from my understanding you would've been infected too. We have our protocol and my men must follow directions. Period."

Squeezing her fists tight, Carrie convinces herself to pull a kamikaze move, "Colonel Renniks how do you feel about the convicted murderer Miguel Mejia being part of the military again?"

The rush of blood to Renniks' face changes his complexion to a dark red. His tucks his chin to his chest looking out through his eye-brows, forming a frown, "That is something that you will have to discuss with General Hamilton. I cannot comment on that."

Carrie's eyes widen as the words register in her mind, "Colonel Renniks, you have just admitted that Miguel Mejia is part of the military, what position does he hold?"

The Colonel looks at all the faces before him holding their breath for his next utterance. Grinding his teeth, he fixes his collar, "Ms. Warren I apologize if somehow you have that idea. If you are about to twist my words around I believe this concludes this interview."

Colonel Renniks drives away leaving Ms. Warren to make some conclusions speaking to the news anchor in the station, "Shawn, I can't believe that the government has allowed a convicted murderer to take any part in an investigation such as this. How can we trust him or anyone else if these are the sorts of people making up this investigative team?"

The elderly news anchor backs up Carrie's comments, "Carrie, I couldn't agree more. Why do any of us need to follow laws that are imposed when a man such as Mejia gets a 'get out of jail free card' because of his political connections? Please stay tuned. We are going to commercial break and returning with an in depth analysis of that question and more."

Entering a darkened room from a sunshine bright living room is Miguel's mother. The light illuminates a metal framed single bed positioned against the far wall in the room. Blankets strewn over the mattress conceal a motionless lump. Walking slowly toward the bed, she places her hand down pressing on the body underneath, "Miguel, there's a woman on the phone and she insists that she speak with you immediately."

The bump comes to life. A hand shoots out from underneath the blankets, pausing for a moment, stretching as far out as possible before folding the thin brown fleece blanket back exposing Miguel's scrunched up face. Fighting against his body's involuntary muscles, he tries to open his eyes. He looks at the clock on the night table, 2:00 p.m., for a moment he pauses, calculating the amount he slept. Pivoting on the bed he lowers his feet down, touching them to the cold floor. Miguel's eyes finally open, seeing his mother holding the phone in front of him.

Reaching out he grabs it, and stretches once more, yawning as he speaks, "Thanks." He lifts the phone to his ear as she retreats out of the room, "Colonel Mejia."

A hyper voice fills the ear piece, "Colonel it's Lieutenant Paula Connie, there is a situation you need to know about. Colonel Renniks admitted that you are working alongside General Hamilton."

Energy fires through Miguel's limbs. Standing in his room, Miguel scans his surroundings, "And?"

"Sir, it's all over the news. It's not good. Public outcry is rampant and there are people in cities around the country protesting. They are demanding your immediate return to jail. Riot troops have held them at bay and are trying to defuse the situation but it's not looking good."

Marching out into the living room, Miguel turns on the television. As the screen comes into focus, Miguel continues listening to the Lieutenant, but her voice trails into white noise as the images of angry rioters protesting down main streets reflect in his eyes. People smashing store front windows, lighting parked cars on fire and launching makeshift missiles of cement and rocks at riot squads has him clenching his fist, "It's happening all over again."

The reporter announces, "Vancouver's downtown core is no stranger to this kind of chaos."

Tear gas canisters are shot into the crowd, slowly filling the street with smoke. The quakes of explosions rock the city block ripping

through the troops lining the streets, launching military personnel everywhere.

Miguel lowers the phone. Seeing the camera zoom in was more
than he could bear. Voices peal in pain, sorrow and anguish, and the
thought of such loss over him has him sick to his stomach. Sitting
on the coffee table Miguel turns his head away from the screen
displaying chunks of dismembered bodies covering the pavement.
Gun fire erupts, momentarily alleviating the cries of woe ripping at
Miguel's soul.

The reporter yells, "Civilians are being gunned down..."

Pacing back and forth in his Ottawa home office, the Prime Minister
bites his nails and strokes his hair back, monitoring the situation on
the television lowered from the ceiling, "For something that was supposed to be ending, it has just gone from bad to worse."

In the same room, seated at a small table dressed in a fine Italian
suit the Prime Minister's aide Clint speaks up, "Mr. Prime Minister,
we clearly don't have control. All of the security measures suggested
by General Hamilton have proved useless in preventing this anarchy
and attack from taking place."

"Give me options Clint, there has to be another way."

Leaning forward Clint stresses his point hitting the table top,
"There isn't any, You know that this is going to keep occurring until
he is back in prison. We must side with public interest and have
Mejia arrested."

"What about the investigative team? How will they react?"

"I'm sure the military and police forces feel the same way. Who's
to say Miguel isn't involved in these attacks or a terrorist himself."

"Hmmm, I think you're on to something. How do you propose
we do it?"

"Sir, we have to catch him off guard. The media must capture the
look on Miguel's face when he's arrested. If we can't find new dirt on
him we'll show the world what kind of an animal he really is."

Walking up the lightweight metal stairs leading to a private jet at
Pearson International Airport, Miguel stops at the top, and looks over
his shoulder, straining his neck, scanning the area. The questions he
posed General Hamilton during the ride over hadn't left his mind.

> "Why would the Prime Minister want me in street
> clothes? Why Vancouver? How am I supposed to
> remain under the radar meeting with him in that

city? This is suicide going to the city that revolted after finding out about my reinstatement."

Hamilton was at a loss, "...if I was the Prime Minister, Vancouver is the last place I would want you showing up. It doesn't make sense either way. If they wanted to arrest you it would've happened already. I don't know what to say Miguel, keep your guard up."

"Welcome aboard, Colonel."

Miguel snaps his head around seeing one of the pilots speaking to him. "Thank you."

He peers around the corner of the doorway before crossing the threshold.

The plane was still in take-off through the blanket of clouds casting grey shadows on the city streets below. Trying to forget his worries Miguel continues to work during the flight, receiving an update.

"Colonel, we have identified the suspect responsible for throwing the bombs that killed our troops in Vancouver as Thomas Singer. He's a thirty-nine-year-old man from Vancouver Island. Our sweep of the area after the incident found his body riddled with bullet wounds. There is also an intelligence report stating he was associated to a group called The Freedom Movement."

"The Freedom Movement?" The plane starts experiencing turbulence, almost shaking the phone out of Miguel's hand.

"Yes sir. The Freedom Movement is an anti-government type org which had been growing for some time across the United States, United Kingdom and Canada until laws and pressure from the government forced them underground."

"Officer Khan, what would have brought them back to life now?"

"Sir, we have only begun to receive information on this group emerging since the introduction of the War Measures Act. It is prime time for this group as they promote the perception of an oppressive government."

Miguel looks out the window, seeing the clouds light up as thunders rumbles through the air, "Ummmm."

"Sir, this group was very militant before they dropped off the radar, and from what I'm hearing people are extremely frustrated with the government. It is easier to convince them that change is needed, regardless how radical."

The Colonel lies back in his chair looking at the ceiling, "Interesting, you definitely have piqued my interest. Have you prepared your report on these findings?"

"No sir, but if you are coming out here right now, I will have it in your hands as soon as you land."

"That will be perfect."

Miguel receives another call as he gazes out the window at the blue sky above the clouds, "Colonel, it's Sergeant Yvan Buligan. We have successfully re-entered Giabatti's residence and have secured a number of items, which are currently under lock and key at the Central Command Center."

"Thanks Yvan. I will advise Lorne of your findings. Him and his team have been assigned to dissect all those files."

"Yes sir."

Perplexed, Miguel staggers around the cabin of the plane inspecting the nooks and crannies while holding his phone to his head, "Colonel Ryan Pegrum, it's Miguel Mejia."

"Miguel, I'm just walking back to my office, do you want to call me back or wait till I get there?"

"Ryan, I'll wait."

Entering his office the Homeland Security Colonel is met by a couple of people standing around waiting for him, "If you could excuse me Captain, no sorry I'm on the phone, I will speak to you as soon as I'm done, yes, yes, thank you."

Pegrum closes the door to his office leaving his secretary and Captain still talking, "Miguel, you still there?"

"Yep."

Sitting in his chair behind his desk, Pegrum grabs a pen and twirls it around his fingers, "I'm glad you called, I'm swamped with meetings over some things popping up here that we really should to talk about."

"Pegs, I have some very interesting info that I believe may be of some assistance to you as well. We identified our bomber from yesterday as a member of a left wing radical movement sweeping across both our nations, called the Freedom Movement. I'll have the report in my hands in a couple of hours. "

Colonel Pegrum leans back in his chair, closing his eyes and rubbing his forehead, "That's not good. I am personally waiting to speak to an old friend who might have some inside information about this group, but I can share with you everything that my team has found out so far."

"That would be great. I'm heading into a political storm, and could use any bit of information as a temporary shelter."

"Of course," Pegrum stands up, shoving his hand into his pocket. He pulls out a key and bends down, opening up a drawer in a wall cabinet behind his desk. His fingers dance across the tops of the files finally stopping, pulling out a file. Opening it up he lays it across his desk, and skims through the documents inside, "So, our terrorist that blew his face off was an active Freedom Movement member a couple years back. We attended his apartment and found the fire department putting out a blaze engulfing the entire complex. Either he had no intention of ever returning or someone wasn't too happy that he didn't come back after driving the truck."

Miguel shakes a panel inside the cabin, "Depending on what happens here shortly we will need to pull in whatever resources we can and start tracking these guys down."

"Miguel it's bigger than that. We revisited some old sources and have been told that the Freedom Movement began making some political ties to middle-eastern extremist groups sharing disgust for our current governmental system."

"What a combination. Basically, we have a group with unlimited numbers out there plotting to destroy western society."

"Exactly. For a makeshift group of conspiracy theorists they now have organized into a militia and pose the largest threat to all of us, with a strong possibility of turning this into a Civil War. This is one fight I would like to walk away from. Rivers of blood will flow through the streets."

Pushing a dolly, Captain Lorne Nolin enters a storage facility gated with criss-crossed metal stretching from the floor to the ceiling of a converted airplane hangar.

Standing blocking the entrance are military police, "Captain unfortunately we cannot allow you to pass, this is a restricted area until further notice."

Lorne is taken aback by the comment, throwing his hands in the air. Pointing back to the main facility where he walked from, "What are you talking about? I just got off the phone with Colonel Mejia and was told to come and collect these items."

Mischievous smirks cross their faces. Looking at each other, one turns engaging the giant, "Colonel Mejia isn't running the show anymore."

Just as Captain Nolin was about to speak he hears a voice from behind him.

"Captain, it's been a long time."

Nolin lets go of the dolly and turns around, seeing General Izzov standing behind him in full uniform. Izzov stood only a couple of inches shorter than him, but with his forge cap on they appeared the same height. As customary, Izzov had his head piece pulled down low shadowing the upper portion of his face. The Captain salutes him, "General? Yes sir, it has been."

Speaking very loudly Izzov starts, "You'll be seeing a lot more of me for the time being. I've been reassigned. Apparently, someone has royally fucked up this investigation and I am here to fix it. Were you aware that one of the prisoners died a couple of hours ago? What level of incompetence is going on here?"

"General, I wasn't aware. All I know is that I was to begin reviewing some important materials with my team, may I gather those items and commence that action, sir?"

Making his voice heard throughout the complex, Izzov moves in closer to Nolin, "Negative! Not until I am brought up to speed on everything that has happened around here. Until then everything is being suspended indefinitely. We may even take another direction; it all depends on what I hear."

Nolin backs away, "Sir?"

Re-adjusting his shoulders a couple of times, Izzov lowers his voice to a normal decibel, "Captain, I am a little premature. Why don't you and your team members begin working on a report identifying everything that you have done until this point and have it on my desk in the morning. I will be recalling all team members to the base tomorrow for a formal briefing."

"Yes, sir."

While walking out of the room Nolin sends Miguel a text message.

Glancing out the window at the clouds blocking the earth from his sight, Miguel picks up his phone reading a new text message from Captain Lorne Nolin, 'General Izzov has taken over the base on orders from Parliament; all actions are frozen until further notice. Did you hear that a prisoner died too?'

Putting his phone down gently on the chair beside him, Miguel inhales until his chest can't expand anymore. Holding in the oxygen for moment, he slowly releases the built up pressure through his mouth pushing every molecule of air out contracting his chiselled abs. He didn't have to ask which prisoner it was, he already knew.

Shaking his head, he couldn't help but feel he was being sucked into another vortex, *It's bad enough there is a civil war about to start but now instead of working together there is the infighting.* Miguel had mentally prepared himself for the bottom to drop out but going through it in real time was always more turbulent. *Why now? We're finally making progress. Who actually killed Giabatti? Which one of Giabatti's associates had the most to lose from the successful conclusion of this war?*

Picking up his phone Miguel wrote back to Nolin, 'Just get my mom and boys off the base and somewhere safe please.'

CHAPTER SEVEN

Crystal white glaciers veil the tops of mammoth rocks protruding from the earth's crust. Vegetation pays homage to the splendour, refusing to climb to such heights, encircling the lower lying areas. Flying above the sporadic cloud cover in the firmament, Miguel catches glimpses of the terrain below.

Even with the limited view, the Colonel was able to get his bearings. He recalls being here on numerous occasions for military training purposes. Dressed in military gear, with a backpack slung on his shoulders, he trekked the entire region as part of special ops geo-caching wilderness survival exercise.

Reaching certain areas unscathed was the goal. However, through this jagged terrain, with trained operatives hunting him, it was never an easy task. Scaling vertical cliffs freestyle was unnerving at the best of times, let alone doing it in the cold with the sparse amount of oxygen at these altitudes. Light headedness was one side effect, headaches and hallucinations were others that weren't welcome when hanging from fingertips several hundred meters above the next landing. The sight of these peaks is a cold reminder knowing it wouldn't be long until the plane touches down.

Grabbing his phone he punches out a series of numbers bringing it to his ear as he walks through the plane.

"General Hamilton speaking."

"General, the truth is beginning to reveal itself. It appears that I have already been replaced and without a doubt as soon as I land will be going back to prison."

Hamilton couldn't respond initially. He paused remembering that everything is recorded. "Ah...They are blaming you for the Vancouver riot, when they should be taking Colonel Renniks to task for his stupidity. Do you know who is replacing you?"

"General Izzov."

David hammers the top of his desk solid oak desk with his closed fist. Rising to his feet, he walks away from his work station opening and closing his fist. "Okay. Miguel I, I, I..."

"General don't worry about it...thank you." With that the phone becomes silent.

A gentle knock on his door has Hamilton turn towards the entrance glaring. The intrusion was his secretary who hid behind the door exposing only a portion of her face, "General, did you need help with anything?"

Hamilton throws his phone down on his desk, "No one will ever know how much he did for his country. Sacrificing his life, marriage, time with his kids, everything for the job and this is how they repay him..."

Hanging up the phone, Miguel surveys the interior of the plane one more time. *Just another day at the office.*

Getting up, he proceeds to the cockpit. Both pilots were buckled in with their head sets on. "Hey guys, what's happening?"

"Colonel, we're just over the Rockies now. We should be landing shortly."

"Thanks."

Leaving the cockpit he heads back to the fuselage; Miguel knows he has little time. By acting now he has a fighting chance to see this through, if for whatever reason he is wrong, his next actions shouldn't jeopardize his situation too badly. The idea of taking over the plane by incapacitating the pilots and flying wherever he wanted crossed his mind, but he knew if they were hunting him, a plane is too easy to track. This has to be done completely under the radar. He removes his single luggage bag from the storage hold along and the two pilots' bags, opening them all up.

Without notice of a malfunction, the back door of the plane opens up convulsing the plane's movements. As the aircraft suffers through its seizure, the pilots clutch onto their joysticks and review the instrument panel looking for signs of trouble, while trying to regain control. Plummeting from its altitude above the clouds, contents of the cabin are sucked out from the vacuum of air. The pilots continue their emergency procedures and radio in the situation.

General Izzov, monitoring the flight from the Command Center had satellite imagery pinpoint the current position of the plane. Bringing the image to the screen he watches the sight of the items tumbling in the open air followed by a male figure falling from the plane.

One of the Command Center operators attempts to make voice contact. "Captain! Captain!"

"Sorry Command Center, we're still here, we're having a bitch of a time regaining control."

Izzov's mouth displays a sadistic grin watching the human body fall from a great height in the sky, until a parachute opens up. The General slams the table with his oversized fist. His gaze fixates on the screen as the cloth opens up, concealing any actions.

He shakes his head as the parachute floats half way down the mountainous terrain. The safety blanket is thrown from side to side landing in the dense pine trees. Focusing on the topography, the General recognizes the area, spitting out to one of his subordinates, "Get Colonel Renniks on the line immediately."

Izzov shouts at another, "Zoom in. I want to see where he goes from there."

"I'm sorry sir, those trees are preventing me from seeing the ground, he could be still stuck in the parachute or he's gone. I don't have him anywhere."

"General, Renniks is on line one."

Izzov runs to the back of the room and snatches the phone off the receiver.

"Colonel, have you heard?"

"General, just. That place is a bitch at the best of times to get there by helicopter. It always has severe and unpredictable wind gusts. Even if you could, by the time you get a team in position he'll be long gone."

The co-pilot unbuckles, and shuffles his feet while clinging to any fixed parts of the plane. He gradually makes his way to the back of the plane, the wind howls through the cabin. Along the way he inspects the cabin shaking his head, "What? How is that possible?"

The fuselage was destroyed, seats missing, and panels gone, the co-pilot finally reaches the back door and struggles with it until he is able to secure it closed. Returning to the cockpit he radios the

Command Center, "He's gone, and the cabin is completely destroyed. All items not secured were sucked out."

General Izzov leaves the room yelling, "For fuck sakes people find him! I've always hated that stupid little spic!"

Reaching inside his jacket, Izzov pulls out his personal phone. Scrolling through his contact list he locates 'Clint' and depresses the talk button walking through the halls alone.

"Clint, we have a problem. Mejia just parachuted from the private jet that you guys booked for him and he is somewhere in the middle of the Rockies."

"What? How didn't we see this happening?" the tiny speaker crackles under the stress of the volume coming through the phone.

Izzov pulls the phone away from his ear momentarily and enters a vacant boardroom, "It appears that he has some loyal friends who are going to be out of a job very soon."

"We can't afford this kind of media attention."

Walking back and forth in the empty room, Izzov starts violently waving his free hand in the air, "You should have let me handle him. At least he would be out of the way."

"General, let's not get caught up on that. We have a problem that needs to be fixed. Now."

Snapping back, the General sarcastically asks, "Are we done playing good guys?"

"What, do you have a plan?"

"Dead or alive, or does it matter?"

"You know what... sure, you have free reign. Just put a stop to it before he does something that winds up on the news."

Izzov strokes the handle of his sidearm, "Perfect but you better keep Hamilton off my back."

"Done. As far as this government is concerned Miguel Mejia is a threat to National Security. Without having control over him, we need to terminate him at all costs."

"That's all I wanted to hear." Pulling out his gun, Izzov sights in an imaginary target.

"We really should be thanking him. That pain in the ass finally did something for us."

"What's that?" Izzov lowers his gun back into his holster.

"He's a deserter now. Any supporters in the military would have to question their loyalty to him now."

"Have you figured out what you're going to say to the press?"

"You know what, I think I do."

Sliding his laptop across the table to the Prime Minister, Clint stares at the leader of the country looking for his approval. The PM remains seated and gently rolls his chair backwards pushing off the floor with his feet. Leaning forward he lowers his eyes away from the screen. Hanging his head, he gazes deep into the floor.

"Clint, is this the only way?"

"I'm afraid so."

"All right. You know I hate doing this."

"I know but there's no other way. If we admit he was in the military, people won't trust you and we risk another uprising. We must give them something else."

"Agreed."

Carrie Warren preps her hair with her hands, as a mob of people gathers behind her mingling about. She lowers her hands and assumes her position, facing the camera holding the microphone in front of her chest, "Carrie Warren reporting from Vancouver city, the location of the Prime Minister's latest address to the nation. It was an emotional speech. He truly appears distraught over the recent riot, passing along heartfelt condolences to the country, in particular the citizens of this beautiful city. However, he urges the country to remain strong. There is an interesting development regarding the Miguel Mejia story. According to the Prime Minister, Miguel Mejia was never reinstated in the military. Instead, he has joined the ranks of the most wanted persons in the world. A prison guard is facing a slew of charges in aiding and abetting Miguel's escape from the penitentiary. Both the yet to be named prison guard and Miguel Mejia are being implicated in the recent terrorist attacks."

General Izzov contacts the west coast team leaders from his office phone, "Captain, we have a situation. Colonel Mejia just went AWOL in the middle of the Rockies and we need him found immediately."

"General, that might be a problem. There will be a delay in our ability to respond, all of the active teams are currently in Vancouver covering the press conference with the Prime Minister and the other teams are bunked down after a long detail the night before."

With a sweep of his hand Izzov throws everything off his desk. Articles fly through the air and land with a crash. "I don't care if they had no sleep, get them up, dressed and find him. He is an embarrassment to the military, police and country."

Punching the top of his desk in a slow cadence, he annunciates each word, "Miguel Mejia is a National Security threat, terminate upon sight. Have I made myself clear Captain?"

After landing their plane at Vancouver International, the pilots who flew Miguel out west inspect the cabin of the plane, "All my shit is gone. Everything got sucked out of the door when that asshole jumped from the plane. I don't even have my wallet. It was in my luggage."

"That's why I always keep mine with me. You just never know." The co-pilot pulls his wallet out of his back pocket tapping it into his opposite hand.

"Great, you're buying drinks tonight. Let's get out of here."

The two pilots descend the small airplane stair case as the airport mechanic approaches pushing a tool chest. While meeting with the mechanic the sound of a car engine gets louder and louder. Turning around they see a military styled jeep loaded with airport security members in tactical clothing enter the hangar and squeal to a stop, fish tailing.

Security members disembark quickly, extract their guns, and run up the stairs entering the plane. Two remain stationary at the base of the entrance scanning the perimeter. Seconds later, members walk out of the plane, and all proceed back to their jeep.

The airplane Captain yells out, "I told your supervisor there was nothing to see."

Without a word they look over at the Captain, enter their jeep and speed away.

The mechanic, a tall lanky man, wearing blue overalls and a baseball hat looks down at the pilots with a wrinkled forehead and begins speaking with a strange accent, caused from the big wad of chewing tobacco stuck in his lower lip, "May I proceed?"

The Captain responds after shaking his head, "Rentacops?"

Turning back to the mechanic, "Yes, it's all yours. We would like to fly out tomorrow, if you could make sure it's sound for the flight back. We will have our people repair the interior."

"Not a problem, I'll have her all fuelled up and waiting for you by the morning," the mechanic replied as he spits into a cup held in his hands.

"Great," the Captain finished, walking away with the co-pilot, he whispers, "Where do they find these people?"

As the captain and co-pilot walk off, the mechanic mutters, "What's all the commotion about?"

Entering the small plane's entrance, the mechanic slouches forward, methodically looking over each component. Touching screw holes, looking at adjoining panel pieces, his face scrunches as he begins speaking aloud, "The wind alone wouldn't have done all this. This has human written all over it."

The mechanic's long staggered steps shake the hull. His hands continue to move from section to section feeling evidence of his conclusion. With a snap, a panel breaks off striking the mechanic in the head. Lowering his head, wincing for a moment he looks back up seeing a flare gun pointed directly in his face. The mechanic falls backwards landing on his tailbone. Choking on the lump of tobacco in his mouth, he tries to sit up to clear his throat spraying the contents of his mouth onto the floor of the plane. Finally able to breathe, he looks up and sees the barrel inches from his face. The mechanic holds his position while raising his arms up out to the sides with his hands open submitting to the man behind the gun.

As the mechanic's eyes focus, his face twitches when he is finally able to see Miguel staring down at him. He stammers, "Ah...you're...you're..."

"Listen, I don't want to hurt you but I need your clothes."

"No...no... no problem... I have no problem with you. I-i-in fact I was one of your supporters. This pin has gotten me in more arguments than I-I-I can remember."

The mechanic twists his body showing Miguel his 'APOK' lapel pin. It was one of Hamilton's ideas to raise money for his legal fund. He didn't like all the attention, but knew he didn't have a penny to his name and wouldn't have been able to afford the expensive lawyer that Hamilton had hired for him.

The long lanky man banters on, "N-n-not too many people would have the balls to do what you did. He was a real piece of shit! I don't know why they made such a big deal about it."

"Can you stop talking, and just give me your clothes."

The mechanic begins stripping off his coveralls, "O-o-oh sorry, I've never been in this kind of situation, I guess I'm just a little nervous."

Miguel moves from one side of the plane to the other peering out the windows, "Buddy, please. If you're going to talk, how about you tell me how to get out of here?"

"Getting out is much easier than getting in. The only thing stopping you from leaving is a mandatory x-ray machine scan to make sure you weren't stealing or smuggling anything. It's pretty quick, as long as you are holding a security pass nobody cares."

The mechanic now in his boxer shorts hands over his oversized coveralls. Accepting the bundle of clothes, Miguel stops and looks at the support pin and glances back at the mechanic.

"Listen buddy, I really appreciate your help." Miguel puts the coveralls on, rolling up the sleeves and pant legs.

Walking behind the mechanic Miguel asks, "Hey, can you go to the cockpit and get me the log?"

Pausing, the mechanic starts to twist his head when Miguel strikes him the back of his neck with the flare gun. The lanky man's knees buckle, his body slumps forward and the tall human frame crashes on the floor of the plane. Miguel bends down examining the gash on the back of his head, "Sorry about the permanent souvenir, but the pain you feel when you wake up will hopefully save you from more aggravation than you could possibly ever know."

Glancing out the window one more time, Miguel pulls the baseball cap down low feeling the thumping of his temples pulse against the elastic band of the profit hat. Peering out from the side of the open door he spots the security cameras and starts his descent. Keeping his head down, the former prisoner walks over to the transport vehicle that towed the plane into the hangar. Bending over detaching the hitch, Miguel hears the screaming of a car engine. Looking up he sees the security jeep flying past the open hangar doors.

The radio crackles to life on the borrowed tool belt. "Hey Josiah, you hear about your hero Apok?"

Seeing the name tag on the front of his newly acquired coveralls, 'Josiah', Miguel detaches the radio and grunts, "Na."

"He's all over the news again, apparently he busted out of jail and is one of the terrorists attacking us. The military are going to hunt him down."

Exhaling, hearing the news, Miguel nods, *So that's how it's going to be.*

Moving over to the transport sliding behind the wheel, Miguel puts the vehicle in motion and pulls out onto the tarmac.

The radio comes to life again, "Josiah what do you think you're doing? You're going to go to jail for being on the tarmac without permission."

Looking down at his foot squashing the gas pedal to the floor, the Spaniard exclaims, "I could run faster."

Glancing over his shoulder, Miguel spots two security jeeps leaving a terminal pointed in his direction. With the fence off in the distance he feels his calf muscles tightening up from pushing so hard on the pedal. Constantly surveying the situation, the Colonel notices that the security vehicles are gaining momentum and closing in on him. Now able to make out their faces, with their guns out, Miguel takes shelter low in the seat. High pitched rings pierce Miguel's ear drums as bullets penetrate the body panels of the vehicle.

Peeking to ensure the vehicle was still on course, he lowers his head as the vehicle rips through the chain linked fence. Grabbing his backpack off the seat, he stands and leaps off as the vehicle rolls over the cliff. The transport vehicle slaps the water, the backlash of fluid sprays up the cliff soaking the rocks. Security jeeps screech to a halt as its human contents spill out peering over the ledge at the water below. Grabbing their radios, they yell out demands.

"That crazy bastard plunged into the ocean. Get some divers and helicopters over here ASAP."

Boats and helicopters heed their call, scouring the area.

Lying in the tall grass rubbing the road rash on his shoulder through a fresh hole in the mechanic's coveralls Miguel disappears, crawling along the coast line monitoring all of the traffic.

Lactic acid burns through Miguel's body stiffening up his muscles. Reaching downtown Vancouver was exhilarating, finally being able to straighten out, limping on the streets. The city's core is eerie, no bumper to bumper traffic, few people walking about. Miguel could see the fear in people's faces as he walks passed the occasional store front. Slipping in and out of back alleys he was met with more people living in the shadows. Receiving directions from a local, the former Colonel makes his way to his first official stop, the Salvation Army.

Bending down tying his shoes, Miguel rubs the grass stains off his knees before standing up. Entering the store he peruses the aisles selecting a variety of items. Feeling eyes burning through his skull, each time he looks up, people turn their heads away. Miguel tucks his shopping list back into his pocket and heads directly to the register removing his backpack. The female behind the counter cowers and starts whimpering as he reaches into the bag. Removing his hand holding a wallet the female cashier exhales.

"Sorry about that sir, we have a no backpacks policy. I thought you were a terrorist."

"A terrorist, no."

"Thank God," she laughs.

Opening up the leather bill fold reveals the photo identification of the private airplane captain, and a wad of cash. Completing the transaction, Miguel walks out and strokes off a couple items off a list he tucks into his back pocket.

Emerging from an alleyway wearing a wig, glasses, and baggy clothes Miguel continues along the roads. Blaring emergency sirens monopolize the sound waves. Within such a short time his ears have stopped twitching, getting accustomed to the noise until one police car rolls by with officers stretching their necks staring at him. The car spins around, and pulls up to the curb. The window on the passenger side of the squad car lowers as one of the two officers yells, "Hey buddy, what are you up to?"

Wrestling with the ideas racing through his mind, Miguel keeps his head down and continues walking. The passenger officer opens up his door stepping out onto the street and yells again, "Hey buddy, I said stop!"

Miguel's heart stops momentarily along with his legs. Sliding the backpack off his shoulders, he drops it to the ground, and closes his eyes for moment taking a deep breath. Feeling the heat from the extra blood coursing through his body, he turns around slowly. The former inmate faces the arresting officer and contemplates an exit plan. Draped over the hood, one officer has his gun in his hands pointed directly at him, as the other officer approaches cautiously with his hand resting on the gun in his holster.

"Where are you heading to in such a hurry?"

The former Colonel sizes up both officers, *They appear to be in relatively good shape, and ready for a battle charging out of the car like that. They're determined.* Miguel swallows deeply and responds trying to delay the procedure as long as possible formulating a plan, "Nowhere, just walking. Did I do something wrong officer?"

"That's what I'm trying to find out. What's in the backpack?"

"What's in the backpack?" Miguel repeated.

The officer clenches the handle of his gun protruding from the holster assuming a gun slinger stance about to draw, "Stop stalling. That's what I asked you. Now what's in the backpack?"

Miguel relaxes, admiring this young man's spirit, "Easy there, nothing much, just my stuff."

"How about you open it up nice and slow?"

Reaching down Miguel pulls on the zippers opening up the compartments. Seeing the pilot's wallet he slips it down further in his bag and starts pulling out some clothes, "Here's some spare clothes and here..."

"Ok just hand me your wallet? I saw you tuck it into bag. I want to know who I'm dealing with."

"I don't have any identification in my wallet."

"Don't give me that bullshit, just hand me your wallet."

Miguel could feel the moisture building in his arm pits as he grabs the wallet out and passes it to the officer's outstretched hand.

A deafening sound shakes store front windows, and shifts the ground as an explosion launches dust and debris in the air only a street away. Screams fight to take over the sound waves, as a stampede of people run across the horizon. The officer pauses glaring at Miguel and drops the wallet on the ground. He jumps into his squad car with his partner. The car squeals off heading down the street toward the recent explosion.

Standing on the edge of a large empty parking lot, Miguel watches from a distance. A long line of people are proceeding through the new security protocols at the local big box general store. The fortified entrance is a bee hive of activity as security processes visitors. Having taken off his backpack, Miguel pulls out his shopping list from his pocket. He scans it one last time before forcing his legs to advance to the check point. With every step his heart beats louder and harder. The light weight cotton t-shirt he had on easily shows the convex lump caused by his heart banging against his chest cavity. Comforted by his skewed appearance as seen in the reflection of store windows, he believes he has a chance to pull this off, yet the bars across the interior of every pane of glass reminds him where he could end up if unsuccessful.

Waiting in the line, he periodically catches the eye of a large muscular security officer manning the entrance. Miguel's head is swivelling, constantly monitoring his surroundings. The muscle bound security guard starts periodically looking at him oddly, forcing Miguel to question himself, *What are you doing? Calm down.* Advancing toward the examination station, Miguel attempts to conceal his appearance by keeping his head down and closing his eyes while the security guard passes a metal detector wand around Miguel's head.

"Miguel! Miguel, is that you?"

The hardened soldier's insides tense rock solid, his eyes jolt open. He tries to control the panic. With his chin tucked into his sternum, Miguel captures the image of a petite female security guard walking towards him from inside the store. Keeping his arms out was all he could do to remain calm.

Still a couple feet away she voices out again, "Oh my God, it is you Miguel!"

Scanning the area, Miguel sees others in the area start looking his way. Like he just swallowed a bowling ball, his stomach weighs down as he braces to carry the weight.

The muscle bound security guard grabs his wrist, "Sir!"

A flip of his wrist releases the grip and Miguel pushes the security guard's hand away. Instinctively he raises both hands and assumes a fighting stance as the petite female jogs past him jumping into the arms of the man standing behind him.

The security guards frowns at Miguel, "You have a problem, buddy? I'm almost finished but I need you to keep your arms up."

"Sorry about that." Miguel raises his arms as he completes the pass.

The security guard waves his wand in the air, "Next."

Toting full bags, Miguel stops on the inside of the general store's doors inspecting the outdoor scenery. Two squad cars are parked just outside. Four officers stand blocking the exit. Diverting to the side Miguel makes his way to a fire exit. Guarding the exit is a tall thin female security officer with a radio and no weapons.

"I'm sorry sir, you have to exit through the front doors."

"Is there any way that you can let me out this door?"

Raising her radio to her mouth she presses the button, "Could I get another officer over to the south side fire exit please?"

Lowering his bags to the floor Miguel frees his hands. Looking over his shoulder he sees another guard in the distance walking toward them.

"Listen lady is there any chance we can make a deal?" Miguel slips the pilot's wallet out of his pocket and opens up the bill fold displaying several bills remaining.

The officer begins to raise her radio. Miguel snatches her hand. "I don't think you understand I'm leaving with or without your permission. The only thing you need to answer is, do you want the money or end up in the hospital for minimum wage."

A lump forms in her throat preventing her from screaming. Her eyes lock onto the Spaniard's dark irises. She senses that he had let go of her hand. She slowly brings the radio up to her mouth and presses the button, "Disregard. It's okay."

Grabbing the remaining bills out of the wallet Miguel puts them into her hands. He picks up his bags and walks out the door looking over his shoulder. Forcing himself outside, he speed walks through the empty side parking lot, reaching lonely side streets. Creeping down a back alley he vanishes from sight.

Behind a dumpster he empties his bags on the ground. Opening a garbage bin Miguel reaches in and removes his backpack. Methodically he starts filling it with his newly acquired items. Manipulating a knife he slices open the plastic cell phone packaging. Using the razor sharp tip of the blade, he pierces and extracts the optical eye and mic from the device. Turning the device on the former Colonel sees the battery life gauge indicating seven percent remaining. Without delay he begins sending coded text messages.

Airport security members continue their examination of the water's edge when surveillance cameras inside the hangar pick up a strange sight. A male dressed only in his underwear hops out of the private plane with his hands and legs tied together falling down the stair case, landing in a heap on the cold cement floor. Zooming in, the security guard manning the station yells, "Hey boss we have a situation in hangar thirteen. It's Josiah, sir. The mechanic we were looking for. He's tied up and bleeding from his head."

At the same time, a military unit reaches the parachute hanging in a tree on the side of a mountain in the Rockies. The harness hosts a makeshift mannequin dressed in Miguel's clothes. The leader speaks through a radio, "General Izzov, what you saw was a diversion. Miguel managed to stay on the plane which means he is now within Vancouver's city limits."

Grimacing Izzov braces himself hearing those words. He hangs up the phone without responding. Every muscle in his body fires, as he starts vibrating. Heaving his desk upside down he sprays its contents throughout his office, "FUCK."

Slamming his office door open against the adjacent wall shatters the glass insert. He turns his head automatically, protecting his face from the miniature sharp shards in the air. The sound silences the

Central Command Center. With all eyes on him, he walks out from his office very slowly. His eyes glow red, "I want Vancouver airport locked down immediately. I want all surveillance footage, and I want to know what Miguel was last seen wearing. Get media to start looping his face on every commercial break. Do you hear me!?"

Izzov stands looking over the room leaning on the railing, as the buzz of activity begins. Easing off the metal railing, the enraged General walks back into his office, crushing the broken glass under his feet. Already tending to his mess is his frail elderly secretary crouching down picking items off the floor. "Lucy, before you clean that up, get me a team of strategists here immediately, this little prick is not going to get away from me."

"Yes, sir." Lucy stands and walks out of the office, as an officer walks over, "General."

Izzov maintains his statue position, staring at his office, "Yes."

"Apparently Mejia escaped from the airport, however we do have one witness who is currently in the hospital."

"I want that witness interrogated immediately. Don't come back until you have better news."

The officer backs away, and Izzov kneels down, picking up a map of Vancouver off the ground. Pointing to the airport he draws an imaginary circle on the map, "All right Miguel, you want to play, let's play."

Cool wet winter weather blows in from the ocean, sprinkling freezing rain over Vancouver. The seasonal temperatures plunge lower with the premature setting of the sun at this time of year. Concealed in the darkness is Miguel dressed in black from head to toe.

Cupping his wrist watch, the Spaniard ignites the fluorescent blue light displaying the time, 19:43hrs. Raising his eyes, he scribbles on a piece of paper the time, monitoring a black Suburban approaching a set of wrought iron gates. A hand shoots out of the driver's side window with a security card, injecting it into a panel. A creaking metal gate swings open, with the emergence of two security guards dressed in standard black combat gear carrying machine guns. They approach and shake hands with the driver. Miguel notes the existence of the video surveillance bubble hanging on the wall above their heads as the vehicle drives into the compound with the sound of a dog barking. Passing by the open gate is another guard with a dog leashed beside him.

Muffling the sound of plastic crackling with his shirt Miguel extracts tablets from the packaging. He begins inserting the medication into meatballs he has lined up on the ground in front of him. Pinching each individual lump of flesh with his thumb and index finger, Miguel stretches back the elastic of a slingshot, launching it over the magnificent stone wall. He sits and waits, reviewing his plan.

> "Daddy, Mommy says you're not coming home for a while. Is that true?"

> Using a shared phone with a line of inmates standing behind him, Miguel is barely able to hold it together wearing his orange prison jump suit. He grips the wall with his outstretched hand, "We will see. Uncle Hamilton is trying to help right now."

> "I can't wait till you come home again, Daddy. I don't like going to that place."

> "Me either."

Looking up at the gate Miguel wipes the moisture away from his eyes, "I'm coming home soon."

Screams curdle the warm blood in all those monitoring the interrogation room with the exception of Izzov's stone cold veins. "Why!!!!!! I don't remember everything."

The monitor behind Izzov shows Rabbath's beaten body as someone wearing a balaclava strikes him again. Izzov spouts out, "He better remember everything that Giabatti told Miguel. He was the only one with him that went to that stupid incinerator room. "

A male Lieutenant asks, "General Izzov does that mean we can let the other police officers go now?"

"No, I want any and all information extracted from them as well. Nothing like the good old fashioned way to pull out information."

"Yes, sir."

Colonel Renniks walks into the area and immediately Izzov questions him, "Colonel, how are we doing in the mainframe? Have they opened those files yet?"

"No sir, they are still trying. Apparently this level of encryption..."

Izzov's face grows redder. "I want results not excuses! Tell me why you're a complete failure!"

Lucy, the General's secretary walks down the hallway towards the monitoring room cringing each time Rabbath screams. Upon seeing Izzov's face, she digs into her purse, "Sir, your high blood pressure. Have you taken your medication recently?"

Glaring at Lucy he stands up, punching the wall, "Yes I have, but how is my pressure supposed to go down when I have incompetent people working under me?"

Inches from Colonel Renniks' face, Izzov's spittle sprays out of his mouth, "What is Miguel up to? Why didn't he jump out of the plane? Why did he risk getting caught in Vancouver? Every second that stupid spic is free I am that much more pissed off."

Lucy interjects, "Sir you're going to end up in the hospital again if you don't calm down."

Izzov glares at her, and she backs away. He turns towards Renniks again, "Colonel Renniks, stay on top of this. I don't want that guy to get a chance to breathe."

"Yes sir."

The rain in Vancouver eases up, but everything is dripping with ice water. Slithering along the wet ground Miguel gets to the edge of the gate behind a hedge. A guard dog walks by the fencing, sniffing as it drags the security guard along. Another Suburban arrives and stops momentarily at the front entrance. Without another second wasted, Miguel rolls under the truck with the cabin concealing his movement from the camera. Under the truck, he tucks his feet into crevices along the belly and wrenches his hands around the other hanging metal organs. The gate opens and a guard approaches the vehicle. The sight of the size ten combat boot standing inches away forces Miguel to hold his breath, trying to eliminate any noise whatsoever. Miguel feels his feet slipping from the oil under spray. His body starts to shake straining every muscle extending his legs even further holding his position off the ground.

"I have a special visitor for the boss."

"I haven't had the privilege of welcoming a visitor in a while." The security guard caresses his gun.

"Whatever, let me just drop her off and I'll come back and talk."

"Sure. You know where I'll be."

The dog starts sniffing by the front of the Suburban. Miguel remains still. His body heat builds, his air supply diminishes. He fixates on the canine as it moves around the truck.

"Hey Tony, move you and your dog, I gotta go."

"Yeah sure. Come on Max let's go." The dog whimpers as it's dragged away.

Tires grip the road and rubber squeaks as they roll onto the interlocking stone ground. The Suburban weaves through the manicured estate, sparsely lit by old fashioned lamp posts lining the path to the medieval stone mansion. Unable to hold on any longer, the vibrations shake Miguel's hands loose. He skids on his back across the solid surface. Staggering to his feet, he presses his hand onto his lower back trying to alleviate some of the pain. Catching a glimpse of eyes staring down at him, he feels the immediate rush of adrenaline into his system before he recognizes them as stone gargoyles. Sprinting off to the side the soldier slides out of sight.

Soaking wet, the Spaniard takes shelter in the dense trees growing throughout the yard. Moving under a large spruce tree positioned closer to the mansion, he drops to the ground, frightening a raccoon. The varmint hisses and snarls at him. Hearing the noise, a security guard starts walking over. The former inmate boots the animal, but it stands its ground snapping and clawing at his boot. Miguel catches a glimpse of the approaching security guard. Standing ten feet away raising his firearm, the former inmate pulls his leg away from the little beast. He lies on the ground, trying to shimmy behind the tree trunk, out of sight.

Another security guard walks over, "Hey Fred, what are you doing?"

Moving his head from side to side looking into the bushes with the rifle mounted flashlight, "I'm going to kill me something tonight."

"You know the boss doesn't like it when you shoot up the yard."

Miguel picks up a chunk of wood and throws it at the snarling vermin. The silenced machine gun's projectiles split the air and the animal's corpse. The raccoon reacts to the pain with a high pitched squeal.

"Fred you better pick that stupid thing up in the morning before you go home."

"Whatever."

Relieved, the former Colonel watches the guards saunter back towards the mansion, and continue their ritual patrols. Taking out his binoculars, Miguel examines the natural stone exterior of the home showcased by spotlights. The two storey building stands at least sixty feet in height and a montage of armed guards circle the home almost every minute. The main entrance is equipped with video surveillance. Wiping the dew off the lens Miguel refocuses his binoculars, seeing another possible entry point – a second level balcony. The masonry of the exterior will allow for an easy climb however the wet conditions worry the Spaniard. Taking out a guard would bring too much attention, and risk the military being called in to assist. This has to be done completely covert. Miguel prepares to move, as another drone guard patrols around the corner of the house.

The guard stops, and raises his firearm, pointing toward Miguel. Taken back by the timing of this irregular action, he lowers his binoculars realizing the guard is only sighting in his gun on the spruce tree. Knowing his plan, Miguel waits as his heart begins to beat a little lighter.

Working with teams he had made risky entrances to places around the globe, knowing he always had back-up no matter what. Here, alone, utilizing less than adequate equipment, the situation wasn't making him feel any better about the odds of success.

As a guard walks out of sight, the Spaniard leaves his hiding place, running towards the hedge at the base of the balcony. He slides on his chest, hydroplaning across the layer of water. Grabbing onto the trunk of the shrubbery he pulls his body behind its foliage as a guard's soggy footsteps come around the corner. The guard walks out of sight allowing Miguel to exhale. He breathes deeply, examining his climb, gauging the possible grips. Using his finger, he maps out his path before commencing, pointing at different foot holds. Once begun he would be completely lit up and exposed, unable to defend himself or take shelter, a perfect target with these trigger happy mad men.

Taking one last look, the Colonel starts to stand when he detects the sloshing of another guard's footsteps in his vicinity. Lowering himself behind the shrub, the guard passes inches from his location. Miguel convinces himself, *It's now or never.*

Younger hands once scaled many walls without hesitation, these unfamiliar hands of an older man shake, reaching for the next grip. That kind of thought gets a man killed. Splashes increase in volume, reaching Miguel's ears. Pressing on, sweat rolls from his forehead scalding his eyes, blinding him. Using his sense of touch the Spaniard continues to climb until his feet slip on the algae-coated rocks. Hanging there, holding on with his fingertips, his eyes bulge and his legs scramble to find traction. Fingernails grate on the rough stone surface and start to crack.

Footsteps close in as he squeezes onto the rock. Blinking rapidly, he barely makes out his destination. His feet lock in. He jumps for the balcony. His chest heaves as his body slams into the side of the house. His arms flail about seeking support as his body slips from the balcony's ledge. Miguel's chest ricochets off the wall and sweat from his head sprays off, landing on the guard's bald head walking underneath his suspended body.

The guard looks up just missing the flinging of the former inmate's body over the side. Rubbing his head the guard sees the fluid on his hand and holds out his hand looking for more rain.

Lying on the balcony floor, Miguel rolls to his feet and shuffles over to the corner nearest the house. He clenches his right fists as hard as he can trying to compensate for the pulsing pain emanating from his left hand. Looking down he sees one of his nails bent backwards, exposing the quick. Droplets of red bodily fluid dye puddles covering the ground. Removing a roll of athletic tape out of his small fanny pouch he presses the adhesive material across his nail, flattening it out. His mandible muscles seize up biting down until he finishes his first aid repair. Miguel massages his jaw until it releases allowing him to breathe heavily again.

Beside him the Spaniard sees the weathered brass door knob only feet away. Yanking onto the handle he feels the locked resistance. With a flick of his wrist, a blade opens with a snap. The former Colonel lowers his body, pausing, hearing the sound of a helicopter in the air. An approaching blinking light forces him to retract into the shadows. Listening to the chugging sound of the engine he confirms the type of aircraft, *Civilian*.

Using the thunder from the chopper engine as a distraction, Miguel forces the door open gaining access to the house. The heat from the home billows out releasing steam in the air. Closing the door he conceals himself behind the oversized drapes, and waits for a response to his action. Blood pumping through his veins remind him he isn't dead yet. Taking a set of low grade night vision goggles out, he reviews the contents of this massive room. The enormous bed with oversized wood pillars at the four corners, and matching furniture was worth more than his previous home. Proceeding to a set of doors on the opposite side of the room Miguel hears hushed voices.

"Sir, I have just received word that Giabatti is in military custody."

"No need to fret. I know."

"You know. No need to fret? Are you serious? We need to leave immediately! They'll be coming for us next."

"No, Christopher. He has been taken care of. That was the first and last time that information will ever come to light. The one man we needed to worry about is no longer an issue. With the military on his heels, I have been assured that Miguel will be captured within a day's time."

"A day?"

"He was last seen a couple of hours ago downtown using a stolen credit card. If you're so worried, double the guards again."

"Sir, I really think we should relocate just for a short period of time, or at least until they find and kill Mejia. Have you alerted the others?"

"No need, this problem is taken care of. Listen we'll talk in the morning. I have a much more attractive guest waiting for me downstairs."

Miguel listens as the two men exit. Twisting the handle of the door, he controls the speed it opens. Stepping through the opening, the former Colonel uses the night vision lenses as he manoeuvres through the room. The room appears to be an office however the decor would be revered by the richest Maharajas. The foreign footsteps continue further away. Captured on the walls of this office are several pictures and credentials, a true shrine.

So Mister Jason Somers, former Premier of British Columbia where do you keep your dirty little secrets? Miguel takes a seat at the desk in the room and scoffs at even more photos displaying celebrities with his unwitting host. The placard on the desk is almost too much 'Premier Jason Somers.' *You really love yourself don't you?*

Miguel barely has time to start going through the desk when he detects the sound of two sets of footsteps approaching. One seems like the snapping of pointy heels colliding with the flooring, accompanied by a deeper snap. He fixes the contents of the drawers so that he can close them. The door starts opening as the Spaniard slips off the chair and under the desk. Crawling on the floor, Miguel peers underneath seeing a woman's feet in stiletto heels and a man's pants covering the top of a pair of dress shoes. Turning around facing the opening Miguel's heart picks up in tempo again. *Nice hiding spot asshole. How are you going to get out of here?*

He forces himself to take a series of long deep breaths slowing his heart rate to a controlled calm until the fragrance of the wood desk comes to his senses. Miguel convinces himself, *no one is going to look under the desk, just relax.*

A familiar female voice begins, "Jason, thank you so much for helping me out with everything."

"Honestly, it was nothing."

"Wow! Is that your room connected to your office?"

"Yes, I spend almost all my time up here. The downstairs is mainly for fundraising events."

"I can't get over how beautiful this place is, it's absolutely gorgeous."

"Thank you, I have an eye for things I like."

"Really, is there anything else that you like?"

The former Colonel pays attention, as their voices lower and transform into sloppy kissing. A sudden bang causes the desk to vibrate as their bodies collide against it knocking items all over the floor.

Screaming and moaning echo in the crevice that is Miguel's sanctuary. Clothing scatters onto the floor as the heavy breathing and mouths slapping forces a smile on the Spaniard's face. He rolls his eyes, thinking, *this is a first.*

Both were not shy in voicing their pleasure and anyone in the house would have recognized the sounds coming from the room. The bare feet of the two eventually cross the floor leading to the bedroom still in one another's embrace. Counting breaths, counting steps, Miguel peeks around the side of the cherry wood hand carved decorations along the side of the desk. Moving between the sexual distractions Miguel hears the sound of handcuffs being put on.

Jason Somers asks, "Are you sure they aren't too tight?"

"It's good."

Peering around the door frame, Miguel slinks into the bedroom, seeing the girl with her hands attached to the headboard looking up at the man mounted on top of her. Using reflections off the shiny items in the room, the soldier sees her close her eyes. Springing to his feet, Miguel takes a step in and punches the former premier in the back of the neck. Somers falls forward, knocking his head against the girl's.

"Ouch, okay that hurt get off me for a second," she whimpered.

The naked man falls aside. The girl's eyes protrude from her face seeing Miguel in the room. Before she is able to scream, his hand covers her mouth. Her muffled screams amuse the guards patrolling the hall, chuckling to themselves.

Miguel whispers, "Carrie if someone comes in here you will be the first person that I kill. Now shut up."

Nodding her head, tears begin flowing down her face. The Spaniard lets go of her face and ties up the former Premier, gagging him.

Carrie whimpers, "Miguel, I am so sorry that I interviewed you like that. I didn't know the warden threatened to…"

Glaring down at her, Miguel squeezes her mouth closed again, "I said shut up."

Throwing a sheet over her naked body the Spaniard explains, "Listen I'm not going to hurt you Warren. Just relax, I'm here for him." He shoves a gag into her mouth. "But I don't trust you at all."

Miguel grabs an MP3 player off the night stand and inserts it into a docking station. Scrolling through the device he locates a folder, 'recently added'. He presses play and turns up the volume allowing the music to mask sounds in the room.

Somers, the former premier, wakes being dragged across his shiny smooth marble floor leading from the bedroom to his office. He notices that his mouth is gagged and he looks up seeing that the doors to the hallway are barricaded. Shock had initially prevented him from feeling the pain, but as the situation became a reality, he notices he was now wearing a housecoat and his hands and feet were tied tightly together with a rope forcing him to be hunched over into the fetal position, exposing his family plan.

Miguel stops, picks Somers up and throws him down onto a large chair. His body ricochets, bouncing from the springs in the seat and his limbs knock together. He screams out in vain.

Moving in close to his captive, the former Colonel speaks loudly in his ear, "Listen here you fucking piece of shit. You so much as whimper without my consent and I will cut you're fucking dick off and feed it to you leaving you to die. If you understand nod your head."

Tears roll down the side of Somers' face, as he nods his head slowly. Barely able to breathe through the gag in his mouth, Somers tries to take in a deep breath making his nose sniffle.

"I want to know everything there is to know about your relationship with Giabatti and a certain associate of his, Alfonso. If you do that I promise you that you will live. Do you understand?"

Again his head slowly nods as more tears stream down his face.

Miguel takes out his personal recording device checking to make sure it is still functioning.

Carrie left alone in the room can see Miguel and the former Premier, but, is unable to hear what is being said because of the music drowning out their words. Her heart had been racing like a horse, which has drained most of her energy. Somehow, in the middle of all of this she believes that she has nothing to fear as she watches the exchange. Her news reporter mind sets in. *Why would Miguel risk his life to overtly attack the former Premier while at home?*

Trying to decipher the situation she pays close attention, reading Miguel's lips as he commences his interrogation of Somers. *What's that?* Had she made a mistake, she believes that she had managed to pick up something about *'Giabatti.'*

CHAPTER EIGHT

Trapped beneath a glass dome, tied down in an upright position, wearing an oxygen mask, Hamilton's refusal to give in is being tested. Radiating dull aches invade every inch of his frame as his joints stiffen up, unable to stretch or alleviate the stress. The cockpit of a fighter jet was not the same place it used to be, as stabbing pains attack his lower back sending volts of electricity up his spine.

Hamilton forces himself to endure it, remembering a tenured career in the field. Enthusiasm and adrenaline pushed him through years of discomfort. Having personally carried tons over the years strapped to his thin frame, he trekked over twisted terrain, leaving him aged and damaged. Staring out over miles of airspace did not provide the same euphoric relief from the afflictions of his youth; instead the scenery was a backdrop of a rapidly deteriorating situation. The bottom has fallen out. The game has changed and quitting is not an option.

Touching down at the military base housing Canada's Central Command Center, Hamilton scales down a miniscule ladder fastened to the side of the plane feeling his spine decompress. Removing the helmet allows his sweat matted hair to breathe. Twisting his upper body from side to side, he stretches out his vertebrae as he spots a military jeep racing across the pavement.

The tires from the jeep kick up loose sand creating a dust cloud following its movements. Metal on metal grinds with a high-pitched squeal as the vehicle comes to a stop. The sound ignites the nerves along Hamilton's spinal cord, contracting muscles, pulling back his shoulders and scrunching his face.

The thump of the pilot's feet hit the ground behind the General. Tilting his head to the side, Hamilton orders, "Captain, once you have it fuelled up, stand by until I am ready to return."

"Yes, sir."

Climbing into the jeep, the grizzled veteran points in the distance, "Corporal, bring me to the Command Center."

Grinding gears puts the vehicle in motion. The driver follows directions without a word. Hamilton has nothing to say beyond that. He's not much of a conversationalist when he's in a mood like this. Adding to his mood were the horrific brakes vibrating the vehicle each time they approached an intersection, not to mention his phone going off every couple of seconds. Reviewing his most recent email message the General jabs his index finger on the screen, "That was the plan all along!"

The Corporal speaks up, "Sir?"

Clenching his jaw, the muscles in his cheeks pulse as Hamilton gradually turns to face the driver. He stares at the young man. The Corporal swallows deep, snaps his eyes back to the road as his body droops at the wheel, "Sorry, sir."

The General releases his mandible, taking a deep breath in through his mouth. He can't allow himself to treat people the way Izzov does. Having spent years working under him he swore he would never follow his example.

"Corporal, don't worry about it. Just get these brakes fixed ASAP." Hamilton forces a grin to his face.

The Corporal's mind eases sitting a little straighter in the seat, "Yes, sir!"

Entering the building Hamilton's strides are long and quick. Dressed in the flight suit carrying his helmet in his hand, the General's body temperature rises as quickly as his pace walking through the hallways. Reaching the Incident Command Post, security guards salute while opening the doors. Hamilton returns the gesture and lowers his head as the cool computer air flows from the portal. Walking into the room, Hamilton spots Izzov hovering over an employee's terminal, "General Izzov, I would like a word with you."

Turning slowly from the computer screen not at all surprised, "David, nice to see you again. What brings you down here?"

Hamilton walks over to meet his co-worker, pointing with the helmet towards his office, "Tom, can we speak in private?"

Eyes in the area skirt temporarily from their monitors to the two military giants.

Izzov's left side of his face curls, forming a half smile, "I don't have time to talk privately General. I am trying to clean up a mess called Mejia, thanks to you. And we have a terrorist group blowing up every country around the globe."

"General Izzov, no need to worry about being busy anymore, I am resuming my post." In a smooth motion Hamilton pulls a folded piece of paper from his pocket and flicks his wrists cracking open the document. Holding it up like a town crier, he displays his letter of authorization from the Prime Minister.

Spitting out a laugh, Izzov's face lightens, "Well you might as well be holding an ancient Roman decree in your hand, because that document means absolutely nothing anymore. You see I'm running the show not you. You were reassigned. If you would like, I could get the Prime Minister on the line right now to put this to rest."

Bending back down Izzov looks at the screen over his subordinate's shoulder, and then lifts his head facing Hamilton, "What, he hasn't been answering your calls? He still answers mine."

Izzov resumes pointing at the screen, "See that..."

General Hamilton stands there, eyeballing Izzov who ignores him. Anger rolls over his body feeling the loss of this political battle. A satisfying mental image of beating Izzov's giant mutated head to a pulp with this aviator helmet plagues his rational thoughts. Slamming the helmet into his opposite hand, a couple of pairs of eyes glance over and retreat to their task. Surveying the room, David begins walking backwards before spinning around and marching out, "This is not over yet."

The soothing sound of a saxophone whining out a jazz melody could not be anymore ironic to the sight in the luxurious home office. The docking station continues to play a soft tune while Somers in his white house coat looks like an old tea bag. Filth from urine and feces has seeped through its porous exterior onto the customized furniture. He quivers as goose bumps ripple over his skin from the gentle stroke of a knife blade over his partially exposed naked body.

"So Mr. Former Premier. Isn't it amazing how much pain the body can endure without leaving a permanent mark? You won't be so lucky if we ever meet again."

Aged dramatically by recent events, Somers' chin continues to displays deep wrinkle creases from hours of crying. Exhausted tear ducts forget how to extract any more fluid from his body as thoughts of the information Miguel coerced out of him, drains any remaining energy out of his body. Slumping to the floor he realizes, *I'm a dead man; it is just a matter of time.*

Retracting his knife from the broken man's body, the former Colonel surveys his surroundings, catching Carrie's eyes witnessing his every move. Musing beside the desk, Miguel's hand glides over his scalp while sitting in the leather reclining captain chair. Rolling on plastic casters across the floor he pulls himself behind the desk accessing the computer's keyboard. Slipping the SD card out of his personal recorder and into the side of the laptop, Miguel starts making copies.

As the computer finalizes the transfer of information, the Spaniard begins digging like a dog through the contents of the desk. Drawer after drawer opens scattering papers across the floor until he finally locates his bone. Raising a second USB drive from a drawer, he injects it into another port and initiates the transfer of information.

Using his pinky finger Miguel scoops up a C cup bra off the desk top. Holding it up, he admires the workmanship as it spins. Rising to his feet, the Spaniard walks around the desk delicately picking up, and examining each piece of Carrie's clothing strewn in the room. Scrunching the clothes together in a ball he places them on the top of the desk and sits back down. He composes an email to General Hamilton and Colonel Pegrum, attaching the Somers interview.

Grabbing Carrie's small black purse, the former Colonel drops his body down low before dumping out the contents on the desk. Rummaging through her items, he spots her cellular phone. Snapping off a piece of tape, he covers up the optical eye. He stands skimming through the phone. Tapping on the touch screen he sends a text and feels the confirmation of its arrival with the vibration in his pouch. Removing both memory sticks from the laptop, the Spaniard places one into his pocket. He moves towards the bedroom palming Carrie's clothes, and looking over his mess.

Somers wouldn't look up as he passed by. Now situated on his knees, the former Premier allows gravity to pull his head down. Hair products that once maintained Somers' hair in perfect form have lost their strength under the weight of sweat coating each strand. The former Premier hopes that Miguel will finish the job and kill him in order to alleviate the stress of the certainty awaiting him.

The reporter's eyes grow in size with every step Miguel takes over to the bedside. She tries to shimmy her body away from the Spaniard, but the restraints wrapped around the bed post prevent any escape.

Still covered with the sheet and gagged she stares at her captor as he speaks, "You've seen and heard too much."

Rocking her head back and forth, her face wrinkles so tight her eyes close and her body starts trembling. She starts slamming the handcuffs against the bed frame trying one last time to free herself as she attempts to scream.

Grabbing her head, Miguel shoves it down into the mattress and holds it in place raising his other hand toward her throat.

She mumbles through the gag and distorted mouth, "you said if I was...ah..."

Somers' voice interrupts her whimpering, "...I gave Giabatti access to my ships and he paid me well for it. I didn't know anything else. It's what we call plausible deniability. I had that until Planet X came on the scene. That's when the waters got muddy."

Miguel shuts off the device tucking it back in his pocket. "Listen to me very carefully. If I let you go you might live, but if I leave you here like this, him and his gangster buddies are going to kill you."

Carrie stops crying, and opens her eyes. She sees Miguel hovering over her, his dark irises pierce through crystal blue eyes into her soul, "Carrie I'm going to let you go. Don't try and be the hero and alert the guards. If for whatever reason they find out. I will kill you. Do you understand me? You won't even reach the main gate."

Her eyes gaze deep into his, nodding assent twice.

Reaching over her body he unlocks the handcuffs from the bed, "I don't know where you got some of your information for that interview in the prison but I was impressed and intrigued. Those military stories were never documented."

Pulling her hands out, she rubs each of her wrists where deep red impressions remain.

"You know better than anyone what I can do. As long as you keep your mouth shut no one will die, this I promise you."

He pushes her pile of clothes over to her, "Get dressed." Miguel proceeds over to the door removing the barriers he had set up.

Sitting on the bed Carrie starts pulling on her clothes. She glances over at Somers and wonders, *Is he really going to let me leave just like that? What about Jason? Is he going to kill him?*

The reporter stands up, buttoning her blouse. Now completely dressed, she starts strutting toward her captor's position. The tapping of her heels could be made out slightly over the music in the background. She glances at Somers through her peripheral vision, avoiding any possibility of making eye contact. Miguel grabs her hand and she pulls back slightly and then releases, frightened what he might do to her if she resists.

He places in her hand a USB drive, "I'm not the bad guy you people think I am. These are the real villains." Miguel turns and cracks open the door, "Remember what I said, not a word."

Fresh air pollutes the passage, reminding her senses of the feces molecules thick in the air. She pauses, looking back at the former Premier still beside himself in fear and abject humiliation. He stares at the floor, not paying any attention to her leaving. Parting distraught, confused and scared, she begins her journey down the hallway, *Can I trust him not to kill anyone? Do I really leave Jason with that maniac? What does he mean real villains? Who could be worse than him?*

Before the door even closes, Miguel starts doubting this decision. *This is it. She is going to squeal.* Pressing a button on a remote control the Spaniard lowers the music volume. He leans against the door holding a chair in one hand while cupping his ear with the other. Hearing her footsteps proceed down the staircase, he detects a voice speak to her. Acid reflux burns Miguel's esophagus.

"Is everything okay Miss Warren? Miss Warren, is everything okay?"

Miguel puts the chair down. He pulls out his knife and cracks open the door. Silently moving down the hallway, the former Colonel grips his knife ready to make a pre-emptive strike. He spots Carrie on the grand marble wrapping staircase trimmed with wrought iron. A security guard with a machine gun hanging over his shoulder stands a couple steps down from her. Carrie drops her head glancing back toward the bedroom, "Yes... yes, I'm sorry; it's been a crazy night."

The guard's face fights back a smile, his muscles contract and he covers up his face with his hand. Miguel could see the dimple in his cheek emerge.

The reporter composes herself and faces the guard again, "Could someone please bring me to my hotel? I have a flight to catch back home in the morning."

"Miss Warren. I will radio a driver for you now."

"Thank you."

"I will escort you to the main entrance. Someone will drive you back to your hotel shortly."

Miguel watches them descend the stairs. He retreats back towards conquered ground. Bracing the door with a chair and a dresser, Miguel stops and listens again. *No feet barrelling this way yet. This may be the first time a news person ever kept their mouth shut.* He reminds himself, *she's not gone yet though.*

Holding onto a window pane, Miguel observes a SUV proceeding down the serpent's path away from the house to the front gate. *Now would be a good time to leave.*

Hours later, Carrie enters the airport and proceeds straight to a small café. Propped up on a stool, she questions her own eyes, ears and senses. Pulling back her sleeves reveals the handcuff marks on her wrists. Grabbing the USB drive out of her purse she inspects it, shaking her head. *This is as real as it gets.*

A jolt to her ribs instigates her nervous energy, propelling her off her seat. "Eeiiiioooo!"

Spinning around she exclaims, "Ah... thanks Sam!"

Carrie ignores foreign eyes turn and glance her way as she embraces Sam tightly. Slowly letting go, she resets and locks onto the handsome man before her. Dressed in a fine looking two piece-suit with a matching East Indian head piece he backs up a step, "Whoa, take it easy Carrie! You okay? I've never seen you like this. What happened?"

"I can't explain here, is there somewhere we can talk?"

His eyebrows wrinkle together, "Yes?"

Heart racing, eyes scanning, and limbs moving, Miguel runs through the dark empty streets, taking shelter in the shadows. The former inmate's feet are moving at only a fraction of the speed his mind is. *There is little time. Have to get as far away from Somers as possible. If Somers is at all smart he's not going to tell a soul because of what happened to Giabatti. When is this going to end? Who can I rely on? Reaching Somers was one thing, but, now I need help. And fast.* The beep of a coded text message stops Miguel mid run. "What the...it's suppose to be on vibrate."

Ducking behind a car on the sidewalk, Miguel pants, takes out the phone examining the coded text. 'See that tiger wearn those sox, or dat angel workn ovr that yank, how bout that blue bird on the mariners boat.'

Miguel nods smiling, "Okay...okay."

Getting back up, he sprints across the road. A police car with a spotlight captures a glimpse of his body entering a treed lot.

"Dispatch, we have a curfew violator entering Vanier park."

Crouching along the shore, Miguel looks at the boats nestled in a marina, sailboats, house boats, yachts and cruisers. *Not exactly what I had in mind.*

Beams of light cut through the night's veil, accompanied by the sound of stomping footsteps approaching. Dropping to his stomach Miguel slides head first into the frigid water. The liquid penetrates his clothing lowering his body temperature and weighing him down. Drifting out away from the shore, Miguel hides among the bumper pads dangling from boats.

Two police officers emerge from the darkness, walking along the waterfront, reaching the marina. They stop and speak to security, "Have you seen anyone come or go from the docks in the last couple minutes?"

"Not that I saw. It's been pretty quiet."

"Open up the gates, we're going to walk around."

"No problem officers, but tenants are permitted to be out on the docks according to the WMA."

"Just open the gates."

"Yes, sir."

Patrol boots hit the docks creaking and cracking the wood planks. The docks sink down splashing into the water. Lights dart across the ocean's restless surface. "Boss, I don't see anything."

"Just keep looking, he's gotta be around here somewhere."

Shuffling along the side of a yacht, Miguel clings to its underbelly. Muscles and joints stiffen, succumbing to the bleak environment. Mucus excretes from his nose across his upper lip over his mouth and flows down his chin mixing in with the water. Shivering, Miguel starts looking around for an escape.

Light illuminates a red rocket. Sitting twenty meters away, among all of these vessels is a high performance speed boat plastered with water sport sponsor emblems. He reads the bold letters across the bow, 'Good Times'.

Quivering, Miguel starts sculling with his hands, accidentally making a splash.

"Did you hear that?"

Gasping for air, the former Colonel finds himself caught between docks and in the open. Over the water, a light flickers nearing his vicinity. Like a boot stepping on his stomach Miguel's diaphragm squeezes the air out of his lungs. Forcing himself, he plunges under water seeing the beam sweep just above him. Pressure instantly builds in his head and chest. His tongue and throat work in concert, wrenching, scrambling for oxygen. Fighting against nature, the Spaniard pushes on, reaching the rear of another boat. Clasping the keel, he moves one hand at a time walking up the side of the boat. Breaking the surface of the water, he tilts his head back and sucks in a belly full of air.

Reaching the stern, he unsteadily pulls himself out of the water resting on the back deck. Water falls from his body splashing into the pool beneath him. Without a moment lost, he lifts the back cover and enters the hull. Securing the thick cover back over the side, he cracks a glow stick. His eyes adjust and images of scuba tanks and accessories come into focus, along with the keys dangling in the ignition.

Shaking, he strips off his wet clothes. The former Colonel begins pulling on a wet suit when his ears capture voices getting louder, "I think I heard something coming from over here."

Grabbing a spear gun, Miguel shoves the glow stick between the seats, and slithers to the back of the boat. Heat permeates through his body once again and the trembling lessens. In the absence of light, the Spaniard's ears compensate, hearing the slapping of tongues mouthing words. The depression of the stern rocks the boat backwards, inconsistent with the light waves floating in from side to side. Suddenly, the cover's snaps sound off in rapid succession. Light fills the hull. Peering over the side is the barrel of a handgun.

Ninja like reflexes grab the frame of the gun stripping it from the officer's grip. An upper cut to the man's face sends him flying backwards landing on the corner of the dock screaming out in agony, "MY BACK! MY BACK!"

Miguel ducks back down as the partner starts launching rounds through the fibreglass boat. A lull in the action has the officer looking over at his partner, "I think I got him."

The other officer rolls onto the dock writhing in pain. "I think something is busted in my back."

"Just hold on. I'm going to get some help."

With his gun covering the boat the officer peers from side to side. Removing one hand from his gun, he reaches up to his radio. Miguel pops up shooting the officer twice in the bullet proof vest. The officer collapses off the dock landing in the water. Swooping with a knife in hand, the Spaniard slices through the ropes anchoring the boat to the dock. He slides across the floor to the ignition. With a growl the twin 454 engines awaken. Setting the boat into motion he rips the cover off as the vessel bounces off others in the area.

Navigating into open water Miguel slams the throttle down roaring out of sight. With his GPS out he points the bow of the boat towards the United States.

Morning streaks of virgin sun shine through the hallways of the Central Command Center, as General Izzov calls to order his first meeting as leader in the auditorium. Alongside the grizzled General is Colonel Renniks. With his arms crossed and chest out, Renniks glares at all those attending until Lieutenant Connie walks in. The Colonel leaves his post and marches over as she checks in her audio visual recording equipment. Standing behind her, as she bends over signing off on a clip board, Renniks examines her body, "Lieutenant."

Connie's spine shivers hearing his voice as she completes the form.

"I understand you are in charge of city restorations. That's part of my portfolio. I want a complete work up on everything you have done on my desk by the end of the day, unless..."

Straightening up she turns around facing him, "No Colonel, don't worry, you'll have your report."

She heads towards the auditorium seats as Renniks' eyes follow her, grinning.

Marching into the room a group of men strut past the check-in and nod at Renniks. Taking to the seats in the back row they begin scanning the auditorium. Pointing at persons seated throughout they whisper to one another, rolling their eyes and laughing.

Izzov takes to the helm, extending his neck from the collar of his shirt. Shadows cover his face from pockmarks under the lights above. His raspy tone echoes in the ears of the listeners as he speaks loudly, "I have been in the military for the past thirty-four years and a serving General for the last ten. In my time, I have never seen such a lack of respect for each of those serving under a supervising officer by having them constantly monitored."

Displayed on a screen behind the General are the gruesome images of military members firing into the Vancouver crowd. Turning around looking at the screen and then back at the audience, he continues, "What idiot would want that kind of information available. And what about our fellow men and women who lost their lives that day, how does Colonel Mejia repay their service as their commanding officer? He flees at the first opportunity away from the base. I cannot comment on General Hamilton's leadership, his credentials speak for themselves. However, his decision to allow a convicted murderer to lead this country's largest investigation is beyond me."

Looking to the side, he orders, "That's enough, shut that off."

Eyeing the crowd, "I'm embarrassed and angry how Miguel left while each of you pours out your heart and soul into an investigation of the utmost importance. Let me assure you that under the careful and responsible guidance of myself and Colonel Renniks, not only will we will put an end to these terrorists, we will also catch this piece of shit deserter."

Clapping from the back of the room starts and spreads, getting louder and louder as others follow suit. Izzov steps back from the podium soaking in the applause. As the noise tapers off, he moves forward again, "We appreciate your devotion to your country. We know that your professionalism and patriotism will push you past this small speed bump. This investigative team and its current status is in good shape. As of this morning the 360 Electronic Surveillance System is completely online..."

A door creaks open, allowing hallway light to ease into the room. Seated on his knees on the bare hardwood floor, a dark tanned man with jet black hair opens his eyes slowly facing the silhouette of a thin man speaking to him from the doorway. "Alfonso, whenever you're ready. Everyone is waiting."

"Thanks Frank. Continue with the briefing. I'll be right out."

Jumping to his feet, Alfonso puts on a pair of white gloves. He stretches them tightly over his hands making them fit properly as he walks out into the hallway. Entering a darkened room he sees ominous plans being formulated. Images of neighbourhoods in major cities shine on the stark white screens.

Alfonso reaches into his pocket and pulls out a laser pointer manipulating the device, "If the population thinks they can hide in their homes, than we will hit their houses."

Everyone in the room turns around seeing the Brazilian speak.

He points the red laser dot on the front of a home with children's toys scattered across the front lawn. "Hitting them at their homes is even easier than public locations. There is less surveillance equipment and less security. As our children have suffered so too will their children suffer."

Images of public figures replace the houses on the screen. "They thought they could oppress us, kill our spirits, force us into submission. Society stood idly by allowing our friends and family members to be jailed and publicly ridiculed. Vengeance will be ours. Western society will collapse. The time of corrupt government heads spreading their tyranny over the population has come to an end."

Miguel discards the scuba tank into the body of water before walking up onto the beach. Dropping to his knees gasping for air he looks up at the glow of the city before him. He relaxes for a moment and takes a couple of deep breaths. Untying the drawstring on his backpack, he dumps the contents out. Dipping back into the water Miguel struggles to put on wet clothes.

The downpour of rain hazes the ground, comforting the Spaniard. He knew if he could barely see in front of him, anyone out in the storm wouldn't be able to see him either. Reaching the exterior of the Seattle Mariner's baseball stadium Safeco Field, he hunkers down under a metal awning.

A black full-sized car with tinted black windows pulls up to the sidewalk. The rear passenger door opens with a black umbrella extending out covering the head of the passenger encountering the weather. The stance and stature identifies this passenger as a man. Wearing a black suit, and galoshes the man leaves the sanctity of his dry tomb. Miguel pulls on his hood recognizing the gait and enters the tempest meeting the man. Within meters of this person the former Colonel reveals his face from the shadows.

"Mejia, get in the car!"

Both men jump into the back seat and barely notice the high performance vehicle speed off, other than the rattle of water pelting the wheel wells. Windshield wipers relentlessly clear the deluge of water with barely a protest of sound. The car's blower hums at high speeds trying to remove the humidity from the air fogging up the windows.

"Colonel Pegrum and I have put our asses on the line meeting with you. Officially we are not meeting. However, unofficially you have our complete support."

Miguel looks at Colonel Pegrum's eyes through the rear-view mirror and turns his head facing General Hamilton, "Ryan, David, I couldn't let them put me back in jail when there's so much at stake. A puppet master is pulling the strings on politicians and crime bosses."

Pegrum manoeuvres the car through the flooding streets. "From listening to your interviews, essentially everyone who ever had anything to do with government construction contracts or passing of laws may be involved. We have to assume that the President or Prime Minister of every country is involved, or anyone around them. This level of sophistication is not something born over night, it would have taken years to cultivate, decades perhaps, even centuries."

"You're not saying...?"

Hamilton interjects, "We're not sure what's going on or who's in charge. These two guys tied to the Freedom Movement are at best grunts if not a distraction. We have gathered and quickly analysed all of their communication records. There wasn't a single person with any political contacts. Simple math estimates the amount of people involved in the attacks we have suffered this far, are in the tens of thousands."

Miguel nods, collecting the information.

Speaking over his shoulder Colonel Pegrum turns the car around another corner, "Miguel, for the time being, I have a place where you can stay inside the city. You're going to need to get some sleep before we start tracking down these assholes."

Hamilton touches his old friend's shoulder, "Miguel, don't get too comfortable. This is far from the Middle East and you have been recently added to the most wanted list."

"General, when have you known me to get comfortable?"

"Don't be a smart ass, the 360 is up and running in almost every country, there are a few things that you need to keep in mind in case you forgot. Every electronic optical eye and microphone is now online. Basically, anything that captures a picture or sound that is transmitted through a computer system is now government moni-tored. If your face or voice is picked up, the system will automatically provide an alert to the nearest Command Center for your capture with your current GPS coordinates. Take this."

"What's this?" Miguel questions, holding up a device similar to a large old cell phone.

"This is a prototype phone that I had made to bypass the system. It changes your voice and emits a signal that scrambles the electronic eye and mic of any device within a short range."

Increasing the blower heat, Pegrum fights against the fog taking over the windshield, "Miguel just stay covered up. Every face is compared to various methods of government information, driver's licence, passport, health card, hunting card, and newly introduced are all major corporation information membership cards, credit cards and anything else that companies possess."

Miguel rubs the couple days of growth on his face, "Thanks for the refresher."

Pegrum looks back at Miguel, "Migs, we're coming up to your stop now. Sorry, we don't have much time to talk. Put your hood on. They will explain inside. Go now, its number twenty-six."

The car slows to a crawl at a stop sign. Miguel throws his hood on and opens the door. Facing the downpour, he starts strolling along the sidewalk. His feet squish out water bubbles through his socks and shoes. Keeping his head down he peeks out of the top corner of his hood looking for his destination.

Stepping into the neighbourhood, Miguel notices that he is entering a cage with a long line of townhouses on either side preventing an easy escape. Cars line both sides of the street, the end result of Blackstar's public-sanctioned transportation protocols, which add to the difficulty of spotting a threat. Rich cars, untouched, sitting in this seedy block causes the former cop to pay close attention. Silhouettes from head rests appear like surveillance team members watching his every move. His eyes scout the area, gripping the handgun in his pocket, ready to face any threat. His nerves are getting to him, he's anxious to reach the safe house undetected.

Spotting a mail box with the French words, 'Les Foux', he looks up spotting the two and six in white letters on the box. "How fitting," Miguel mumbles.

The front gate creaks with his hand pushing on the 'No Trespassers, No Solicitors' sign. Miguel eyes the pathway. The cement interlocking stonework lies beneath three inches of water pooling in the depression. Window coverings conceal the interior from sight. Attached to the top floor of this two story townhouse, a surveillance camera peers down at him. Dropping his head, he reaches for the stainless steel door handle. Turning it slowly releases the mechanism. The door swings open gently, squeaking under its own weight.

Hand on gun, Miguel strains his head forward while still outside the door. His senses pick up plastic scraping metal and the flashing of a television or computer screen in the distance. *No shoes at the entrance, very odd.* Sizzling is heard as Miguel steps inside. Gun out, rounding the first corner, a voice asks, "You want some soup, Colonel?"

Lowering the gun, the former inmate relaxes, "Sure Captain, when did you switch to chicken noodle soup?"

"Are You Serious? Carrie this is crazy!" Sam jumps up from his seat shouting at Carrie inside a miniature office.

Covering her ears for a moment, she yells back, "Sam, relax! I know. What do I do? You are the only one I trust."

He struggles to straighten his seat before sitting back down, "Carrie, I will never forget that you helped me through journalism school while I was working full time at my father's store but this is some serious shit."

"How do you think I feel?"

"Well, you're the one who decided to sleep with this guy to cover a story. Now look what you got yourself into."

Carrie moves her head to the right, "Awwwww." Turning back she glares at her friend, "Fuck you, Sam! Why do you think we broke up? Like you never slept with someone while you were covering a story?"

Deflated, folding his head into his chest, "Sorry Carrie. That was out of line. I'm just scared. If anyone gets word about this I would be ruined, you too. Who do you think they will believe me, you or them?"

"Sam how can we ignore this? This is massive."

"People are going to die over that kind of information, Carrie. You're going to be crucified for leaving and not telling anyone."

"And if I did he would have killed everyone, including me. I don't think I had a choice. After I left I went back to my hotel and listened to the interviews, Somers and then to Giabatti. I needed to talk to you again. Since my mom died you always seem to be the voice of reason when my life is falling apart."

"Parental issues are one thing, schooling another, even when you told me what you saw after the first attack I can deal with, but this – this is far from the celebrity gossip news that I usually cover. I'm sorry."

Sam starts rubbing her back as she leans forward with her head in her hands. "Have you even talked to him since you left?"

Carrie takes a deep breath, "No."

"You don't even know if he is alive or dead? Funny, nothing has been on the news either."

"That is weird. I'm supposed to return to Toronto on the next flight to cover the power being turned back on. I will call him from there."

Pointing at the USB drive on the desk top, "Carrie whatever you do with that, just make sure you know what you're talking about. Fighting a government cover-up never ends well. They have unlimited resources at their disposal."

"I was there and saw the look on Jason Somers' face, he's guilty. He wouldn't even look at me and that is his voice absolutely, which confirms what the other voice says."

"Okay, okay. I am only trying to get you to think rationally. You can't cover this, at least not yet. You will have to do some more work confirming what is on the audio before you do that."

She looks down at her watch and grabs the memory device off the desk, "I've gotta go Sam. Thanks for the talk. Sorry for bugging you. I will send you a copy of these recordings." She gets up out of her chair and hugs Sam tightly, going onto her toes to kiss him on the cheek.

"Don't bother. I don't want any part of that. Leave me with my fluff stories thank you very much. At least celebrities don't want to see me dead."

The visual flying over the Rockies was a symphony for Somers' eyes. The mixture of the rich green forests, intermitted with the crystalline blue lakes, churning froth of the rivers and silky flow of streams, were interrupted by massive mountains stretching to the sky. Disturbing the tranquility of the moment was the loud sound of the engine suspending the metal bubble in the air despite wearing the standard helicopter earphones to hear the pilot. Dropping in altitude, the chopper angles to the right rounding another peak of the Big Sky terrain.

Descending through the mist, a manicured estate rested inside the crevice of an open pit mine. A replica 15th century stone castle occupied a large portion of the property with several similar smaller buildings. A black air strip divided the grounds in two, with a hangar opposite the castle. Flying to the back side of the castle between the mountain and the building itself, sat six helipads with only one vacant spot.

The sight of the grounds raised Somers' heart rate. Opening up his hands he wiped away the built up sweat from his palms onto his black pants. His mind kept running over the events of the preceding twenty-four hours. His aide, Christopher, leaned over grabbing his shoulder and points at the castle, "It's beautiful!"

Somers' closest friend Christopher was the only person who saw him tied up. Despite their relationship the former Premier couldn't bring himself to tell the truth, oddly enough Christopher bought the story without a fuss.

With all of his time in politics, he couldn't remember a single time he felt this nervous. His heart beat in synch with the spinning helicopter's blades. Cognizant that streams of sweat ran from his armpit down his rib cage and were soaked up by his shirt tucked in his waist band, he composed a blank stare that he believed showed strength. The suit jacket acted as his security blanket, comforting him, concealing his true body functions. The sunglasses covered the look of panic in his eyes as the pilot completed the landing procedure.

Exiting the helicopter Somers follows his aide's lead. As they approach one of the castle's entrances, shaved bald men wearing dark sunglasses and charcoal suits stood holding open doors. Waiting on the inside of the doors was a single male standing at attention wearing white gloves. Somers' gulps.

Security cameras pivot into position monitoring the movements taking place throughout the magnificent complex and elsewhere. Displayed on a monitor is the landing and movement of the former Premier and his associate. Mics scattered throughout building record all of the sounds and interactions taking place. Persons manning the room watch as Somers and Christopher are greeted by the man standing inside the entrance speaking with a southern American accent, "Mr. Somers and associate, welcome. My name is Benson. I will be your escort. If you could please follow me, your host will meet up with you shortly."

Somers nods and begins following the man through the grand edifice with twenty foot ceilings. Escorted to a trophy room where a fire gently lights the space, the former Premier notices his aide remove his sunglasses walking through the room. Unable to see five feet in front of his face, Somers tilts his head down looking over his sunglass frames. Comforted by his inability to see his companion's facial features, he slips a finger behind his glasses and pulls them off, exposing his eyes. Navigating around items in the room, he continues to a set of high-backed leather chairs opposite others set up in the center. Joining his friend, Somers takes a seat as Benson asks, "Would you care for a beverage while you wait?"

"Double scotch on the rocks for me and a Vodka seven for my friend," Somers responded.

In the surveillance room, fluctuating gauges and bar graphs begin providing specific details on the screens. "His body temp and pulse keeps going up, it's like he's running a marathon. I think he's going to have a heart attack."

"Let's see how he reacts."

The murmur of Somers' low voice whispering to Christopher turns to a deafening silence hearing the clip-clop of footsteps enter the room. Straightening up in his chair the former Premier takes notice of a gorgeous female, wearing a tight-fitting white blouse and a short black skirt, headed in their direction. Her bleached blonde hair feathers in the wind created in the speed of her walk. The sound of her high heel shoes accent her movements. She finally lowers herself onto one of the chairs opposite the two men and crosses her legs. Following closely behind her is Benson now carrying three drinks. He hands them to each person present.

A soft British accent escapes from the female's perfectly shaped lips, "Gentlemen, nice of you to make the trip. Unfortunately I have been busy and couldn't spare the time to go see you this time. There is a lot happening and we need to be timely with our advances."

Running her fingers through her blonde hair she taps on her earpiece. The gesture is noted in the surveillance room, "All is a go."

Mimicking her pose, Somers crosses his legs in a manly fashion, "Miss Lindsay, we are a little surprised with the urgency in your request to meet. As I am sure you're aware the riot was a success, which forced the current government to clean out the lead investigator and install a more favourable one. We are about to begin the campaign with the selected new regional government leader. I have called in favours and have used the Planet X surplus to get what we need to make it happen. It will start as soon as I get the go ahead from your office. With Toronto starting to stabilize and utility services coming back on line, our campaign there should be a success as well."

"Jason is everything all right, you seem tense."

Beads of sweat form on his brow and begin to roll down his face. Somers stomps his elevated leg down, "I am quite all right."

Lindsay pokes again, "Is this plan upsetting you?"

Gripping onto the leather chair arms, he makes fists and pulls his body forward to the edge of his seat, "No, not at all! I've been involved long before you ever came on the scene! If it wasn't for me you wouldn't have had the success you have had in my country!"

She continues to receive information from the surveillance room, "Jasmine his vital signs peaked when you called him out, but settled the more he spoke. I don't think he is going to tell us."

Nodding Lindsay continues, "Jason, has there been anything that has happened that may compromise our situation?"

His blood boils, streams of sweat flow down the former Premier's ribs soaking through his shirt wetting the top area of his pants, "Why would you even ask such a thing? I have a vested interest in this proceeding, if there was something, I would have told you already."

Lindsay looks at her guest unconvinced. Another update streams through her ear piece, "Just stand by, you are getting some help now."

Biding time, Lindsay continues, "This is true. Unfortunately, we have heard of a little speed bump called Mr. Giabatti."

Just the mention of that name has Somers panicking. He loses his ability to remain angry and starts to relent, "Yes...yes...Well there is nothing to worry about. I have already had him neutralized and he won't be causing anyone any more problems."

"What about your visit with Miguel?" Lindsay brings the martini glass to her lips drinking the last of her beverage staring at Somers with a silhouette moving across the ceiling behind him.

The former Premier glances at her, then to Christopher and back to Lindsay. "Ah. Ah. Ah. I never."

A tap on Somers shoulders has him look down, seeing a rope disappear from sight wrapping around his neck. Instinctively he fights trying to loosen the noose. Christopher rushes to his friend's side. The former Premier's arms and feet flail about when a thrust to his mid section has the former Premier stop and look down seeing Christopher's hand pull back, holding a knife coated in blood. His eyes lose focus, blurring Lindsay and Christopher standing side by side, before they close. His body slumps over the arm of the chair.

Benson walks out from behind the chair, rope in hand.

Clapping her hands together once, Jasmine holds them up to her mouth, "Very good boys. Benson, could you please be a dear and clean up this mess? The master isn't going to be pleased with his bodily fluids all over the furniture."

"Yes, my lady."

Benson rolls Somers' body off the chair dropping him to the ground. Using the rope, he drags him out of the room leaving a trail of smeared blood across the polished floors.

Miss Lindsay smiles at Somers' friend, "Chris, well done. You have definitely proven yourself as a valued asset. You were right to inform me of what had happened. Your further assistance by completing the tasks required will definitely earn you a seat at the master's table."

She grabs her necklace lifting it up exposing a USB drive dangling as a pendant from the chain concealed between her breasts. Removing the drive she slips her hand into his, releasing the device,

"Chris, this contains all of the information that you need. Please return to Vancouver and make sure that everything runs smoothly. As far as anyone is concerned your former boss is still around calling the shots. You were his right hand man; they will listen to you like you were him."

In the darkened surveillance room, male figures turn their chairs away from the screens to face one another. The screens behind them show Miss Lindsay hanging onto Christopher's arm, escorting him from the room while speaking into his ear.

A relaxed hoarse voice begins, "We are close, but that email Miguel sent out is problematic. We cannot allow them to derail us now. No mistakes. Do you hear me? No mistakes."

Alphonso's Brazilian accented voice replies, "That situation doesn't pose us any significant risks. As it stands now they don't know who to trust. Before they can elicit any assistance I will see to it that they are eliminated. And as for Miguel, well, when he surfaces he will die one way or another."

CHAPTER NINE

Leaving the warmth and comfort of her first class seat, Carrie passes through coach, noticing its vacant status. As she walks down the concourse an airline employee smiles, "Welcome back to Toronto, Miss Warren."

"Thank you."

Waiting for her luggage, every noise she made stood out as did those of the few people scattered in the massive empty space. Each cough, sniffle or whisper was no longer white noise; it had a face. A shiver pulses through her body. Carrie looks down at her arm pulling back her sleeve, revealing the textured surface created by goose bumps. *What I would give for the congestion and confusion right now.* Avoiding eye contact, she overhears two refined older men comment on the situation.

"I have never seen air travel this low."

"It is definitely at its worst ever."

"These attacks have created an uncanny ripple effect."

"I don't know how long these companies are going to last at this rate."

Spotting her bag spit out on the carousel she walks over, lugging it off the track. Dropping it onto the floor, she extends a handle from the top and begins towing it behind her. Automatic doors open as Carrie walks through them leading to the public area, when she feels the rumble of her name in her chest and ears. Stopping mid-stride she looks around.

"Miss Carrie Warren. Oh, Miss Carrie Warren."

Quickly turning around, she spots a familiar smiling face advancing towards her. Carrie's face brightens, smiling from ear to ear, "Steve."

There was no comparison; she didn't know any other men matching him. Steve was without a doubt the most cheerful man she knew, and the only one matching his description. Standing well under five foot five inches in height, she couldn't remember ever seeing Steve without a full face beard or without his dark aviator glasses on his head covering his green eyes. Somehow it made him feel cool and taller but he'd never admit it. Although his stature was well below that of the average man, Steve's baritone voice moused every other man's voice she knew. He could have easily made a living in radio but his passion was flying. She loved being around him, perhaps it was his cheery disposition or his crazy unconventional sense of humour that often made her seek out a local bathroom so she wouldn't wet herself laughing.

"Miss Warren, I'm glad you stopped, I would hate for you to see me run. It's not a pretty sight."

As if on cue that familiar laugh he brings out of her bursts out of her gut, followed by an embarrassing snort, "Thanks for the warning Steve, I've had a crazy day. I don't know if I could handle that."

"Really though, the big man wants me to bring you to the station immediately. He must be wearing his girlfriend's thong today because he's pretty bitchy. I guess I would be too, all that ass hair getting caught in the elastic band being wedged against my butt."

Laughing and snorting Carrie fights to catch her breath, "That's just nasty."

"So my dear, do we have a date? We can fly off into the sunset wearing matching thongs. Don't worry I brought an extra pair of thongs for you, in case you're going Commando."

Shaking her head, covering up her nose with her hand as she snorts again, "Steve. Matching thongs?"

"They're mine. Slightly used, but don't worry I washed the shit stains off of them."

She bends over laughing forcing the few people in the airport to walk around her. Her infectious belly laugh echoes off the walls, forcing smiles to their scowled faces.

"So what do you say, Miss Warren? Can I have the honour of sweeping you off your feet again?" Lowering himself to one knee, he raises his hand up to her.

Putting one of her hands into his, she wipes away tears from her cheeks, "You had me at slightly used."

Kissing the back of her hand, he lets go, jumps up, and grabs her luggage. "All right, all right."

Steve starts walking away, pulling her bag and looking over his shoulder, "It's pretty exciting in the city today. I haven't felt a buzz like this ever!"

Landing on the roof of the WBC building, Carrie leans over, kissing Steve on the cheek. "Thanks Steve."

"Till we meet again my brave little Commando."

The door to the helicopter is opened by a man shouting into the cab, "Hurry up Carrie, you need to get downstairs right away, there's a military transport waiting for you."

Steve salutes Carrie as she removes her head gear and closes the door.

Carrie begins her coverage holding a box of French fries and a bottle of water in her hands, "Operation Take Back Toronto is in full effect as dozens of vendors are handing out free food and drinks to those in attendance. Despite the daily bombings around the world, people have gathered here for some long awaited good news, with the promise that there would be no attacks within the celebration's secured perimeter."

Shawn Gurl picks up on cue, "Take Back Toronto, or TBT as it is now called, has been promoted as a peaceful fight against terrorism. Companies have spared no expense releasing powerful commercials. Here is one of the more controversial pieces."

A hospital bed comes into focus and lying there is an elderly man, withered to skin and bones as his heart monitor goes flat line. A camera zooms into a single house, the lawn is over grown, and the camera continues to zoom through the wall into the house's basement. A family of four sit around a table as a young child crosses another day off a calendar, "Dad how long do we have to keep hiding in our..."

A bomb erupts, destroying the entire neighbourhood. A slow, steady baritone voice begins speaking, "Death finds us all."

People of every race playing sports take to the screen, replaced with others at social gatherings, talking and laughing, as the voice returns, "You only have one life. Enjoy it. Join the Take Back Toronto celebration." An athletic company's logo fills the screen.

Shawn pivots around, facing the camera and shaking his head, "What a message. The response has seen a constant flow of bus fleets transporting thousands of people from cities around the country to take part in this massive celebration. This event will go down as one of the largest celebrations ever witnessed."

Carrie comes into focus surrounded by a crowd of people smiling for the camera. "Shawn, there is an energy in the crowd that is simply electrifying! This is a positive sign showing the world that we can regain the advantage in a situation that has been spiralling out of control. With people around the globe watching from a distance, even those thousands of miles away can feel the sense of accomplishment, especially considering that this was the flashpoint of the new war on terror."

The illusion of a speedy recovery is being attributed to the generous donations of certain corporations funding the project rather than tax based government agencies.

Lieutenant Paula Connie stands off to the side in her military uniform, surveying all the happy faces of everyone present. She feels a sense of optimism, seeing the multitudes who have not given up hope. Tilting her head back she looks above a huge stage, as gusts of wind snap open corporate insignias printed on banners and flags hanging for all to see. She listens to the cheers of the crowd, and allows herself to take partial ownership of them.

After all, it was left up to her to get the city up and running and she employed any and all resources available. She orchestrated the combination of these corporations' abundance of energy and powered the meagre government resources she was allotted. She could not believe how willing these companies were to go out of pocket for this cause, but she figured with a city this big out of service, everyone was losing money. The faster it comes on line, the faster they can start profiting again.

Dry ice fogs the stage. Stage lights move in unison to an overture of music, gathering everyone's attention. The Mayor of Toronto appears through the smoke, standing in front of the crowd. An oversized grin appears on his face transmitted onto large screens positioned on either side of the stage. The crowd bursts into cheering seeing his feigned enthusiasm. However, if they had seen the Giabatti interview, they would question if it was brought on from a heavy dose of Planet X.

Sipping slowly on an expensive bottle of water, he clears his throat and begins his address to the people. "Our city has suffered a horrible blow. Dear citizens, you have been through so much, yet being here tonight is a clear demonstration of your resolve. With the engaged assistance of these corporations, we have been working to give Torontonians back their city. I would like to introduce a spokesperson that made it his mission to get this city back up and running. This man needs no introduction with his countless hours of charity work around the globe. He personally took on this project, pushing his company and others to step up to the plate. And step up they did. Working together they knocked this out of the park. Without further ado, I would like to bring to the stage, Reficuel Nomed."

The spokesperson runs up to the podium to thunderous applause. Reficuel reaches the mic and begins scanning the crowd. He unbuttons his wool trench coat flaunting his regular sized frame wearing a finely made pinstriped suit. Standing behind the podium, leaning forward he grasps each side of the lectern as if to pick it up. His slicked back black hair shines under the spotlights contrasting starkly with his clean shaven pale face. "Hello Toronto and the world! I cannot express how excited I am to be here."

Reficuel continues speaking over the cheers of the gathering. "Tonight will be remembered for years to come. First, I want the stage lights dimmed please."

The lights lower leaving everyone in darkness lit only by the stars in the sky and the pink crescent moon. His voice almost becomes giddy reciting his memorized speech as the band sets the tone with some prearranged background music, "In the beginning we suffered tragedy and saw that it was bad. Instead of giving up we worked and worked to try to make things right again and knew that it was good. In the end we decided that it was time that Toronto received...LIGHT!"

At that very moment street lamps begin to flicker, high rise buildings lining the streets came to life with illumination. With the fabricated dawning of a new day the multitudes of people gathered roar in applause, shaking the ground. Mammoth sized speakers amplify a band playing music as they are elevated on a lift over everyone in the throng.

Conducting the crowd like a rock star, Reficuel takes to the mic yelling, "How is that for good news? You're welcome. I just thought I would brighten your life a little bit. Another thing that will make you smile will be that for those living within the city and abroad, I am announcing a two-month hiatus on energy bills of any kind."

The assembly can't believe their ears and scream for joy.

Pointing up at the banners and flags waving in the wind, Reficuel continues, "This is a token of our thanks. Thank you for your patience and thank you for your resolve not to give in. You people are the best! Don't ever forget it!"

The crowd begins shouting his name. "Reficuel. Reficuel. Reficuel."

"Now, how is that for a holiday present?"

The people keep yelling praises. Many could not even hear what he was saying anymore but Reficuel kept talking, the news companies broadcasting the celebration caught every word. "This is your celebration, enjoy it. Public transit will be working all night and security measures will ensure the safety of all here. For those of you who are not down here yet, we will be here all night; don't miss the celebration of a lifetime. Come on down."

In the mob, Carrie smiles as she yells into the mic trying to be heard over the noise cupping her hand over one ear, "Shawn this is ten years worth of New Year's Eve celebrations all at once. Sir, what do you have to say about the energy here today?"

The man shouts into the mic as the masses rock him back and forth crowding around him. Faces poke into view of the camera smiling as they pass by, "It just keeps getting brighter and brighter. I never thought I would love streetlights so much."

Carrie brings the mic back to her face, "I was told earlier today that this would be the biggest loudest event ever, Steve you were right. I have never seen or felt this kind of energy in all of my life. This is truly a day to celebrate!"

A cheap brass plated chandelier with its five miniature bulbs removes the dullness from a long narrow living room. The off-white walls wrap around the perimeter untouched by art, colour or article. An old tube television flickers in the corner showcasing a news channel and assisting in illuminating the area. Nestled in the shadows around a small corner is a matching couch to the recliner situated in the middle of the room. The smell of burnt dust permeates from the electric baseboard heaters as condensation drips down the interior of the tinted black glass patio door collecting in a towel lying across the bottom on the linoleum floor.

Miguel sits at the table under the lights, eating chicken noodle soup and crackers. Gravity slowly draws the excess water from Miguel's clothes creating a puddle encircling the floor under his chair.

Entering the room from the attached kitchen Captain Nolin clunks his bowl of soup on the table and looks at his friend, "Are you sure you don't want to change first?"

"I'll change after I'm done eating. I'm starving."

"Like I was saying after I had your mom, and... and your... and your boys flown off the base, General Izzov terminated me from the team, saying that he should have me brought up on charges for treason for contacting you. I was being relocated when General Hamilton arrived and asked me to join him. Along the way he arranged for someone to pick up your boys and bring them to a better location."

"So you know where my boys are?" Miguel interrupted.

"No, but Hamilton does, he moved them to a secured facility, your mom is living with Lisa right now."

"Lisa? My ex-wife?"

"My boys aren't with my mom or my ex-wife?"

"Miguel, please. It's okay. You know you can trust Hamilton. You wouldn't be out of prison if it wasn't for him."

"I haven't spent any time with them since I was released. I need to see them."

"With the situation the way it is right now you'll be putting yourself in danger of getting caught."

"Lorne, I need to see them."

"Once we figure out what's going on, you'll have all the time in the world."

Walking up a set of stairs, Miss Lindsay's white fur coats drags across each stone covered riser. Five security guards surround her, forming the points of a star as she talks on the telephone, "Another eleven countries have formed public allegiances with Mr. Reficuel Nomed. I think we need to act quicker than anticipated...Yes of course. We should be able to persuade him to...I'm sure you'll find out shortly if this works or not."

Miss Lindsay reaches the platform, guards hold back a man waiting at the top dressed in a tuxedo and wearing white gloves. She removes her jacket showcasing an elegant purple gown highlighting her physique. "I am just meeting with him now. I will call you back soon."

Shutting off her phone she reaches into her jacket before handing it to her bodyguard and slips two envelopes out of the pocket. Jasmine approaches the man and hands him the documents, "This one is for you with instructions for the other one."

The man accepts the envelopes, nods and walks away. Miss Lindsay's guards open the door allowing opera music to flood out onto the platform. Grasping one of her guard's arms she closes her eyes, "Don't you just love that?"

Snapping his head around and reaching for his gun resting on the table top, Miguel prepares to arm himself after hearing a sound come from the basement. Slapping his hand and pinning it in place is Nolin's massive paw.

Turning back around, facing his friend, the Spaniard looks for an explanation.

"Relax, it's only Colin. When he comes up I'll introduce you to him. I'm sure you'll like him. He was a former Olympic sprinter."

Lorne releases Miguel's hand and continues eating his soup. Clanging his spoon against the metal bowl, Lorne scoops up another spoonful and raises it to his mouth slurping the hot liquid between words, "He served with Pegrum as a SEAL and gave it all up for computers."

Miguel's face wrinkled trying to understand the connection.

While speaking, Nolin gets up and walks out of the room, "Well sort of. Colin got into some hot water trying to teach his bosses a lesson."

He returns with a binder, sliding it across the table. Miguel flips opens up the book skimming through the plastic protected pages while his friend continues.

"After years of bitching over the inferior firewalls set up on military sites he unleashed a crippling computer virus halting operations for a day. Once the system reset itself, they charged him. As you can see he got off." Nolin points to an article marked 'Classified'.

Quietly reading aloud, Miguel's finger follows along through the article, "Chief Warrant Officer Colin Brunet was acquitted today on several charges that kept him imprisoned until now. During the trial, Brunet was able to prove his intentions were not malicious, but simply to open the eyes of supervisors. It was the American Constitution that freed Brunet from bondage. The quote being, '...But when a long train of abuses and usurpations, pursuing invariably the same object evinces a design to reduce them under absolute despotism, it is their right, it is their duty to throw off such government, and to provide new guards for their future security...'."

Impressed, the former Colonel nods approvingly while Nolin continues with the biography, "From there he walked away from the military and bounced around, hired by various computer companies on a contract basis until…"

For the first time since being released from prison the Spaniard finally feels at peace with his environment. Hearing every word, he sits there soaking wet, as his mind relaxes. With each spoonful of hot chicken noodle soup, Miguel's tense muscles loosen as the warm noodles slide down his throat heating his stomach. The simple meal felt like a feast.

"Now, currently police around the globe are searching for Colin."

Before Miguel had time to register the worry on his face Nolin adds, "No need to fret Migs. Colin has everything under control. Him and Pegs go way back, this is only one of several safe houses they own together off the grid. I couldn't think of a better place. Finish up, go upstairs and change and I'll introduce you. You'll recognize your room; I left something special for you on your night stand."

After changing his clothes Miguel follows his large friend down a set of creaky wooden stairs into the basement. The dehumidifier's exhaust fan vibrates and shakes, slaving to extract the moisture from the air. Behind a hot water tank and several boxes in the corner of the open space was a sectioned off office. The door was open, allowing the dim light inside to illuminate the exterior of the room. The ceiling in the basement was low forcing Nolin to hunch over as he walked to his destination.

Pulses of energy fly through the Spaniard's grey matter trying to understand his present situation. Running his fingers along the wall he recognizes that the typical cement was covered with thick metal plates. Thoughts begin crossing his mind that have him second guessing everything. He starts mentally kicking himself for leaving his gun upstairs in his room. Rubbing his hands on his pants, he tries to remove any signs of his anxiety. Straining his ears he hears the faint tapping of a keyboard inside the room. He watches Nolin lower himself even further entering the office space.

Stopping short of the door, he peeks in through the opening allowing him an opportunity to run if need be. He sees Nolin waving him into the room. Behind the Captain he sees a desk and a dull shine from a screen situated in the area. Inching closer he scans the room from top to bottom still unable to see another person anywhere in the room. Miguel's gut starts wrenching, keeping him on guard.

"Colin, I would like to introduce you to my other paranoid friend."

Strolling out from behind the desk, and away from Nolin's shadow, a dark man approaches the doorway. Although short in stature he appeared like a solid block of man-made steel, definitely no stranger to the gym.

Advancing into the room Miguel extends his hand, feeling horrible that he didn't trust his friend.

"Great to finally meet you, Miguel. I feel like I already know you. Lorne wouldn't shut up, giving me your complete day by day biography." Colin spoke with a soft Jamaican accent.

Giving his neck and back a rest Nolin drops his oversized framed body into a soft chair beside the desk, "What's wrong with that? I like being thorough."

"I can't tell you how much I appreciate your help right now Colin."

"Come in, come in, sit down. I was just tooling up a couple programs that I've been working on. If you want a drink grab something out of the fridge." He points to a corner in the room where an old fridge stands untouched by time.

Returning to his chair in front of the computer Colin adds, "Just let me save my work before I forget."

Sitting up straight with his hand extended Lorne requests, "Hey Migs, before you sit down can you get me a drink out of the fridge? Colin, I was just telling him about your computer business."

"Which part?"

"I didn't get to the good stuff yet."

Grabbing a beer out of the fridge, Miguel passes it to Lorne, "The last thing I heard was that you're wanted but he didn't say why?"

Looking up from his computer as Miguel finally sits, Colin responds, "Power, Miguel, power."

Accessing the internet, Colin explains as he types, "After leaving the military my computer business introduced me to some interesting people. The Freedom Movement really showed me a side that I never thought of. Things that everyone takes for granted and don't question."

"Like?"

Powered with adrenaline the Jamaican spoke faster, "For example, everything in the industrialized world is now being made for less – food, cars, homes, electronics – everything except energy. Yet, energy costs keep going up. How is that possible?"

The former Olympian spins his monitor around showing the New York Stock Exchange, "Look on the stock market, the energy companies' stocks are through the roof because everyone needs energy and they hold all of the cards. With so much being automated there are fewer employees, meaning less wages need to be paid. So, why does the cost keep increasing? That's when I decided to do something about it."

Stretching his neck looking at the screen Colin types, pulling up news article after article, "I perfected my version of Magnetic energy and started selling it when the government shut me down with regulation bullshit and a backlog of red tape. I spent hundreds of thousands of dollars to push it through the court system and in the end I lost the fight. They don't want this to ever come into existence. Once I realized that, I cut my losses and hit YouTube, broadcasting to everyone how easy it can be to cheaply cut your electricity bill to almost nothing. If I couldn't make money, neither were they."

"I had heard that people were experimenting with that."

Spinning the computer back around, a series of quick taps brought more information to light, "Now look at the spike in their stocks when they introduced that new law making it illegal to generate and store energy in non-registered formats. The government and the energy companies are hand in hand sharing the wealth while we pay."

Pressing a button, Colin shutdown his computer, "When I first started looking into energy generation I explored old technology that was never mainstreamed. Icons such as Thomas Edison, Nikola Tesla and others who did more in the 1800s than they have done since that time. Now out of fear of losing their empire these multi-billionaires pay off government officials to shut down anyone who is a threat."

A huge grin stretches across Nolin's face listening to Colin.

Sceptical, Miguel questions, "You're talking about sustainable free energy? You perfected sustainable free energy and you're still alive to talk about it? Either you're the craziest person I know or my new best friend."

Blinking a couple of times Colin stares at Nolin. Lorne lowers his head, afraid of the response knowing how defensive this SEAL can get if he perceives that someone is questioning his validity, "Colin just show him."

Vibrating with energy Colin gets up and waves Miguel to follow, "Come on."

The Spaniard slowly gets to his feet, looking at his friend, "Where are we going?"

"Just follow me," Colin orders. "I guess you have no reference for the history of electronics?"

"Extremely limited."

Exiting his little office, Colin crosses the basement floor to a fuse panel, "So I guess you didn't know they had a magnetic motored car in 1899 that was capable of doing over 65mph or that, in the 1960s there was a race between companies to see who could develop the strongest magnetic energy, all of which was never followed through."

Trailing behind, Lorne interrupts, unable to remain silent, "Imagine where we would be today if we continued working on that technology. No pollution, no smog, and most of all no energy companies metering us to power our homes and cars."

Picking up where he left off Colin continues, "Considering the technological advances within the last fifty years, I knew that I could easily improve on what they did."

Opening the fuse panel door revealed a technological marvel. Colin places his palm on a small screen. Lowering his face down, he looks into an optical eye, while simultaneously entering a password with his free hand. The suction sound of an air pressurized metal door opens. "Here is my baby. It's not much to look at, but underneath that shell is literally a world of power."

What appeared like a wall was actually a door. It pivoted outwards allowing a loud low hum to resonate through the air. Miguel walks in inspecting the eight foot by four foot, by five foot device. Industrial sized cables lead upwards through the house floor and side to side through the metal reinforced cement walls. "Okay, you have my attention. So with this new law you're definitely a wanted man."

"Extremely, and I still make them, but only for a select clientele."

Nolin interjects, "Brilliant. I told you..."

Following a train of thought Miguel speaks over Nolin, "Hold on a sec. You must be who Pegrum was talking about, his friend that goes to these Freedom Movement meetings? What made you stop going in the first place?"

"Bumbaclots! Crippled by fear; they lost sight of the cause. Their ideology is somewhat sound but they have no idea of how to take the movement from the underground to the general public. I wasn't going to waste my time waiting for police to arrest us all, so I stopped going."

Sliding his back against the metal wall, Miguel sits on his heels, "The writing was on the wall years back. With each violent protest, governments gained the political backing to outlaw any such events. Wasn't there a bunch of groups before, like the Sovereigns, Freeman, Travellers, and Gypsies?"

Leaning against his generator Colin crosses his arms, "There were, but after the eviction of the Dale Farm residents in England, governments across Europe and the world began establishing new laws specifically targeting anyone not adhering by society's formal laws. Failure to pledge allegiance to the country's laws resulted in indefinite prison sentences until they conceded or were able to locate a country that would accept them as a refugee. Once that happened those groups ceased to exist."

Looking to both men, Miguel seeks clarification, "Dale Farm?"

Getting a nod from Colin, Lorne answers, "Dale Farm was a huge standoff that resulted in numerous Travellers being injured and killed. Those laws pushed all anti-government movements underground. The Freedom Movement emerged slowly joining groups, races and sexes to one cause. Remaining underground they eventually gained momentum. The recent attacks and the invocation of the world-wide War Measures Act have added fuel to the flames, allowing them to recruit thousands of new people."

Rubbing his forehead Miguel attempts to put everything into perspective. Facing the inventor, he questions, "Colin, how hard would it be for you to start going to meetings again?"

The jagged skyline in Canada's capital city began to shadow the last remaining rays of the sky's brilliant golden light as it fades away, leaving only darkness. Street lamps scantily illuminate the carpet of pavement below leaving many areas in the umbra. Transports creep into the city through check points, their powerful engines chug along echoing off concrete establishments as they cart fresh supplies to restock shelves.

An Asian female military officer riding shotgun starts to tremble, raising her machine gun at the ready, breathing heavily in through her nose and out her mouth she waits for the endorphins to kick in to calm her mind. While pivoting from side to side, she peers through the mounted night-vision scope, as the monotone voice of her superior occupies her thoughts repeating the same nightly message,

> "…we are experiencing daily explosions in cities around the globe. Everyone must be on high alert no matter how many successful deliveries you've made. Each of our fallen officers could not foresee what was about to happen and if they were, are now unable to pass along any words of wisdom."

She had definitely heard better pep talks and every night he would repeat those words and more, "… driving the highways should pose no difficulties. With all of the sensors and video equipment on the trucks if you don't pick up a threat your guardian angel here in the CCC will. As shotgun operators you must stay vigilant and watch for anything. The slow speeds and stagnant turns make each of you easy targets. The mandatory curfew is still in effect, so if you feel for a moment that someone is a threat to you and your transport, you are authorized to dispatch them with extreme prejudice."

She recalls how many applauded when General Izzov announced his decision to rid the twenty-four hour mandatory recording equipment. She agreed, under these tense times why add to the stress by being micromanaged like that. She knew a friend who accidentally shot some citizens and all non-official video footage mysteriously disappeared. Right or wrong she was happy that her friend didn't go to jail. That didn't ease her mind at all though. She knows like each shotgun operator knows that they're playing Russian roulette, it just a matter of time before the gun goes bang.

The CCC officer in charge receives an urgent message and announces over the sound of all those at their workstations, "Attention people we have activity in the nation's capital. We have more cryptic chatter being intercepted upon our trucks entering the capital city."

The loudspeaker blares allowing everyone to hear. Activity stops as heads tilt, stop and listen to the static noise of garbled voices speaking back and forth, "Jah bin…lice sary…pean mals…exp ficial rac ary cess…."

The Officer in charge yells over the noise, "What's the frequency?"

A technician lowers his ear piece and turns looking at the Officer, "Sir, it's still those old CB radios."

The Officer growls. Spinning around, he yells to the back of the room, "What's going on? What are they saying? Come on. It's our people out there."

"Sorry sir, I can't make out what they're saying. They change their words every time out."

Slowly pivoting looking at the map, he walks over and points to the transports highlighted on the map, "So, if our trucks are entering here, where are they, why can't we triangulate their locations?"

Another monitor speaks up, "We're trying sir, but their exchanges are so short it's impossible to get a fix on them."

The officer in charge wrings his hands, looking at the satellite image on the big screen, "Do we have anything new to report to Colonel Renniks?"

"Until we capture one of these members I'm afraid that we are at a loss figuring out what they are up to."

Slapping the metal pole the officer in charge yells back, "And how is that supposed to happen when we can't figure what they are saying or where they are hiding?"

"I don't know, sir."

Exhaling loudly, he rolls his eyes. The exhausted officer in charge replies, "Exactly. Just get me Colonel Renniks on the line. I'll be in my office."

The officer walks into his office and slams the door, "I'm sure he's going to be thrilled."

As the call connects, the CCC officer in charge grimaces as the phone is answered. He begins telling Renniks of the ongoing situation and Renniks charges at him over the phone. The little ear piece speaker crackles under the force of the volume breaking through the line.

"I don't give a fuck what you do! Send in a fleet of men and find them. They are short distance radios whoever is using them has to be around there somewhere! Kick in every door if you have to."

The officer in charge sits at his desk and zooms in on a map of the city, looking at the neighbourhoods, "Colonel Renniks, yes, we know that, but there are endless possibilities where they could be hiding."

"So what? Concentrate the men where I tell you, not to their districts. I am sick of hearing this bullshit. Find them or find a new job."

Dressed in his uniform Colonel Edward Renniks places his cellular phone on the white tablecloth in front of him. The table is set; the restaurant is elegant and a beautiful woman sits across the table from him. People at surrounding tables try not to make eye contact, having been forced to overhear the Colonel's side of the conversation. Even the physique of the blonde goddess wearing a purple, sleeveless dress is lost to them. They are embarrassed for whoever the Colonel was abusing on the phone. Renniks, however, is oblivious, and begins to speak to his dinner companion, "Sorry about that Jasmine. I'm sure you know how frustrating it is to work with incompetent people."

Miss Lindsay responds in her soft spoken British accent rolling her eyes, "Unfortunately, I've had a couple of occasions. I do hope they are able to handle this."

Looking over at Jasmine's hypnotic blue eyes and sexy smile he responds straightening up his back, "They should be able to or they shouldn't be in this field."

General Izzov sizzles the end of a cigarette as he inhales, feeling the carbon waste drift through his lungs. Lowering the cigarette from his mouth he exhales loudly, blowing the smoke into the air. The cloud distorts the view of the room around him. Wearing his uniform, seated in a turn of the century deep leather arm chair, he butts out his cigarette in an ash tray balanced on the chair arm. Looking intently at the ash tray, he starts to play with it, "Gravity is an interesting enemy. It gives you this false sense of safety. We won't drift off into space because gravity protects us. We can drive our cars without hitting a flying aircraft."

He pauses, and looks up with eyes reddened by broken veins. He gently shoves the ash tray over the edge of the arm, "Then one day you find it's betrayed you as you hang over the edge of a cliff. Have you ever hung off an edge of a cliff?"

Standing up quickly the strain of his voice echoes around the room, "Why are you dangling this country over the edge? Hamilton is an idealist and doesn't share our respect for the order of things. He is constantly trying to reinvent the wheel. As your lead advisor for the military you should have checked with me before making that decision."

The General lowers himself back down into his chair, gazing through the smoke-filled room at the Prime Minister and his aide Clint.

Getting his back up the Prime Minister leans forward in his chair, aggressively addressing the General, "Who are you kidding Izzov, you're a politician with limited to no active duty time. This is a real problem and one we need resolved quickly with limited chatter. Hamilton helped implement the Blackstar protocol years back and he has a solid reputation for going in, getting the problem fixed and moving on. Besides, when he is not working in some other country he always returns here, which tells me where his devotion lies."

Unshaken, Izzov moves the ash tray to the coffee table and rests his torso and head into the cushioned chair's high back, "Sure, he loves the country, but he lives by his own rules of engagement, like letting the little spic out of the box. He is more loyal to him than to you or I. This is bigger than any quick fix he has ever done, this is global."

Still on the edge of his seat the Prime Minister comes back, "Well, I listened to you and had him assigned to the Joint Forces Intelligence Team, so you could take over. The riot in Vancouver was something I wish didn't happen. Now I committed myself to a lie that could easily surface."

Clint looks over at the General and slightly shakes his head no.

The aged General responds, "Prime Minister, using authorities granted under the War Measures Act I am in the process of dealing with the loose ends. Under Martial Law treason is dealt with a lot harsher. Don't worry, one clear example of that will straighten everyone else out."

Sliding his body back onto the chair the Prime Minister waves his hand in the air, "General, don't say anymore, just do what you have to. The biggest questions I have to answer are, where is Miguel now, and why hasn't he been caught yet?"

"With all due respect he is someone who has specialized in the infiltration of other countries. Until now he wasn't an easy person to track. Thanks to Hamilton, we have a system in place that will alert us wherever that little piece of shit is holed up. I guess bringing the General back wasn't a total loss, with his technology we will finally be rid of that disease Mejia."

"General, personally I never want to hear his name again."

"I couldn't agree more. There is another matter that needs your attention."

"Yes?"

"The Joint Forces Intelligence Unit has determined that the Freedom Movement has been gaining momentum and they are responsible for the attacks in Washington and in our own Vancouver riot."

The Prime Minister's eyes bulge out, "Really? Of all of the terrorist groups out there, it is our own people attacking us!"

"That is what Intelligence is confirming as we speak."

"So what's the next move?"

"Identifying them has proven to be more difficult than anticipated. Right now every country is working from the same information.

Many have begun widespread arrests and are interrogating suspected members. I suggest we do the same."

The aide interjects, speaking directly to the Prime Minister, "This demographic does not affect us. Their numbers are low, and besides, they were never our supporters. If the General starts bringing in these people no one should be any the wiser and we will deny any such actions have taken place. These people gained no sympathy from the law-abiding citizens when we began taking land and property away from them."

"All right, General, if I'm denying that these arrests are taking place, our members must be dressed accordingly. No one gets anything that they can use on us."

Lighting another cigarette and exhaling a large puff of smoke, he stands up and pivots preparing to leave, speaking over his shoulder, "Absolutely."

Shawn Gurl's voice announces, "Now out to Carrie Warren on the streets of Montreal."

"Thank you, Shawn. A startling revelation has occurred since these explosions began so many days ago. 911 call centers are now so overwhelmed by crime calls, they won't dispatch police to anything less than that involving immediate death. All other incidents such as assaults, breaking and entering, and vandalism are put on the back burner, likely never to be investigated."

Lifting up a piece of paper and reading from it, Carrie continues, "We were provided the following information from a serving police officer who wishes to remain anonymous: 'we are constantly responding to life and death situations hourly. It has now become common to be involved in at least one gun fight a shift. If the evidence isn't there when we get there it is pretty much a dead issue. The back log of events are weeks old'."

Putting the paper away Carrie continues, "Stepping up to fill the void of community safety has been newly formed Neighbourhood Watch programs. Members in the community have grown tired of the lack of police support and constant crime filling their streets. Taking action, citizens grouped together forming new Neighbourhood Watch Programs that roam the streets despite the mandatory curfew."

Turning and looking beside her, Carrie says, "Speaking with us today is Tuccio Cosina."

Standing alongside Carrie is a large framed middle-aged man wearing a bright orange fluorescent ball cap with the letters NWP on the front of it. "Tuccio, what was the driving force behind you assisting with the development of this program, which has been seen out past curfew and your members risking imprisonment?"

"Carrie, first off, I would like to thank you for having me on your program today. You have done such a wonderful job covering the news since this began. We all support the hard work you have been doing."

"Thank you, Mr. Cosina."

"Basically, Carrie it's simple. I couldn't stand by any longer and tolerate the madness infesting the streets. I run a meat shop downtown and I've been robbed eight times, besides that I know other people who have been robbed too. It's just gone crazy everywhere. I figured if I was going to die, I might as well die fighting. It was time we stood up and put a stop to it, if not for us, for the kids trying to grow up."

"How did you introduce the program?"

Pointing to people around him they cheer as the butcher continues, "A bunch of us small business owners began talking to our political leaders and out of those conversations we decided that if the police can't do anything for us than we must."

"Since beginning the NWP have you noticed a decrease in the infestation you claim was taking over your streets?"

"Carrie it has been overwhelming how much we have been doing. We don't have statistics but I can say that the robberies have gone down dramatically."

"Have you caught anyone committing any crimes and if so, what did you do with them if you haven't been calling the police?"

Pulling out a piece of paper from his pocket, he slips on a pair of reading glasses and responds loosely reading from the sheet, "We're not vigilantes nor are we a lynch mob. We are basically the police for our neighbourhood, without the pay. If you think about it, the police are a government agency built to care for the people. The government is elected and receives power and authority from the support of the people. In our case our neighbourhood supports us, one hundred percent. So we have created our own government agency called the Neighbourhood Watch Program. We take care of our problems our way, which is also supported by the community and that is all I will say about that."

A quick pan of the camera shows ordinary people behind Mr. Cosina as he puts his piece of paper away. The others around him also wearing the NWP fluorescent clothing, cheer. Carrie continues,

"Okay...your neighbourhood has been credited for the beginning of the program however it appears to have spread throughout several countries. Are you at all surprised that you have had that kind of effect?"

"Not at all Carrie. People have to feel safe and those of us that are able must protect not only ourselves but those around us. I am sure everyone feels that way or it wouldn't have spread so far so fast."

"So what's the sense in the community now?"

"These Neighbourhood Watch Programs are actually creating community bonds that haven't been seen for decades. There is a common goal and everyone is getting to know their neighbour and really supporting one another. It's all about relationships and for too long we have been primarily occupied with our own problems and not dealing with problems together."

"Interesting...there appears to be a lot of planning and work despite no one getting paid. How do the police treat you guys?"

"Carrie the payment for us is being able to feel safe to walk around the neighbourhood again. As for the police, well they are so busy dealing with the bigger things that occur, that they don't have time to stop and engage us much. Besides most police officers living in our neighbourhood are members themselves when they are not at work. They completely support the program, I guess that is why we are not chastised or hassled for being out past curfew, I'm sure it's like that in other neighbourhoods too."

Another evening's curfew in Vancouver comes in like a subway train, emptying the streets of life, with the exception of the Neighbourhood Watch patrollers. The transports carrying supplies begin to enter the city. In order to avoid an ambush they resort to their own selected routes to reach their destination.

Driving through the streets, a young man riding shotgun wipes tears away from his cheeks using his shoulder. Looking over at the driver, the soldier gains solace, breathing out heavily, knowing he has concealed his emotions. Gripping his machine gun's handles he peers out through his night-vision scope. The hue of various shades of green and black distort in his mind reliving the disturbing briefing given minutes ago by his Sergeant.

> "Ladies and gentlemen, if we could all stand for a moment of silence. Tonight in the nation's capital we had another loss."

The image of a young Asian female with her hair pulled back in a bun dressed in the military fatigues appeared on the screen. At the same time his zest for life evaporated, his thoughts ran rampant, *How can that be? I just spoke to her three hours ago.*

His Sergeant's hollow voice continued, "Private Kim Li was an excellent officer who had spent time with numerous regiments, including a short duration with ours prior to the attacks. Intelligence identified that this threat came in the form of a Neighbourhood Watch patroller dressed in the normal fluorescent vest."

Blinking a couple of times, the young man shook off his thoughts, trying to remain focused, but his mind slips again to an evening stroll through the park with Kim. Hand in hand they walked along a lit path to a small bridge over a stream, with the moon shining in the sky, dropping to one knee, "Kim will you..."

She shouts, "Yes! Yes!" Tackling him to the ground.

A smile crosses his face briefly as he comes back to reality looking through the scope as tears wet the inside of the optical lens. He knows that all their future plans were dashed. *After this situation stabilized she was going to quit the military and finish her schooling to be a teacher. We were going to have a normal life.*

The driver catches the young military man crying, "Hey buddy, are you all right?"

Taking out a rag, the young man cleans his night-vision lens and then wipes his nose. "Yeah everything is just peachy. I'm just here on another suicide mission waiting for some asshole to blow us up. What does it matter anymore?"

"Come on buddy, twenty years driving truck and I haven't had so much as a flat tire. You're safe with me."

"That makes me feel so much better."

The truck rumbles through the city streets going in and out of each passing street lamp's light. Looking out the windows, the shotgun operator catches an apparition standing in the shadows. Snapped back into reality he brings his eye down to his night-vision scope, scanning the area. His eyes capture the reflection of a single fluorescent vest walking around the corner of a building. "Hey, where is his partner? This is it! Turn, Turn Turn!"

Immediately he pokes his gun out the side of the truck and begins shooting just as another person wearing a fluorescent vest comes into sight. Both fall, ravaged by metal jacket projectiles ripping through their flesh and shattering their bones.

The concussion of bullets spraying out the side rings in the transport operator's ears as he cranks the wheel. The truck shifts to the left making the sharp right turn. Protesting rubber tires screech, creating ungodly sounds. Increasing speed, in the midst of making the turn causes the truck to slam into the side of a building crushing bricks, barely keeping the truck upright and on course. Shattered masonry and loose mortar crumble onto the truck and ground. Wire belts in some tires snap, launching rubber fragments across the road adding to the debris field. The truck and trailer bounce back and forth taking out parking meters and small trees along the sidewalk.

The shotgun operator gazes through his scope at the two people left lying on the ground.

Overcome with grief he screams, "What have I done? What have I done? FUCK!!!!"

The truck driver yells, "What do I do? What do I do? What's going on?"

Taking his side arm out he places the gun under his chin and pulls the trigger. Blood sprays throughout the cab of the truck coating the interior of the windshield. The truck driver, stunned by the tragedy exclaims, "What the?"

Screaming into the mic, "This is truck one oh three we're under attack! My shotgun operator is dead! What do I do?"

"Truck one oh three this is the CCC, continue to your destination, we're sending in air support. We will reassess the situation once you are safely away."

Running from nearby streets are two more fluorescent vests. Reaching the scene they see the annihilated store fronts and watch the transport truck speed away. Following the debris they spot the members on the ground. Sprinting to their location, they slide on the ground. "Page! Jimmy!"

"Holy shit! She's dead, John!"

"I see that Kevin! Oh, please don't die, come on Jimmy speak to me." Ripping off his shirt, John presses down into one of many holes leaking blood over all over the sidewalk.

"Dispatch this is Kevin, we need help immediately Jimmy and Page have been shot."

Jimmy raises his arms holding onto Kevin's arms, his only response is a sucking chest wound before his arms fall cold.

The radio crackles again, "What's your location?"

John sits back on his heels, looking at his blood soaked hands and seeing the two lifeless bodies in front of him.

"I repeat, what's your location?"

John shakes his head and starts yelling, "Ahhhhhhh!"

"They're gone dispatch. They're gone." Kevin takes off his jacket and lays it over Page's faceless head.

Doors in the neighbourhood slowly start to open. People start to exit and gather on the street. A chain reaction of calls commences. The entire neighbourhood exits their homes seeing what occurred. As more people approach, crying is loud and emotions run high.

The monitoring section of the CCC intercepting all communication is alarmed at all the calls coming from the Vancouver neighbourhood.

A private runs over to the Officer in charge, "Sir, there's a situation arising out of the shooting in Vancouver."

"What's that?"

"We have been intercepting a lot of chatter regarding the incident. We may have a revolt on our hands."

The officer in charge yells for the room to hear, "Bring up satellite imagery of the shooting scene in Vancouver."

Staring at the screen the officer in charge is speechless and the private speaks up. "As you can see sir, there is a considerable amount of people there and the chatter we have been listening too suggests they are going to launch an attack."

Renniks' back is bare outside of the blankets, he rolls over exposing the naked Jasmine Lindsay who lies under him as he reaches for his ringing cell phone on the end table. Looking at the number on the screen, he presses a button and speaks into the device, "This had better be good."

Jasmine places her head near Renniks' ear, listening to the conversation, "Sorry to bother you sir, but we have a neighbourhood on the brink of a revolt from an over zealous shotgun operator who ended his own life after shooting two innocent Neighbourhood Watch civilians."

"Listen to me very carefully, these civilians shot at our officer first and before he succumbed to his injuries he killed the two terrorists. He's a hero. Now go in there and round up anyone breaching the mandatory curfew."

"Sir, you don't understand. That's not how it happened."

"What is wrong with you? I don't care what happened. They're all breaching martial law. If these patrollers weren't out in the first place this wouldn't have happened. The law is pretty black and white. Either you are breaking it or you are abiding by it. Handle this, and don't fucking interrupt me again."

CHAPTER TEN

Flickering incandescent bulbs strobe the crowded musty Seattle basement, as thunder cracks and rain pelts the exterior walls in waves. Colin clasps both hands around a steaming ceramic mug filled with coffee that radiates heat up his arms. With his body hunched over the escaping vapours, every joule of energy warms his shivering core sitting on the metal folding chair. Water drips from his wet clothes splashing into a large puddle covering the concrete floor under his feet. Adding to the sounds that ricochet off the bare cement walls are Colin's chattering teeth.

The former SEAL feels as though he's back in the corps, submersed in ice cold water, learning how to work through the pain. He can still hear his sergeant's yell vibrating in his ears, "Suck it up Brunet, a true soldier never shows fear or pain." Colin smirks, rubbing his coffee cup, "Damn cold."

Competing with the hum of a dehumidifier is a man speaking to the crowd. A diverse group of thirty men and women gathered here tonight despite another evening's torrential downpour. Sandwiched between two people Colin leans forward allowing for shoulder room. Feeling, slowly returns, allowing his nose to detect a multitude of odours lingering in the air. An elderly woman sitting in front of him shifts her body, vibrating the tin chair adding methane to the chemical compounds sticking to his nostrils.

Colin tilts his body back, smiling and shaking his head from side to side. The two people beside him pay no attention. Their gaze remains fixated on the speaker whose veins alongside his temples and neck protrude as he shrills at the audience. Witnessing the speaker's thin bony structure almost disappear as he walks behind a supporting pole, Colin pays close attention to his details. Flesh draping from his cheek bones indent around his mouth, and his eyes bulge from their sockets, scanning the room. Prancing around engaging the crowd, the tie around his neck shifts and flaps with his movements, and his dress pants wrap loosely around broom handle-sized legs.

"We all have a story that brings us here tonight. After twenty-five years as a government accountant sworn to secrecy, I have more than one. Make no mistake, I want you to analyse, and question every piece of information you hear tonight. I guarantee that after you have certified its validity we will be of one accord."

Spotting a government agency sticker on the side of the projector transmitting blatant security breaches and overt anti-government propaganda, Colin began developing respect for this man, "Ballsy. Very ballsy."

Looking around the room, the former Olympian notices that all of the basement windows are barely large enough for a child to squeeze through. In the event this soiree gets raided Colin knows they're all screwed. Surveying the crowd, *It only takes one mole to send a text and it's over.*

Watching eyes follow the speaker's every move followed by the jotting down of quotes and information, it was impossible to tell who, if any, would be working with the government. Everyone appears on the same page, heads nods together while one lady seated at the front stands up clapping, "Amen, brother. The truth will set you free."

The speaker wasn't swayed or distracted by these outbursts, it energized him. He marches around the audience shouting louder.

> Colin's eyes blink and reopen to see his mother finish singing, "Amen sister Brunet. Praise his name! Praise..His..Name!" A preacher dressed in a cheap polyester suit yelled as he walks to the pulpit wiping his brow with a white towel. Sweat continues to roll down from his jerry curled black hair as he hugs her. His mother steps down from the stage under a large canvas canopy, sweltering in the humidity from the sun torching the ground outside another home-based Sunday church service. Grabbing her index finger with his tiny hand, Colin followed her out to the shade of a tree where she taught Sunday school to all of the

little boys and girls. She began each lesson with the
Ten Commandments.

A homemade sling shot broken in two on the floor
was directly in front of Colin as the sweaty preacher
with no shirt yells, "Just because your mama's gone
doesn't mean you can do whatever you want. Now
get over here. What did she teach you?"

Colin walks over slowly lowering his trousers,
mumbling, "Thou Shall Not Kill."

"I can't hear you." The preacher pulls off his belt
and extends his arm way back. "Say it with me ten
times. Thou Shall Not Kill!" The strap slaps against
his back-side jolting his body as the man kept
screaming in his ear.

The words morphed into Colin's Commander's
stutter, "Brunet kill-kill-kill those sons of bitches.
That truck is a hostile target. P – p – pull that
trigger, son." Peering through the scope he saw
the human shields covering the truck made up
of women and children. From this distance Colin
replaced their faces with that of the preacher
belting him, depressing the trigger erased his sweaty
face from sight.

The former SEAL's hands start to shake, as someone next to him
touches his shoulder asking, "Are you still cold? Do you need
more coffee?"

Colin glances over, snapped back to the basement meeting, "I'm
okay thank you."

The speaker carries on, "...Over the years the allure of riches was
exchanged for the keys to the country. Slowly but steadily corporations made a peaceful invasion of our culture infecting every facet.
The momentum of this movement led to a more subtle sophisticated
kind of propaganda developed by their marketing directors in the
form of advertising."

Fanning her face with her hat, the lady at the front exclaims, "Selling our souls to the devil."

Bright colourful hues enrich the white screen, captivating the audience's attention. "Through these commercial ads, they established a new standard of living seducing a large portion of society. The industrial age eliminated thousands of jobs in the rural areas. Now the majority lives within the cities, unable to cultivate enough food to sustain their own lives, relying on 'the system' to provide nourishment."

Pressing a button shuts off the projector as the speaker asks, "Who here has ever hunted or fished? Raise your hands."

Scanning the room he sees half of the room with their arms extended upwards. "You." Pointing to a man in the middle of the room. "Sir, what's your name?"

"Uhumm, it's Gavin." The man points to the name tag stuck to his chest.

Walking around the room, looking at everybody, the speaker continues, "Gavin did you know that you can't even go fishing with your children unless you have a licence?"

"Yeah, it's been that way for some time."

"Really?" He stops and turns back.

"As long as I can remember."

"So with this licence do they teach you how to do it properly or make sure you know what you're doing?"

"No."

"What does this licence do for you?"

"Allows me to go fishing."

"So with your licence you can catch as many fish as you want?"

"No, there are limitations."

"Does that make any sense to you? How can they regulate our ability to feed ourselves, yet allow fishing vessels to net entire bodies of water for profit?"

The audience members shake their heads.

"Who here has children?"

The majority of people lift their hands.

Walking over to a female sitting beside Colin, "Madam, are your children in school?"

"Yes, they are."

"Have they ever had problems in school with a bully or even a teacher?"

"I have two boys and one girl, of course they have."

Laughing the speaker asks, "Well put. Okay, did the children defend themselves in those situations?"

"Initially, yes."

"What were they told?"

"Tell a teacher."

"Did that resolve the matter?"

"No, it continued, I've had several meetings with the teachers and the principal."

"So what was the next course of action?"

"My one son kept getting in trouble and would spend time at the office, the other put up with the nonsense and didn't retaliate. Both are frustrated and angry."

"Frustrated and angry, how true that is to us all. Your one son because he defends himself he is punished. That is the way things are going. Telling us to give in. To give up. Don't do a thing out of fear of trouble, call the authorities to deal with problems because we are all too incapable or stupid to deal with our own issues."

The speaker walks back to the front and grabs a man sitting there, "Sir! When was the last time you were allowed to be a man? When was the last time you changed your diaper? Wait you don't need to do that anymore the government is in that business now, keeping you helpless and dependent on big daddy."

Turning the projector back on, news articles replace the commercials, keeping the speaker on pace explaining the relevance, "Our fundamental right to bear arms has been under attack, we have been bombarded with news that society is out of control, so unsafe that in order to protect you or I, the government needs to take everything away, from everybody."

Walking over to the table grabbing a glass of water, the speaker takes a drink. He slams down his empty glass and shouts, "This is more than a right, it is a duty each American citizen is charged or empowered to enforce! The Founding Fathers had given us that right recognizing that government or rulers can spiral out of control. With every right and weapon removed the corporations and government are enslaving the population to their rule. With each protest that turned violent, rolled out more news and laws oppressing us, citing the related dangers to the public, taking away even more rights."

Slouched shoulders, vacant smiles, and side mouth chatter signified the conclusion of the meeting. The congregation mingled about wearing the 'My name is...' sticker on their chest where they scribbled their first name and their profession. Lost in their own inadequacy to do anything about this monster machine called government they talk amongst themselves.

Colin walks over to the table pouring himself another cup of coffee hearing the cheerleader from the front of the crowd speaking to one of the quiet females that was sitting beside him, "What is there to do? What can we do?"

The quiet female agrees, "It's all so confusing. The world has grown so reliant on the government that we are prisoners to a system with no easy way to correct it. What do you think, Colin?"

Everyone knew who Colin was by reputation, at least, the only one he allows them to know. He was a former high level athlete who had founded a reliable free power motor that almost everyone in the room had in place in their home now. With each conversation Colin speaks and deals in shades of gray, only admitting he was at one time a computer engineer working for all of the major corporations, keeping them oblivious to his military background.

"There are so many levels and so many different intricacies that I would need a map to know where or how to begin. This is far from my computer background."

"God bless you Colin, I cannot tell you how thankful we are everyday when we use your power source. For someone who developed free energy you're extremely modest. I'm sure you could figure out a way if you thought about it." The cheerleader spouted.

Standing next to the coffee table, men and women, young and old, walk up thanking Colin for his contribution to 'the cause' and the thousands of dollars worth of free energy as they pour themselves a new cup. Kept busy carrying on piece-meal conversations with various individuals Colin scans the little groups around him discussing the evening's information. They are brainstorming, trying to come up with a winning solution to the government and how to stop hiding in basements with these meetings.

Once the pot of coffee dried up and the only evidence of home-made bakery were the sugary impressions of crullers and chocolate croissants left on ripped wax paper, the basement slowly emptied. Colin made his way to the staircase just as the frail speaker wearing the same 'My Name Is' sticker with a scribbled 'Frank' under it approached him. While unpeeling the paper from a muffin he began, "Colin thanks for coming back, it was great to see you out again. No one here tonight has sacrificed as much as you. Did you enjoy the information tonight?"

"Frank, sure it was interesting but yet again, you have no plan. Nothing has changed. This is exactly why I stopped coming. It's like sitting at home watching the news, nothing changes so why even watch?"

Starting to get animated the scarecrow flails his free arm in the air, "The news! Bah the news! What is so newsworthy of the news?"

"Hold on Frank, don't blow a gasket, I understand everything you said, but what can I or anyone do about what you said tonight?"

"If you were the leader of this group," pointing at all of the empty chairs, "looking through the crowd tonight, what would you do? Look at me."

Frank raises his toothpicks for arms and puts them down, continuing, "Can I ask you a couple of questions?"

"Sure."

"When the government came in saying that your eco-friendly generators didn't pass through government regulated standards and shut you down, how did you feel? When they came and dismantled your company, what was the first thing running through your head?"

Colin clutches onto his coffee mug even tighter, "Do you even need to ask?"

"Humour me please. I just risked everything. At least explain what happened, I never heard."

"Sure, that's fair. Take a seat."

Colin grabs a chair and hands it to Frank and then takes one for himself. Both sit down as Colin begins, "Frank they took my designs, my computers and my prototype for testing and never returned them. I had paid private labs to test it and ensured that they were safe, I thought I had nothing to fear. After their supposed independent testing, scientists provided a report slamming my machine in every way stating that it was unsafe for humans. They refused to release any of my items, shutting down my company. I lost it all."

Breaking off a small chunk of muffin and shoving it into his concave cheek, Frank shakes his head, "I couldn't even imagine. You devoted yourself to something that you believed in and trusted it would work out. What action did you take other than the failed lawsuit?"

"What could I do? Legal or illegal, I started selling it to anyone that wanted one."

"Now your device is outlawed. You're labelled a criminal, and so is anyone who has one. How are you going to fight them when they find and arrest you?"

"I don't plan on going without a battle."

"Realistically either you will be imprisoned or killed, and that is what I'm getting at. Individually we fall victim one by one waiting for someone to come get us. Collectively, if we attacked instead of retaliating they wouldn't have the resources and we would win. Am I wrong Chief Warrant Officer Brunet?"

The former Olympian's leg muscles flex slightly screeching the chair an inch backwards across the floor, "What? What did you just say?"

"Colin, I have access to a lot of information. My ass is on the line every time I host one of these parties, I have to know exactly who I have in my home before I open my big mouth."

"How? It's..."

"Classified I know...it wasn't easy to come by, but I've known for a while."

The inventor squints, his forehead wrinkles as he looks at Frank's eyes through the crow's feet along his face.

"Colin, I can't imagine the frustration you must be feeling. After living your life protecting your country they stab you in the back not once, but twice, because you have morals and values. Some system!"

Shifting in his chair Colin squirms as the visions of all of the faces of those he has killed come to mind.

"You are not the only one. Why do you think I hold these meetings almost every night? To answer your earlier question, Colin, we are not without action. Like the founding fathers Jefferson, Hancock, Washington, Franklin we need to make sure that whoever is involved can be relied upon. Like them if we don't succeed we will be deemed to have committed treason and will be sentenced to death."

Through a muffled pause, "Uhumm, I get it."

"Colin if you want to know more, go to the marina near 2203 Alaskan Way by one this morning, you'll know the one. Through the centuries brave bold leaders have had to sacrifice everything to correct the balance of power. You could be one of those leaders..."

A battle against gravity resonates through a vortex of wind created by the media helicopter hanging over the crowd. The multitude of faces look skyward, the wind extracts tears from squinted eyes, blurring their vision of the camera recording and distributing their facial image to everyone in the world. The male helicopter news reporter shouts over the noise hanging out the side of the helicopter broadcasting the images.

"Surprisingly, despite being documented out past curfew, this crowd hasn't been distracted or dissuaded from continuing their stance. This rally is going to be precedent setting, since everyone is currently under martial law. It will either lead to further similar breaches if not suppressed or it will be yet another painful reminder why the law must be followed."

The co-pilot taps the reporter's shoulder, pointing in the distance to a long line of headlights approaching their location. Camera in hand the news reporter spins around, and zooms in, spotting a caravan of black panel vans. Speaking loudly he explains what he's seeing, "These trucks are not here for a convention, they are filled to the brim with military and police personnel prepared to quell this movement. I fear that this situation is going to get a whole lot worse in a few minutes. We still have no information on what had triggered this sleepy neighbourhood to disregard the curfew laws."

The military and police personnel inside the vans had no idea what had started the rally, nor was there a desire to question orders. Periodically, balaclava-ed eyes stare at the photos of fallen friends taped to the inside of the van, a reminder of the protest only days ago. Each member has mixed emotions arriving at this location, anger being the most prevalent, associated to their co-workers' needless deaths. Fear of being the next dead officer also flashes through their minds, making them cognizant not to take any chances. The sound of their supervisor's voice in their radio ear pieces attempts to keep everyone on the same page, "…if you fear for your safety or the safety of anyone else, act appropriately. The law is clear, these people are breaking the law. It's up to us to clean up the mess. Just remember it is better to be tried in a court by twelve than carried by six."

Like the blood staining the sidewalk, negative emotions spill across the streets surrounding the dead bodies. Weeping, crying, anger, resentment, are picked up by the constantly running video equipment. Conversations in the crowd continue to hum, "Edison, do you think the cops and military are coming to arrest all of us right now?"

"After shooting our Neighbourhood Watch patrollers, they'd better not."

A group of young men walk up joining the crowd, "What's going on, Edison?"

Edison nods at the group, "Hey guys," and points at the media helicopter, "One of their stupid shotgun transports killed a couple of our neighbourhood watch members."

"Is that right?" A young man reaches down grabbing a piece of mortar off the ground and propels it through the air striking the bottom of the helicopter.

The pilot jerks on the controls spotting another projectile incoming.

"Wh-wh-wh-WHOA!" the reporter screamed. His foot slipped from the side of the helicopter, throwing his body forward and tumbling from the open helicopter door toward the gathered masses.

Viewers from around the globe hypnotized by the events unfolding clench muscles at the sight. Families gazing at televisions in livings rooms gasp, watching the video feed hearing the reporter's screams. A cab driver sits motionless at a green light without protest from the paying customer, both enthralled by the footage streaming through the cab driver's phone.

The group of young males laugh seeing the helicopter fly away dangling a reporter and his camera by his safety strap.

Blocks away, the south side camera captures the chirp of the black panel vans' tires coming to an immediate stop. Sliding van doors slam open; battle armoured officers debark onto the street. They take to a line formation waiting for further instructions. Hidden in the shadows, snipers scale rooftops with their commander speaking through their radios, "Sierra team are you in position?"

Peering through the eye of the scope they see the bulging mass, "Sierra team in position."

"Sierra team what's the status on the crowd?"

"Sir, emotions are pretty high, but I haven't spotted any weapons."

"Sierra team keep me apprised of any change, we don't need another incident."

"Sir, yes sir."

Walking in the Central Command Center speaking through his ear piece, General Izzov returns a salute to the officers holding open the doors, "...Clint, tell the Prime Minister I am just walking in the building as we speak...yes, assure him that I will deal with this situation myself...of course I will keep you apprised."

Standing at the helm holding onto the railing over the information pit, Izzov pulls the device from his ear as the Central Command Center officer in charge advances toward his location.

"General..."

Interrupting the officer, Izzov chastises him without even glancing his way. His eyes remained glued to the large screen, "Officer there had better be a good reason why you didn't deal with this situation before it got to this point."

"Sir...I...I..."

"Get out of my sight!" roared the General.

The officer backs away and retreats out of the area. The room becomes silent.

Taking a long deep breath with everyone looking at him, Izzov's eyes bulge from their sockets glaring at everyone before him, "Implement the 360 and send a text to every phone in that direct area saying, 'We know who you are and that you are involved in an after curfew violation.' Then cross reference that list and photos with the ones from the other riot. We will take out our trouble makers one at a time if need be."

A shaking hand rises from a computer terminal. "General?"

"Soldier, are you okay? Why are you shaking like that?"

"The 360 can isolate that area but that doesn't mean that every device it locates is out of their homes. There could be some in their homes legally."

Gritting his teeth and clenching the railing, Izzov shouts, "Send that message! Failure to comply will result in immediate termination!"

The soldier sits down and starts working, as everyone else waits for the next command.

Izzov yells, "Ensure that those troops know that not a single person is to get by our line. Keep them isolated to that area."

As directed, every phone in the area begins buzzing, beeping and ringing. One by one everyone with a device looks at the message on their screen and compares it with others. Surprise gives way to shock manifesting in tremulous hands holding their phones. Mucus begins dripping from their noses as a bulge develops in their throats creating an obstruction to those swallowing deeply. The idea of jail begins entering their minds making many legs weak. Others transform their fear into anger and rage, gripping their phones, and yelling at them.

A Neighbourhood Watch member receives another message after receiving the first one. The photo of the former Premier's aide Christopher shows up on the screen followed by a message, 'Kyle get everybody out of there peacefully. If not, you and everyone present will be jailed tonight. They are sending in the whole army right now.'

Grabbing a megaphone, Kyle elevates his medium-sized body standing on a knocked over news paper dispenser. Pressing his trimmed goatee beard against the plastic mouth piece he announces,

"My fellow neighbours please hear me now. You have every right to be scared or angry, but, I beg of you, do not let anger overwhelm you to do something that you will regret. Now is not the time for battle, now is the time to support one another as we mourn the loss of two of our family, neighbours and community members. We have all received this message to instil fear, knowing that fear may cause us to do something worthy of their attention."

Looking up and pointing to the helicopters hovering above, "Considering all of the attention we have right now they want to justify their response and show the world that we are nothing more than a bunch of criminals violating imposed military law. This incident is a surprise to us all and we need to address it, but not now, not like this. We have two dead friends lying on the cold cement, let's carry them home and lay them to rest respectfully. Please honour their sacrifice by containing whatever pent up emotions you have over this incident and any others and return to your homes in peace. There will be a time, but, not yet."

His voice softens in intensity. "Not now. Thank you."

Bending down to pick up his fallen friends, the leader begins humming Amazing Grace. The crowd begins to help the struggling leader shoulder the weight. Others follow along in song, as the slow steady walk towards their homes allows those in the procession to view the scene, the pooled blood, the shredded brick walls; the NWP's last stand. The masses dissipate like a kettle's steam in the air, returning to their homes.

Watching the screen seeing the fleeting numbers, Izzov's head rocks backwards, "Fear makes cowards of us all." Mumbling under his breath, he grins, "Run along little boys and girls."

Releasing the metal bar, puffing out his chest General Izzov marches around the CCC, "Is it something I said?" he jokes, laughing out loud. "Did you see the looks on their faces? It was priceless! Bunch of cowards." Looking over at one of the stations, "Did we get any matches with the riot?"

"Yes, General. The complete list is being sent to your secure email address now."

"Perfect." Skimming through the list quickly on his handheld device, he looks up, "Have the contingent of soldiers remain in the area until every one of them has returned to their nice cozy warm homes. Prepare the special teams. I think it's time to take the fight to a whole new level."

Sidewalks spit dust as the rumble of diesel powered engines echoes off the buildings as the military vehicles speed through. The glow of a new morning silhouettes the mountain ranges in the distance, barely illuminating the men dressed in black surrounding various homes in the now quiet neighbourhood. Clanging boots kick at the side of a black van as two neighbourhood watch members bound and gagged try in vain to alert their friends. A thick and heavy heel of the guarding officer lands on their faces one after the other, ending that shallow bit of heroics.

Simultaneously, splintering door frames and shattering windows fill the air, as adrenaline-fuelled teams crash through the main entrance of homes. A stampede of combat boots sounded off moments before the arrests of everyone in sight commenced. Bellowing screams are short lived by those arrested. A human body slams through double paned glass windows creating an explosion piercing through the misting morning air. Melted sand particles land in shards and debris as bare feet slam to the ground sprinting out of sight yelling. Leaving bloody footprints in their wake, military officers give chase.

Awakening to the noise, an older man jumps out of bed peering from the corner of a window, questioning his own eyes. Masked men tackle, beat and cart off lifeless bodies throwing them into panel vans. Hiding behind curtains the man trembles with fear. Panic grips his body hearing more screams, "Help! Please!" and a thud silencing them. Jittery eyes bounce around the room searching for answers, his mind spins, burning rubber like a race car tire seeking traction, finding one solution.

Muscles tighten, mind sets, and the man jogs to his closet pulling out a baseball bat. He runs to the door. With a jolt he throws the door open, and sprints toward the first group of machine gun toting men carrying a body. A foul sweep with his bat clobbers one masked military officer in the head. Falling to the ground, dropping their cargo the second masked man fumbles reaching for his gun as the bat caves in his face. Turning, spotting the panel vans he howls out pointing with his bat, "Attack."

Neighbourhood doors begin flying open and people flow, running from their lit entrances, half dressed, carrying golf clubs, kitchen knives, and pieces of lumber. The community charges in battle against hardened army soldiers.

Bullets begin spraying through the air wounding and killing many in the open when a soldier's body explodes blood all over side walk. His hardened body drops, emptying more bodily fluid under his black clothing to spill across the pavement. The military leader spots new civilian warriors brandishing rifles firing at his men. He yells into the radio while shooting suppressive fire, "Abort. Abort. Let's get out of here!"

Dropping bound bodies on the ground, and running for the trucks more military members are shot, before the vans beat a hasty retreat.

Pedestrians stop and crowd in front of electronics stores watching the illuminated television screens through the panes of glass and metal bars. Public transit commuters monitor breaking news on mobile devices. Others listen to the news streaming over radio waves.

Shawn Gurl's voice is full of energy as he begins, "Friendly Neighbourhood Terrorist Sleeper Cells. Think you know your neighbour, think again. Military and police following up on last night's attempted rally in Vancouver acted swiftly in the early morning hours, executing arrest warrants for active members in a sleeper terrorist organization called the Freedom Movement. Apparently, two members of that movement attempted to hijack a transport truck carrying goods into the city. This resulted in the two members being gunned down before the shotgun operator fell victim to the injuries he sustained during the confrontation."

Images from helicopters show swarms of people gathered in the streets, "The leaders of the terrorist Freedom Movement took advantage of their friends' deaths prompting a rally to lay siege to the city yet again. Over one thousand people joined in and out of that number thirty were identified as the instigators and were to be arrested this morning."

Amateur video footage takes to the screen showing a melee of people gathered in the streets, "This morning as military and police were effecting the arrests of these Freedom Movement terrorists they were attacked from the community supporting these men and women resulting in more casualties on both sides. The final tally has not been released; however, there are several military and police members in critical condition, not to mention the civilian casualties. Ambulance and police refused to enter this area at the time in fear of another ambush. This neighbourhood has since erupted and people from everywhere continue to join this group taking to the streets. As they walk through the streets more and more people converge adding to the numbers. It appears as though they are headed downtown carrying everything from rifles, handguns to baseball bats and other makeshift weapons. We will continue to monitor these actions as they unfold throughout the day."

Watching the recent news broadcast, Nolin explains, seeing Miguel shaking his head, "It's a tactic used since the dawn of mankind. They did the same thing in Egypt during the time of the Pharaohs and in Greece to overthrow the Caesars. Now to control what we think it's easy to hide the truth from an unsuspecting population, who are unaware of who the real enemy is?"

Standing up and pacing back and forth the former Colonel adds, "Make the enemy your neighbour and people will run to big brother to save them."

"Exactly, hence the crowd control and government power domination. Say goodbye to basic rights and freedoms because we just handed them up on a silver platter."

Rubbing his unshaven face, Miguel looks over at Lorne, "Where could he be? It's morning already and Colin's still not home."

"Maybe he got caught up in that toga you saw him in." Nolin smirked.

Pointing out the door, "They black bagged Colin's face and shoved him onto a yacht. He could be anywhere by now. And I didn't get a chance to video the boat, how are we supposed to find it again?"

"Miguel, relax. Talk about a control freak. He's a talented operative, just have a little patience."

Sitting back into the reclining chair Miguel's head sinks into the top pillow. He pulls a vintage forty-five caliber handgun out of his waist band and lays it on his lap.

Lorne stares at the gun on Miguel's lap, "I can't decide what I like more, the laptop he gave me or the gun..."

"Shhhhh," the former Colonel moves off the chair and takes a position around the corner of the front door.

Walking in the door Colin shouts out, "I'm home." And slams the door closed.

Leaving his position of concealment Miguel approaches him, "Colin, how was that? What was with the toga?"

"Don't even talk to me about that."

Lorne fills up his coffee mug, "You guys want some?"

Colin shakes his head, "No, not a chance, I really want to go to bed."

Rubbing his eyes Miguel agrees, "Sounds like a plan, but first we need to know what happened."

The former Olympian grabs a bottle of water out of the fridge, "All right, here it is. Crazy that something this big could have been kept quiet for so long. The Freedom Movement acted as a testing ground weeding out potential new members for a secret group of people trying change the world."

White knuckled fingers pry open the water bottle cap spilling some of the contents in the process. Colin tips back the bottle into his mouth, sucking back a mouthful of water before continuing, "After we left the dock we were on the boat for about an hour before it stopped and we were escorted off one at a time. There was a huge bonfire and everyone wore masks except us, the new recruits. We had to stand there as they marched past us one at a time. If anyone had a problem with us they had the opportunity to voice their opinion. It's a one way ticket into the group or certain death. There was no turning back once we were on that boat."

Colin grabs a chair joining Nolin at the dining table as Miguel wakens, hanging on every word, "They call themselves the Sons of Liberty. They have remained in secret existence since the American Revolution. Their sole purpose is to act as a watch dog over the government living by the motto 'I prefer dangerous freedom over peaceful slavery,' as quoted by Thomas Jefferson. This group was responsible for the Boston Tea Party."

"Patsies," Miguel mumbles.

"What's that Miguel?" Lorne asks.

"The Freedom Movement, they're just a bunch of patsies."

Colin continues, "Something like that, or a distraction. The Sons of Liberty all believe that collateral damage is necessary and cannot be avoided. They accept that families will die in what they call a noble death for a better tomorrow."

Miguel grumbles, "Twisted bunch of self righteous..."

Standing up from his chair Colin glares down at his two friends, "Before you guys start judging them hear me out. How are they any different than us? How many families have you killed personally or seen in chunks walking through war zones, knowing full well that our government officials authorized the air force to carpet bomb a region?"

The Spaniard leans back, the white in his eyes pop out of their sockets, "Listen, I didn't mean to..."

"Upset me! I'm well past upset Miguel! What makes it okay that we go into other countries devastating their population? Because our government says so? Because we got paid? Who put you behind bars,

Miguel? Who attacked me? Tell me they know best, I dare you. I dare you!"

Lorne steps between Colin's glare and Miguel's returning stare, "Okay Colin, just take it easy, we're on the same team."

Colin picks up a chair and whips it against the wall busting through the drywall. "Ahhhhh. How can we fight these people? They might be doing the world a favour, but at the same time how can we allow more innocents to die for another cause?"

Lorne takes a deep breath and looks back at Miguel and returns looking at Colin, speaking soft and slow, "I think we all need to get some sleep. We will talk about this when we get up."

"Sure, I could use some rest." Colin hangs his head shuffling his feet over to the stairs when he stops and turns around. "One more thing. They are having an open meeting tonight and the same rules apply. If one of you wants, come along and hear for yourself."

"I can't but maybe Miguel will join you."

"Let me sleep on it. I don't think it would be a good idea that I go. If they recognize me I won't be coming back."

That evening, Carrie sits beside Shawn in the studio as the newscast sets to begin. With her head down she speaks on her cell phone. "Sam, if you need anything just give me a call anytime. I mean it. I can't lose you too." Raising a tissue to her face, she absorbs the tears falling from her eyes.

Crackling through the little speaker Sam speaks loudly, "Carrie, I'm a survivor. I lived in the Middle East. I think I can handle this. Just make sure everyone sees that footage."

Shawn Gurl bumps Carrie's arm, "Come on."

"Sam, I've got to go." Lowering the tissue and dropping her phone to the floor she sits up tall. Carrie's face strengthens as she goes into character. The red light on the camera comes on and she begins, "Mayhem, absolute anarchy, thousands of people converged on the downtown core of Vancouver laying waste to anything and anyone of government status."

Shawn continues, "What initially started as a protest quickly turned violent when the first couple of civilians were shot after Molotov cocktails were thrown at a barricaded line manned by police and military. The crowd charged with a force of pent up anger and energy never captured before. They pressed on despite people around them being shot and killed. It evolved into genocide for anyone wearing a uniform."

Carrie takes her cue following Shawn, "We have just received the following videos from someone within the city during the uprising."

Bloodshot eyes, sweaty brows and war cries howl through the streets, as the crunching, cracking and smashing of military members and civilians struggle for supremacy. Gun powder coats the air with its white glow under the sun's rays and the streets pile up with bodies dead and injured.

Retreating military members run for their lives given chase by thousands of civilians who pulverize them into the ground. Civilians strip corpses of their gear flapping it over their head like flags of victory, before moving on to the next confrontation. Vehicles driven through the crowd are stopped and flipped over with civilians thrashing the occupants.

A bouncing camera shows a handful of military members enter a clothing store and exit dressed in clean new clothes joining the crowd marching through the streets.

Warren carries on, "Our correspondent that provided the video described the events, that government employees were all seen as a part of those oppressing the public. There was no thought or concern that the cameras were capturing their faces as the masses took part in ousting those they believed were in power. People were angry and fed up with being picked on."

Another camera's red light notifies Shawn to pick up the dialogue, "All government buildings were set ablaze and continue to burn throughout the night with no firefighters responding to the many calls. Although for the most part the infrastructure was intact the city was on fire. Anarchy is the disease that swept over Vancouver leaving it in ruins."

High energy music blasts through Paula Connie's head phones as she works out, pumping her sweat-covered thighs to the beat. Watching a television while on a spinning bike in the base gym she remains in touch with the news in Vancouver and skims over her idea of a response to such a situation. A quick glance over her handlebars into the mirror terminates the euphoric feelings from the endorphins flooding her mind as she recognizes Colonel Renniks walking towards her.

Tapping her on her shoulder she speeds up, monitoring him through the mirror spotting his dumb grin outlined by the feeble goatee he is now growing. Rolling her eyes she begins to slow down before stopping and getting off the bike. Taking the ear phones out of her ears, beads of sweat begin multiplying over her entire body.

Panting, Connie addresses him, "Yes sir."

"Lieutenant, the General would like to see you at once." Pointing at the television, "I think you know what it's about."

"Yes, sir. I will go and take a shower before I meet him."

"He is not that patient. Come as you are, I will give you a ride." She watches his eyes scan her body from head to toe and back again.

"Yes sir." She returns waiting for his eyes to complete their survey. *Seriously Renniks take a picture. It will last longer,* she said to herself walking passed him. *There is no way in hell ever.*

> She remembers, after he made Colonel, she was teamed up with him working on a project. They took a break for supper and at the conclusion of the meal they returned to work. On the way back to their office they proceeded through a secluded hallway when he grabbed her ass and moved in for a kiss. She knocked his hand off her shoulder, swept his legs and released his body, crashing his back into the ground, knocking the wind out of his chest. Standing over him with her combat boot raised about to stomp on his testicles she warned him, "Colonel or no Colonel, if you ever touch my ass again I will crush your manhood permanently."

Ever since, he appeared to be aroused even more. And whenever he was around, he just stared at her like he was appraising a piece of meat, oblivious to protocol. She wouldn't let that distract her from gaining the experience from being involved in projects that she had been assigned to, regardless of his noxious aura.

Paula knows that General Izzov is no different. He is just an older, uglier piece of shit with no practical experience. Sure, he appears smart but he has no idea about practical operations. All his advice or counsel comes from those around him. He gathers a nest of kiss-ass advisors who would do anything for him. Perhaps, the sign of a good leader, but because everyone around him was so afraid to get on his bad side they always deferred to his decision, regardless of how poor it was.

It was painful speaking to him, aside from him constantly staring at her breasts; he wouldn't know what she was talking about. She always had to repeat herself to one of his little groupies later. Now, going to see him in her sports bra, this was going to be interesting. *Man, I miss Hamilton.*

The ringing of the boat buoys chime in the void of darkness, swayed by the current. Decaying fish scents loiter in the mist descending on the Anthony's Pier sixty-six marina as waves lap against boat hulls rocking them into the docks.

Speaking to himself, stationed off in the distance with a video recording device in hand, Nolin maintains visual of Miguel and Colin with another ten people dressed in black. *Looks like the curfew is keeping everyone inside. Only people out are us and the SOB SOLs.*

A military vehicle arrives on site. *Oh shit Miguel. This isn't good.*

The vehicle's horn honks, summoning a security guard out of his booth carrying a pot of coffee. Mugs extended out the military vehicle window are filled as they exchange words with the security guard, "This curfew has killed all of the after hour restaurants."

"I know. Don't worry, we always have a pot on."

"Thanks. We will be back in a bit." The vehicle drives off.

He zooms in on Frank who shows up out of the shadows bouncing with excitement. Bringing the camera into focus he gets good footage. One by one Frank escorts them into a shed where they come out wearing nothing but a toga. Holding his breath Nolin contains a percolating chuckle in his throat capturing Miguel and Colin in their togas. He whispers, "This is a keeper."

An ocean cruiser yacht enters the marina, pulling up to the dock. The roar of the engines fight against the waves it created coming in. Gently it presses against the docks, creaking and cracking. Each new recruit is black bagged and escorted on board being brought down into the hull. Sweeping the camera over the scene Nolin records everything he can. *Whoever these guys are they are well financed and obviously tied in with this marina.*

The camera's eye automatically adjusts the focus as Lorne tries to get the boat's serial number through the mist. *Looks like I've got some work to do.*

CHAPTER ELEVEN

The poor audio recording of a man's voice narrates the scene captured from his mobile phone, "No words can describe what I see. Atrocity, catastrophe, mayhem, words are merely just words until your eyes actually witness the state of this once magnificent city. Crows pick at human bodies lying on city streets like road kill. Rotting flesh assaults my nostrils with a putrid diarrheal odour. Black soot fills the air with a toxic gas that burns my eyes and throat."

Wrapping her arms around her legs Carrie pulls them against her body. She rocks in her office chair, staring at her tablet playing video from Vancouver.

"Where are you, Sam?" her voice crackles, as she sniffles. Pressing talk on her phone she hears the service provider's automated message again. "The cellular number you have called is not available. Please call again."

"Damn it." She throws the phone down on her desk. Mascara trickles down her cheeks as she pulls another tissue from the box, blowing her nose. Wiping away tears she smears make-up across her face, "Sam, you better be okay."

The man's voice continues with the choppy video. "Without emergency crews coming to assist NWP, members wearing their fluorescent orange vests are charged with the removal of the dead. Seen here tossing brutalized bodies into the back of pickup trucks, seagulls and crows circle above in massive numbers. With the number of dead, they will likely be thrown together into a pit never to be identified again."

Spray-painted on the side of the pickup truck are the words, 'Never Forget.'

Sniffling, wiping the droplets off her nose, Carrie whimpers, "Oh Sam, please be okay."

A disgusting feeling of relief crosses her mind, glad that she got out of the city before it happened and awful for feeling this way, knowing Sam is trapped somewhere in there. Tears run unchecked down her face as she pictures one of the lifeless bodies being Sam's. While sobbing she hears her name being summoned,

"Carrie Warren report to studio two."

Releasing her legs she straightens up and snatches another tissue from the box, drying her face. Lugging her body down the hall, with every stride Carrie feels the weight of the moment, the fear for the innocent, the anguish of personal cowardice.

I wonder if these feelings are anything like walking in quicksand. Stopping suddenly, her head lowers, with her hand instinctively pressing against the center of her chest with the sudden realization of just how ironically cold that 'quicksand' word is. Bogged down physically, every perilous movement sinks you deeper into a slow suffocating death. There is nothing quick about that at all. A peevish voice beckons her again over the PA, "Carrie Warren attend studio two, please!"

Snapping back into forward motion she picks up her pace. A female stage hand wearing a headset and holding a clip board spots Carrie down the hall, "She's almost here."

The stage hand props the door open, and notices Carrie using a crumpled tissue in her hand to clean her face.

"What happened, Carrie?" she asks in a voice of collective fear, as the reporter walks in through the open door.

The stage hand yells, "Makeup! Tammy get your ass over here now."

The stage hand follows the reporter and pulls a tissue from her pocket, handing it over.

Accepting the tissue, Carrie dabs her cheeks noting people coming to her aid, "Thanks Sarah, thanks Tammy, thanks guys. I'm okay. Seriously. I was just having a moment. I'm ready, honestly I am. I just need Tammy to help me clean up and I will be right as rain."

A broken nervous giggle slips out of her mouth as another tear escapes, rolling down her face. Fighting against her inner emotions, she feels her face contorting into a cry. Taking control of the moment she adjusts and shows off her classic Warren smile.

The voice of the male producer breaks up the 'love in' trying to keep people on schedule, "Forget it, we don't have time. Just get her on the set. Carrie, use it for the broadcast. People will eat up that emotion. Let's go people. The world is waiting to watch."

Camera crew members silently cheer Carrie on, "Come on you can do it."

Unintentionally, Warren evokes a plethora of tears from viewers who watch in High Definition the tears streaming down her face as her voice begins to crack.

"Welcome to another segment of 'Behind the Wall.' Here in the studio with me today is, is, S – S – Sam..."

She lowers her face into her hands sobbing. Tammy runs up to the stage with a box of tissue whispering, "Here you go Carrie. Take your time."

Carrie nods sniffling and Tammy backs away from the stage. Carrie lifts her face squeezing her fists tight into little balls, trying to muscle her way through this, "I'm, I'm so sorry. Uhummm. Here, here with me is a-a-a professor from McGill University."

As the camera pans out, Carrie walks off the stage, coming into focus is her guest. The television screen displays with an electronic banner showing his name and credentials. The professor, a thin set man looks over at Carrie's empty seat and then looks at the camera patting down his comb over, "Yes, well. My name is Samuel Schultz, and I was asked to talk about the Vancouver incident. Backed by social media, the world has united to rally around the citizens of Vancouver. What started out as a simple curfew violation has quickly evolved into a global political nightmare, with the inevitability of a civil war..."

Within the city of Vancouver, crowds congregate around grocery stores under tents, where, music plays, food is served and warmth is readily available. The venue is completely lit and functioning regardless of the power outage. Homemade signs hang everywhere in the area displaying 'Never Forget.' NWP members armed with firearms occupy the stores preventing any looting of food. Using megaphones NWP members rally the people.

Evolving from the small rally after the death of the two NWP members, Kyle was nominated and chosen to be the leader of the Vancouver City Neighbourhood Watch Programs. Dressed in his fluorescent vest and matching ball cap, he stands on a table in front of a huge crowd speaking through a megaphone, "Friends, relatives, neighbours, mark this day, and 'Never Forget' the faces of those who made the ultimate sacrifice. Don't let their heroism be in vain. 'Never Forget' what pushed you to stand against tyranny. Mark this day and 'Never Forget' that today is the first day you are truly FREE!"

A reserved applause begins and ends quickly.

Lowering his megaphone for a moment he bends down and grabs a bottle of water off the table. Taking a swig, he stands up again, "Many people have come up to me saying 'Kyle I'm scared, I don't know what's going to happen next.' I'm here to tell you, it's okay to be scared. Don't lose hope because you're scared. If we give in to fear, they have already won."

Jumping off the table, Kyle walks amongst the crowd speaking into his megaphone with it tilted into the air, "'Never Forget' it was fear that controlled us in the past. It was fear that they used and held over us, much like our free energy here today. Use free energy and 'go to jail.' Blindly we followed, threatened and fearful that we would lose our limited freedom."

Reaching the center of the crowd, Kyle sees a monster of a man standing head and shoulders over everyone else. The NWP member waves at the man to lower himself, and whispers in his ear. The man bends down, allowing Kyle onto his shoulders before he stands, "I walk among you and see the bravest bunch of people that this world has ever seen. Being brave is about defying fear. It's about saying, 'I fear but I won't let fear stop me.' 'Never Forget' together we are Strong! Together we are Brave! Together we are FREE!"

The multitude erupts into a roar cheering, "Never Forget."

Kyle gets off the man's shoulders and walks back through the crowd. People shake his hand and hug him. He jumps up on a picnic table raising his megaphone, "The world over has seen our stand and from what I hear they are joining us. They know we will not stand by and be bullied anymore. If you will allow me, I would like to negotiate peace talks for our city and for us as citizens."

A grainy video takes shape on Carrie's tablet as she watches an amateur video update from Vancouver, "This band of misfits and vigilantes are sending one of their so-called community leaders out to discuss peaceful negotiations with the military. Here comes a huge truck. Stand by — just watch the video."

Driving along the Vancouver streets is a red extended cab pickup truck with a lift kit raising the bottom of the truck another two feet off the ground. Very slowly it continues through the street as the crowd separates to allow passage. Kyle walks over to the truck and steps on one of the oversized tires, climbing up and into the cab of the vehicle. Waving his fluorescent ball cap in the air, the people ignite into applause as the truck proceeds down the street.

A white flag flaps in the wind, hanging ten feet above the cab of the truck from a pole implanted in the cargo box. Thirty motorcycles accompany the truck as they lumber through dishevelled streets making their way out of the city limits towards a military blockade.

"We will soon see if this has any effect. I can't imagine how this is going to end. Stay tuned..."

With the blockade in the distance Kyle lowers his ocular apparatus and speaks to the driver, "Stop the truck."

"Why what's wrong?"

"Just stop the truck for a second."

The brakes on the beast squeal to a stop. Kyle gets up, negotiating his body from the cab of the truck into the box without touching the ground.

The motorcycle riders gather around and remove their helmets as Kyle begins to speak, "Gentlemen, this is it. I want you guys to stay here and use this." He tosses his ocular device to one of the drivers. "The blockade is just at the horizon. Considering the military already busted in my door trying to arrest me, I might not make it out of there. If I don't return in a half hour notify everyone you can. I hope it doesn't come to that. Never Forget! Never Forget!"

The riders watch as Kyle re-enters the truck and proceeds to the blockade. Using the zoom lens, one of the motorcycle members monitors the activity around the truck. Initially, a robot exits the compound as the two remain in the truck. Following shortly behind is a small team of military officers. At gun point Kyle and the driver descend gradually from the truck with their hands over their heads. "Guys it doesn't look good. Kyle and his driver just got arrested. They are being escorted back behind the wall..."

Empty candy wrappers cover the entire dining table where Nolin set up shop with his computer. Sheets of paper were pinned to the wall with scribbles of information highlighted by arrows. Quick choppy movements kept Nolin moving around the living room before he dropped to his chair typing away, finding another clue. Pressing print he rips the paper from his machine. Scratching out another message, he gets up and tacks it to the wall.

A gust of wind flaps the papers hanging on the walls shortly after hearing the sound of the creaking front door. A fresh coffee smell rushes out from the house greeting Nolin's roommates upon their return. Miguel and Colin hear Nolin munching on food mumbling out, "Please tell me you're not still wearing those togas."

Colin rounds the corner looking at Nolin with a trail of crumbs from his mouth to his lap. "So?" Nolin said, shoving the last bit of the candy bar into his mouth pointing at the empty chairs at the dining table, garbling out, "I'm dying to hear how you made out last night."

The duo joins Nolin at the table. Colin sits down resting his body into the back of the chair spreading out his legs. Miguel turns a chair around sitting on it backwards with his body leaning on the top of the back of the chair and his arms around the sides resting his head on his hands.

The Spaniard scratches his chin, "Dying is the right word. Standing in those stupid togas, I never appreciated the warmth of a fire as much as I did last night. Colin endorsed me but they didn't accept it. Instead they did a march and someone recognized me. Within a moment we were both black bagged being dragged away when a voice spoke up."

Paying full attention Nolin's eyes widen, "Do you know who it was?'

Looking at his friend and over at Colin, Miguel shakes his head, "No, they never revealed themselves. Laying there soaking up cold and dirt this man comes right up to us and says he supports our joining. I thought those would be the last words I heard before a bang."

Drawn in, looking for more information Nolin stares at the men across from him, "So they accepted you both as members?"

Looking over at Miguel momentarily the former SEAL answers Lorne, "Not exactly. We are probationary members. We will be called upon to do some acts of 'justice' to prove our worth to the clan. They have our phone numbers and we should be receiving a text when the next meeting is going to be."

Scanning the papers hanging on the wall Lorne reviews his notes, "Finding out who vouched for you and why will be added to our list of things to do. What is their end game?"

Miguel tilts his head back studying the ceiling thinking, "I know that voice. It was so familiar. It isn't coming to me."

Pointing to the walls full of paper Lorne prepares to explain, "Well, as you can see I did some research of my own last night.

Perhaps I can shed some light on the situation that you guys are in. You'll never guess…"

Situated at his desk in his chambers, the Prime Minister opens an envelope pulling out the paper insert. Reading the words etched onto the paper, he slouches in his chair. Running his fingers through his hair, he looks up, seeing a man dressed in black before him.

A Brazilian accent speaks through a thin balaclava concealing his face, "Mr. Prime Minister, you have to ask yourself some very important questions. With all of the security in place, how did I get passed your guards, or more importantly, who within your staff is working for me and let me in? Either way make no mistake you and your family with die if you fail to comply."

A knock at his closed chamber door preceded it opening slowly. The Brazilian hides behind the door and pulls out a knife.

A female revealed her face in the crack of the door, "Scott, is everything okay?"

The Prime Minister's face is petrified and he manages to eek out, "J-j-just."

The female opens the door further, starting to walk in, "Scott, what's wrong?"

Jumping to his feet, "Gwen, just stay right there please! I have work to do! You're disrupting me! Leave right now!"

"What?"

"Can you go get the kids ready? We're leaving Ottawa tonight!"

Reluctantly, she walks out the door pulling it shut behind her, as a cold gust of wind blows through the office moving papers.

Scanning his office Scott saw nothing but the open window…

Masses shout through the streets with the sight of the oversized pickup truck returning and waving a white flag on its mast, "Never Forget. Never Forget. Never Forget."

Kyle exits his seat with a huge smile. Jumping into the box of the truck he looks at the crowd gathering around. Standing tall he shouts out, "They want to listen to us now. Power to the people!"

The crowd jubilantly echoes, "Power to the people!"

Formally dressed in her military uniform Lieutenant Paula Connie sits in the back of a military jet, examining Vancouver city maps and military reports on the situation that are strewn across a customized work station. She is managing the security detail surrounding the barricade and camp. Trying to determine the best approach to combat the civil unrest and return the city back to order she continues to work. Vibrating against her work station desk is her phone receiving a text message. Glancing down she sees that it's from her friend Jennifer. Picking up the phone she reads, 'Good luck in Vancouver gf.'

Paula types back looking over at Reficuel, 'Going to need a miracle. This pretty boy doesn't have what it takes to please these ppl.'

Her screen flashes to life again, 'Just be careful these ppl attacked and killed how many govt workers already. Who's to say they aren't settn up to attack that barricade? Is it true that they received a shipment of weapons?'

Paula responds, 'Not sure what to believe. But I don't think that they will be fooled for a moment by this guy's expensive suits, hair, or his slippery talk.'

Jennifer sends another message, 'How about you? Does he have what it takes to put you to bed?'

'U kno I'm busy. I got work to do.'

'That wasn't a denial. Who else is with you?'

Paula looks around the cabin, seeing Renniks sitting there talking to Reficuel, no doubt working another political scheme. He shifts in his seat turning right around looking at her, giving that devilish smile. *Man I hate him.* Paula lowers her head turning up her music drowning out any chance he would try to talk to her. Peering over her shoulder she notices reclined, reading a gossip magazine, is Carrie Warren.

Paula replies to Jennifer's message, 'Renniks, and Carrie Warren.'

Jennifer doesn't miss a beat and fires another message back, 'Ouch tough crowd. Well you better make ur move b4 Warren does. She's on fire right now. If you strike out with the rich cat you know you will always have Renniks as a fall back plan if you get lonely out there.'

'Why do I even talk to you?'

Jennifer responds, 'who else is going to remind you that ur human with needs and not a robot.'

Paula's phone receives another message from Jennifer, 'anyways i will let u get back to work. I gotta go. Let me know when you're back.'

'Will do thx'

Putting down her phone Paula picks up her ultra mini device, changing the song. Holding the machine in her hand she takes a second appreciating it, remembering the salesman's speech when she bought it at the electronics store, "Countless hours of music, waterproof, the ability to take a picture on the go, or record several hours of audio and video if need be, this thing does everything." Tucking it back into her pocket with the ear buds still plugged into her ear canals she flips through another report.

Carrie reclines on the leather covered seat flipping through a fashion magazine, a tear streams down her face as she finishes an article written by Sam Merchant. Putting the magazine down she picks up her phone scrolling through pictures of her and Sam, and re-reads their last text messages. Closing that screen she opens up another message, 'Congrats Carrie, ur ratings were never higher. Not bad for someone who spent most of the time off the camera CW.' She still can't believe that Wilson is sending her to cover this historic truce considering she walked off camera during her last televised broadcast. He didn't even ask her to explain why she did it.

The reporter closes her eyes nestling her head into the seat. She has been on the go for days on end with no relief in sight. It's moments like these when she longs to take back her decision to get involved working political stories, wishing she had followed Sam with his entrepreneurial endeavours.

Holding her purse like a teddy bear, she starts to doze, when flashes of the former Premier tied up in his house coat come to her mind. Opening up her eyes, she starts pinching the side of her purse until she locks onto the shape of the memory stick that Miguel gave her. The last thing she wants is to inadvertently run into the former Premier while covering this story. Carrie tries to answer the questions coming to mind, *What would I say? How can I even look at him knowing what he has done? Why didn't I alert anyone or call when I got back home?*

"Awww." Carrie grumbled, picking up the fashion magazine. She starts reading another article.

General Izzov marches up a flight of sculpted stone steps leading to the front doors of the Prime Minister's castle in the mountains near Montreal. He knew that this place existed but never personally attended until now. After the riot in Vancouver the Prime Minister fled from his usual home in the city. Izzov recalls how distraught the PM sounded on the phone when he summoned him to this locale. Clint wasn't much assistance either. The General wonders, *I'm not taking the blame for Vancouver. This is Hamilton and Miguel's fault.*

Snapping his hand up to salute the guards he watches one of them use his palm print to open the front doors. Walking with him they open a door leading to a den. Izzov marvels at the size of each room, high reaching ceilings add an illusion of increased size. Built at the turn of the twentieth century before the First World War, the residence has been kept up ever since, minus the Victorian style decor. After a century of standing here, it still looks completely sound.

Strutting around the den, Izzov examines the contents. Picking up trinkets he recalls personally rubber stamping additional funding that was required to ensure the security measures were second to none. He had forgotten all about one of the follow-up reports until now –

'With the development of better aircraft, in the event of an airborne attack the basement has been fitted with a cavern leading deep into the mountain to a sophisticated bomb shelter. Larger than the house, it contains every amenity available to sustain life for up to a year if not stocked up for longer. All food contained in the cupboards is vacuum sealed. Water bottles are kept in a dark cool room maintaining their longevity including a well system that boasts an onsite water purification system. The design had been copied from several other countries with similar safe houses able to withstand such an attack.'

Clint walks into the room. Izzov immediately puts down a small statue and advances toward him. Leaning over speaking quick and low the General demands, "You gotta give me something. What's going on?"

Bewildered, Clint raises one eyebrow at a time looking side to side, "I don't know. He hasn't said a word to me since the Vancouver thing. He just packed up his family and came out here and has been spending time with them ever since, refusing to talk to me or anyone else about anything involved in that situation."

"That's not…"

Abruptly a door flies open, bouncing off the door stop, and in walks the Prime Minister, his face unshaven and hair dishevelled. He advances slamming the door shut, making his way to a set of unoccupied chairs in the center of the room.

"General, thank you for coming up here. I know there is a lot going on that needs your direct attention but I am considering something that has never been done before in the history of our nation."

Moving towards his host the General is apprehensive, looking at the Prime Minister's stained shirt, questioning his sanity, "Yes, Mister Prime Minister what is it?"

The Prime Minister reaches into his pant pocket grasping an envelope as beads of sweat pollute his forehead, "Hmmm, it is with deep contemplation with my family that I have decided to do what's best for this country and give up the Prime Minister's office."

Clint interjects as the General stops and ponders the implications, "Mister Prime Minister, Scott, you can't be serious!"

Prime Minister yells, "I am! I don't think I've ever been more serious in my life!"

Sitting down and resting against the high cushioned back of the chair, the Prime Minister continues speaking calmly, "Gentlemen, please, sit down."

The aide speaks as the General takes a seat, "Scott, just hang in there. I know it looks horrible but in a short time we have learned so much. This has been a long time coming but we finally have some activists in custody and are questioning them now. We will have more answers soon."

The Prime Minister rests on the arm of the chair speaking over the side, "Clint, General, what are we doing? What is our goal?"

Clint responds, "Uhhh, well, we're trying to restore peace and prevent further terrorist attacks."

"Very noble causes, they are ones that I support one hundred percent. Did you know my oldest daughter is twenty years old this year?"

Both Clint and Izzov look at one another and wait. The Prime Minister takes out his wallet extracting a picture and looks at it. He passes it to the General, "Twenty years old. When she was going through her teen years she tested me and her mother. Do want to know what happened?"

"She moved out," the aide responds.

"Exactly. At seventeen years old she moved in with one of her friend's older sisters."

Handing the picture back to the Prime Minister, Izzov questions, "Mister Prime Minister, I don't see how this applies to our situation."

"General, neither did I until this morning. It's been three years and in that time she finished high school, and now she's in university. She won."

Shoving the picture back into his wallet, he takes out another one. "She proved that she knew what she was doing. That she didn't need us making all of her decisions for her. We fought so hard that we nearly lost her, instead of understanding her and coming to some peaceful solution."

"With all due respect Mister Prime Minister, I don't think..."

"What Clint? What? World War I, World War II, our troops went to war voluntarily. I could never understand why my great-great grandfather at the age of seventeen forged his documents and hitchhiked to a neighbouring town to enlist in the army. What to fight in a war that had already claimed the lives of his three older brothers. He had heard that the army needed more men, and he wasn't going to let his brothers' cause lose because they couldn't find soldiers. He went on to become a Captain before resigning."

"Mister Prime Minister, I'm sorry but I don't understand how the two stories connect."

"Like my daughter the people of this nation are screaming out that they don't need us to be their parents anymore and the more we try the more they resent us. If we fail to treat them as equals they will become like my great-great grandfather. They will fight regardless of how scary this new world appears and will continue to fight against all odds. Gentlemen, we have to let go, or risk murdering our own citizens to win a war we cannot win. I will not authorize our troops to kill our own citizens, unless they attack us first."

The Prime Minister releases the contraction of his muscles keeping him upright and falls into the back of the chair. "Hhhhhh, I have spoken to all of my colleagues personally and have instructed them all to leave the cities and hold fast at their cottages or second homes in the country. They are no more inclined to stay than I am. The last thing we want is more families suffering because of our reluctance to submit."

Sliding to the edge of his seat the General shouts, "Mister Prime Minister that's it? We're just going to give up? What about all the soldiers that died trying to keep this country safe?"

"General, I understand your frustration but I believe this is what is best for our people. When the time comes I will relinquish my title, and I ask that you do the same."

"Mister Prime Minister, it's not that simple. We are part of a global political group fighting against this terrorist group. We can't just pull out. There are people depending on us."

"General, negotiations have already begun. There are other countries conceding as well. As you can see by my shirt I was in the kitchen helping out right before you got here. Before returning to your base could I interest you in staying for supper? If you need to work I can open up my office. There you will have access to everything you do while at the CCC."

The General stands up and lowers his head. It appears to be out of respect, but in reality it is to conceal the smirk on his face, "Mister Prime Minister, I really must return to the base of operations, thank you."

The Prime Minister stands up. "I understand, General. Gentlemen, if you could excuse me, I have years of catching up to do with my children."

He shakes both of their hands, and exits the room speaking to his aide, "Clint would you be so kind to escort the General out?"

"Of course, sir."

"Thank you," the PM responds, closing the door behind him.

Clint looks at Izzov knowing exactly what he's thinking, "Okay Tom, we don't have any time to waste."

Buttoning up a navy blue wool military style double-breasted jacket Reficuel covers up his off white knit sweater. Black jeans extend from the bottom of his jacket leading to a pair of stylish shoes. Greased back hair loosely rests in long strands on top and along the sides of his narrow head. Sunglasses glide effortlessly over his ears as he swaggers from his room proceeding to the conference room. He greets saluting officers walking the grounds, "Great evening gentlemen!"

"Reficuel, wait up!" Renniks commands, increasing his stride length and speed.

"Colonel Renniks, are you ready to make history?"

"Born ready." Renniks holds the door open to the conference room allowing Reficuel to enter first.

Breaking through the threshold Reficuel spots Lieutenant Paula Connie standing around a table with a number of officers. Colonel Renniks bumps her shoulder with his hand leaving it on her body, "Lieutenant, after we're done making history tonight, how about you and me make history."

Reaching up, she slides her smooth skinned hand over his and gently cups it. All of the men around the table start laughing. She twists her body with a slight pivot, cracking the ligaments in Renniks' arm buckling him at the knees. Now facing him, pressing down on the joints leading from his wrist, she pushes his arm back forcing him onto his ass and lets go.

"Owww. Total Burn." The men again burst into laughter.

"You certainly have a way with the ladies Renniks," jokes Reficuel.

Renniks face crinkles, glaring at everyone laughing. He recovers from the temporary discomfort she induced on his arm, and shakes it out. Standing up, he straightens his jacket pulling on the bottom.

Connie brushes them off, gesturing with her hand, "This is not about history, this is about the present. I don't have time for idle chit chat. If that is your game, please see the reporter, she is here to document your history. Now if you don't mind Colonel, Mister Nomed, I would like to go back to my work."

Sheepishly Reficuel and Colonel Renniks walk over to where Carrie Warren is being fitted with her recording devices. She is in a better mood and has gathered her composure since the plane trip. With the buzz of activity she realizes why she loves covering the news. The excitement of this meeting will forever be remembered and she is honoured to be the one chosen to cover it. And not from a distance, she is going to stand right there and watch the entire process. Beaming, she greets Reficuel and Renniks with a big smile. Her eyes radiate with energy, sparkling under the artificial lighting, "Don't you guys look good Mr. Nomed, Colonel Renniks."

Rebounding from his humiliating experience with Paula, Reficuel is now full of himself once again, "Thank you, Ms. Warren, I feel good about today."

Glancing back at Lieutenant Paula Connie, not getting a moment of her attention, he turns and continues speaking to Carrie.

Rattling doors, stomping feet, and jovial voices sing out as the unobstructed sun streaks through the spaces between homes across Seattle streets. A warm front gently blows in from the ocean encouraging curious minds to join in the festivities. Men, women and children walk through the streets banging on every door inviting more out of their homes and into the celebration congesting the downtown core.

Resounding thumps on Colin's front door wake the trio. The former SEAL peers out the curtained second floor window. His eyes spot a host of people standing in his postage stamp sized front yard spilling out on the sidewalk. Just beyond his fenced front yard, hundreds walk by, "Guys it's one of my neighbours, the one from the Freedom Movement meetings. Just a sec. Frank's here too. I can't see his face but he's the only guy that looks like a three hundred year old zombie."

The neighbour yells out looking up at the windows on the second floor. "Colin. Come on man. This is crazy you gotta get your ass away from that computer. I know you're in there. We aren't leaving until you come out."

Crawling slowly to Colin's side, Miguel whispers, "Oh shit. Colin this is it. You're being called. This is going to be your act of justice to solidify your entry into the SOL."

Quietly Nolin takes off running down the stairs. He scoops up documents on the living room floor and rips his charts and pictures off the wall, shoving them in a box. Lifting the box he returns upstairs skipping risers in his ascent.

The Spaniard spots Captain Nolin's return, "Lorne are we good?"

Breathing heavily Lorne nods.

Orchestrating a plan, Miguel directs while looking out the window, "Okay Colin. Go open the door and see what they want; tell him, you just need to get dressed."

"Are you sure, I could have already left?"

Keeping his voice low, Miguel responds, "I think they've been watching your place. At the very least they know you're home."

"Roger." Wrapping a towel around his waist he covers up his man parts. Colin descends from the second floor. Cracking open the front door, the neighbour immediately announces, "Mr. Brunet, I knew you were home. Go grab Miguel. We have to go."

The former Colonel's ears perk up. He initiates his descent in his boxer shorts, making eye contact with Colin. As if by telepathy Colin knows exactly what Miguel is thinking, 'These guys are definitely Sons of Liberty, how else would they know he was here with Colin.'

Grabbing the door opening it further, Miguel displays his red boxer shorts greeting everyone standing at the front door, "Hey guys."

The neighbour looks him up and down, "Nice shorts. Come on, we have to go."

"Give us a break, we just woke up. Can we get dressed at least? Five minutes?" Colin pleaded.

Grabbing a pot of coffee, Miguel fills it up with water asking, "Does anyone want coffee? I'm going to start a fresh pot."

The neighbour glances back at Frank who has his back to the house, "No, I'm good. We really must hurry."

Patting his neighbour on the back the inventor understands, "Yeah, yeah of course."

Miguel runs upstairs in his boxer shorts, leaving Colin with the uninvited guests.

Looking over his neighbour's receding hair line, the former SEAL observes Frank's bony neck pivoting from left to right watching the masses pass him.

Reaching the upstairs room, Mejia spots Nolin inside his bedroom capturing their images on the surveillance camera mounted to the outside of the home. Snatching crumpled jeans from the floor Miguel snaps them out straight. He jumps into his pants and fastens his belt. He bends forward and picks up a t-shirt and sweater off the floor, pulling them over his head. He hears, "Psst."

Looking over at his friend, Miguel sees a miniature device resting in his outstretched palm. Grabbing it from Lorne's hand he pushes it into his front pants pocket. Walking toward the door he stops and backs up a couple paces. Sidestepping towards his bed he kisses his fingers and touches the framed picture of his children on his night stand.

Stretching over his bed, Miguel's hand slides under his pillow. Moving from side to side his hand stops. He pulls it back. In his hand is the vintage firearm. Quietly he removes the magazine, checks for ammunition and replaces it into the handle of the gun. Tucking it into the small of his back, he slowly returns down the stairs. Feeling the metal handle of the gun grating his skin, he reaches behind and tucks in his t-shirt providing a little barrier.

Reaching the bottom riser Colin winks at Miguel and steps away, "If you could excuse me."

Walking over to the sink Miguel cracks a banana from the bunch. "You guys should have given us a heads up. A little text like, 'hey we're coming over'."

Glaring at Miguel the neighbour responds, "You should just count yourself lucky, period."

Miguel pauses, wiggling his fingers around the metal fridge handle, delaying his pull, imagining a satisfying mental image, *bludgeoning him using this handle, would be messy but gratifying.* Opening the fridge and grabbing the milk Miguel turns around smiling at the man now standing in the entrance and slaps the container of milk on the counter. Ripping open his banana he stares down the man. Chomping down on the textured white surface Miguel garbles out, "I do, do you?"

The man scoffs blowing out air from the corner of his mouth. He turns around looking up the stairs. "Hey what happened here?" Pointing to an array of broken porcelain over the living room floor.

Miguel glimpses over, "I accidently knocked something off the table." The Spaniard opens the cupboard over the stove and pulls down two thermos mugs filling them with a potent mixture of black syrup. Colin's massive quads rumble the flight of stairs as he sprints down fully dressed. Handing Colin a mug the duo's eyes lock for a moment.

"Okay. Great. Let's go." The former Colonel says as he lowers himself down tying his shoes. Standing up he grabs the remaining banana and shoves it into his mouth. Snatching his mug from the counter he walks out the door. Colin follows closely behind pausing for a moment to lock the door. People walking by cheer seeing more recruits for the rally join in.

Miguel stops and looks around. His eyes widen thinking to himself, *this is suicide. My face is going to be captured by the pentagon within seconds being out here with all these people. Hopefully the Vancouver incident will keep the military out of the celebration.*

The neighbour questions Miguel, "What's wrong with you?"

Speaking with a mouthful of banana Miguel mumbles out, "Nothing just surprised at all the people taking part in this."

"History in the making my friend. History in the making."

Frank turns around grinning from ear to ear.

With every step along the patio stone walkway the gun shifts, stabbing Miguel in the back. Reaching the street, walking past Frank, Miguel runs his hand along the bottom seam of his sweater by his back. His index finger tucks under the cotton cover grazing the blue steel frame, adjusting it slightly.

Choking down his banana Miguel winces as an unchewed portion gradually slides down his throat.

The neighbour asks, "Colin, I've followed your directions but I'm still having problems with the power converter. I keep shorting out, do you think you will be able to come over and take a look at it?"

"Power converter eh? Hmmm. You know what that could be? That could be the solenoid. Are you sure you connected the solenoid properly? If you didn't..."

The Spaniard smiles listening to Colin entertain their courters speaking about his invention. It was only hours ago Colin had a much different tune –

> "What are you saying Nolin? That they're only using me." Colin shouted lunging at Lorne seated on his dining room chair.

> Lorne calmly replies looking his friend in the eyes, "I'm not hiding anything, you've heard what I said. It speaks for itself."

> Colin relinquishes his aggressive stance, walking away. With a sweep of his hand he threw a lamp off an end table against a wall, shattering and

shooting debris throughout the living room, "They're using me!"

"They're using everybody. Yachts, marinas, islands, countries, it's a worldwide operation."

Sitting on the very edge of his couch, Colin's legs started shaking, with his hands clenched into fists, "I'll kill them. I'll kill every last one of them."

Miguel rolls out a map over top of Lorne's mess of papers across the table top, and starts plotting using a marker. "Lorne, are you sure?"

Nolin's head snaps around glaring at Miguel who continues to speak, "I was just checking, because based on everything that's happened, the world has been divided into quadrants, and North America is the last piece of the puzzle."

"Of course, but let me solidify some of this supposition before we do anything that we might regret. Colonel Pegrum is flying out to meet me and he's bringing his Pentagon computer tomorrow."

Trees flash past the windows of the stretched limousine. There is absolutely no road noise heard inside this sanctuary.

"Huh." A lone male grunts as a television deliberately protrudes from the limousine's bar cabinet, with its screen already activated.

Carrie's image comes into focus as her voice continues without pause, "...large crowds gather in downtown cores in cities around the world, contravening martial law. Seen here, ecstatic celebrations erupted when Reficuel and the Vancouver community leader shook hands, restoring energy back to the city. Everywhere, festivities continue with new hope of a change in governments. Vancouver is now an example of courage, hope and determination."

A picture of Reficuel takes to the screen. A video montage scrolls showing the billionaire shaking hands with world leaders at different times and places, "Leading the procession of praise for the Vancouver movement is the CEO of the world's largest energy corporation among his other assets, Reficuel Nomed. His controversial stance has been heavily criticized by politicians at all levels however his support among the commoners is gaining ground like an avalanche. Whether it is his constant charity work that inspires others into action or his laborious commitment to working until a project is done, barely into his forties Reficuel has developed his businesses with respect and admiration from all. When asked what his secret to success was, he calmly replied, "I will let you know when I get there." Chuckling, "Seriously though, there's always more I can do, I constantly strive to push myself to work harder, and it doesn't hurt to be very lucky either. That's why I commit to help out when and where I can."

"An extremely modest position, for the world's poster boy for success and generosity," Carrie responds.

"So where did this icon of industry develop?" Carrie's face fades into flashing pictures of Reficuel and his younger self, "Raised in an American military family he moved around the world, adapting in every city devoting himself to soaking up the language, culture and customs. While attending fine schools abroad, Reficuel gained friendships with the children of powerful people who took him in as one of their own despite his families' meagre financial situation."

Charity organization emblems litter the screen, "Without knowing it, these relations gave him his first beginnings where he put his nose to the grind stone and worked his way to the top. During his rise, Reficuel maintained his family's traditions of giving both time and money to the destitute. He himself began various charitable organizations which have grown to help many around the world."

The images fade away showing Carrie's face again, "Now people everywhere are beginning to see Reficuel Nomed as more than a just corporate image but as a natural leader and one who will change the political landscape of this world for years to come..."

The television screens fades to black, eliminating most of the ambient light illuminating the cabin of the limousine. Coming into the light is a lone male figure preparing to have a conversation with someone on the other side of the earpiece, "Call Christopher," he directs.

The ringing of the phone is answered abruptly by Christopher almost in a panic, "Yes sir!"

"Christopher, very good PR work. I really like Kyle, he was a good choice. I was a little concerned how quickly things got out of hand before we were ready, but it looks like you managed to keep a lid on it."

"Thank you, sir."

Pulling a piece of paper off a printer the man folds it in three sliding it into an envelope, "Make sure you tell your friend to come see me. We don't have much time now."

"Of course, sir."

Frank moves through the crowd smiling, patting people's backs and shaking hands. Miguel stands being bumped and moved as people shuffle through the streets. *This is our test, recruiting new members to his basement Freedom Movement meetings? What is this guy up to?*

The skeleton of a man is lifted by his drones onto a transit shelter. Like a conductor working an orchestra, Frank's arms flail about as he screams at the top of his lungs, "Who is the one man that can bring change to this corrupt society? Who is the one man who, through his actions, has supported us and shown us to fight for what we believe in?"

Punching his fists into the air, Frank yells, "Reficuel! Reficuel! Reficuel!"

The energy through the crowd builds as they follow along chanting. Firecrackers start popping as screams and stomping feet shake the ground, "Reficuel! Reficuel! Reficuel!"

Miguel grins nodding looking over at Colin. The former SEAL looks down at his phone and looks over at Miguel, winking while joining the crowd in the chanting.

The Spaniard reads his friend's response, 'I'm starting to believe my Sasquatch friend more and more.'

Staring at the scarecrow's feeble limbs gaining the strength of thousands, Miguel types out a message to Nolin, 'Start packing. We're leaving tonight.' Miguel's eyes catch Frank's for a second, *This is going to hurt more than you know.*

CHAPTER TWELVE

Acid burns through Connie's mucus membrane disintegrating her thin stomach wall. Another growl reminds the Lieutenant that her body is devouring itself, starved from real sustenance. Torturing ideas invade her mind knowing that she isn't out of the woods yet. She would have to endure at least another hour of political stroking before being able to escape. She props her upper body up with her hands on her hips and attempts to push past the shooting pain invading her mid section as her nose detects the culinary scents emanating from the mess hall. *It isn't going to end well for anyone if I don't get something to eat soon.* Her stomach snarls at her again as she recognizes the odour of barbeque chicken, clasping her belt buckle, "Oh man."

"Did you say something Lieutenant?" A male officer wearing Captain insignias on his tunic asks.

Touching her stomach, "Negative, sir. Gentlemen, if you could excuse me?"

The hum of chatter fades into sporadic cheers and yelps over the base as she leaves the Conference Hall.

"Congratulations Lieutenant Connie." An officer exclaims as he slows and begins to extend his hand.

Gaining momentum, Paula marches passed the officer in full stride speaking out of the side of her mouth, "Thank you, sir."

Finally reaching the mess hall, the Lieutenant enters a long line up, "Oh great."

Standing in line, waiting her turn, Connie hears the typical mess hall banter of several voices speaking. Instead of the normal male bravado occupying the air space, her ears keep pinging with the sound of, 'Reficuel this, and Reficuel that.'

Entering the kitchen she reads the options written in colourful calligraphy, 'Chicken Delicacy or Smoked Salmon compliments of Reficuel.' Grumbling, she proceeds to grab her food. Walking out of the kitchen Connie slides into a seat, finally taking a break. Beside her, a table full of men discuss politics.

"Reficuel seems like if he could, he would do something about this whole world situation."

"I can't believe him."

"What are you talking about?"

"Will you let me finish? I can't believe him, how he walked around talking to everybody asking how we are coping with everything. No one else has asked us. Not once have our supervisors ever done that."

"You're right. What, we're just supposed to carry on and pretend that the Vancouver riot never happened?"

"Exactly, not only did he ask questions but he listened and responded without worrying about some made up political answer."

"Give respect, get respect."

"And he understands what's it's like to be on our side."

"He should, his dad was military."

"That's one guy that I would vote for."

"Yeah, me too."

"Awwwww." Connie sounds off, chomping down on her last piece of chicken, ripping it from her fork. With only half a bun remaining on her plate she glances around the room at her smiling co-workers. The food filling her stomach hasn't changed her mood. *Am I being overly critical? Why does he make my stomach turn? After all, he has it all, looks, money, fame.*

A magazine left on the table beside her features Reficuel on the cover. 'Poster boy of the future; what makes this billionaire tick?' Pushing the magazine away, she sits there for a half a second before she reaches across the table pulling it back. Opening it up, she reads Reficuel's story. 'Charities...'

"What? He gave away how much?" She moved her head even closer to the print. Closing the magazine, 'Just the thought of Renniks cozying up to Reficuel makes me want to vomit.'

A group of five privates walk towards an empty table next to her. The scowl on her face warded them off. She turns her head looking at them continue to another table. *Am I a bitch to everyone? After every-thing Reficuel's done I treat him like shit.*

> Paula's mind flashes back to only a couple of minutes ago when she was in the conference room. The billionaire walked up behind her as she was monitoring the pickup truck with the white mast on it travelling back towards the city, "Lieutenant, I just wanted to thank you. You have kept me safe in Toronto and now in Vancouver. Would you join me for a drink tonight?"
>
> "Mr. Nomed."
>
> "Before you say no, understand that this is strictly professional. At the end of any successful business venture I always celebrate. At least let me buy you one drink."
>
> "Strictly professional?"
>
> "Absolutely. Just one drink."
>
> "So everyone is going to be there then."
>
> "No, this is me personally thanking the one person responsible for truly running the ship."
>
> "Okay."
>
> "Very well, eight o'clock tonight."

Grabbing the remaining half bun off her plate, she pulls at it tearing chunks off. Popping them into her mouth she contemplates what she is going to talk to him about during their 'one drink'.

A lone officer enters the mess hall with quick long strides and slides off his hat. Gasping for air, he scans the room. His eyes lock onto Connie, and he rushes to her side out of breath with a flushed face.

Paula stands dropping the remaining chunk of bread, "Yes Corporal, what is it?"

"Lieutenant, Reficuel has just left. He wanted me to tell you he had forgotten about an important engagement that he really must attend to."

"Who authorized the landing and departure of his personal aircraft on the base?"

"Colonel Renniks."

"That...that...that." Putting her head down, she it rocks it from side to side. Picking up her food tray, she releases it clanging against the table. Taking in a deep breath, she tilts her head back up seeing the Corporal's eyes widen, "That will be all, Corporal."

Grabbing her tray, Connie walks over to dispose of it mumbling to herself, "That son of a bitch. I've had it with his bullshit."

Her boots pound the ground with each step. Short, forced breaths exit her mouth as her eyes skim over the faces of those in her path. Like pin tumblers aligning in a lock mechanism, her mind unlocks the chain of events with perfect clarity. Her stride shortens and sluggishly she comes to a stop. "If Renniks and Reficuel want to play underhanded, so can I."

Connie resumes movement diverting herself toward the base's command center with a sinister smile.

Back at work, alone at the dining room table, Nolin hears his phone ring. Patting down the papers strewn over the table top he locates a familiar bump. Digging through the pile, Lorne finds his device and easily translates a coded text from Colonel Pegrum, 'IF u See Mxw = WS u.' "Oh shit they picked up Miguel in Seattle!"

Nolin stands up pacing back and forth. He clears out of that screen and prepares to send a message when his phone vibrates in his hand displaying a new message, "What is going on?"

Reading the new message, 'MC u Want SU u 2 seek.' "Come on Miguel get your face out of there, you're better than that. Look around they have you surrounded."

The Captain again clears out of the screen. He types and sends a message when a third message rings through. Before opening up the message he hopes aloud, "Please tell me you guys made it out of there."

Reading the message wavers the large military veteran. 'SU u has ppl there = AOD u.'

The screen becomes blurry as his hand flutters. He lowers his phone stumbling through the living room, collapsing on a chair, "Son of a bitch. It's over."

Tossing the phone onto the table, his eyes skim through the room. His mind tries to decipher recent events, when he notices the screen on his phone still activated. "What the hell?"

Curiously he leans forward reading the screen, "Message Sent?"

Grabbing the phone Lorne presses a button with no response. He presses another, and another and another, "Oh no. Fuck. Fuck. Fuck!"

Running upstairs he enters Miguel's room and spots the framed picture of his kids. Snatching it off of the night stand, he runs down the hall grabs a large mountaineering backpack and returns downstairs. Frantically Nolin throws whatever he can into his bag. Jogging out the door he hears it slam behind him as he glances back at the house. "Sorry guys." Sprinting down the street, he keeps scanning his surroundings.

Eyeing his phone Pegrum starts taping the screen with no response. He looks up. Staring at him from the front of the room a five star General nods his way, "Colonel Ryan Pegrum, is there something you want to tell us?"

Coping with the ensuing pressure headache crushing his mind Ryan closes his eyes, "Fucking assholes."

"I'm sorry Colonel I didn't hear that."

Looking at his General, Pegrum's mind solves the mystery of the questions, *Why all of a sudden was I required to stay in Washington? Why was this meeting so important?*

The glass walls encircling the room allowed Ryan to see the Military Police advancing. Calculating the odds of surviving a fight out here, Pegrum stands up, places his phone on the table top and raises his hands out to the sides, "Just get it done General."

Wearing his running gear, Hamilton sneaks out the back door to face glacier coated mountains. Stepping onto the path during this early evening, the General's cushioned soles crunch the crystallized earth under his weight while an ocean breeze sweeps the fresh aroma of pine trees into his nose. Pressing start on his wrist stopwatch, the military leader sets his limbs into motion. Immediately, the aches and pains of a wretched career infuse his body with each stride, haunting every ligament, reminding him where missions had gone awry, faces killed, and the games played.

This was much needed alone time. He refused to allow the mental torture he'd put himself through and the wisdom he'd acquired to be lost in a sea of gray. After a full day pouring over intelligence information, all the countries' delegates retired to the lounge for cocktails and networking. A necessary evil, however, tonight the General decided he would get his run in before eating and then indulge in a fine bottle of Brandy, complemented with hand rolled cigars and political gossip.

Fifty-nine minutes displayed on the General's watch as he rounds a mountain range with the base meters in front of him. Picking up his pace, sweat streams down his face, his knees crack shooting pain up his body. Bearing down Hamilton lowers his head for a moment absorbing the anguish of speeding up. "Aw. Aw. Aw." Looking down at his watch he urges his body to go faster. A formidable gust of wind knocks him backwards.

Hamilton's eyes quiver trying to focus through distorted vision. A high pitch ringing fills his ears. "AWWWWW!"

Agony sheers through his body. Pain pulses from his right arm. Lethargically turning his head to the side, he sees a massive mangled piece of sedimentary rock crushing his strong hand. Swallowing deep Hamilton tastes blood running down his throat. Monstrous flames replace the once solid building with its debris coating the ground in front of him.

Slowly Hamilton rolls his body towards the stone and his pinned arm. Flexing his abs he raises his feet and lays them against the rock. He braces himself accepting the pain engulfing his mind and body. His rubber soles squeak as he wiggles them into position on the stone's surface. Grimacing, he mentally prepares for the ensuing torture. Thrusting his legs straight his body slides across the icy surface yanking and tearing his arm's ligaments and muscles, "FUCK!"

Dropping his feet, lying on his side, the blood from his nose runs down his cheek as he watches emergency vehicle lights dance in the night sky...

The pulse of an electronic device pulls Miguel's attention away from the crowd of people around him in downtown Seattle. Reading the message on its lit screen, he shuffles his feet to a stop. 'NURu IFu!'

The coded words seize his mind while his core muscles tighten. Juggling eyes rise, fully cognizant of the situation he finds himself in. Jostling bodies knock him about as Miguel scans the faces in the crowd. Elevated above the hordes standing on a bench was Frank.

With his arm extended holding his phone he records Miguel's movements in the crowd. "That piece of shit!"

Snapping his head frontwards Miguel spots Colin corralled by the Sons of Liberty deeper in the crowd. The former SEAL looks back at Miguel with a look of panic in his eyes and yells, "GO!"

Hurling his phone in the air Miguel jets in the opposite direction. The plastic chunk of hardware tumbles through space finding its mark: Frank's face – just above his eye.

Battling against the current of people walking through the street, he moves his body around those in the crowd. Occasionally leaping up, his head swivels from side to side, scanning faces. Looking to the sky he spots a helicopter. "Oh shit." With his head up, he accidentally bumps into a group of males wearing leather jackets.

Someone yells out, "Take it easy buddy," followed by a shove. Knocked off balance, he collides with someone else. Catching himself, clinging to a leather jacket, Miguel starts to stand up when they shout, "Slow down asshole." And a hand punches him in the face. He hits the ground on all fours tasting the blood coating his gums. The crowd laughs.

Shaking off the punch, Miguel stands looking behind him. His dark eyes spot a head flowing against the masses following his lead. The Spaniard tries to cut through the mob when a big burly man steps in his path and points in the opposite direction, "Little man, everyone is moving that way. Now start stepping."

Glancing over his shoulder Miguel sees the approaching hit man when he feels the large man jabbing his chest shouting, "Go on. Move it little man."

The crowd forms a circle around him. Unknown faces smile in anticipation of the confrontation. Miguel licks his bloody lips and steps up to the grinning burly man who spouts out, "What are you gonna do little man?"

Thick red spit flies from Miguel's mouth covering the burly man's face. Simultaneously the Spaniard's sinks his knee deep into big man's midsection. The man crashes to the ground with a thud. Immediately, the crowd disperses bunching behind Miguel holding off the trailing attacker, as the former prisoner runs away.

Dodging around a family walking with their children, Miguel trips over the stroller's wheels and falls to the ground. His gun escapes from his waistband and slides across the pavement. A female yells, "Gun!"

He springs to his feet, moving toward the hardware when a hand grabs him by the collar yanking him backwards poking a stiff piece of metal into his kidneys. "Gotcha Colonel! Move and you're a dead man. Eagle, this is Wolf, I've got him, Charlie team move in on my location."

The bulging mass starts yelling, "Cop! Cop! Cop!"

Closing in, forming a wall of human flesh, the crowd circles around Miguel and Wolf. The hit man's eyes widen gaining intensity realizing his peril. He radio's for help, "Wolf to Charlie team I'm about to fight a mob. Move in. Move in now!"

Miguel sweeps his hand behind his back grabbing the gun hand. He moves it away as a bullet fires out ricocheting off the ground. The crowd drops and starts panicking, separating. Miguel lowers his body and twists, releasing the henchman's grip on his clothes. An executed elbow strike lands across the man's jaw incapacitating him. Releasing the limp body, Miguel scoops up Wolf's gun and dodges as a red laser sight loses him through the crowd.

Fast approaching a flea market area, tents line both sides of the road. Miguel sees a male's eyes light up and focus on his movements. The man is alone and speaking openly but he isn't wearing a headset. Miguel keeps glancing back but the guy isn't approaching. Pivoting around Miguel spots more young, well built men slow from a run and enter the market. Their heads pan from side to side. Ducking under the canopies of cloth, Miguel moves from one booth to the next as the men congregate and start their approach.

Walking away from the Sons of Liberty flowing with the crowd, Colin is followed closely by Frank.

Pressing his hand against his face, Frank tries to stop the bleeding as he warns the former SEAL, "Colin you have every right as a Freedom member to walk away, but as a Son of Liberty you're in it 'til death do you part."

Halting his movements, Colin faces the confident scrawny man standing behind him. Frank smiles, "You don't have a choice. You're a great asset but don't make me have to tell you a second time."

All of a sudden Frank is bent over. His one hand flat on the ground holds his body from falling over onto the pavement while the other grips his abdomen. Frank's stomach is forcing gut-wrenching sounds out of his mouth. Colin provided no warning before delivering a devastating jab to the thin man's solar plexus. Now gasping for air, trying to relax the contraction of his diaphragm, Frank's head is only a couple feet from the ground. Reaching down grasping his throat Colin squeezes the remaining life right out of his puny body.

Straightening out his feeble frame Colin forces Frank to look him in the eyes, "You Son of a Bitch!"

Out of his peripheral Colin catches the Sons of Liberty rushing to Frank's rescue. Releasing the slimy creature from his clutches, Brunet takes off running as fast as he can, leaping over obstacles along the way.

Standing over someone working their computer terminal in the middle of the Vancouver base Command Center, Paula Connie surveys the hive of activity. Hearing the chime on her cellular device she grabs it, reading the message. Her hand transforms into a claw. Her fingernails grate against the smooth plastic as she marches out of the room.

A strange sensation overcomes her chest. It was as though someone shoved their hand through her rib cab and was squeezing her heart. Her eyes glaze over, she blinks clearing the excess fluid reading the message again.

'A bombing in Greenland has devastated the Joint Forces Intelligence group. Among the dead stationed at this facility was General David Hamilton of the Canadian military.'

Hamilton's voice breaks the silence, "Lieutenant Connie what are you still doing here, I told you to go home."

Computer keys jingle under her quick hands as she navigates through piles of information, "Yes sir I know but there are a bunch of people depending on me to finish this on time."

Cautiously approaching her, Hamilton lowers his voice, "Lieutenant, Paula, your brother just died. I think we can manage until you come back."

Standing up walking over to a wall sized monitor, Connie begins plotting, "General Hamilton with all due respect I'd rather keep working and prevent more people from dying than take time off and spend it in a funeral home."

"Lieutenant, that's an order not a request. Your family needs you more than we do right now. Don't let them down. If I catch you back in here before Monday I will personally court martial you."

Paula's jaw clenches as she looks to the sky, "Don't worry General, I won't let you down."

The doorway of a sliding pocket door fills with the presence of an elegant woman's body. Turning to close the door, she exposes her profile identifying herself as Ms. Lindsay. With the door closed she begins approaching an illuminated desk top on the opposite side of the room. Reaching the area she walks behind a man standing at the table's side. His head was above a desk top light focused on the table. Resting her hand on his shoulder, she leans over whispering in his ear, "Everything is in place. There are a couple of loose ends that should be resolved shortly."

The robust male removes an envelope from his pocket handing it to Jasmine, "Excellent. Ms. Lindsay ensure that the angels do their thing. Get this to Shane immediately."

The rotten egg smell of burnt sulphur lingers in the air as night swoops over Seattle. Explosions are met with a cheer from the droves of people filtering through the streets seeing the colourful streams of light descend from the sky. As more fireworks burst, crowds start chanting, "Reficuel. Reficuel."

Wrapping a shawl around his head and body Miguel's heart pounds against his chest as he walks out from a tent. Joining the masses filtering through the streets he attempts to make a stealthy escape. Approaching a group of military and police officers coming to arrest him, he lowers his head. Looking down at his blue jeans and running shoes exposed from the bottom of the shawl, he hopes with his face covered he will be able to pass by undetected. Captured in his peripheral Miguel sees undercover teams in plain clothes invade booths. Approaching the outer perimeter a number of men stand scanning faces. Miguel leans against a large man stumbling along the street drinking a beer. The man wraps his arm around Miguel and grabs his ass, "H-h-hey hon-honey, I like, I like your dress."

Miguel tucks his head against the man's chest. The man pulls him in tight, yelling "Ref. Ref. Ref."

Skirting through the check point Miguel keeps walking with his escort.

Away from eyesight, lost in the crowd, the Spaniard spins out of the large man clutches speaking normally, "Thanks buddy."

Snapping knees and an aching back remind the former Colonel of how long it's been since he was this busy. *Staying active is easier than slowing down.* Still wrapped in the shawl, Miguel crouches in a darkened corner watching the front of a home. Incense from wood burning fireplaces reminds him of happier days with his boys, hanging out by the lake cooking hotdogs and marshmallows. A tear rolls down his face. "I'll come see you guys soon, I promise."

The murmur of voices and the creaking of a door redirects Miguel's attention. Leisurely, people began showing up and entering the home. The Spaniard coaxes himself to have patience, *Hold on. Just hold on.* Occupying the time, he starts methodically disassembling and assembling his new gun barely making a sound.

"Dad, can I try?"

"Me too Dad, can I try?"

Turning around Miguel sees two bright-eyed boys standing behind him in their pyjamas, "Hey, aren't you guys supposed to be in bed? Mom's going to kill me if you guys get dirty."

"Please, Dad, we'll be careful. We promise."

Pulling out two stools, he slaps the tops, "Sure, but one at a time."

The older boy props himself up on one stool with a huge toothless grin, "Dad, what do I do first?"

Miguel grabs the younger one and picks him up, sitting him down on the stool on the other side, "Remember, never point a gun at anyone. And anytime you touch a gun you have to make sure it's not loaded, so pull that back."

"Can you help me?"

"Of course."

The youngster tugs at Miguel's shirt, "Love you Dad."

Hours passed without motion. The torture of distant memories flood over Miguel, reminding him of his passes and fails as a father. The sound of an elongating spring followed by the snap of the door awoke Miguel out of his daydream. Looking at the screen door Miguel watches men and women exit the residence going their separate ways. As quickly as they exited the residence they vanished in the darkness.

Cupping his watch the former inmate checks the time, *the witching hour is almost here.*

Stretching from side to side, Miguel closes his eyes, taking several deep breaths. Replacing the slide back on his gun, he locks it in place and inserts the magazine. Someone leaving the residence walks by. He drops to the ground, concealing his position. As they pass, he starts to crawl across the neighbour's lawn when the front door opens one more time. Jerking to a stop, he looks around. Out walks a thin tall man. His gait and movement clearly identify him as Frank. Miguel lowers himself back down maintaining his visual of the thin man, *where are you going now?*

The door snaps closed again, walking on the front porch was another man. Backlighting prevented Miguel from seeing any features other than it is a man and he is short and stocky.

"Wait up," yells the unidentified man.

Proceeding to the backyard Frank calls back, "Come on, hurry up."

The unidentified man runs down the stairs following Frank's lead to a detached double car garage located in the back yard. Miguel's heart races and sweat begins to trickle down his forehead as he reigns in his enthusiasm, *whoa easy there. Slow down. Let them get settled.*

Leading his movements with his handgun, Miguel creeps through the shadows. The hum of an exhaust fan drowns out the sand crunching under his feet. Reaching the side door of the garage he sees the motion sensor light staring down at him. Each move he makes is snail slow, preventing the light from turning on. Peripheral vision constantly scopes out his surroundings, keeping his movements undetectable. Inching towards the side door, Miguel stops. He hears the door rattle followed by a scraping sound. Raising his gun smoothly toward the noise, he prepares for the moment. The sound dissipates away from the door going deeper into the garage.

Standing beside the door, Miguel slowly twists the door knob compressing the metal springs in the handle. The mechanism releases. Holding the door from opening, he takes a couple of deep breaths listening to his thumping heart, *one, two, three.*

Pouncing through the opening into the garage the former Colonel quickly scans the room with his firearm raised. Not a soul could be seen. A very bright light shines from the ground at the far end of the room. Miguel's head swivels back and forth around the room as he crosses to the other side. Looking in the direction of the bright lights, Miguel sees a hidden basement under the cement floor.

Nearly blinded, Miguel pauses for moment as his eyes adjust to the brilliance. Step by step the Spaniard enters the belly of the beast. His eyes notice a homemade door constructed with thick plastic vapour barrier stretched over a wood frame. A skunk smell begins to make itself known.

Miguel hears Frank ask, "What do you think?"

"This is the best yet."

"I'm glad you approve."

"What do the other guys think?"

"Do you care?"

"No, not really."

Miguel recognizes the second male's voice, *it's the voice that vouched for me at the bonfire.* Opening the door with speed, he gets inside and sees what he smelled only seconds ago, a marijuana grow operation. The two men tending to the plants are smoking a joint laughing, oblivious to his presence. He approaches, gun in hand announcing, "Get on the fucking ground!"

Petrified, both men jump and turn. As the second male's face comes into focus Miguel's expression changes from pissed off to that of disappointment and shock.

"Shane?"

Shane stands there frozen. Frank smirks, snapping Miguel back into action, "I said GET ON THE GROUND!"

The former Colonel punches Frank's face using the barrel end of the gun, folding his feeble frame.

Seated on his behind, Frank rubs his forehead rocking his body back and forth, "Humf…You're a dead man Miguel. You hear me? YOU ARE A DEAD MAN!"

Shane dressed in a white wife beater shirt and jeans, slowly lowers himself keeping his hands raised.

> Miguel's mind races back in time… dressed in brand new military fatigues standing inside a Quonset hut with bunk beds lining the room as far as the eye could see, a young man shoots out his hand, "Miguel is it? I'm Shane, Shane Miller. Looks like were sharing a bunk for the next few months. You want top or bottom?"

Miguel looks at the man now before him. The years have not been kind. Although still stocky and well built, track marks cover his arms and scars age his face. He reminds Miguel of several embalmed members he had seen over his years. Gray hairs secured their dominance, taking over his once brown locks.

Shane runs his hand across the marks on his arms, "Yeah, these are new. After Christa died I had a bad go."

Frank touches the side of his head with his fingers, and pulls them away covered in blood, "Where were you when he had to bury his wife and unborn child?"

"Frank, that's enough," ordered Shane.

Miguel lowers his gun, "Shane I tried finding where you moved to."

Sitting back on his calves as if in a dojo, Shane consoles him, "Miguel, don't worry about it. A lot has changed since then."

Raising his gun up, Miguel spins around quickly and comes back on Frank. He was partially comforted that the noise he heard was only the oscillating fans shaking the plants, "Shane, I want to help you."

The junky's eyes bulge out of his skull, "No Miguel! You can't! How are you going to help me? Are you going to take away that empty stabbing pain that I feel every fucking day?"

Lowering his gun down to one side Miguel squats down, "Shane, listen, I know how you…"

"Miguel! Don't! You can't…you can't…You can't even help yourself! The Sons of Liberty are going to change everything so that no one ever has to go through what I did."

Pointing at Frank with his gun the Spaniard tries to educate his old friend, "These guys are the disease destroying everything right now, and before that, they killed how many people with Planet X or whatever kind of drugs they could get their hands on."

Calmed down, resting on his heels Shane responds, "They have done more for me and this world than you or I ever have."

"That's bullshit and you know it."

"Is the world a better place because of what the great Miguel Mejia did, or did you let me, your wife and your kids down? Wait, you don't have to answer that, I already know."

"Shane not everyone is able to be saved from the years of sub-liminal brain washing," voiced Frank. As Frank continues speaking, Miguel sidesteps a circle around the two checking out the entire operation. Behind plants along the far wall, he caught a glimpse of a room in the back. Inside the room on the table are similar devices that the terrorist bombers used.

Pointing his gun at his friend, Miguel exclaims, "Shane, it was you. You built those bombs."

"Miguel, they let Christa die because of a lawsuit. A fucking lawsuit, Miguel! You know this system needs to be torn down and rebuilt. And I am doing something about it."

Standing up defiantly, with his hands in the air, Shane turns around very slowly until he completes a full rotation. Facing Miguel again, he lowers one hand and pulls out of his pant pocket a pair of white gloves.

"Shane, I'm not screwing around. Get your ass on the ground."

Pulling each glove on very slowly Shane reminisces, "Miguel as you can see I have no weapons. I remember how you used to pray before each mission. I hope you prayed tonight." He starts walking toward Miguel who stood blocking the only exit.

Backing up Miguel pleads, "Shane, sit down. Sit down. Fuck Shane!"

Swallowing deep, keeping his gun on target Miguel pulls the trigger. Without a sound or reaction, Miguel's eyes bulge, catching the fire in Shane's irises. The Spaniard immediately reaches up to rack the slide.

Capitalizing on that split second, Shane's eyes widen focusing on his task. Shooting towards Miguel's body the junky grabs the back of Miguel's legs. In a violently smooth motion Shane slams the former Colonel's back against the cement floor knocking the gun out of his hand.

"Ahhhh." The wind expels out of Miguel's lungs.

Fighting for breath and to survive Miguel kicks at Shane trying to create some distance. The junky squirms over Miguel's body and starts dropping elbows on Miguel's head before he can raise his arms for protection.

Wrapping his legs around Shane's upper body, Miguel tries to keep him at bay while catching his breath. He pulls the junky off of his chest, just as Shane swiftly spins around and slithers out of his grip. The junky gets behind the Spaniard and locks a death grip around his neck. Miguel claws at his arm trying to breathe. Shane's arms are in position and he starts squeezing the life out of the former Colonel. Miguel's one hand pulls at his arm while the other one quickly searches the area. As Miguel's movements begin to slow, Shane pulls harder on his neck suffocating him. Desperately, Miguel starts punching at Shane's arm. Blood starts spraying over their faces.

Releasing his grip Shane yells out, "Awwww!" The Junky examines his mangled forearm impaled with a stake. Shane grabs the piece of bamboo, yanking it out just as Miguel begins to rain down a flurry of fists pounding Shane's head into the cement floor.

Slicing through the air, a shovel ends Miguel's fight for victory and sends his body crashing down. Frank raises the spade above his head again slamming it down on Miguel's back. Shane wobbles to his feet.

Scurrying away, Miguel tries to escape.

Snatching the shovel from Frank's hands Shane orders, "Give me that! Migs, I can't believe you tried to shoot me and you actually stabbed me. After everything we've been through this is the thanks I get."

Slamming the spade against Miguel's legs between words Shane yells, "I thought...we...could...be...partners again.."

With each strike Miguel grunts in agony.

Rolling to his back the Spaniard faces his old friend, "Shane. Just finish it."

"No problem."

Shane drags a plant out sliding it across the floor. He lifts the shovel above his head. "Like father, like sons."

Miguel sprays Shane in the face with a hose, and sweeps his legs, dropping the junky's body onto the ground. The Spaniard rolls over, snatching a plant. In a series of quick movements Miguel wraps the plant around Shane's neck. Coughing, fighting for air, Shane struggles to release the plant from collapsing his Adam's apple. Frank bends over and picks up the discarded shovel.

Scanning the area, Miguel sees Frank fast approaching. He wrenches with every muscle fiber pulling tighter on the plant for a second. With Frank about to strike he kicks Shane's body away and slides across the floor.

Spotting the faulty gun, Miguel lunges his body towards it as the shovel narrowly misses him smashing off the ground.

In the split second it took Frank to raise the shovel realigning his aim, Miguel grabbed the gun and in one motion yanked on the slide racking the action, rolling to his back.

Vertigo sets in on the scrawny man as he stands staring into the barrel's abyss. He collapses onto the floor dropping the shovel.

Shane pulls the plant off his neck and stands up.

Lying on his back Miguel pivots around screaming, "Shane don't. I don't want to kill you."

Shane rips off his shirt revealing a full chest tattoo of a decrepit horsemen with a banner under it 'Pestilence'. Wiping his blurry eyes with his raggedy shirt, he throws it away, sneering, "I always regarded you with a certain level of respect but that is just sad."

Walking over licking his lips, Shane circles around Miguel. Spinning on his back keeping Shane in his sights Miguel has his finger on the trigger. Shane underlines the tattoo banner on his chest, "You're the dead man."

Shane crouches to leap as Miguel pulls the trigger again. Explosion after explosion erupts from the barrel, launching metal rounds through Shane's body causing chunks of the cement above to crumble down. The junky's body falls backwards destroying a couple plants behind him as he lands to the floor.

Miguel limps to his feet grimacing with each step. Hunched over his friend's lifeless body he watches him expel his last breath. The former Colonel peers over his gun sights seeing his old friend's blood coating the untreated cement floor, soaking into the porous surface.

Wheezing and trembling, Frank shimmies across the concrete floor staring at Miguel. The limited colour remaining in Frank's pale skin vanishes as simultaneously his lips turn a shade of blue. The thermometer hanging on the wall shows one hundred degrees Fahrenheit, yet Frank's body continued to quake as though he fell through ice into freezing water.

The tears in Miguel's eyes vaporize as his temper reaches its boiling point.

Frank's eyes lock onto the Spaniard as he breaks the silence, "It's time to pay the reaper!"

CHAPTER THIRTEEN

Torn pieces of beige masking tape grip onto store windows through-out New York's Times Square holding up messages, 'Reficuel, the rightful leader to rule.' Double Decker buses and taxis honk passing by with praise from their passengers...

Walking up the steps towards England's Palace of Westminster a middle-aged man dressed in a suit carries a folded newspaper under his arm with the front page article titled, 'Reficuel: the People's Fuel'...

Signs on wooden stakes wave in the crowd gathered outside of the Taj-Mahal in India that is bellowing out, "Reficuel"...

Marching through Mexico City streets people wear white shirts with smeared black ink messages across the front and back, while shouting their slogan, "Liberarnos Reficuel"...

Facebook messages and YouTube videos burn through fiber optic cables igniting the world on fire with people claiming their allegiance to Reficuel. Techno savvy commercials display Reficuel's image flying around the world in a superhero cape...

"Reficuel! Reficuel!" Carrie Warren's voice shouts during another broadcast. "If you permit me to use a mathematical term, Reficuel is the common denominator for every major city across the world. Regardless of language, religion or ethnicity they scream his name. He stands as the face of a welcomed new political age."

Knobby snow tires galloping down the bare highway send vibrations rippling up Paula's arms, while the sound of each tread striking the ground resonates in her ears, overpowering the factory stereo system. Trying to overcome the numbing sensation in her limbs Paula keeps readjusting her grip, squeezing the steering wheel. Her eyes strain, peering into the darkness, scanning for black ice hiding along her path while she reminds herself that she is doing the right thing.

> "Stop telling me what you think is best for me and let me make my own decisions." Paula argues punching the cow hide covered rear car seat of a luxurious vehicle.

> Dark male eyes glare through the reflection in a rear view mirror, "I will not allow you to throw your life away on a whim."

> Paula fires back refusing to blink staring back at those eyes, "Dad, it's hardly a whim, I've thought..."

> The eyes squint as the voice behind them interrupts her, "Paula, you're at the top of the Dean's list. I'm sorry but people with that kind of future don't join the military."

> "Are you really listening to yourself? You'd rather trust the fate of the country, and world in the hands of less than qualified people? They need good people too."

> A female in the front passenger seat with brown wavy hair leans over resting her arm on the male driver's shoulder, mumbling, "Joseph, I told you that all that community service wasn't going to do her any good."

> Shrugging off the front passenger the male glances in the rear view mirror so she could see the anger in his eyes, "That's it, if I can't reason with you I'm taking matters into my own hands. I'm calling Schneider myself, this ends today."

"Don't you dare! Father or not, if you interfere
with my job..."

Paula shakes her head from side to side awakening her senses out
of a daydream. She looks down at her military tablet displaying two
blinking blue dots on a road map of the north west United States.
Touching the one dot, a pop up window displays the speed at two
hundred and twenty-three kilometers per hour, "Richy Rich, where
are you going in such a hurry?"

Pushing her foot further into the floor Paula recalls the events
leading to her trip –

> "Forget it Paula. Do you know how much shit
> we're in if you get caught. I won't do it." A man in
> a military uniform rolls his chair away from her and
> back under the keyboard of his computer.

> She grabs the sides of his chair, "Henry, how long
> have we been friends?"

> Henry ignores her and keeps working, "Don't
> give me that friend bullshit. This is illegal and you
> know it."

> She bends down whispering in his ear, "Illegal?
> That never stopped you before. You know I have
> good shit on you."

> Spinning around on his chair, Henry grits his teeth,
> "You little bitch."

> Interlocking her hands as if praying, Paula looks
> down at him, "I promise this is the last time. I
> need a dedicated satellite monitoring Reficuel's
> chopper ASAP..."

Something so simple can have such serious repercussions. She knew
she had put one of her best friend's jobs on the line as well as her
own. She convinces herself, "Nobody's going to find out."

Looking at her phone, she sees the message relating the information about General Hamilton, "You were a great man. You stood for what you believed in."

> Outside a military tent withstanding a downpour, Paula's uniform hangs down drenched as she speaks through the open flap as a younger Hamilton glares at her, "Colonel Hamilton, I apologize, I attempted to go through the chain of command but it's broken, sir and if you want your troops to survive you need to hear what I've got to say."

It was at that moment she endeared herself to him and ostracised herself from many promotions. Closing the screen she questions, "As soon as I finish with Mr. Nomed, I will devote myself to your cause, I promise."

Questions invade her mind, *Who could have bombed that location? That's no regular terrorist strike. It's obviously military, and someone at a high level.*

She couldn't explain her thought process right now, not even to herself. Unable to pinpoint what it was exactly was driving her mad, she jokes, as she twiddles a knife between her fingers, "Guess this is what I get for working with computers all my life. Those high frequency emissions have finally disintegrated the logical side of my mind."

Looking down at her tablet Paula continues following the screen's directions like a beacon.

Beep. Beep. Beep. "Connection terminated." The tablet's automated voice announced.

"What the hell?"

Paula looks down at the tablet screen. The only dot remaining was her own. "What happened? Did he crash?"

She pulls the car over and picks up her tablet zooming in at the mountain ranges. "No helicopter, no crash. That's odd. Where did it go? There is nothing around there."

Entering the last known geographical position into her GPS she continues her investigation, at the very least into the disappearance of the world's most celebrated man.

A four by four SUV enters a narrow forested uncharted trail off an interstate. Fog lights illuminate a harsh dark mud-filled path as the whine of the engine creeps the vehicle splashing, cracking and crunching through the terrain jostling its occupants about. Finally reaching an opening, off to the side of the road a log cabin comes into view. The fog descends on the cabin covering the roof with clouds. The vehicle slows to a stop. The driver's door opens and unsteady feet hit the slippery ground. Proceeding to the back of the vehicle, footsteps break the suction with each step on the viscous surface. Opening the back hatch the compression of the shock slows its rise. As the door extends upwards, the interior light illuminates Frank's tall skinny frame hunched over with his hands and feet tied together and his mouth gagged. The gag is secured with duct tape, wrapped several times around the perimeter of his head.

Frank's bloody face recognizes Miguel. The scarecrow's eyes scream out in terror as his throat convulses sending out a high-pitched squeal in the air.

The former Colonel jabs Frank's throat with his index finger causing him to start snorting. Reaching in, the Spaniard heaves the skeletal frame onto his shoulder. Limping toward the cabin, the bony body bounces against his Traps with each step. The cabin door swings open and a large framed body blocks part of the ambient light escaping from inside.

"You need help with that Colonel?" Nolin asked as he walks down the stairs.

"No, I'm good." Miguel pushed past his friend. He enters the cabin and drops his package on the floor with a thump. Frank's eyes widen seeing Colin approach and Nolin shrimping them all.

"I know I'm hard up when I'm happy to see you two." Miguel struggles to lower his aching body into a chair.

Kneeling down, Colin looks into Frank's eyes, "Miguel, I like that you came bearing a gift. Is this to make up for the safe house that I lost?"

Sheepishly Nolin adds, "I already apologized to Colin but I fear that Colonel Pegrum, if not already arrested, will be soon as will General Hamilton."

Miguel waves his hand in the air, "Lorne don't worry about it. It was a set-up from the start. We were supposed to fail. Me and my newfound friend here had a little chat and there is much more than meets the eye to this whole situation. We don't have much time either. Shane was building bombs for them."

Looking at Miguel's busted body, Nolin questions, "Shane? Shane? Shane Miller did that to you?"

Touching his swollen broken nose, Miguel replies, "Yeah. He was the voice from the Sons of Liberty meeting."

"So, where does that leave us now?"

With a bounce in her step Carrie leaves Studio one and removes an elastic from her pocket. Running fingers through her hair, she shakes her long wavy strands, gripping onto them she pulls them back and fastens them into a ponytail. A huge smile beams across her face as she struts down the hallway of the studio to her dressing room.

"Great job, Carrie," a stage hand announced walking by.

Another agrees, "Yeah, awesome job Carrie."

"Thanks guys, I appreciate that."

A female in a skirt suit sticks her head out a studio door yelling down the hall, "Remember Warren, we need you in an hour on set three."

Effortlessly Carrie pivots around on her toes, "Thank you Luanda, I'll see you then."

Walking in through her dressing room door to a bouquet of flowers on her desk, Carrie giggles, "Honestly, what a crazy ride."

"There you are." She grabs her phone off the desk seeing several new messages. Skimming through the list she pauses seeing a number she doesn't recognize. Clicking a button, the message opens and immediately Carrie loses her vitality, collapsing onto a chair dropping the phone to the floor.

Slouching in her chair motionless she stares at the dressing room wall. Her eyes flutter to life as she bends sideways, slowly inching over the edge of her chair allowing the phone to come into view, 'Cover the real story look at the USB I gave u. I got more if you want it'.

Reaching down she picks up her phone, "I got more...Who would have been his next target after Jason Somers?"

Grabbing a pen Carrie starts doodling. *The most wanted dangerous man in the world and I'm just going to go meet with him. Have I gone insane to even think about it? If I get caught with him it's over, it's all over.*

Her sketch of a flower turns into words as she scribbles out question after question. She had no control as her curiosity continues to build. *The biggest story in the world and I'm sitting on it. How would I get away? I'm booked solid.*

She grabbed the side of her purse pinching the memory device through the material. *Getting more information wouldn't hurt. Doesn't mean I have to act on it.*

Carrie stood up and started pacing back and forth holding her phone, *I can't believe I'm even thinking about it. I would have to go alone.*

Without another thought her fingers race, responding to the text, 'Sure I will take a look. Pick a time and place.'

Black men's dress shoes clop across a marble floor, accentuated by military boots in escort. Two solid oak doors open allowing dance music bass beats to escape this lavish court. The beats thump down the hall into their chests. In the center of the court a tanned young man wearing sunglasses and a pair of shorts sips on a drink while floating across the water of an in-ground pool. Sprawled out on lawn chairs are bikini clad women soaking in the rays.

A military officer carrying a machine gun strapped over his shoulder announces, "Monsieur le Président."

Paddling around, the half-dressed man sits up seeing a stocky man dressed in a black dress shirt and a black suit with a white tie standing poolside. The man adjusts the dark sunglasses on his face as the President shouts out in a French accent, "Quelle surprise. What an honour. Madagascar welcomes you, please take a seat."

The military officer escorts the stocky man to the bar in the shade of a canapé and palm trees.

A servant hands the President a towel as he climbs the stairs coming out of the water. "It's been a long time Alfonso. I was beginning to think you guys had lost your interest."

The military officers walk over and waken the women. Walking out escorted by the military officers, the concubines blow kisses to the President.

"A bientôt mes filles," the President waves at the ladies before the door closes.

Wearing white gloves Alfonso reaches inside his suit jacket and pulls out an envelope, holding it out toward the President. The President takes the straw out of his drink and downs the fluid before slamming down his empty glass on the bar, "Magnifique!"

Reaching, he snatches the envelope while sitting down on a bar stool, "C'est quoi ça?"

The Brazilian remains mute as the President rips opens the envelope and reads the enclosed letter, "Incroyable! You expect me to go along with this? This, this bullshit! This is all I get after what I've done?"

Crumpling up the paper he throws it in Alfonso's face. "Guards! Guards!"

Soldiers brandishing guns come running back as the President continues to yell, "Get this man out of my sight. If he hesitates shoot him in the back and ship him home in a body bag."

Straightening his jacket, Alfonso pulls on the lapels and marches towards the guards.

The President spouts off watching the white-gloved man walk away as he summons his servant with a wave of his hand, "Alfonso, you'll never get the support you need without me. Go back and tell your boss that nothing will proceed until he comes here personally and renegotiates our terms. If he fails to do this I will tell the world."

Nodding, Alfonso leaves the courtyard as the oak doors slam shut. The servant walks up to the President handing him another drink from a silver tray.

The President grabs the glass and gulps it down immediately. He looks around, and starts choking, gasping for air. Falling to his knees, the President claws at his throat barely making a sound. He looks up at the servant standing over him wearing white gloves with the tray under his arm.

"Adieu, Monsieur le Président."

Bows sliding over a host of violin and cello strings brighten the mood with a soft melody while majestic chandeliers warm the grand auditorium with a gentle light. Mingling about the black tie affair is an array of cultures displaying the pomp and pageantry of the world's finest clothes and jewellery.

"This is absolutely delightful, Charles." An older woman marvels, looking around the room.

An elderly black man dressed in military garb swirls his wine glass, and holds it up towards his face breathing in the aroma before taking a mouthful. "Soirées are soirées Mrs. Lexington. Charles, I for one will be much more satisfied once we have established ourselves."

Exhaling a puff of smoke into the air, Charles clutches a cigar in one hand while posting his body on his other resting on a cane. "Well said Roland, I too had my doubts and was beginning to question the validity of the reports I was receiving. This has cost me more than double what was originally discussed."

"General Inabinet, Mr. Lexington, I can assure you that we are very much established and the reports are accurate. You will get back far more than what you put into the program."

Turning about, Jasmine Lindsay's face comes into focus standing behind them as she swooshes her blonde locks around her neck with a twist of her head. Mr. Inabinet stutters, "Miss Lindsay, I, I, was just saying."

"I heard exactly what you said. Please gentlemen, reserve your scepticism until after tonight."

A voice announces over speakers in the room, "Ladies and Gentlemen please move towards your respective seats in the auditorium. We are about to begin."

Miss Lindsay looks at the two men, "If you could excuse me."

Sauntering away Jasmine's complete physique comes into focus wearing a red gown that swings on her hips.

Mrs. Lexington sticks her nose up in the air, "Really Charles, must you stare? It's like you've never seen a woman before."

Wait staff take to the top of the auditorium making sure each person has a full drink with them. Following the reception, they cleared the room, picking up left over plates and other dishes before retiring for the night. Armed guards secure the doors and remain outside.

The auditorium lights dimmed as the glow of stage lights became brighter.

"Welcome all."

The black curtains at the front of the stage open. People anxious to see who or what was behind them see nothing, just black emptiness. The crowd studies the stage confused, not seeing a thing. Suddenly, a face appears in the middle of the darkness to a gasp from the crowd. Dressed in black from head to toe, is the poster boy now showing his billion dollar smile.

"Don't you just love theatrics? Much like that, we have remained in the darkness watching and waiting and are now slowly revealing ourselves. After years of planning and developing we finally have what it takes to make this work and convince the world that they are the ones who wanted this. Wielding the power of illusion we have created the possibility of a fictional world, embodying fairness, equality and understanding."

Walking around, he looks at everyone in attendance, "The money each of you has spent on Research and Development is about to pay off. The constant allure of easy cash, roped in even the most devout person. Answer this survey, win one thousand dollars here, answer this and get a free t-shirt, they can't help themselves, all the while giving us all of the information we ever needed. The privatization of every major commodity fuelled our drive and information gathering ability. The only opportunities the general public had were the ones we gave them. The result…"

Pausing looking at the crowd as they waited, "…we established a behaviour matrix, a behaviour analytic if you like, quantifying habits and manipulating them to our cause. For too long we have bribed, threatened and schmoozed our way into countries, constantly giving kickbacks from government contracts to greedy political leaders. They controlled the borders and could oust us at any time using laws created to keep us on a tight leash. Instead, we have assembled with one united goal: to tear down these walls and enter a new era. No more political corruption, no more coups for power, no more countries claiming bankruptcy and world markets fluctuating due to public uncertainty. It has to end and it will!"

A screen behind Reficuel displays the world with RN flashing from every major country in the world. "Together, we will form the ultimate system like none before it in the history of the planet. We stand to change the world forever. We will lead and control the minds of the public, maintaining our sovereignty. We will accomplish what every leader before us has tried and failed. Alexander the Great although mighty will forever be remembered in history lessons, but we will live on as we rule the globe!"

Colin leans over the back seat of the SUV poking Frank's ribs with his handgun, forcing pig-like squeals out of his gagged mouth.

"Colin, you're giving me a headache. Will you cut it out?" Miguel pleaded.

"I really don't like us carting someone around who wanted to kill us, hearing everything we say." Colin slides back around.

"The only reason he's alive is because he cooperated. I promised I wouldn't kill him and he knows too much so we can't let him go. If this is a dead end.."

Nolin interjects, "Hold off on finishing that sentence Miguel. I knew we should have told you."

"Told me what?"

Pulling out his tablet Nolin taps on the screen. The pixels illuminate bringing a map into focus, "This isn't exactly a perfect science. Triangulating based on the information contained in the existing cell network gives us an approximate location of Frank's contact's geographical location."

"I thought you told me that you could put them within five hundred meters."

Leaning forward between the two front bucket seats Colin adds, "It's a little trickier than that. The phone is giving off two sets of readings, one is the GPS coordinates, which would tell us exactly where they are, and the second is the tower locations."

Pointing at his tablet's map Nolin continues, "As of right now, one of the sets of readings appears erroneous."

Pulling the vehicle to the side of the road Miguel looks down at the fuel needle wavering over the 'E'. He rubs his temples, "Hold up, what do you mean?"

Tilting the tablet towards Miguel, Nolin explains, "It looks like they altered their physical location. Like tracing a land line phone number that keeps jumping home addresses. One set of coordinates shows them half way around the world while one set of coordinates puts them about seventy-five miles away from us right now."

Colin reaches forward tapping on the closest coordinate, "And when we use SAT imagery there is nothing there."

Putting the truck back on the road Miguel peers at the gas gauge again, "If we don't get gas soon we'll be stuck walking around the country. I don't understand why you wouldn't have told me back at the cabin."

Sitting against the back seat Colin raises his feet stretching them out across the opening, "Miguel, I'm glad you brought up the I don't understand speech because, I for one don't understand why you had to give up the location of another one of my safe houses. A few days with you and I've lost two of my homes. Why was it so important that this news reporter receives a copy of the information that we just extracted from dear old Frank?"

Pointing to a road sign coming up on the right Miguel announces, "Big Sky is not that far away. If this is truly the place by the time we get there we don't have much time to pull it together. No doubt there's a ton of security and if for whatever reason we don't succeed at least someone has an account of what's really was going on. If she rolls with it great! If not, well, I'm sorry."

Closing his eyes resting his head against the headrest Colin returns, "All I've got to say is, Miguel you owe me, huge, and Nolin you sure as hell owe me."

Shifting around in his seat Nolin stares at Colin, "Yeah right, how many times did I carry your ass when you were out partying and could hardly stand the next day? I took care of everything while you cowered under the table lying on the floor nursing your self-inflicted flu."

"That only happened one time, and besides how does that compare to a house? It doesn't. You owe me..."

Remaining quiet Miguel smiles listening to the guys banter back and forth. It was like hearing his boys argue. *It will be over soon and I'll come see you I promise.*

Scanning the horizon the only lights visible were the stars above. Reflections of her high beams brought an orange fluorescent sign into focus, 'Construction Zone – Detour next right.' Connie depresses the brakes stopping her car just shy of the intersection seeing Jersey barriers set up across the road. She grabs the tablet and begins mapping her course.

"I've got about twenty miles left going straight down this road, if I take the detour I won't come anywhere near it."

She looks up at the wall in her way, "What's going on? It's not construction season."

Twisting the key backwards the car's engine rattles to a stop. Opening up the driver's side door, Paula steps out onto the pavement. A gust of vapour billows out from the car's interior as the warmth reacts to the crisp cold mountain air. Ice begins forming on the Lieutenant's eyelashes as she walks over to the obstruction, peering over the top. Her flashlight shows that the road is completely torn up. She shines her light to the left and right of the concrete wall spotting six feet deep ditches. Her only option now is on foot.

Prepared for the occasion, Connie assembles her gear for the journey. Given her rank and tenure in the military she managed to acquire quite an array of equipment. Despite being dressed in white from head to toe, parka, toque, gloves and wind pants she feels naked without her gun. She feels the void space on her hip. Pulling the draw straps on her backpack, she tightens her luggage against her shoulders. Grabbing the handle of her favourite knife in its sheath, she grins, "I guess it's just you and me."

Meep. The horn from the car sounds with the locking of the doors. She commences her expedition taking the first step behind the barrier.

Intoxicating fumes hang heavy in the air at a mom and pop gas station at the break of dawn. Miguel stands outside the vehicle filling the tank as Colin and Nolin go over the map of the area again. *This is it. We're close.* Miguel thought to himself.

A slide show of faces invades Miguel's mind. Destitute victims begging to live. An array of cultures scream out in their native tongue, "Help." The crying fades to laughter from unrelenting tyrannical leaders eliminating anyone opposing their rule. Outright philosophical genocide deemed to be lawful extermination in the world court.

Racing through the streets of a village taking on enemy fire, Miguel squeezes the trigger on the military jeep's mounted fifty caliber machine gun. Miguel's hands barely hold on as it shakes his entire body. The whiz of bullets flying by his head sustains his fight to withstand the vibrations, rattling out deadly projectiles leaving a wake of dead bodies behind him. The mental video replays, and the frames slow down allowing him to capture in life's magnificent colours of the faces of those dying by his hands.

The trigger on the gas pump snaps and releases the pressure. Miguel blinks a couple of times looking down at his hand clenching the gas pump handle tight. Forcing his hand to let go he stretches out his arm against the vehicle and puts the gas cap on.

Sticking his head into the cabin of the SUV Miguel orders, "Colin, one hundred bucks."

"Please would be nice."

Miguel shakes his hand looking at him. Colin reaches into his pocket and pulls out a wad of cash peeling off a few bills. "Here."

Entering a small dilapidated building, Miguel makes sure his sweater's hood is on, attempting to conceal some of his features.

An old man behind the counter extends a withered hand out, accepting the money and ringing it into the register while speaking to the Spaniard, "I see that you guys are heading out east. It's a damn shame that mining company came in and bought up that old ski chalet along with ten thousand square miles of land. It's probably costing you guys maybe half a day's drive and at least another tank of gas to get back on track. They have been working on that stupid thing for the past ten years and I don't think they have produced one nugget out of it. They promised they would open the roads again when they were done, but that was all a bunch of bullshit."

"It's okay we'll get where we are going soon enough." Miguel looks out the front window towards the truck before turning back.

Handing back the change the old man closes the till, "Just a damn shame."

Lowering his voice a bit the old man leans over the counter, "Some folks 'round here think it is a military base. Lots of choppers coming and going but no more big trucks. Fact is, after a couple years they tore up the roads and put a fence 'round the whole thing. How is that for a mining operation?"

"Really?" Miguel mused, now more interested in what he had to say and hunching over the counter.

The old man continues, "Yep, me and my ol' lady thought it would bring all kinds of business our way. At first it did but like I said, no more trucks. Haven't seen a truck in years. Guess there's always hope."

Straightening up Miguel realizes that he heard the conclusion of the old man's suspicions. Turning around he pushes on the door allowing a gust of wind to enter the building rattling items hung on the walls, "Sorry to hear that. Thanks for the advice though."

"Don't worry about us sonny. Good thing you stopped. There isn't a pump house for a long ways." The old man finished as Miguel let go of the door, allowing it close by itself.

Jumping back into the four by four truck he exclaims, "We're definitely on the right track."

Nolin looks up from the map displayed on the tablet, "Yep. We only have about an hour left before we are as far as we can go by vehicle."

Starting the engine Miguel puts the truck in gear, "That's good because we are running out of time before people start really wondering where Frank and Shane are."

Positioned on an edge of a valley absorbing the spectacular view, Paula breathes heavily, stopping for a moment as her eyes adjust to the sun cresting over the mountains to the east, illuminating the area. Tear ducts release some of their contents as her eyes submit to the light's strength; squinting, the glitter of the snow-capped peaks was like diamonds over a tapestry of trees, rocks and patches of water.

Stripping off her backpack, she's reaches into a pocket, pulling out a set of military issued electronic binoculars and scans the area. Pointing the lens directly at Reficuel's last known GPS coordinates she saw nothing. Her index finger presses firmly on the side of her device as she pivots her head taking in the landscape. "What is that?"

She lowers the binoculars, peering over at a mountain with her naked eyes. She covers them up again, looking at the electronic display with a pulsing bar graph, "That's odd."

Sitting down on a rock, Connie arches her back to the sound of her joints and bones cracking. Rolling her shoulders backwards she tilts her head from side to side and retrieves a device from her pocket. Entering a new set of GPS coordinates into it she surveys the valley, "What's with this place? Ten miles behind a barrier and no signs of any life? What's going on here?"

Connie sends a text to Henry, 'N E thing?'

Immediately her phone's screen lights up, 'Nada'.

Taking her knife out Connie tosses it against a tree. Walking up to retrieve her weapon her face wrinkles as she thinks, *Why would he come out here when every city in the world wants him to grace them with his presence? How did we lose an entire helicopter?*

Throwing the knife again, "That's it I need to get some sleep."

Paula shakes her head as she walks up pulling the knife out of the same hole smiling, "Most definitely need some sleep when shit like that pops up in my head."

Grabbing her backpack she moves under a pine tree and lies down. Closing her eyes she smiles slightly, *a modern day Bermuda triangle? I'm such an idiot.*

With the slamming of a car door, Carrie twitches and shakes sitting in the driver's seat. Vehicles flash by the rental company sticker affixed to the driver's side window. The compact car rocks with the passing of another vehicle while Carrie's hands fumble trying to insert the key into the ignition.

Turning the key over, the fan blows cool air throughout the car. "Brrrrrr."

Carrie squeezes her cold wet muddied legs up against her body and starts rubbing them with frozen hands. Her teeth chatter as she reclines her seat back.

Finally feeling like she could move her fingers without them breaking, Carrie reaches into her jacket pocket pulling out a new USB drive and phone. Placing the phone down, she holds the USB drive in her hand, "That was stupid. I hope you are worth all of the trouble. I can't believe he stood me up leaving me this package at an abandoned cottage in the bush."

Standing in front of an oversized desk in a barren room is Reficuel. Like a guard at Buckingham Palace he holds his position at attention.

Floating around his head are clouds of sweet incense billowing up from the mahogany top. The chair positioned behind the desk rocks forward as white-gloved hands jet out from either side of the chair grabbing hold of the table top steadying himself from pivoting or rocking again. The man speaks, his accented hoarse voice echoes off the unadorned dark walls.

"Good speech last night. I was thoroughly impressed. You cannot lose focus though. I want you to return and get out there as much as possible. The world is crying for you right now. I want them begging for you. I want the news to splash your name like God in church. The people will find comfort in knowing you are around."

"Yes sir, whatever you wish."

"I've already taken the liberty of having your helicopter warmed up. Your pilot is waiting for you now."

"Thank you."

CHAPTER FOURTEEN

Size nine combat boots sidestep, avoiding a patch of green grass, the wearer cognizant of a puddle of water underneath its immediate dry surface. The sound of twigs snapping, leaves crunching and thin ice cracking tests Miguel's memory of the last time he was on a trek. While jogging he periodically hops up, yanking on the backpack's shoulder straps readjusting the tension on the lump of mass fastened to his body. Him, and his companions were saddled with more gear than they ever were in the military, lugging an equal amount typically carried by a full reconnaissance team. With each step they fought the sensation of their shoulders being ripped from their bodies or their knees buckling under the weight. Gasping for air, Miguel sucks in as much oxygen as his body will allow, speaking through a burned out esophagus, "These coordinates better be bang on."

His reply came in the form of two approving wheezing grunts. "Hu.Hu."

Pressing on, the former Colonel peers down at his GPS as a branch whips his face. Snapping the twig he glances back at his men, "Less than fifteen minutes."

As his strides shorten, coming to a stop, the Spaniard leans his chest against a tree trunk. His body throbs with pain. His associates stomp to a standstill posting their bodies on outstretched arms against a rock formation. Standing behind a tree situated on a ridge over a valley, Miguel scans the landscape, panting, "According to your coordinates... it's supposed to be somewhere down in this valley."

The former Colonel pivots around keeping his weight against the tree. Ever so slightly he lowers himself to the ground, his backpack grates against the bark. Shifting his torso from side to side he struggles to pull his arms out from the imbedded shoulder straps. Finally getting the right movement he slips one arm out and wiggles to release his body from the other. Slowing tilting his head back against his backpack he closes his eyes feeling the anguish of every muscle fiber.

Reaching up to his chest pocket, Miguel removes a plastic tube, placing it on his lap. Popping off the cap, he reaches in and pulls out a cloth. He unfolds it exposing a number of tablets. Pinching a couple of pills together he drops them into his mouth and swallows. With one hand he replaces the cloth and with the other hand rubs his legs, grimacing. Peering over at his two friends, he sees beads of sweat form and trickle down their faces. Each expelled breath hangs thick in the air, evidence of the below freezing temperatures. The wind whistles through the trees swaying the tops back and forth creaking and cracking.

Colin glances over at Lorne sucking on a Ventolin inhaler and whispers, "You all right Nolin?"

Lowering his puffer alongside his massive frame, he breathes out, "I've been keeping up with you haven't I?"

With his GPS in his hand Miguel crawls over to Lorne and Colin, "Okay geniuses, where is everyone? We're inside the radius that you provided and there is nothing here, no buildings, no vehicles where...?

Eyes widen as each of them look at one another feeling a tremor.

Miguel slides across the snow towards the ridge facing the sound.

The two other men strap on their backpacks responding to a series of hand gestures by the former Colonel. Their feet start moving, retreating back into the depths of the forest.

Adrenaline pulses through Miguel's body, shimmying away from the ridge. He snatches his backpack, grabs his rifle, and follows his friends.

Sprinting through branches, twigs and brush, the thunderous sound continues to increase in volume. Diving under a rock ledge Miguel turns over as loose sand and snow cloud the area. Slicing through the debris his eyes spot a helicopter flying out from the valley and over their location.

Without a sound they listen as the engine noise dissipates in the distance.

Removing his goggles, Colin cleans the lenses, "Whew."

Pulling off his protective eye wear, Miguel stares at his two companions, "I wouldn't believe it if I didn't see it."

Nolin questions, "What?"

Grabbing Miguel's shoulder Lorne insists, "What?"

Staring out into oblivion Miguel responds, "Down in the valley at the base of this mountain there is a village hidden behind a rock wall in the mist. Lorne give me those binos."

Removing his pack, Nolin immediately opens a pocket, pulling out a sophisticated set of binoculars. "Here."

"Just leave your packs. We'll travel light from here."

Sprawled out on the edge of the ridge, Miguel keeps the binos glued to his face scanning the valley. "Gentlemen, we were extremely lucky. They have a well fortified establishment down there surrounded by electrical devices placed sporadically around their perimeter."

Handing off the ocular device, Lorne reaches over as Colin snatches them first. Holding them up to his eyes he voices, "That's impressive."

Passing the binos to Lorne, Colin questions, "What's the plan, boss?"

"Yeah, how are we going to approach this situation?" Nolin asked, handing the device back to the Spaniard.

Raising the ocular devices up, Miguel surveys the entire area again. He ducks his head and starts crawling away from the ridge, "Shit. Shit. Shit. We've been spotted! Turn that signal suppressor on and follow me."

Jumping to his feet, Miguel takes off as fast as he can, circling away from the village. Through a haze of movements the Spaniard's aches and pains disappear. His beating heart courses blood through his body. With every bound he feels the crunch of the frozen surface under his feet. His sprint speed fluctuates keeping his bearings. *Have they already alerted the others? Are we close enough? Are we going into an ambush?* Thoughts run through his mind as fast as his legs are moving.

Bounding onto a rock, Miguel's boot glides off the lustrous ice-coated surface launching his body into the air. His boots gain altitude as his head plunges downward, striking the solid surface with a thud.

Colin stops as Miguel rolls to the side. Brunet spots the former Colonel's white tuque change to the colour red, asking, "Migs, you…"

The Spaniard gets to his hands and knees, shakes his head and starts running again.

Galloping through the bush, trees fade into oblivion. Miguel's mind wanders into his recesses. He sees and hears his boys burning in a house fire, "Help Daddy help!"

Behind bars, helpless, Miguel watches in horror as the flames engulf the place he once called home, "Daddy please help us, Daddy!"

Miguel finds himself trapped inside the burning house running from room to room unable to find his boys.

Stopping abruptly, Miguel spins around looking at his surroundings. Shaking off the dizzy sensation, he sees the first sign of human life within the valley: a discarded white and grey mountaineering backpack on the ground. Lowering himself to the ground Miguel examines the footwear impressions. Springing back up he sets to run again when Lorne tugs on his white jacket, "Migs, I don't know if you've noticed but we've got company."

Turning around Miguel watches Nolin point to a grey coyote blending into the scenery. The animal stares at them from a distance concealing most of its body behind a tree, "You know they don't travel alone."

The former Colonel orders, "We can't afford to waste any ammo. Don't shoot unless you absolutely have to, come on let's go."

Holding his assault rifle at the ready Miguel continues to chase the footprints in the snow. A cadence of footprints per stride kept Miguel moving forward until they vanished.

The steely-eyed warrior scans the unnaturally quiet horizon sweeping his hand over his head removing his blood-soaked tuque. Birds and animals are eerily absent. Miguel's index finger covers the trigger as venous red fluid gushes down his neck.

The sound of Miguel's thumping heart prominently drowns out the frozen silence ahead. Slowing down time and holding off the natural response to run, Miguel's breathing quickens. With each shuffle step forward, the Spaniard feels the granular texture of the icy surface through the soles of his boots. His eyes capture the intricate designs of falling snow flakes. His ears pick up a high pitched metal ping in the distance. Bile fumes fill his nostrils, the burn of its ascension leaves a bitter taste in his mouth as he swallows the stomach acid back down.

> Standing at the door of a house, Miguel reaches down, accepting his police uniform from his preteen, "Why do you have to go work?"

> "I go to work so I can make money to take care of you guys."

His younger one clutches Miguel's leg, and looks up at him and through the hole of two missing front teeth lisps out, "Daddy aren't you scared of all those bad guys?"

Miguel wraps his arms around his two boys, "Come here you guys."

Holding his boys close, he explains, "Sometimes I'm scared, but if I don't fight these bad guys then who will? There are little boys and girls who don't have a daddy or mommy to protect them. I go to work to protect anyone who needs help from these scary people."

"We love you, Daddy."

Lowering his face inches from the ground Miguel scans the crystallized surface with his eyes. Moving in one direction he hears his men advancing behind him. A canine's howl echoes through the trees.

Lorne whispers as he slides into position, "I've got your back."

The Spaniard gains control of his breathing. Calmed down, he repositions when a female voice breaks silence, "It's a shame that such a persistent man is in a hurry to die."

Instinctively Miguel drops to a prone position minimizing his vertical profile. His group does the same.

Miguel returns, "Death comes to us all. I like to meet it on my terms."

A moment of silence is followed by the same female voice, "Miguel?"

The former Colonel's body temperature skyrockets. Beads of sweat overtake his face dripping down off his nose, as an aura of steam circles his head. Miguel makes eye contact with his men, exchanging hand gestures.

"Colonel Miguel Mejia is that you?" she asks again.

Colin and Lorne slide their bellies across the snow and away.

Miguel attempts to distract her, "Back up isn't coming if that is what you're stalling for. We have been jamming your transmissions since the beginning."

Paula scoffs, "You better tell your men to stay with you. If they move any closer I will kill you first."

A jolt of weight lands on Miguel's back, snapping it. Growling and yanking at his jacket's hood the beast starts choking him. Miguel tries to face the animal but its jaw starts ripping at the back of his skull trying to bite his neck. Another one locks down on his gun arm ripping the jacket.

Charging from behind a tree Paula throws her knife, sinking deep into one of the coyotes' necks. Yelping the dog staggers away and falls dead. Grabbing another knife from her belt she advances. About to plunge the knife into the back of the other canine, the sound of suppressed pops polka dot the chest of her target keeping her at bay.

Frozen, staring at Miguel's crew, Connie yells, "Behind you!"

Spinning around Colin and Lorne dispatch another five charging dogs as Paula hovers over Miguel scouting for more.

Miguel coughs and collapses onto his back. He unzips his jacket. Rolling to his hands and knees he wobbles to his feet and staggers his body over to a tree. Dropping his body against a tree, he crumples at its base. He jerks his head forward feeling the pain at the back of his skull.

"Lieutenant Paula Connie?" recognizing her, Nolin lowers his weapon.

Colin, watching the interaction rolls his eyes keeping his gun pointed at Paula, "Miguel, if you don't mind I want to make sure she is who she says she is."

Nodding his head, Miguel looks at his torn jacket. "I think it's fair to say you're not reporting to the village, but, what are you doing here?"

Paula contemplates, and reluctantly responds, "Reficuel."

Miguel peers over at Lorne and Colin.

"Reficuel's chopper disappeared from SAT visual in this area, I was investigating a possible crash."

Carrie Warren's mind began spinning. She rips off her ear phones, drops her laptop on the floor and stumbles to the plane's miniature washroom. Flipping open the toilet lid she hangs over the bowl gagging. Yellow bile drips from her lips into the cavern. Tearing a piece of paper towel out of the dispenser, she wipes her face. Before leaving, she checks her face in the mirror. Opening the door she steps out and returns to her seat when she spots a stewardess picking up her laptop.

"Hey! What are you doing?" Carrie demanded.

"Oh! Miss Warren, nothing. Your computer was on the aisle floor, I was just putting it up on your seat."

Carrie approaches the stewardess, "Here just pass it to me. I can take that, thank you."

The murmur of two voices speaking in hushed tones captures Carrie's attention. *Are they talking about me?*

She strains to get a glimpse of them but the rows of empty seats obstruct her view. Another stewardess walks by. Carrie glares, following her movements. *What is she up to?*

Standing at her seat, she looks around the plane cabin one more time before she sits and opens the laptop. Slipping her headset on, she hears only static. Sliding the USB drive out of the port she places it in her purse pocket with the other one.

Like a dry sponge in a pool of water, motionless, she lets her mind absorb the information. *This guy is killing me. I can't believe how paranoid I am now.*

Scribbling on a napkin, 'SOL 1,000,000 members???' She pauses thinking, *Who is there to trust? What can I trust?*

The reporter begins questioning the information, "This is all it is, information. These are certain people's accounts for what was happening, and supposedly what they did, saw or were told."

This wouldn't hold water in court nor would it be sufficient to convince me if I hadn't seen Miguel interrogate the former Premier with my own two eyes.

"Miss Warren, could I interest you in a beverage?" a stewardess asked.

Blinking a couple of times, Carrie faces the woman standing over her, "What's that?"

"A beverage, could I interest you in a beverage?"

"No thank you."

Glancing down at her hands clutching onto her purse, she pinches the pocket concealing the dual USB drives. *I was introduced to Jason Somers through Clifford Wilson. Is he involved in this global conspiracy too? If so, presenting this news story would be suicide, both vocationally and literally. Who else would be willing to protect me, other than the most wanted man in the world?*

Jogging up to her car, parked on the side of a barren road, Connie strips off her backpack tossing it into the back seat. Unzipping her jacket she pauses, staring at the blood on her sleeve, she looks over her shoulder at the wilderness. Pulling her arms out of the jacket she turns the sleeves inside out and drapes the piece of outerwear over the front passenger seat.

She drops her butt in the driver's seat, and jabs the car keys into the ignition. Cranking hard on the steering wheel she makes a u-turn and punches her foot down on the gas pedal. The car responds, revving the rpms and squealing its tires, kicking up gravel as it heads north. Slamming her fist into the steering wheel she yells, "Sons of bitches!"

No sooner had Reficuel taken to the skies in his helicopter from the Big Sky mountains then transport trucks with his name in large letters began arriving in cities around the world. Workers under his direction began distributing food from the back of trucks to people everywhere.

Later that night, a hang glider descends through New York's Manhattan streets. A wireless video camera displays the scene from a bird's eye view on large screens in front of a capacity crowd in Times Square while anthem music blares. The glider swoops in, landing on a couple of transport trailers parked in the middle of an intersection at the same time fireworks blast over the crowd. Reficuel dismounts from the glider with a roar of excitement. Television crews in place monitor every action, displaying them on the four storey screens behind him,

"Good Evening New York! I hear that you're looking for a change!"

He raises his hand to his ear walking from side to side of his stage while people crowded around for blocks erupt into cheering.

"First, we need to change how we see things."

Reficuel points at one of the military officers and waves him over to his location. The mob, seeing the military officer, starts showing their dissatisfaction. Loud 'boos' replace the joyous greeting the billionaire just received. Nomed raises his hands in front of him waving them downward trying to quiet the masses, "Officer would you be so kind as to remove all of your clothes?"

The military officer steps back. Without a microphone, no one was able to hear what the officer responded to the most influential person in the world.

Turning to the crowd, Reficuel's venomous smile shines bright, "He wants to know if I am serious? I have to answer that question with another. When have you ever heard about me not being serious?"

Everyone standing in the streets starts chanting, "Strip. Strip. Strip."

The officer received an approving head nod from his command-ing officer. Reluctantly the officer begins removing his clothing. The billionaire's energy continued to grow as he walked circles around the man. The populace screams louder.

In among the media crowd Carrie announces, "Shawn, I'm not sure what Reficuel is up to but viewers at home please beware if there are young eyes in the room."

Resembling a traffic cop Reficuel raises his hand, "That's fine officer you don't have to take off your underwear."

The mob jeers.

Grabbing the officer by the elbow Reficuel pulls him along, walking from side to side of his stage, "Like I said, first we need to change how we see things."

Examining the well built man standing there in his boxer shorts. "I can tell you if you don't have a wife or girlfriend I am sure that you will have no problem after tonight. Will you look at this guy? Ladies give him a hand."

Laughing and whistling bellows from the multitude.

"Officer could you come here for a moment? I know it's cold but if you could indulge me."

Looking out to the crowd pointing to the man standing before them, "What do you see? Do you see a military officer or do you see a man just like you and me?"

Spinning him around, Reficuel shows off the near naked military man to the crowd and the world, "Thank you officer you may get dressed again."

The throng of people cheer at this opening.

"Because he wears that uniform doesn't make him a good guy or a bad guy. He is a man wearing clothes. Believe it or not he is here to protect you and me. We have to stop fighting each other. Government employee or not we are all countrymen...and women, sorry about that ladies. He has a job and he has to follow orders like all of us to bring home money to feed and clothe his family."

Captivated by his enthusiasm, people revere him as a brilliant leader and chants of his name begin all over again. The noise becomes overwhelming. Reficuel stops speaking and motions with his index finger to his lips to quiet the crowd. As the chanting subsides he raises his voice,

"Thank you. Thank you. I can't tell you how touching it is to have your support. Community members, I cannot count how many times I've gone to foreign countries where its citizenry were suffering, and I tried to ease their pain, with food and negotiating with their leaders. Now, looking out at citizens of this wonderful city and over the world, I am not blind, I see the pain and suffering. I want to make things right."

A swarm of hands clap howling, "He is our fuel, Reficuel."

"Thank you. Thank you. Millions of people keep asking me to be a political leader. They are tired of the rhetoric from ineffective, absent and in most cases corrupt leaders. These leaders once elected become tyrants forcing their will on the masses. I've been told that the company I manage has a reputation for being an excellent place to work; fair, honest, respectable and profitable. I've heard that there are some who wish a country and the world could be run the same way. And I thought, why not, WHY NOT?"

Stomping their feet and clapping their hands the crowd erupts screaming, "Reficuel! Reficuel!"

Absorbing the praise of the masses he waits before speaking again. The cheers slowly quiet as he continues, "Why can't countries or the world stand for those qualities? Over the years these so called leaders have run countries into the ground or near bankruptcy while continuing to gouge citizens for more and more tax money. Where is all that money going I must ask?"

The masses yell, "Yeah!"

Reficuel stops walking around. He looks over the crowd, slowly staring in the eyes of everyone he can. The shine in his eyes, the white silky teeth form part of his effortless smile, "I stand here before you today and say, no more. No more will you be forced to accept none other than what you should deserve."

A helicopter drops down from the sky, an aide runs up connecting a wire to a harness on his back. Raising him over the mob lining the streets, the sound of superhero music starts playing in the background as he addresses the populace once more, "I respect your wishes and the wishes of so many who, like you, want change. I humbly accept your proposal and I will negotiate talks with community leaders and the elected governments to establish order. This I promise."

Carrie announces with an explosion of cheering, and chants of Reficuel from the crowd, "Ready or not here he comes. Reficuel the most powerful man on the globe has just announced he will undertake to establish world order..."

Miguel and his team successfully patrolled the entire perimeter finding vulnerable locations. A sketch of the area sits in front of them as they begin deliberations on the most tactical way of approaching the situation. The former Colonel starts, "We know that there are motion sensors and cameras set up at these locations."

He points to the map at all of their locations. "The open pit mine is fairly deep with the excavated rocks making a solid perimeter around the top. Our main target appears to be the largest building at the base of the mountain…"

The spray of hot water penetrates Paula's skin standing in a shower stall. Engulfing her mind like the steam filling the bathroom are the events that followed her visit with Miguel.

> The voice of General Izzov rings through her mind like a dream, "Lieutenant Paula Connie, a certain Reficuel Nomed attributes the success of the Vancouver negotiations with your planning and security out west. Congratulations, you have finally made Captain."

> Standing there with an outstretched hand, Izzov waited to congratulate her. Frozen in disbelief she finally snapped out of it and grabbed hold of his hand giving it a good jolt, "Thank you, General Izzov."

> The leader of the military continued to eye his subordinate, toggling from her eyes to her chest, "I also heard that immediately after negotiations you decided to take a couple of days off."

> Paula's face flushes for a moment, "Yes sir."

> "Good idea. It's always good to get away when you can."

Her hands press into the shower wall as she hunches over allowing the weight of the water clinging to her hair to pull her head down, stretching the muscles in her back. *Can this information be true? Can these people really be involved?*

Turning off the water, Connie grabs a towel, bundling herself in it and walks out to her bedroom. She sits on the end of her bed staring at her cell phone on the night stand. Her towel falls off as her mind continues to dwell on information. *If all these people are involved, what chances do we have to succeed?* A shiver pulls her mind back to the present. Reaching down she grabs her towel wrapping it around her body again, lying back on her bed she gazes at the smooth textured ceiling with a glossy finish. "Wow. Our whole way of life is subconsciously reinforcing this mindset. We go to such great lengths to deceive ourselves. A little plaster, paint and voilà, a whole new atmosphere and never once changing the structure."

Paula rolls over grabbing her cell phone, and opens it. She scrolls through her contacts finding the billionaire's name. Taking a deep breath she presses talk and lifts the phone to her ear, hearing it ring.

Night had long fallen and the hauntingly eerie sound of canines crying out fills the air. Pistol in hand, Miguel's eyes glance from side to side. Reaching back he slides his hand under his tuque lightly brushing a new set of stitches on his head. Feeling the scabby dried blood, he mumbles, "Thanks Paula."

A dull green backlight outlines the digits on the Spaniard's watch, 02:02hrs. Crawling out from underneath the evergreen tree Miguel stands up, walking over to his two comrades lying down. Their eyes flash open.

Colin sits up, peeling himself out of his sleeping bag, "Time to go, Colonel?"

Miguel nods as Nolin rolls to his hands and knees performing a cat stretch cracking his back. Packing up camp, the anxiety gnaws at Miguel's gut. He forces himself to eat, opening up a banana after stuffing a protein bar down his throat. Nolin comes up behind Miguel and grabs his shoulder with his massive hand, squeezing, "This is going to work, trust me."

Colin grabs his watch, "Come on guys. We need to get a move on. In five, four, three, two, one, now."

Automatically all three synchronize their watches. Miguel passes out a rolled up piece of paper, "Here is your sketch, mapping out our objective. Make no mistake, this is our fight. We have the element of surprise. I'd rather die here today than live a lifetime of regret knowing we could have stopped this factious group from slaughtering people at will."

Colin and Nolin nod their heads, solemnly agreeing with Miguel.

The former Colonel continues, "That being said I don't see why a little extra help wouldn't hurt."

As each of them went their way, a portion of the final words spoken by Miguel echoed in their ears, somehow comforting them... "Yea, though I walk through the valley of the shadow of death, I will fear no evil, for you are with me..." They had heard these words before at countless funerals but it was the first time it meant so much. Did they really believe or was this their way of taking out the last insurance policy in the event things went really bad?

Miguel stood still watching his friends divide and fade into the darkness. Taking the first step on his journey, he begins weaving in and around trees, thinking how strange it is that he still clings to that passage in the Bible. Thankfully, no one questioned him because he didn't have an easy answer. After all, where was God when he killed in the name of his country? His reply is one so convoluted that in the end no one would understand it... Simply put, it gave him solace no matter what mission he went on.

Monitors in the surveillance room located at the mountain-side castle receive a series of motion alarms. Hearing the alarm, a security guard sits up and begins panning an infrared camera in the affected area. As the camera spins into position, the guard complacently utters, "What is it this time? A deer? Another skunk?"

His counterpart seated at another station exclaims, "I can't believe we get paid to do this."

"Wait a sec...we actually have someone."

The camera's image displays Nolin bent over, his back to the camera.

"I don't believe it. We actually have someone on the grounds."

"Not another Green-peacer. It's been a while since the last guy came out here and went missing permanently."

"Yep, those nasty cougars," the second security guard snickers.

The Prime Minister runs his hand through his salt and pepper hair. Holding onto his neck he looks around the entire cabin as the plane shakes. Despite being escorted by a barrage of military officers, including General Izzov, Colonel Renniks and Captain Connie, he was extremely nervous. A flight attendant comes into the cabin, "We are entering Switzerland now and will be landing shortly. Please fasten your seatbelts we may experience some turbulence."

Gazing out of from her window seat, Paula's eyes widen taking in the eerie sight. The entire airport is shut down with military and police personnel from every country swarming over every inch.

Entering the terminal Paula remains with the Prime Minister as he mingles about with various leaders preparing to accept Reficuel as their replacement.

Who in here is paid off and who is doing it out of fear? What is going to happen to the world if Reficuel is taken out?

As thoughts continue to ricochet off the inside of her skull, nausea sets in and her throat starts pulsing. Walking out to the helicopter Paula looks up at the mountains. A cool crisp gust of wind enters her body squeezing out a shiver. *Breathe, Paula, breathe,* she tells herself. Inhaling a long and steady stream of air she feels the restriction of her clothes with her inflated chest. Expelling slowly she takes control of herself. Last in the line entering the helicopter she pauses, taking in one more helping of the unspoiled oxygen.

Peering at her watch, *What am I doing? In only a few hours this world will never be the same.* Looking over at the Prime Minister she smiles, thinking, and, *If I could scream I would.*

Paula's stomach drops as the helicopter lifts off the tarmac. She tries to coax herself, *Just look out the window and enjoy the scenery.*

Staring through the pane of glass, the mountainous backdrop is overshadowed by the activity saturating the streets to her destination. Climbing the mountains' elevation leading to the castle, the location of this momentous occasion, placards wave showing their support for Reficuel. Paula closes her eyes grabbing her stomach, *This is not good.*

"Hello all, I'm Shawn Gurl live on location in the Swiss Alps where we see helicopter after helicopter dropping off their precious cargo consisting of various world leaders. Among these politicians preparing for the event, every celebrity worth their weight in gold will be at this beautiful castle. A military blockade holds back thousands of spectators gathered here waiting to welcome with a joyous celebration the first true leader of the world."

In the distance, Connie studies the castle beginning to take shape. The beauty of the stone construction, turrets and huge arched entranceways are darkened by the barbed wire strung like Christmas lights around the building. People in military garb carrying automatic weapons line the upper walls, not to mention the iron clad vehicles patrolling the grounds. The enclosure appears more like a prison than the nerve center of the public revolution coming into fruition. Although not provided the opportunity to contemplate the beauty of the landscape, Paula is secretly appreciative of the additional security measures, considering if she manages to achieve her undertaking.

Get a grip. She chides herself landing in the courtyard. As they approach another security checkpoint she immediately she feels the pressure building giving her a splitting headache.

"What's the matter with you Paula?" Renniks shouted out.

Paula's insides twist, her palms begin to sweat as she looks up at the Colonel who captured everyone's attention with his comment.

"You look nervous. What are you up to?"

"Nothing." Paula spits out.

"Whatever. I've never seen you look so nervous."

Izzov hits Rennik's shoulder commanding, "Colonel Renniks just leave her alone. Reficuel asked for her personally to be here."

A reflection in a window reaches the new Captain's eyes, *Renniks is right, I do look like shit. I haven't slept for days.*

A television positioned on the security desk displays a news report, "Switzerland is an ideal place to negotiate the termination of debts, being a neutral country and the holder of the world's wealth. The concept promised by Reficuel – having one government – would mean no more debt. Only hours from now Reficuel is going to accept the biggest responsibility ever taken on by a human being: to lead the world."

And somehow in the midst of all this I'm supposed to unravel the web of deceit and reveal the true monster hiding in the dark? Paula questions her abilities for the first time in years.

Eyeballing those officially working security points, her 20/20 vision started suffering, their faces were becoming blurry. *This assignment is definitely out of my range of expertise. Wait for it any moment they are going to arrest me for treason.*

An armed guard escorts Captain Paula Connie down a long hallway. Passing by a closing door, she catches a glimpse of Carrie Warren unpacking. Memorizing the location she continues to follow her escort. Stopping short of a door the armed guard turns around, "This is it. You're expected to be in the great hall by 7 p.m. sharp."

Opening the door she sees a large bouquet of flowers on a table in the middle of the room with a note, 'Welcome to the Palace in the sky.' She drops her baggage, and goes into the washroom to throw some water on her face. Leaning on her elbows, she hovers over the sink looking in the mirror, "Paula, you better know what you're doing."

Drying her face she prepares for stage one of her mission. Retracing her steps to Carrie's location, she knocks on the solid wood door. A brute of a man wearing a security tag with 'media' in yellow highlights cracks open the entrance. Staring into Paula's eyes, he asks, "Yes, may I help you?"

"Could I speak to Carrie for a moment?"

The man turns his head toward Carrie, "There is someone here to see you. Do you feel like company?" He swings open the door revealing Paula Connie standing there in her military garb. Carrie, resting on a chair beside a desk, was reviewing notes. She peers over her papers seeing Connie. An expression of confusion clouds her face for a moment before she wipes it away with a warm smile, "Come in, come in."

Paula approaches Carrie and carefully opens up her hand surreptitiously showing a USB drive resting in her palm, "Could we speak alone?"

Carrie nearly faints. She physically braces herself holding onto the armrests of the chair. Lowering her face for a moment she looks up, "Of course, Eddy could you get me a drink, I would like to speak to the Captain alone for a second."

Montana State Police receive a call from a concerned motorist, "There is a four by four SUV off the road in the forest near the mining operation. I walked up to help out but I think the person inside is dead."

Police squad cars respond to the location and park on the road. The officers follow the tire tracks to the forest area where they find the vehicle still running.

One whispers, shining his light on the tailpipe, "Nothing tied to the tailpipe."

Approaching the side of the vehicle their light barely cuts through the tinted windows. Stepping closer to the vehicle a foul odour emanates from its interior. Bracing to endure the smell they get closer.

"Man that stinks. Suicide for sure!"

Holding a flashlight against the window the light finally illuminates the contents. Their minds interpret the images before their eyes. Outstretched in the back of the vehicle, was a skeletal figure of a man with his hands handcuffed to posts, his mangled face and soiled clothing spoke volumes, "Oh shit, this is a murder."

Shining the lights over the dead man's face, his eyes twitch to life. Frank screams as he raises his body upright. The police officers stumble back a few paces and pull out their guns in haste. The frail man screams in a shaky voice, "Please help me."

The police officers look at each other in the same responsive manner, as Frank begs, "Please help me before they come back. There are three men who did this to me."

Immediately one officer scans the ground with his flashlight exposing footprints in the snow. Following the trail leads him towards the mining operation. The other officer grabs his radio, "This is Golf-six-three-seven this is not a ten forty-five. I repeat it is not a ten forty-five. We have an abduction. We need additional officers to cordon off the area to search for suspects and send an ambulance here ASAP."

CHAPTER FIFTEEN

Standing outside a room in civilian clothes Connie feels her skin crawl, *Am I really going through with this?*

Bodyguards blocking the entrance show her half cocked grins, with lust in their eyes as they stare at her entire package. Normally displaying a reserved and rigid demeanour with lines tightly fastened, Captain Connie itches to correct all of the imperfections. She resists her instincts to fix her barely held together messy ponytail. With every movement, strands of hair brush across the back of her neck feeling like a spider crawling across her skin. Wearing some of Carrie Warren's clothing the shirt she wore hung loosely on her shoulders exposing the crest of her firm cleavage being gawked at by these brutes. The stretchy jeans revealed every curve and restricted her movement, a tactical error. Most irritating of all was a coating of cream and other additives smeared across her face accentuating her almond shaped hazel eyes and plump red lips. Her pores feel as though they're suffocating. As she stands, waiting, every now and again she forms claws with her hands ready to tear to shreds her hair, clothes and face.

A large bodyguard opens the door looking over at Paula, "He will see you now Captain Connie."

"Thank you." She forces a smile to her face as she walks past the other guards and enters the room.

Reficuel meets her at the door and delays his introduction, taking in the sight before him, "Lieutenant... sorry Captain, I apologize that I stood you up the other night. I had a pressing work related engagement that I had completely forgotten. I promise I will make it up to you. Please come in, sit down," he said, motioning to a little bistro table set up by a balcony overlooking the valley.

She follows his lead over to the table, "Mr. Nomed we have worked together long enough. You can call me Paula."

The billionaire pulls out Connie's chair allowing her to sit down, "And likewise Paula you can call me Reficuel, everyone else does." Laughing initially at his attempt to make a joke and then really laughing at the pathetic form in which it was delivered, he joins her sitting at the table. "I'm sorry, that was horrible."

Reciprocating with a fake laugh, Paula thinks, *What am I doing? If I can't pull it together he is going to know that I'm not genuine. Come on girl.*

Feeling the heat from her body building up, she breaks the ice, "I can't imagine how you're feeling. I have butterflies in my stomach just thinking about waking up tomorrow to a united world. It's so exciting."

Scanning the room, Reficuel returns looking at her, "It certainly is, I can't believe it sometimes myself."

"Reficuel, I never had an opportunity to apologize for being such a bitch when we were outside of Vancouver. I want you to know that I really appreciate everything you have done. I can't explain why I was like that. I am so, so sorry."

"It's okay. I have worked with thousands of people around the world and some people don't handle stressful situations well."

Thinking to herself, *Ouch that hurt; if he only knew the real reason why I am here. The mere presence of him in the room makes me want to vomit.*

Swallowing his insult was tough. She smiled at him, nodding her head trying to demonstrate a sheepish look, concealing the anger building inside, *How dare he? This was going to be even harder than I thought.*

Reficuel continues as he pours each of them a glass of wine. "It has been an insane ride. But the day is almost at hand when the real work begins. If you will permit me, I have a confession to make."

Shocked and puzzled at what exactly was going to come out of his mouth Connie is curious to hear what he has to say. After all, the possibilities could be endless, *I have deceived the world or I am not what I seem. Stop thinking like that and just let him speak.*

"What on the earth could you have to say?" Gazing deep in his eyes Paula lifts her glass sipping on the beverage and puts it down, tilting her head ever so slightly.

"I have been attracted to you for some time, and have enjoyed spending time with you, but right now I must admit that I am a little overwhelmed. Given what is on the line I must ask that we postpone this date if I can use that word, and resume it after everything has been completed. I hope you understand."

She couldn't believe it. That is the last thing he was supposed to say. She has to act faster than she thought, *What were some of the flirtatious things Carrie told me to do?* She reaches over grabbing his leg rubbing it, "I'm sorry. I didn't mean to cause you any alarm. I was hoping we could spend some time together. I want you to know..."

Interrupting her, Reficuel rushes to speak, distractedly looking around the room again. In a softer tone he tries to comfort her, "Paula, I can't tell you how much I have enjoyed working with you, with everything. I do want to spend some time with you, but not here, not like this. When this is over, I will take you someplace you have never been before. I will make it up to you, I promise."

As he finished speaking, he stood forcing the Captain to retract her arm slowly from his leg. "Please understand, I have too much on my mind right now to be distracted, no matter what. Paula please, I really do want to see you again."

Leaning against the back of the chair Paula is brought back in time recalling the last time she had been rejected. It was high school all over again. Even though she didn't feel hurt by his dismissal it was the thought of failure that bothers her and registers on her face. *Miguel is counting on me to get to him and prevent this from happening.* She begins contemplating her options, *What do I do now? Do I attack him? Do I let him go? Do I try one more time?* Her mind races as she places her hands under the table top. She scrolls through all of the advice that Carrie gave her trying to find the appropriate reaction to this situation.

Standing up Paula takes a step forward, "I am so sorry, I completely understand." Walking up to him face to face, "I am going to hold you to your word. And how about this for my word, I promise I won't disappoint you."

As the words leave her mouth she leans over, her vanilla perfume infuses the air. She puts her hand on his shoulder and gently brushes her lips against his cheek. Her solid breasts press into his chest. In the stillness of the moment, she was able to sense his heart racing. She pulls back slowly, locking eyes with him for a split second before slipping her hand off his shoulder, running her fingers down his arm along his chest and catching his hand giving it a slight squeeze.

Turning to walk toward the door she catches a glimpse of him gazing at her, flirtatiously she finishes, "You know where to find me."

Torn in his thoughts, Reficuel begins to follow her toward the door, "Paula, don't go far, as soon as this is done I'll be looking for you."

She opens the door, peers over her shoulder, "I hope so." She continues out and down the hall with the security guards' stares locked on her retreating figure.

Renniks walks out of a back room, with the biggest smirk on his face, "You've got to be kidding me. No wonder she was so nervous. What is it? The money, the power? I can't believe it. You're on the verge of cracking the toughest nut on the tree my friend. I must admit I am attracted to you, what was that?"

Embarrassed, Reficuel responds, "What? Do you think I came off too needy?"

"Whatever works my friend, whatever works. All I have to say is after they turn over the power to you, instead of talking to all those losers, don't hesitate for a moment. If you do, you might never have a chance. What I would give to be you tapping that ass... You should've taken advantage of that right now. She would have never known I was here. You could have let me watch."

Under the star-filled sky, Nolin takes out his map and looks over his route using a red light. Asterisks mark several spots on the piece of paper. He had completed setting his charges and was waiting impatiently at the rendezvous coordinates for Miguel and Colin. Following the lines of the other two routes he looks around the valley and sits down rubbing his stomach, *Put on a couple extra pounds and I get the fat kid route.*

Nestling underneath a large pine tree overlooking the valley, Nolin sits down to rest his body. He glances around again expecting to hear or see Miguel or Colin approaching, *man I don't like this. No communication. Fine in theory, horrible in the field. What if they get attacked by these blood thirsty canines again or worse?*

Fatigue begins overcoming Nolin's senses. He keeps turning around thinking he could hear something behind his location. The solitude and time was eating away at him. Tucking his assault rifle in the branches above his head he pulls out a candy bar, trying to stay awake nibbling on it.

A team of mercenaries dressed in winter whites from head to toe sit in the bushes watching Nolin. All of their tools match their outfits including their firearms, which are spray painted the colour of the snow. Using whisper mics they radio the town below, "Delta team to base, don't know who this guy is, or why he would be here by himself. We haven't seen anyone else around, have you?"

Responding from the control room the supervisor stands looking at the screens, while the two other security officers continue scanning areas around the base, "Delta team, that's a negative. He's the only human that tripped our system. We haven't seen anyone else, and there haven't been any radio transmissions. If he's not meeting up with anyone capture him and we'll question him in the morning, after looking around in the daylight to see what he was up to."

The team leader responds, peering through infrared lenses, "Roger that. It shouldn't be long now, he is fighting the inevitable. He's under a pine tree and his eyes keep closing."

Scanning the monitors the security leader closes, "At your leisure then."

"Yes sir."

The crunching of snow gets Nolin's attention. He spins around the trunk of the tree to see a cold metal gun barrel pointing at his face. Holding up his hand he removes the red laser sight shinning in his eyes. On the opposite end of the gun Lorne sees a new face. His body tenses, examining the situation. The Captain looks over his shoulder, seeing the shadow of his gun only inches away. More men exit the forested area dressed in white pointing guns at him. The mammoth man tries to warn Miguel and Colin, yelling out "Don't shoot! Don't shoot!" He raises his arms in the air demonstrating he has no weapons in his hands.

The leader looks down pointing at his half empty backpack, "I don't know what you're doing here, but we're going to find out one way or another."

Speaking loudly Nolin continues to voice his distress alarm, "I am a conservationist, I'm here studying and preparing a report on the species here."

One of the members points out with his laser scope a handgun attached to his hip, "You really expect us to believe that?"

Nolin looks down and laughs, "There are wolves, bears and mountain lions in these parts. I wanted something to protect myself and the guy at the gun store told me this was a good one."

The leader looks at his members, "Get him up and cuffed. I'm not wasting any more time with this bullshit. Where are all your little friends?"

"I work alone. There is nobody with me."

As the members assist Nolin, the leader speaks again, "We will find out very shortly. Any hint of bullshit out of you and you will die, you understand? Delta team to base we have our package. We will be returning to base camp soon."

Proceeding down the mountain, the mercenary team leader turns around and kicks Nolin in the testicles. Lorne slumps over, landing on the ground face first and letting out an awful moan. The leader bends over grabbing Nolin by the hair pulling his head up, "Listen here you piece of shit. Captain Lorne Nolin where are your two friends?"

Unable to respond, Nolin braces, feeling the after effects ripple through his body. Not only was he lifted off the ground from the leader's size ten boot to his balls, with his hands cuffed behind his back when he fell his face slammed against a rock breaking his cheek bone. Lying in a fetal position Lorne begins gagging and throwing up.

The mercenary leader speaks again into his whisper mic, "Delta team to base, yes sir, of course."

He looks up at his men, "You heard that. Be on the lookout for anything. Miguel and Colin may be tracking us as we speak."

The leader starts positioning his men, "You and you take positions to the northwest, you and you cover off northeast and you and you watch the south side. We are going to stay put until reinforcements come up. Meanwhile, I have the pleasure of interrogating our prisoner."

Forcing the cold steel barrel of his handgun into Nolin's mouth the leader threatens, "If you don't tell me what the fuck is going on, you're a dead man."

Nolin gags as the barrel sight scratches the back of his throat. Grunting out noise Lorne tries to speak.

Ripping the gun out of his mouth, the leader slices open Nolin's cheek, "You better talk because you're a dead man if you don't."

An iron taste coats his tongue as his mouth fills with blood. Nolin swallows deep a couple of times.

The crosshairs of a scope sway over the horizon trying to focus on the team leader's head before it drops again. Miguel steadies his arm, "Come on asshole."

Mustering up everything he could, Nolin forces out a whisper, "So... are...you."

The leader's cool demeanour transforms into a maniac. Rapidly and repetitively he drives the butt end of the blue steel weapon into Nolin's face, spraying blood across the rock's surface. Nolin grunts and moans with each strike.

The brutality of the sound waves created from the beating has Miguel's eye burning red as it pierces through the scope, "Don't die on me old man just hold on."

Standing up, the leader points his gun down at Nolin's head and starts pulling the trigger, "You first."

The leader's head comes into view. Miguel breathes out slowly and smoothly as he squeezes the trigger.

The crack of two gun shots pelt the air with noise. Echoes ricochet off the mountain ranges.

Seeing the muzzle flash from Miguel's gun, two security members respond immediately, opening fire in his direction.

The remaining team members glance over their shoulder surveying the action. In their peripheral they see their leader's limp body lying on the ground headless. Scattered across the blanket of snow were remnants of his skull, and blood staining the ground. Within moments, the mercenaries find their senses overloaded.

A hail storm of bullets riddle the area from another angle. Rocks and wood chips add to the confusion. Two more men succumb to the surprise assault. One of the mercenaries breaks radio silence; the sound of gun fire in the background supports his demand, "We need reinforcements now. We're pinned down and we've lost three already including Walter."

Blaring from the town below a panic alarm sounds off.

A mercenary slides over on his stomach grabbing Nolin by the throat compressing his voice box, "Get up. I said, get up!"

Squeezing out a gargling choking voice Nolin exclaims, "If you're going to kill me, kill me."

Frustrated with the lack of cooperation the mercenary starts kicking Nolin in the face. He raises his gun and just as he pulls the trigger a peal of thunder vibrates the solid rock foundation.

Explosion after explosion vibrates through the air and the earth, overpowering the panic alarm sounding off in the base. People in the village, scurry in all different directions. Running for their lives, those outdoors pause, and brace as a rain storm of rocks come crashing down over top of them.

The remaining mercenaries attempt to escape the pending doom, abandoning Nolin's limp body.

The explosions placed around a fault line in the mountain directly above the town had freed tens of thousands of tons of rock. The shower the town received was only the beginning. Dislodging this huge crag, gravity was its silent co-conspirator. Picking up momentum the tumbling stone crumbles trees and vegetation in its path creating a snowball effect launching wood and other debris in the air. Colliding with other rock formations it catapults gravel into space as the landslide continues to move.

Swelling distorts Nolin's face, forcing his eyes closed. Lying on his side bleeding from a fresh bullet wound to his shoulder he knows exactly what Miguel and Colin did. Surrounded by three dead mercenaries Nolin slithers over their dead bodies trying to get to his feet. Compounding his own movements, the ground shaking underneath his body reminds him of his detached orbital bone, jaw and nose. Still handcuffed hearing the tormenting of sounds of impending doom, Nolin silently agrees it is the only way. He had hoped that it wouldn't have come to this but he accepts his fate.

Tossing the remote aside, Miguel and Colin stand up and watch the mercenaries in winter whites running for cover. Without effort, triggers pull, staining their virgin white clothes. Before the last body falls Miguel captures a glimpse of the rocks tumbling down the hill. Colin grabs his arm pulling him towards an indentation. Breaking Colin's grip the Spaniard sprints toward Nolin.

Leaping over a crevasse Miguel takes a rock the size of a softball in the back knocking him to the ground. Inches from shelter he sees Nolin's body only feet away. The shadow of the mammoth jagged stone looms closer as a spray of wood chips pelts Miguel's face, "NOLIN!"

Nolin quivers, lying there deafened by the horrific sounds rumbling nearby. He braces to greet death. Without delay the reaper came with a violent strength snatching his body launching his carcass through the air. Boulders smash into his skull as his mind relieves him of the misery by slipping out of consciousness.

Helicopters in the town below are destroyed as they attempt to take flight from the helipad by the avalanche now impacting the manicured grounds of the town. The airport runway lies in ruins, with obstacles and articles littering its paths. A thick cloud of dust blackens the entire man-made basin. A deathly silence falls over the village, no alarm sounds, no voices heard, only the occasional crumble of rocks submitting under the weight of the moment.

Slicing through the dust and debris is Colin's cry, "Miguel! Lorne!"

A high-pitched ringing in his ears has him off balance as he stumbles around coughing. He keeps calling out his friends' names. A gust of wind forces his eyes shut. As the gale dissipates, Colin's pupils slowly re-emerge from under cover taking in a powerful sight. Stunned for a moment, he realizes he is there alone, with a levelled unobstructed view of the entire mountain side. Falling to his knees, blood flows from underneath his dredlocks along his temple and drips to the ground. Hanging his head he slouches forward.

A grunt pierces the revered hush. Colin braces as he gets to his feet. Covered in rubble a human lump slowly extends from a crevasse in the rock. "Colin..(cough).. Colin."

The former Olympian recognizes the Spaniard's voice. He staggers over to him, as Miguel demands, "Help me!"

From out of the crevasse Mejia lifts Nolin's limp upper body passing it to Colin. Together they place him onto the flattened rock surface. Removing the handcuffs, the beaten giant wakes yelling, "What the hell? AWWWWWWWWW!"

Initially forgetting what had just happened, Nolin is quickly reminded by the pain. Miguel administers a morphine needle to alleviate the Captain's misery while attempting to console him, "Lorne it's going to be okay. We're going to get you out of here."

Looking at Nolin, broken, beaten and disfigured, Miguel feels responsible for his friend's suffering.

Colin helps prop Nolin up with his backpack as he begins to calm down. Lorne's attempt at a smile rivals Quasimodo with the multitude of injuries and swelling, as he mumbles, "I think it worked."

Dressing some of the injuries on his face the Spaniard adds, "Lorne, you definitely know your stuff. If you could see what happened you would know we didn't have enough explosives to do all this."

The former Colonel turns to Colin for some support, "Lorne, Colin is going to stay with you until we can get you out of here. Considering they detonated explosives on themselves there shouldn't be much resistance down there."

Drawing their attention are the sound waves of a helicopter in the distance. Colin grabs his binoculars surveying the sky, "It's a police chopper. I think they found our little friend."

Stretching out his hand, Nolin feels around eventually grabbing hold of Miguel and pulling him in, "Grab Colin and go. You don't have much time. Get down there and finish this for your boys, for Hamilton and for me!

Harnessed in, wearing goggles and gas mask Miguel looks at Colin through the smoke lingering in the air, "I don't like this, no safety rope, only one descender, are you sure that little spike is going to hold?"

"We only had one full pack left, luckily some of Lorne's materials were left in that indentation or only one of us would have a mask. Don't worry about it. Just trust me. It will hold."

"You know I hate that word."

Ignoring Miguel, the former SEAL jumps from the ledge with a zip starting down the cliff.

Reaching into his pocket he pulls out a folded piece of paper and opens it up. Looking at the picture of his boys, he bears down. "Almost done."

Slipping the picture in his pocket, his zips it up. Miguel begins walking backwards, staring at the little peg that Colin hammered into the rock. Holding tightly to the rope the Spaniard leans back slowly, loading the line with his weight. The harness hugs his legs and body as the tension increases. Holding his breath Miguel pushes off the ledge descending down the mountain side.

Sliding down the rope, Miguel feels the heat building on the descender. He looks at the piece of hardware and notices it starting to bend. Rapidly glancing around the former Colonel comes to grip with a daunting situation. Half way down the two hundred foot drop and his hardware is starting to buckle. An approaching helicopter twists the cover of smoke. With seconds left before falling he decides to get as close to the ground while his gear is working. He releases his tension allowing for a near free fall. The rope zips through the device building heat through the friction. Monitoring the descender he spots it melting. It folds in two and snaps away.

In a last ditch effort Miguel grabs onto the rope rushing by his face. Clenching with one hand the Spaniard's decent is too fast. Heat burns through his gloved hand melting skin just as he manages to switch hands. Squeezing with every fiber of his body, he wraps his feet around the rope, slowing his body to a stop.

Inches from the ground he releases, feeling the burn in his palms. He extends his fingers trying to release the pain while gasping for air through the enclosed gas mask.

Approaching through the smoke Colin asks, "You okay?"

Showing the rope burns in his palm, Colin responds taking off his backpack, "I told you it would hold."

Miguel pulls off his gloves, and accepts a couple of clothes provided by Colin. Wrapping his hands he prepares for the entry.

A cloud lingers in the air. An expedited equipment check ensured their firearms fitted with flashlights were still functioning, shooting beams through the airborne dirt particles. Miguel and Colin began moving, keeping themselves close to one another. Side by side they advance, walking slowly toward the once magnificent complex. With the pile of debris now on the ground the men easily enter the second floor of the main building through a balcony. Portions of the roof were taken out allowing more light in as they carefully make their way around the edifice.

Staggering around a corner, an older man cowers under the lights of the two military men yelling through their face shields, "Get on the ground, get on the ground now!"

Coughing, the man lowers himself to the ground. He begins spitting up blood.

Cautiously Colin approaches the man and zipties his hands. Inspecting his body, he was unable to see an injury.

The Spaniard pulls out his digital recorder, "What happened to you?"

"When the alarm sounded off, I followed some friends running with the security force. I followed them to the basement where there is a cavern leading under the mountain to a bomb shelter. The security force put on masks and started shooting anyone standing. I ran for my life back through the mansion. That's when the sprinkler systems went off and I, I..awww"

Pressing his fingers against the man's neck Colin checked his vital signs. "He's gone Migs. This is fucked. Blowing up their own place; executing anyone around; and bio agents killing off any survivors."

Shutting off his recorder Miguel orders, "Come on Colin, we don't have much time. We need to find someone else before they die. We need answers."

Running through the mansion, they come across corpse after corpse lying in puddles of blood. Reaching the basement the duo slowed their movements. Flashlights mounted on their firearms slice through the blackness, illuminating more horrors.

Without sympathy Miguel comments on the incident, "Isn't it ironic that these people who plotted and killed thousands died like this? Obviously, they were equally expendable."

"We have a problem."

Taking a couple of steps back Colin's flashlight shines upon a huge safe-like door at the base of the stairs. He moves in and rubs his gloved hand across the surface. "Oh yeah, this is some quality work right here."

Spinning around looking at all the bodies scattered on the floor, Miguel orders, "Okay Colin, start grabbing ID out of these people's pockets. Maybe we can piece together something."

Exiting through the maze, Miguel and Colin enter a new room. An infirmary by design and décor, gurneys and IV poles made up the scene. People trying to escape hang lifeless from their beds. Walking around the room, Miguel spots someone looking vaguely familiar. The brilliance from the gun's mounted light showed the man's face bubbling out blood from his mouth and nose.

Dropping his gun to his side, Miguel grabs the man's neck feeling for a pulse and then starts shaking the dead body, "How could you? I trusted you! Fuck!"

Hearing the commotion , Colin approaches illuminating Miguel's latest victim. Without a word he recognizes the bloodied face of General David Hamilton. Gently he places his hand on Miguel's shoulder and gradually increases the pressure, trying to coax him away from the corpse. "Migs, we really got to move, we don't have much time left."

Miguel's eyes flicker and his head turns, looking back at his companion.

Tapping the Spaniard's shoulder Colin reminds him, "Come on, we've still got to get Lorne some help."

Relaxing the muscles in his forearms, Miguel pulls his hands away from the General's throat and nods. Lifting his gun back up to the ready, the Spaniard begins walking towards the exit.

Slowly following the Spaniard, Colin points his gun's light at the dead man once more, shaking his head.

Reaching the second floor of the building, Miguel and Colin crawl through another balcony and scout the basin. The cloud of smoke had mostly settled leaving a light fog. The sound of the police helicopter hovering above them, thunders through the mist. The power of the mounted spot light is watered down by the cloud's particles deflecting its rays. Without another moment lost the duo race across the grounds kicking up a trail of dust behind them.

Approaching the hangar on the opposite side of the pit, Miguel observes that its doors are wide open. Inside, they see four men lying dead around the base of a shiny serviced helicopter on a dolly. Grabbing the dolly they pull it out into the open.

Colin steps in front of Miguel heading for the operator's seat, "I've got another place not too far from here let me…"

Continual bursts of light illuminate the night sky over the Swiss castle nestled along the ridge of a mountain.

"A brilliant fireworks display marks the beginning of a new era here at the inaugural ceremony of Reficuel Nomed who is accepting the responsibility of the world. The who's who around the globe has paid handsomely to be in attendance, while a myriad of musical talent is about to take the stage to entertain the crowd. As the celebration continues I will bring the people celebrating the event inside the castle to you, sharing their warmest wishes. Enjoy the show, back to you Shawn."

Shawn Gurl faces the camera from within the crowd outside the castle, "That was Carrie Warren coming to you live from behind the wall setting the stage for big changes about to come. We will continue to show you more live footage of the festivities in a moment."

Mingling amongst all of the dignitaries Reficuel speaks with the Prime Minister of England, "This is a great day, I appreciate your support, it…"

Colonel Renniks grabs Reficuel by the shoulder pulling him back, whispering in his ear.

At the same time, Paula Connie cuts through the crowd turning heads as she goes, trying to intercept Reficuel. She spots the world leader's demeanour switch instantly from his on demand model smile to horror, as he turns around to face Renniks. Immediately he leaves the Prime Minister of England and the crowd, staggering through the festivities bumping his way towards an exit. She hurries to his side, as quickly as she could move in a set of borrowed high heels from Carrie. Grabbing his arm she speaks, "Reficuel stop."

His head bobbles around seeing her wearing a red gown, looking like a princess within this castle. He attempts a smile but the weight of what Renniks just told him contorts his facial muscles into a frown. He doesn't say a word. He stares blankly into her eyes.

Grabbing his hand the new Captain turns her body slightly from side to side swinging her hair with the momentum, "I dressed up for the occasion."

"Paula, I am so sorry. I really have to go-go-go… take this call."

Reficuel begins to move again, the fear in his eyes was not lost on her. She knew something had happened and figured that Miguel had likely succeeded with his attack.

"Can I go with you?" she shouted out.

Unable to respond, the pressure of the moment collapses his ability to make sense out of his predicament. The new leader of the world turns away and spots his lead bodyguard enter the center of the celebration. Nomed grabs hold of his lead man's shoulder and follows him out of sight.

Weaving in and out of the celebrities and politicians Paula rushes out to the main area outside of the hall. Military security forces stood guard at each entrance while others made frequent patrols of interior of the complex. Walking around, scanning faces, she wonders, *How on earth am I going to find him when I need him.*

"Signorina Connie."

Spinning around she recognizes the man standing behind her. The Italian accent and the hair coming out of the collar of his shirt were only a couple of the more obvious features separating him from the others.

"Captain Yvan Buligan. I think our mutual friend was successful, I need him alone. Like right now."

"Of course." Pivoting, he grabs his radio and takes off in a jog.

Following slowly behind with the staccato clip of her heels Paula finally stops. "Awwwwww."

Throwing off her shoes she hikes up her gown and runs across the stone floor.

The large wooden door to Reficuel's castle bedroom opens slowly, with Mr. Nomed walking in followed by his bodyguard.

Sitting at the bistro table inside the room, Izzov raises a glass of wine shouting, "Congratulations, Your Excellency. Unfortunately we have a problem that needs to be addressed immediately."

With a motion of his hand, Reficuel's bodyguard walks out into the hallway, closing the door, "I heard. General Izzov, weren't you supposed to take care of that for us?"

"We can run around pointing fingers or we can focus on damage control. Frank Strauss gave Miguel an audio recording detailing the operation, tying you to the Sons of Liberty. With all of the audio recordings he has , Miguel could expose our organization. Apparently, he killed Shane in the process and somehow managed to find our Big Sky ski chalet."

Joining the General at the table Reficuel sits down and pours himself a drink, "Is that all? I thought it was more devastating than that. Who's going to listen to Miguel? He is a loose canon, a rogue agent. Nobody trusts him."

"I wouldn't be so sure. If Hamilton was in his back pocket there are more."

"So what? A couple of military guys. What good.."

"Hold on. What's that sound?"

Muffled by the large stone walls were grunts, moans and screams from the hallway, "We're under attack."

Izzov jumps to his feet grabbing hold of Reficuel and pulls him towards another door, "Come on! We'll take the back entrance out to the courtyard."

Throwing open the back door, sounds from the staircase mimic those in the hall. The General slams the door shut and locks it. Pulling out his side arm he scans the room...

Thuds increase in volume as Paula approaches Reficuel's area of the castle. The clang of a gun falling on the sedimentary floor vibrates the noise down the hall to her ears. Rounding a corner her eyes confirm her mind's interpretations of sound. Yvan and his team had executed a surprise assault on Reficuel's personal bodyguards. The sound of the music playing from the Great Hall drowned out the guards screams for help.

She reaches down, grabbing one of the guns that had been dislodged and runs to the outside of Reficuel's door, hitting it open.

Izzov's voice yells out from inside the room, "We're under attack."

"Reficuel. It's Captain Connie. We know about everything. It's over."

The same voice shouts, "It's General Izzov, we're under attack send troops immediately."

"Reficuel, we know you're one of the Sons of Liberty."

Again the General's voice demands assistance, "Mr. Nomed's room now. Send everyone."

Paula pops her head around the corner surveying the situation, and pulls it back as fast.

Pop, pop, pop. Gun powdered projectiles stop half way through the cement wall shaking loose dust on Paula's side of the barrier. Her hand pressed against the wall transmits the vibrations up her arm. She pulls away crouching down even further away from the high blasts.

An alarm sounds, the music stops and the stampede of feet running continues to gain in volume. Hiking up her dress Connie takes her knife off a garter belt and starts cutting the gown's length well above her knees.

Inside the room, Reficuel's voice starts shaking, stepping over to the balcony's stone ledge, "Izzov its over! We're done. For the good of the cause you have to push me over the edge. I can't do it myself!"

Gun in hand, Izzov glances over and rushes to his side ordering, "Shut up! We have a whole army coming to protect you. As leader of the world, grow some balls."

Shots ricochet off the room's walls above the General's head as Paula fires in the room.

Facing the room's entrance again, Izzov fires more shots, which lodge into the wall and door.

"Izzov, do as I tell you! I know too much. If they catch me we'll all go down!"

A crowd outside in the courtyard looks upwards towards the balcony. Unable to hear what's being said they begin video recording the leader of the world standing on his balcony.

"General, we don't have much time. Do it now!"

Looking over his shoulder at the entrance to the room, Izzov grabs Reficuel by the back of the neck and the belt and heaves him over the side. Unable to release the man from his grasp, Reficuel's weight pulled the large man halfway over the ledge before he let go. Clinging to the sides, the General steadies his body from falling.

Running to the falling man's aid the crowd screams, "NOOO!!!"

Others, frozen in disbelief, captured the events on their devices. The General's face shocked at what he had done, hangs over the ledge.

The freefalling hundred and eighty pound frame slams awkwardly onto the cobblestone court. A pool of blood immediately begins to fill the cracks on the ground.

Taking advantage of the lull in the action Captain Connie peeks around the door frame. Spotting Izzov peering over the balcony, she advances toward a large stone pillar in the room. Her bare feet slap against the tiled floor, catching the General's attention.

Turning around, Izzov raises his gun. Paula's heart sinks. Running for cover she depresses the trigger, firing several shots.

While raising his firearm the General pulls the trigger on his automatic weapon, shattering a line across the marble floor.

Chugging for air Connie yells out from behind the pillar, "General, just put down the gun!"

Unable to lift his gun any higher Izzov looks down at his shoulder, seeing blood seeping through his jacket. Fighting the pain he tries to lift the gun again, screaming, "Oye!"

Bullets spray the stone pillar, chipping away at its size.

Transitioning the gun to his opposite hand, Paula hears the clang of the weapon being moved around. Raising her gun she darts out and fires another couple of shots. The sudden appearance of another person in the room has her spin around gun on target. She sees Yvan Buligan standing at the door, lowering his smoking gun. Glancing at her momentarily, he again focuses on the General. Connie walks towards Izzov, who is lying in a heap. Energy pulses through his body, twitching his limbs.

Slow methodical steps lead Paula to the General's side, as she witnesses the blood pulse out the side of his head and his chest. She knew he would be short lived. Keeping her gun on the General, she peers over the balcony, seeing Reficuel's broken body lying motionless. Drunken people congregate around the leader's body. The experience sobers them, as screeches for medical assistance bellow through the courtyard.

Retracting her head from over the balcony, Connie sits down at the bistro table and reaches underneath the table top. Opening up her hand she takes a deep breath and presses stop on her recording device.

Out in the hall, charging soldiers yell, "Get down! Get down! Get down!"

A lump in her throat grows as she prepares for the attack. Looking at the device in her hand she questions, *Who's going investigate this? If this is my only evidence, any supporter of Reficuel would make sure it never existed.* Looking down at her bare thighs she shakes her head, "I'm not cut out for this spy bullshit."

Soldiers peer into the room demanding, "Get on the ground! Get on the ground now!"

Connie raises her empty hands over her head and slowly lowers her body to the ground.

Dressed in a beautiful evening gown Carrie Warren's image fills the screens as she announces the breaking news to everyone outside of the castle walls. "Calamity struck the celebration when the newly-elected world leader Reficuel Nomed suffered a horrible accident. We are not being given too much information at this time but we have been told that sometime during the celebration Reficuel Nomed fell into a coma after striking his head and breaking his legs. The joys of the celebration have turned to sorrow as the world now has to wait until their saviour recovers. He is in stable condition at a Switzerland medical facility and is set to be airlifted to England to be cared for by the world's finest medical staff. At this moment doctors are not saying how long this champion of men may be out of commission."

A knock at a large wooden door is answered by Colonel Renniks. He swings open the large slab of wood, seeing Miss Lindsay standing in front of him. Wearing her evening gown with long white gloves pulled over her elbows, she begins immediately, "I heard your boss is dead and girlfriend Paula got arrested."

Sticking his head out of the door, he looks up and down the hall spotting security patrol officers marching around, "Get in here."

Grabbing her wrist he pulls her into to his room and slams the door. He starts speaking in a low but forceful voice, "What the hell do you think you're doing?"

Opening up her handbag, her fingers leaf through a couple envelopes bearing names written in calligraphy. Pulling out his addressed envelope, she attempts to hand it over, "You have new instructions."

Stepping away from her outstretched hand, he stammers, "He's, he's, he's here."

Dressed in a skirt suit Carrie Warren begins a new broadcast, "In a bold move, the United Nations met and have been in deliberations trying to decide on a replacement leader until the poster boy for fairness, equality and respect has recovered. They announced, before going into talks that martial law would be lifted and people would be permitted to return to business as usual."

"Mourners around the world unite in candle light vigils praying for the speedy recovery of Reficuel Nomed. Media from around the globe continue to cover the event while the question on everyone's mind is, will he survive?"

"Celebrities chime in songs and famous bands are writing memorials, planning a worldwide concert tour of peace and unity in the fallen leader's name."

Shawn Gurl begins his narration of recent events with images filling the screens, "Cities across the world are saddened by this incident. People of every denomination are performing rituals in hopes of reviving the one man they revered as a compassionate leader. Taking to the streets we met with thousands who have gathered, sending well wishes to Reficuel. Among the mourners there is no shortage of sceptical people voicing their opinions. Here is an earlier interview by Carrie Warren from Switzerland."

Video footage shows Carrie stopping a couple on the street, "What country are you from and what have you to say about the unfortunate accident suffered by Reficuel?"

"We're Americans, and this is yet another government conspiracy cover up. This wonderful man was becoming too powerful so they took him out, just like JFK."

Shawn returns speaking, "A lot of emotion in the last twenty-four hours and this is definitely being felt around the world. Personally, I don't think we have seen the last of Reficuel, with everyone pulling for him, I have no doubt he will make a comeback…"

A grand court room with a panel of high ranking military officials elevated over the room stare down from their pulpit at Captain Paula Connie dressed in military uniform sitting handcuffed in the interview box.

A ranking officer struts around the body of the court, "Captain Paula Connie, let me see if I understand you correctly, you received information from a wanted convicted criminal and acted on it, laying siege to the world's newly elected leader?"

"Yes sir, that is correct."

"Captain, you stand before this secret World Court hearing stating that you orchestrated a coup based on evidence but there was no evidence was there?"

"That's not true. I received audio recordings of interrogations that I used to help me form my belief."

Twirling his glasses in his hand, "Oh yes, Exhibit Twelve, these audio recordings. There were three, is that correct?"

Paula looks at the panel, "Yes, three interviews."

The prosecutor slides on his glasses grabbing a pad of paper from his table reading over his notes looking very smug, "Were you able to verify the authenticity of these interviews before acting?"

"No, but they..."

Interrupting her, he whips off his glasses and strides over to her booth, "No! So let's break this down. Interview number one supposedly, is by a one Mr. Nicholas Giabatti, a long-time convicted criminal. Someone who has lied on numerous occasions to save his own life was being beaten to near death before saying something that appeased his accuser. Captain, is this one of the interviews that you used to build credibility for this story?"

"Yes, I found..."

Walking away, interrupting her again, "Interview number two. Mr. Jason Somers. No one has seen or heard from him since this interview, likely killed by the cold-blooded murderer Miguel Mejia."

A lawyer stands up, "Objection."

Turning around facing the panel, "Very well, Mr. Somers, no one has seen or heard from him since he too was tortured by this crazed man?"

Gritting her teeth, "I believe that is the information you have received."

"Interview number three, the most damning against Mr. Nomed, yet the person identified on the recording states his name is Frank Strauss from Seattle. According to American records no such person exists."

"That is what I was told."

"So Miss Connie what real evidence did you have?"

Paula's face flushes, as she pauses and looks around the courtroom, "Is there any way that I may be permitted to go to the washroom, before I answer that question?"

CHAPTER SIXTEEN

In the weeks and months following Reficuel's injuries, the media routinely reported on the situation:

"Captain Paula Connie and a team of specialized agents are being attributed with killing the man who attempted to kill the world leader Reficuel. No memorial service will be held for the late Canadian General Izzov, who was recorded by multiple celebrities throwing Mr. Nomed from his open balcony."

"Two weeks after the attempted assassination of the first true world leader, a computer virus dubbed 'the Apocalypse' has frozen computers around the globe, playing an audio recording linking and naming Reficuel Nomed as the leader of a left wing terrorist group called the Sons of Liberty."

"A week after the Apocalypse computer virus halted global trading it struck again. This time it displayed a list of multi-millionaire investors that supported Reficuel Nomed. Included on the list was former Canadian military General David Hamilton. Police have confirmed that all the people named on the list died after an earthquake rocked the Montana region resulting in a landslide that destroyed a luxurious ski resort, trapping and killing everyone present."

"United Nations representatives continue to delay the first official Worldwide election due to the ongoing cyber investigation. They refuse to comment on details contained in the virus that spread over the internet."

"Riots broke out in cities around the globe demanding answers to the computer virus Apocalypse accusations and the opportunity to vote."

"Bombings that had subsided during the rise of Reficuel Nomed have once again gripped cities around the globe."

"Six months after the Switzerland incident, military and police have made sweeping arrests connecting several hundred people to a coup that resulted in the formation of a one world government. There is still no comment whether or not Reficuel Nomed was in fact connected to the group in any way."

"Speculation and mystery continue to surround the event now approaching its first anniversary."

"Despite the controversy surrounding Reficuel on whether he's innocent or guilty of the accusations stemming from the computer virus, many citizens are pleading that he recovers to help stop the bombings occurring throughout the world."

Knocking on a door frame, Carrie Warren sticks her head through the opening. Shawn Gurl sitting at his desk looks up, "Carrie what brings you down here?"

Sluggishly walking over towards the elderly man she fumbles with her purse. "No hard feelings Shawn, I won't be taking the anchor spot away from you. I'm leaving the station. I wish you well."

She turns around and walks out of the room as Shawn stares at her leaving. He yells at her, jumping to his feet to chase after her, "Carrie hold on."

Getting his foot out the door he meets her coming back, "Are you seriously giving up your anchor spot to write gossip stories?"

"Not that you care but something like that. You wouldn't understand. Good luck with everything."

"Thanks I guess."

The soothing voice of Shawn Gurl narrates the images encompassing the screens as people move about haphazardly paying attention to the message, "Under the United Nations rule, the World Court convened again today as they continue the inquest into the people and the subsequent events that gripped the world a year ago. Since Reficuel Nomed's dramatic rise to power, the world has become aware of a society that is said to be a threat to every man, woman and child – the Sons of Liberty. At this time, nearly three thousand members have been arrested. This group of idealists were ultimately responsible for the bombings that shook numerous cities to their core. Testimony entered this far from several former members reveal much about this secret society, however it falls short of answering the multitude of questions on everyone's minds."

A young male sits perched on a stool centered in a packed café taking in the fresh smell of Colombian coffee beans brewing, and addresses those present, "I am here to tell you what no news cast will dare speak of. The media waters down its daily doses of information and we're so busy that we can't take the time to notice but it's all in front of our eyes."

Standing up, he walks around the coffee house, "Through televised interviews with defunct members now in custody we have learned of the existence of the Sons of Liberty. Now what you don't hear is that this society has remained dormant for some time, rebuilding after their last unsuccessful attempt to gain power in the 1930s, at that time using a pseudonym. Estimates during that era calculated that the group had over a million loyal members. Only recently have they reverted back to the name that brought them attention during the American Revolution."

A male voice heckles from the back, "How do you know? Are you a member?"

Another shouts out, "There's no evidence that they are the same group."

The young man walks closer to the voices speaking loudly skimming many faces as he speaks, "No, I'm not a member, but my father was."

A hush takes over the crowd as the young man continues, "In the 1930s during the Great Depression, members of the banking community among others tried to seduce Major General Butler with support and money in order to gain his loyalty ousting President Roosevelt. Compare those facts and circumstances with the American Revolution and Reficuel Nomed's rise. They are carbon copies: society in decline, social distress, and wealthy people vying for power."

An energy bubble bursts, scattering chunks of human flesh among splintered wood and shards of glass lying in the streets.

A pair of hands wearing white gloves snaps a remote in half discarding it into a waste receptacle while walking away from the area.

A television blares the news, "Hell on earth is how many are describing the relentless bombings keeping everyone on high alert. New protocols are reigning in many luxuries that we used to take for granted. With confirmation of an active secret society actively plotting to take control, special investigative teams operating under the United Nations' General Ryan Pegrum have been established. They continue to piece together the puzzle in order to unmask those that continue to commit these heinous acts. In other news, the World Court continues to wait to hear from three crucial witnesses in connection to the Sons of Liberty investigation. Topping the most wanted list are these three men, Miguel Mejia, Lorne Nolin and Colin Brunet. Covering the first World election campaign is our reporter Carrie Warren. Carrie."

The television shows a political rally, enthusiasts chanting, waving flags and pointing at banners hanging on walls as Carrie's voice begins before she comes into focus, "Thanks Moses, the Freedom Movement seen here in jubilation were at one time thought of as a disorganized lot of elaborate conspiracy theorists. Moments after the World Court cleared them of any involvement in the Sons of Liberty coup, they solidified into a significant political party across the North American continent. Current polls in North American ridings suggest when voting stations open that the long standing favourite Liberalist party under the leadership of Ms. Jasmine Lindsay need to worry..."

A soft woman's voice says, "Off."

The screen blackens along with everything around it. A full moon's ambient light enters the room from a balcony window shadowing lines on a hot tub positioned with a view overlooking a mountain range and the Great Wall of China lining the country side.

A hoarse male's voice speaks, "Amazing what the right information in the wrong hands can do."

Ms. Lindsay stands, raising her upper body out of the water with the excess water dripping from her hair and limbs landing back in the pool. Her magnificent wet physique reflects a warm glow as she moves from one corner of the tub to the man on the opposite side. Lowering her body back into the water she caresses him, running her fingers through his thick black hair, "What do I have to do to make sure you let me win the election?"

Outside a small home, in the splendour of sunlight in a cramped back yard, laughter, splashing and sizzling, form a symphony of sound. The smell of steak grilling on the barbeque fills the air in the smoke billowing off to the side, while people take part in playing around and in an above ground pool. Standing, tending to the meat, while speaking on an oversized mobile phone is Paula Connie, "...I'm still looking into it. It's not easy."

"You have to get us home somehow. I have to visit my boys. It's been too long." Miguel repositions the framed picture of his boys on the desk.

"Miguel, with security restrictions everywhere and the World Court putting out witness warrants on you and your friends, I'm doing everything I can do. Trust me, I will look into this."

Miguel cringes, "Don't say that."

"Don't say what?"

The Spaniard closes his eyes and runs his fingers over the scar on his head that Paula had sewn up for him. He shakes his head, "Never mind."

"You guys have other things requiring your immediate attention than worrying about that right now. Just let me work this out."

"I don't like it. Believing in those operating the World Court or the politicians heading the United Nations is something I can't afford to do."

Paula starts flipping burgers, "We have to start somewhere. I trusted them and look at me. I've been cleared. Not everyone is going to betray us like Hamilton did. Until you have information on these people, we have no alternative but to trust them and abide by their rules. Concentrate on the present and forget about the past."

"Easy for you to say. You're the one accredited with saving Reficuel, although I can't understand why."

"The people want to believe in something. Is the truth worth it? What would happen if we told them everything?"

"This coming from the girl who is playing by a pool back home while we are stuck in the middle of a war."

"Don't give me that bullshit Miguel. I stuck my head out on the line trusting you, now you better start trusting me. Find Mr. X and you'll find all of your answers. Until then, let me and Pegrum work on the politics."

"Sorry Paula. I was out of line. You're right."

"Damn straight I'm right. Seriously, don't worry about it. Just do what you do best and let me do what I do best. Together we should be able to put this to rest, once and for all. Tell the fellas I haven't forgotten about them either."

"Thanks again, with any luck we'll see you soon."

"God speed, Miguel."

Industrial noise is heard outside the small dark dirty room, as Miguel shuts off his oversized mobile phone. He looks up to see two familiar faces.

Colin, sitting on a counter top, readjusts his bullet proof vest, ripping the Velcro and reattaching it. Nolin stands, leaning on the counter beside Colin inspecting the large scar on his face in the reflection of himself in a mirror. Both stop and look at the Spaniard, waiting.

Miguel stands and grabs his bullet proof vest, slipping it over his head. He answers the inquisitive looks on their faces, "Connie's looking into it. She says she is on top of things and wishes us well."

Nolin stands up tall, looking down at Miguel, "Migs, that doesn't answer anything. We haven't been home in over a year. I'm fed up. Fed up! I need a light at the end of the tunnel. Maybe I will just turn myself in and see how it works out. It worked for Paula."

Cranking his head upwards, Miguel looks his friend in the eyes, "Let's just finish this last mission and re-evaluate where we're sitting. The sooner we find X the sooner we can all relax and go home."

Colin hops off the counter, "Well I guess we better go to work, right old man." He slaps Nolin's shoulder and starts out the door.

Nolin grunts as he turns to follow Colin.

All three walk out of the room to a grungy four bay garage. Parked inside the building are military grade vehicles and in the corner sitting at a table are a group of others dressed in the same military gear.

Walking in front of the group Miguel begins, "Hopefully, that gave each of you a chance to review our action plan for today. As you can see, this is our only chance to get this guy. After six months we finally have Mr. X coming to personally to deliver the explosives. This guy will open up the opportunity to gain ground on the main target. He will have others on board for protection. If this truck goes boom, us and a good portion of the block will be evaporated."

Miguel points at a map, "We only have one stop to make. Our friendly is going to be meeting us here. Colin and I will go and speak with him personally. We're going to wire him up. We'll radio Lorne who will be monitoring all of our movements. He will direct you guys when to start rolling. So, be ready to move. Once we start there will be no pit stops until this ride is over. Any comments, questions or concerns?"

Yvan Buligan speaks out, "Apok, I love you to death, but with you involved, this has all the ingredients of a shit sandwich."

Brad Scanlon stands up, "As much as I agree with Bully, me and my team are ready to move."

Miguel sees Colin and Nolin nod, agreeing with the comments. Miguel dismisses them, "Thanks for sharing Yvan! Now let's eat."

"I'm just saying," Yvan starts laughing, shaking his head as he leaves the table. Bewildered looks on faces from those still at the table gaze around, not finding the information they desire to clarify the statement.

Colin and Miguel climb on board a van and exit the building.

Nolin looks over at Yvan Buligan, "Bully, you can't help yourself can you?"

"Come on. I'm just stating known facts. Everyone calls him Apok; you would think he was used to it by now."

Buligan spots Young Blood walking over to him, "Leonard what's up? You have that look on your face."

The young Asian male, a stark contrast to Buligan, boasts a baby face with no sign of facial hair. He is tall and slender. Yvan, short and stocky had only allowed a single day's facial hair growth go unshaven and it already appeared more like a beard. Leonard questions, "Bully, what's with Apok?"

"Nothing, Young Blood, he just gets really stressed out worrying about missions like this. He wants to make sure everybody comes back in one piece."

"No, I mean why do you guys call him that? Me and the other guys never understood the meaning."

"Oh that." Yvan looks at Lorne Nolin who shakes his head no. Rolling his eyes, Buligan continues, "Back in the day, when you were just a baby, this crazy son of a bitch was in the prime of his life. He was a lot like you. Except every mission he went on turned into a blood bath, total annihilation. Seldom were there any bad guys left standing. He started reciting Bible verses to himself before every mission. Guys started teasing him saying that he was praying for the apocalypse."

"The what?"

"Apocalypse. You know, the end of the world, total destruction, the four horsemen, the grim reaper. Anyways everyone started calling him Apok. He never really took to the name until one day, you remember that Brad?"

"How could I forget? I don't think he'll ever really forgive us for it."

Young blood questions, "What?"

Bully continues, "When we were at Blackwater training some of the newbies, a bunch of us decided to take a break and go to Mexico for a weekend. We were drunk from the moment we got there. Miguel was wasted. I think he was actually passed out when we all decided to go for tattoos."

Listening intently to the story Young Blood leans in, "No way."

"Yep. When he woke up he was pretty pissed. I don't know why he was so mad, his tattoo turned out better than everyone else's."

Bully pulls back his sleeve revealing a distorted raunchy tattoo under the hair on his arm.

Leonard, seeing the tattoo, makes a disjointed face.

Brad adds, "Deep down I think he likes the tat, but for the next while I slept with one eye open."

Miguel's voice breaks the radio silence, "Nolin, send the trucks, we're ready to go."

"Roger Apok, the trucks will pick you guys up at the rendez-vous point."

"Roger." Miguel quickly checks over his apparel and equipment, while Colin does the same.

"Okay Colin, we got to get going. They're going to be here any minute now."

Climbing out onto a rusty old fire escape, hearing the ancient metal creaking, Miguel wonders if it was going hold him and Colin. Exiting a high rise apartment building, with another building only a few feet away, there was a limited view of their surroundings. With garbage everywhere, the constant noise level, Asian street signs, and a distinct smell, their senses confirmed that they were in China.

While Miguel descends the stairs, he looks around, and his mind begins reliving a similar experience. Despite all of the horrific things he has seen over the years, one will forever haunt him no matter what he does. He has tried to forget it because of the emotional pain it brings back. Pushing it back into his subconscious and focusing on the task at hand sometimes proves to be futile.

The scenery here didn't help him either; it's a carbon copy of that night years ago. His memory plays back the scene like a movie on a loop, rushing every associated memory of that incident back to the present.

> Sitting in a jail cell receiving his mail from the guards, he examines an envelope noticing that it had already been opened and read. He reaches in and pulls out the piece of paper inside. Unfolding

the sheet he sees the words etched on the white lined paper clear in his mind.

'Dear Mr. Miguel Mejia, Even though the world has turned its back on you, I want you to know that you will always be in our hearts and prayers. My husband and I are so thankful to you. You brought our little girl back to us. Mere words cannot express how much she means to us. When she was kidnapped we weren't sure if we would ever see her alive again. Those twenty-four hours not knowing and fearing the worst, trying to mentally prepare for that news was more than I could handle. When we received word that she was alive I was overjoyed. I want you to know that if it wasn't for your heroic actions our baby girl would have suffered the same fate as his other victims, and for that we can never thank you enough. She is doing remarkably well considering the ordeal. She is finally making friends and her nightmares have now stopped. The doctors say that she is young and the amount of love and support she has at home will go a long way to seeing her, not forget, but cope with her situation. Every night she prays and thanks God for you. Hopefully, we will bring her to the jail to see you next month. Again, thank you so much, you have truly made this world a better place. Love always Nicole, Nick and Ruth.'

Reaching the bottom of the staircase Miguel rushes into a truck built like a tank and takes a seat in the back. Colin turns to Miguel sensing his distress, "Apok, you okay?"

"Yeah, I'm fine."

Tapping his knee Colin reminds him, "Boss, we have ten minutes before we get there, get your game face on."

Sitting back into the seat, Miguel nods his head before laying back watching the street scenery flash by as his mind wanders off again, whispering to himself. "Apok."

Initially called Apocalypse, Miguel never thought much of the name at first but accepted it. Over time, it was shortened to APOC. The Greek meaning of the word meant, 'to uncover or remove the veil'. He recalls the last time someone called him that before his arrest. Running up the flight of stairs in a neighbourhood like the one they just left. His old partner Saduj Toiracsi nips at his heels and his mind.

"Apok, what are you doing? We are supposed to be in position to arrest the biggest X dealer. The team is counting on us."

"I don't have time to explain. Just stick with me. There is a little girl that needs our help." Miguel walks quickly down a long dark hallway in an apartment building, counting each door he passes on his left.

"Apok come on, just call another car to come by, we should be with the team." Toiracsi continued, pressing his point.

Finally, finding the door Miguel starts pounding on it. "If this fucking guy doesn't answer the door, I'm going to boot it in."

"This is mental, what I am doing here? What are you doing? We don't have a warrant for this place, Miguel snap out of it." Toiracsi paces back and forth and rubs his forehead.

Pounding on the door again, Miguel is physically grabbed by Saduj, "That's it. Come on Migs. This isn't funny. Let's go."

Miguel pushes his partner off of him, "If you want to go, Go! Someone here really needs our help."

The door clangs ajar, showing a chain strung across the opening, permitting only a small view of the interior, "Yes, can I help you?"

Inside, Miguel sees a shirtless man dressed in a pair of jeans with the belt undone and his messy hair. The man focuses on Miguel's police badge hanging around his neck on a chain, beads of sweat begin forming all over his face.

Miguel's eyes light up recognizing the man, realizing he had found the right place, "Open the door, I know what you're doing in there, we're the police, open the door."

Stuttering out, "C-c-c-come, come back when you have a warrant, cop." He closes the door as he finishes his sentence. Miguel boots the door, ripping the chain right out of the frame. The door strikes the man squarely in the head sending him flying backwards. Wasting no time he makes his entry into the apartment.

Standing at the doorway Toiracsi doesn't even enter the apartment. "Miguel, are you fucking crazy?"

Handcuffing the stunned man on the ground, Miguel demands, "Where is she?"

Receiving no response he punches the handcuffed man in the face. Miguel leaps to his feet and spins around going further into the apartment.

Creaking open a bedroom door, Miguel enters the room meeting the sight he will never get out of his mind. Slapped in the face with a sickly body odour smell, he presses on. His ears pick up the broken whimpering. A petrified tiny girl snaps her head around hearing the door open and wails seeing him walk near her. The absolute fear in her innocent eyes drives a stake through Miguel's heart. Ripping off his sweater, Miguel covers up the little girl's naked body and starts to untie her bruised wrists from the bed frame, "It's okay, he won't hurt you anymore. It's okay. I got you."

Gently picking her up, he walks out to the main entrance where he sees his partner still at the threshold. The handcuffed man starts yelling, "I'm sorry! I'm sorry!"

Handing the little girl over to Saduj, Miguel instructs, "Bring her downstairs. She doesn't need to be here anymore. Get an ambulance here immediately and call this in. I will stay here with this piece of shit."

Shocked at what just happened, Toiracsi listens and does exactly what he is told.

Brought back to the present by a squeeze to his thigh, Colin whispers, "Apok, we're here."

The team sits stationary in the vehicles, coiled and ready to strike. Miguel sits up and monitors the situation. He begins quarterbacking the play, "Okay, here comes our cube van, it is picking up our boy… they are leaving now… Move out and don't lose that rig."

Speaking through a crackly radio system Nolin speaks up, "Don't worry about following too close, I have everything under control. Just stay back we don't want to spook them. I will let you know where they're going."

Monitoring the screen Nolin calls out their directions, "In thirty meters make a left hand turn. They are just ahead of you guys. Our boy is doing fine. Sounds like there are five of them on board. I'm still waiting on voice recognition."

Narrow streets crammed with vehicles clog the passage and the team continues its slow pursuit of the cube van. Reaching a large apartment complex on the opposite side of city the cube van proceeds to the back of the building.

"Apok, it's Mr. X. Perfect match."

Miguel advises, "Okay men, this is it, and it looks like they're going into an underground parking garage."

"We're going to need a truck in there to make sure we don't lose a signal." Nolin demanded.

The Spaniard prepares his team, "Roger that, my team will enter the underground, Bully and Scanner set up to intercept whatever happens out here. We can't let him get away."

Entering the underground Miguel's transport amplifies the signal to Nolin's computer. Everyone sits in anticipation of the next move.

Nolin's voice comes across as big and strong as his body, "Hook line and sinker. The deal is done; they just showed the explosives and handed over the keys to the truck… They are entering a black Mercedes Benz parked on parking level three. They're leaving now."

Picking up the play Miguel instructs, "Okay we got them. They are passing us now… it's now or never. We will follow them out, Team Scanner and Bully you come in and block the exit… Wait, wait hold on…. they just parked their car on P1 and entered the stairway on the north east side of the garage… Scanner, move your team in through the building and cover off that exit. Bully, keep your team in your transport and get ready to move if they have someone waiting outside. The cube van is exiting right now."

Leaning forward, Miguel radios to the others. "Okay, we're moving, stairwell northeast corner of the building, engage anyone coming up."

Addressing the crew in his vehicle Miguel instructs, "Colin and I will force them up to Scanlon, you guys follow that cube van. We can't let it get away."

Scanlon's team vacates their vehicle. Boots pound the apartment building floor as they shuffle into position. Running through the halls rifles raised, they glance over unsuspecting citizens that scream out in terror, falling to the ground. Approaching a corner one member posts and quickly scans the hallway, "All clear. Move, move, move!"

Leapfrogging through the complex, Scanlon's team continues to the stairwell.

Miguel follows the suspects up the flight of stairs, hearing glass break. He pauses, "This is Apok. We're in the stairway. Did you hear a window get blown out?"

"Scanlon here, yes sir, just below us, these stairs appear to have windows along one side all the way down."

Miguel and Colin start running up the stairs, "Go, go, go!"

The chase is on. Miguel and Colin reach the ground floor and see four men off in the distance approaching a parked car on the road. Setting up behind a cement barrier Colin begins to take aim.

"Colin, we need to take them out gently."

"Of course, gently." Peering through his sight, Colin prepares to fire.

An explosion rocks the building and the fleeing suspects don't even slow their strides, opening the doors to the vehicle about to leave the area. The parking garage collapses on itself. Miguel spins around seeing a concrete cinder block on a collision course with Colin. He reaches down, grabbing Colin and yanks him out of the way. The piece of cement craters the ground where Colin's body was just a moment ago.

Miguel impatiently radios, "TEAM SCANLON. YOU OKAY?"

Colin shakes off Miguel's death grip and repositions. He resumes lining up the cross hairs.

"APOK, don't worry, I got your back." Bully yells out over the radio. The armoured truck screeches around a side street, coming into view.

Scanlon yells over the radio, "Awww. I lost half my team. They went down with the parking garage. I need evac immediately."

Nolin responds, "Evac coming. Stand by."

The terrorists aim at the speeding truck, Crack. Crack. Crack. Crack. Casings dispensing from rifles litter the ground at their feet.

Yvan slams his truck into the front of the getaway car. The inertia launches the car backwards crushing one of the suspects standing behind it. The flying vehicle continues through the air and smashes into another car parked on the street.

The three remaining suspects fall to the ground, avoiding the impact. Picking up a sight picture Colin squeezes the trigger severing a henchman's arm, and disabling his legs.

Another spins around, spraying the area with bullets.

Colin ducks behind cover, as Miguel dives onto the ground and raises his rifle, returning fire. Chips and chunks of the remaining cement wall shower Miguel's back.

Buligan tries to exit his armoured vehicle slamming his body against the door. Rolling onto his side he kicks the door, cracking it open slightly.

One suspect with jet black hair watches Bully's slow progress from the underbelly of a truck parked on the street. He rolls to his feet and runs off.

Bully yells over the radio. "Apok. One is getting away. Running east!"

The action on the gun recoils into Miguel's shoulder as he hurls bullet after bullet at another suspect leaping for cover behind a cement barrier. While in flight projectiles shred through the suspect's legs tossing bone fragments into the city streets. His body collapses on the ground as he shrills in pain, "Ayieeee!"

Releasing the trigger, Miguel looks up, spotting the last remaining suspect running through a crowd of people gathering to investigate the commotion.

Colin jumps to his feet and his quads explode into action chasing the fleeing suspect. Miguel drops his rifle, following Brunet. Straggling behind, the added discomfort of running with all of the gear slows Miguel's stride. Watching from a distance the Spaniard sees Brunet bounding over cars and kicking off a panel van, changing direction. Trying to keep, up Miguel moves and dodges bicycles, operating through the street.

Driven, refusing to fail, Colin pushes himself harder. His boots barely touch the ground as he flies through the air.

The fleeing suspect keeps looking back, seeing the former Olympian gaining ground.

Struggling around a corner, Miguel is breathing heavy. He catches a glimpse of Colin as he darts down a crowded alley.

The suspect runs up a wall and pushes off, jumping upwards. His hands snag the bottom rung of an emergency ladder hanging fifteen feet off the ground. He starts pulling himself up, climbing the ladder with his hands. Colin jumps up and catches the man's dangling legs.

Hanging there, the suspect tries to squirm out of Colin's clutches. The suspect's fist grip on the rung of the ladder weakens. Slowly, his hand opens releasing the two suspended bodies. Like a cat, Colin lands on his feet. His body crouches down, absorbing the fall. The suspect's heels drive into Brunet's back smashing Colin's face into the ground. Falling to the side and rolling to his feet, the suspect turns and sees Miguel approaching through the masses.

Without a clear shot, Miguel gives chase. The suspect sprints away, with the Spaniard closing the distance. A civilian sweeping the sidewalk stops and stares, seeing the suspect flash past him. Following close behind, Miguel snatches the broom out of the civilian's hands. Running out of energy, Miguel speeds up and tosses the broom through the air like a spear. The thin bamboo broom-handle slips between the suspect's legs and trips him up, bringing him down hard on his head. The fleeing man struggles to shake off his disorientation. Getting to his hands and knees, he pauses for a moment when Miguel runs up and kicks him in the ribs.

Falling back down, the suspect winces in pain, gasping for air. Turning around, facing the Spaniard, Renniks forces a smile to his face between breaths and reaches up yanking off a black wig. Miguel raises his gun pointing it at Edward's face.

Fighting to speak between breaths, Renniks sits up and whispers, "Do it. Do it." He screams, "Do It!"

Miguel walks closer, pulling the gun tight to his chest while keeping it pointed at Edward.

"You're still a worthless piece of shit, Miguel."

Lowering his gun, Miguel sees the other team members arriving and starts to back away.

"Look at all these young faces, Apok. Them being here with you just sealed their fate. If you follow this man you will die. Do you hear me? You Will Die!"

Spinning around Miguel swats Renniks in the head with his gun. Jolted sideways Renniks falls to the ground. Straddling Renniks' body Miguel pulls back his hand to hit him again. Not offering any resistance, Renniks smiles through bloody gums. Miguel lowers his hand and starts to walk away.

Renniks starts laughing, "Miguel you're nothing but a coward. Your boys..."

Spinning around Miguel shoots out a round house kick, snapping Renniks' head sideways. The traitor falls to the ground unconscious.

Looking down at Renniks' head bleeding over the ground, Miguel communicates over the radio, "We have all parties secured, but we need a cleanup crew sent to our location."

"Crew is en route. Get those guys out of there and back here for interrogation." General Pegrum responded over the air.

Inside a central base, Miguel walks into the observation room overlooking the interrogation. Renniks' head is completely bandaged up, making him appear as if he was wearing a turban. Sitting down, Miguel speaks to General Pegrum who is watching the entire interview, "Has he said anything yet?"

"Lots, but nothing of any use."

"What about the others?"

"Well, we spent the first bit reminding them that they can speak English, and now they are swearing that they don't know anything. They were paid to accompany Renniks for a delivery. That's all they know."

"They had no part in shooting up downtown Beijing? Nice. These grunts are getting more stupid and or harder to question."

Agreeing, Pegrum nods, "They are definitely adapting to our techniques."

Sitting back, Miguel watches the interrogation when Renniks begins pleading, "I don't know anything. Please. Please. Please believe me."

Hearing him brought back more memories of that worthless piece of shit child rapist.

Pacing back and forth, Miguel demands, "Shut up."

Sitting on the floor of his apartment the rapist starts crying. "Please sir, understand. Please sir. Sir. Sir!"

Continuing to pace, Miguel yells again, "I said SHUT UP!"

The image of the beaten little girl's body engraved in his memory kept getting more pronounced each time he spoke. Every muscle in Miguel's face tenses, his eyebrows contort.

"I can't help myself. It's a sickness. Please get me some help."

Miguel jolts to a stop. "That's it."

He reaches down, grabs the man's head of hair and drags him into his bedroom.

The man screams kicking his legs, "No, no, no. Stop it. Please."

Squeezing the rapist's face Miguel pivots his head around the room, pointing his eyes to his walls. The grotesque pictures force Miguel to look away. Swallowing the vomit building in his mouth the

Spaniard chokes out, "What's this? You can't help yourself? You fucking piece of shit."

He releases the rapist's clean shaven face. Looking at his gloves, he sees the sweat and bodily fluids of this maggot covering his hands.

The man pleads, "Please, please I need help. I need help. I'm sick, I know that. It's a sickness."

Miguel's head was spinning. He couldn't pay attention to anything in the room. Had he been able to tolerate looking up he would have clearly seen the laptop computer's digital eye recording the entire event.

Thinking of his military days, Miguel remembers being directly responsible for missions that resulted in or required the killing of all kinds of men for many different reasons. Each mission he stood behind and didn't question. They weren't his own. They were someone else's, thousands of miles away, never being truly affected by the decisions. Standing here with this savage, who, Miguel had personally seen raping a tiny helpless little girl, thoughts of his own kids invade his mind. *What would I do if anyone would ever do that to them? Allowing men like this to live puts everyone's children at risk.* Miguel unsnaps his gun out of his holster and raises it to the man's head.

Squealing the man continues, "Please sir, Please, Sir, Don't do this please. Sir. Please sir. Please sir, I beg you. I need help. This is a sickness. I need a doctor!" Miguel quickly reviewed the countless similar men he had caught as a police officer breaching their parole or probation for similar offences and knew they couldn't be helped. He positions himself with both hands on the gun, staring down the sight at the child rapist.

Looking directly into the rapist's eyes Miguel inadvertently catches his own reflection as he softly
pulls the trigger saying, "The doctor is here."

"Miguel, that's it, were calling it a day. You need a ride back?" General
Ryan Pegrum stands as Renniks is dragged from the interrogation room.

Sucked out of the recesses of his mind, Miguel comes back to the
present, "Ah, Ah, no thanks. I'm heading back to the barn. There's a
couple of things I need to go over again."

"This is supposed to be a happy moment. I know this isn't the best
timing, but I finally have your letter. You, Lorne and Colin can go
home." Reaching into his jacket General Pegrum pulls out a folded
piece of paper and holds it out. "Paula left her party when she got the
call and picked it up herself. This is only a faxed copy but it's real."

Shaking, Miguel reaches over and accepts the piece of paper.
Opening up the document he reads the text, and rubs his scalp,
holding back his emotions.

The General steps out of the room, walking down the hallway
with Miguel slowly behind. He stops and turns around to face the
Spaniard, "I know you won't listen, but don't beat yourself up about
this assignment. There was nothing more you could have done today.
Scanlon's men knew the risks as did everyone else on the team."

"Ryan, it just never gets any easier." Keeping his head down,
Miguel walks away.

Back at the warehouse, Miguel sits at his desk with the portfolios
of Scanlon's men with red marker written in the corner 'Killed In
Action' when he hears a bang on the metal garage doors. Ignoring
the noise he keeps reviewing the details of the mission, when another
bang distracts him again. Turning his head to the surveillance camera
screens he sees a young boy with a mushroom hair cut standing
outside the garage doors. "Brandon?"

Moving over to the camera system Miguel zooms in on the boy.
*Brandon, is that you? Wait. Who is that? What's he doing? What's a twelve
year old doing out here in the industrial zone?* The boy dances around
in his tattered clothes and bangs on the door a third time, yelling
in Mandarin.

Scanning the area around the building using infrared and heat
vision technology Miguel finds nothing but his motorcycle and a
couple of vacant cars.

The young boy bangs on the door again. With each passing second the little boy's face looks more and more panicked. He hits the door again.

Miguel walks to the man door, and opens it cautiously. The boy approaches him, and reaches into his pocket. Pulling out an envelope, the little boy extends the package up to Miguel.

Reluctantly, Miguel reaches down and pinches the envelope between his index finger and his middle finger. With his other hand he pulls the envelope through his fingers feeling nothing but paper. Flipping the envelope over, the Colonel sees bold letters, 'MIGUEL MEJIA.'

Immediately, his heart kick starts the flow of adrenaline through his body. Swivelling his head from side to side he scans the area and grabs the boy's arm, pulling him inside the garage speaking in Mandarin, "Where did you get this?"

The boy starts crying, "A man wearing white gloves gave that to me."

"White gloves?"

"He told me if I didn't give that to you he was going to kill me."

Releasing the boy's arm, Miguel looks at the envelope again. He holds it up to the light. Snapping open the blade of a knife, he slices open a corner and slides the enclosed paper out. Rotating the paper up right he reads the note.

'WWW.APOK.CA. You had one minute to escape when you opened the door.'

Panic grips him momentarily. He looks over his shoulder at his boys' picture on his desk. The little boy sobbing in front of him draws his attention back around. Miguel lets go of the envelope, snatches the boy into his arms and runs out the door. Sitting the boy on his motorcycle seat behind him, his little arms clutch around Miguel's waist. Scanning his surroundings Miguel starts the engine and with a couple of quick revs, squeals away from the building. An ear shattering blast erupts and the building disintegrates. The energy force grows out from the explosion knocking him and the boy off the bike tumbling across the ground.

"Hot, cold, hot, hot, hot. You found us Daddy."
Jumping from behind a couple of cardboard boxes two little boys grab Miguel's arms. "You're the best daddy in the whole wide world."

> Together they walk out into a brightly lit room,
> forcing him to squint.

Blinking a couple of times Miguel wakes up seeing the brilliant glow of fluorescent lights captured in the ceiling. Feeling intense pain shooting throughout his body, his other senses slowly respond. His eyes gradually come into focus seeing a hospital room setting. A murmur of sounds filtering through the paper thin walls transform into footsteps, talking and electronic beeps. Rolling his eyes over his bare-chested body he sees the product of an emergency room hospital team. Legs suspended off the bed held in place with metal pins shooting through gauze patched quads squash any thoughts of getting up and leaving here on a couple pain killing tablets. The additional weight to his arms are old plaster casts covering his forearms with white-rolled bandages wrapped around his uppers arms and shoulders soaking up blood. Poking into his skin are needles attached to hanging bags of fluid. Turning his head proves to be painful. Closing his eyes doesn't alleviate the pain, only the solitude.

The Spaniard's eyes flutter back open and through the haze of the dilating pupils he sees a netbook computer sitting on a rolling hospital table. Clunking his casted arm onto the side rail of the bed he winces, accepting the pain. Leaning forward, he reaches for the computer. Extended out, holding his breath, his index finger and middle finger scratch at the air before landing on a corner of the desk. The wheels on the table barely move. Miguel twists his body, pulling at the pins through his legs. Biting his lip, he pushes out further grabbing the table, pulling it closer to the bed.

Laying back into the thin foam mattress Miguel takes a couple of deep breaths relaxing for a moment. Glancing at his legs he sees blood dripping through the gauze onto the bed. Flipping open the laptop screen, the computer comes alive. Plaster scrapes across the plastic as Miguel accesses the internet. Tapping keys, the screen displays, www. apok.ca. Pressing enter, the screens transforms into flames roaring inside a fireplace and an accented hoarse voice begins speaking;

"Miguel, Miguel, Miguel. What am I going to do with you? You're definitely outside the norm. I wasn't sure you were going to make it. I saw you hesitate and think about grabbing that precious picture of yours. Lucky you didn't, we wouldn't be talking right now."

Staring at the screen, Miguel turns up the volume, "You definitely make it interesting, never knowing what you're going to do. You quitting the military, or killing that unarmed man. Who would have guessed? What really boggles my mind is all of the people around you that feed into your delusional world. Why do they patronize you? Your children are dead. While you were in prison your house burnt to the ground and old Fireman Rick swooped in to take your woman away. Do you still suffer from those nightmares, Miguel?"

> Chained to the floor of an interview room, the Spaniard dressed in orange sat across from a detective who spoke softly, "...the house next to yours was a clandestine drug lab. It exploded and, took out your home. Unfortunately, your boys were at home being babysat at the time. I'm sorry Miguel."

Fury builds up. Miguel's muscle flex so hard his body starts to shake. Under the veil of bandages stitches rip and blood seeps through the layers of gauze.

"Why do you fight? To see their empty urns? Their photographs? One final goodbye? How will that help you? Is it to remind yourself that YOU left them helpless and defenceless? Or is it to investigate the botched work yourself? They never did find their bodies did they, or did they even tell you that? Are they still alive or do you know? Miguel, mind your bandages, it looks like you're bleeding."

Emotions run rampant over Miguel's body as he surveys the room through teary eyes trying to find the video link. He scratches at his eyes, initially trying to rub his eyes with the back of his hands but the casts grate across his skin.

"I'm sure it's just killing you that you can't find me. With all your strength and resources, surely you should know who I am by now. No? How is this for a clue? I am every person with an ulterior motive. I am anyone who needs something more than what they have. I am General Hamilton trying to free a friend, and before you die I will be you. You see I had a good thing going with Hamilton until you came back into the picture. So now instead of him working for me, I want you. No one really knows anyone do they, Miguel? I am very happy that you received a pardon. That opens up a lot of possibilities."

The flames on the computer screen morph into two boxes, one black and the other red.

"I like to gamble Miguel, do you? I don't think death scares you like failure. But to test my theory here it is. Click on the black box and when you are all healed you will receive notice of what you are to do, do it and your family and friends will live. Click the red box and your family and friends will die gurgling on their own blood in a bed beside yours. You have ten seconds to make a decision."

Miguel reaches forward, touching the mouse pad with his finger. He slides the cursor over the screen as the faceless man begins the countdown, "Ten, nine, eight, seven, six, five, four…"

With the cursor in the middle of the two boxes Miguel's mind wrestles through the medication to think clearly.

"Three, two, one."

The cursor sweeps across the screen and clicks the black button.

The colours from the computer screen begin to fade as the raspy voice exhales, "Too Easy. Now I own you, Dim Mak."

ACKNOWLEDGEMENTS

From the very beginning of this process one person has stood behind me and assisted in every way possible. Without your support I'm not sure if I would have been able to complete APOK. Thanks mom (Catherine Walton). Your countless hours of proofing some very rough drafts didn't go unnoticed. I really appreciate your help during the writing and publishing process.

My lifelong family friend, my brother Danney Hamilton, what an editor you have been. You are terrific! I can't imagine where I would be without your coaching and guidance. You truly understood what I was trying to say and you pushed me to do better. Thank you so much.

My cousin Carrie Duncan the photographer that managed to capture the essence of the book before anyone really knew I had written one. You supported my early work and took photographs that attracted a lot of attention. You're the best.

I big shout out to Billy Argel. Although we have never met, I am truly grateful that you're allowing me to use the Sniper font for the book cover and all commercial applications. You did a great job. Thank you.

My promotional minded friends, I can't tell you how much it meant to me to have your support with all the brainstorming sessions big or small that provoked some wicked ideas. Thanks, Jasen Topp, Crystal Topp, Joshua Waugh, Reg Dava, Kyle Kanstein, Jenn Knox, Aaron Barton and Joanne Rosato.

To those that came out personally to the early promotional events, I am humbled by your generosity. Taking the time out of your busy schedules showed me how much you care. Thanks, Reg Dava, Colin Giles, Colin Duncan, Pete Huyssen, Maxim Doneval, Tara Giles, Carrie Duncan, Lindsey Carrier, Lynn Cowman, Ron Walton, Lynda Walton, Kyle Kanstein, Jenn Knox, Jesse Major, Bonnie Major.

Gratitude is too small a word to express what it meant to me to have the phenomenal support provided by my family and friends who reviewed draft chapters, helped me promote, advertise and get the book to the market. Trying to live up to your expectations has forced me to work harder to meet them and more. Hopefully I have made you proud of something that you helped develop into the final product;

Ron Wood, Colin Duncan, Brad Spratt, Yvan Godin, John Buligan, Mark Pritchard, Lindsey Carrier, Lorna Judd, Joann Dupuis, Karen Brunet, Sheryl Eason, Rick Tarnowski, Glen Hamilton Jr., Adam Judd, Lorne Judd, Mackenzie Judd, Bonnie Major, Andy McDougall, Tyler Pallister, Greg Sadler, Stephen McCormack, Michelle Pierce, Jasen Topp, Ron Walton, FASSH, Joanne Rosato, Jean Facciol, Mike Mobbs, Jenn Knox, Joshua Waugh, Steve Travers, David Light, Karen Jokinen, Moses Khan, Ryan Huxter, Ward Foster, Chris Yap-Young, Jeremy Daniels, Laura Emery, Andrea Cogswell, Janette McIntosh, Karyne Brown, HAPU, Joseph Chamberlain, Denise Yee, Bill McLeod, Shane Racicot, Alexandra Grant, Jody Martin, Melanie Kavanaugh, Rob Morris, Chris Lewis, Tom Shantz, James Hargreaves, Connie Amartey.

FriesenPress' Carmen Sum, Rupert Home, Mary and everyone within the company, helping me bring my dream to life thank you. Your work, patience and guidance has been essential to the process.

Last and far from least is my beautiful wife Stephanie, and my two awesome boys Kwintin and Joshua. They have experienced every part of this journey with me. You guys are the best family I could ever dream of. I couldn't have done this without you. Thanks for your understanding, support and patience.

Above all, I would like to thank God for everything; from the family and friends to the crazy experiences and all of the off the wall adventures that I've lived which have inspired the writing of APOK.

After a near death accident rendered police officer Michael Walton unable to return to work, he was faced with the real possibility that he may never wear a badge again. The seasoned officer turned his complete focus to writing, a dream he had put off for far too long. Although his lengthy and decorated career as an officer had provided him with much fodder for writing, he had never found the time to write. Stuck between bed-rest, physiotherapy, and medical appointments he finally had the opportunity to compose the novel that had long been brewing below the surface.

No stranger to the sensation of adrenaline pumping through his veins while in the midst of car chases, house raids, gunpoint take downs, wire taps, and undercover operations, Walton didn't hold back as he put pen to paper writing this action-packed tome. Having faced the challenges of drug enforcement, gang land turf war, child rape and murder, firearms trafficking, and internal affairs, his accident was his greatest fight yet. He knew he had to push himself to keep his mind and body strong. Thirteen years in the trenches as a police officer with two performance commendations in 2001 and 2002, as well as two Commissioner Commendations in 2007 and 2009 for his contributions as an investigator, certainly gave him the skills to soldier on.

The first draft of *APOK* was completed in late 2011, and the story has since been transformed from a rough around the edges' hero's tale to an epic novel of intrigue, international conflict and terrorist agendas.

CPSIA information can be obtained at www.ICGtesting.com
Printed in the USA
LVOW101705090713

342071LV00003B/285/P